# The Truth in Their Blood

## The Progeny of Devils book 1

Viktor Bloodstone

**FORTRESS PUBLISHING, INC.**

WWW.FORTRESSPUBLISHINGINC.COM

*The Truth in Their Blood*
© 2022 Fortress Publishing, Inc.
ISBN: 978-0-9887991-8-9


Edited by: Catherine Jordan

This book is available for wholesale through the publisher, Fortress Publishing, Inc.

PUBLISHED BY:
Fortress Publishing, Inc.
1200 Market Street
Unit 17 / Box 137
Lemoyne, PA 17043


WWW.FORTRESSPUBLISHINGINC.COM

# CHAPTER 01

*March 24th, New York*

Personal entropy asserted itself in a variety of ways. Sleeping through an alarm. Missing the bus. Stepping in a mud puddle. For Celina Davenport, it was an email. She knew better, knew she shouldn't open strange emails, and should never reply to them, but the allure of learning more about her birth parents was far too great, the mystery too enticing.

Maybe this entropy was some form of cosmic rebalancing? If Celina ever felt the need for a life motto, it would be "status quo." She moved from points A to B to C in crisp, straight lines. If she strayed too far from that path, she'd inevitably grow uncomfortable and hurry back on track, keeping points D, E, and F in sight. It was what life had taught her to do – she felt it easier to embrace the status quo than fight against it.

The day started as expected. Up by 7:00, sensible breakfast while listening to a podcast, fifteen minutes with a crossword puzzle, then a three-block walk to the café by 8:00. Every Monday through Saturday. Today was too nice, though, too smooth, so she should have known the universe would correct her course.

The last remnants of snow disappeared as Spring asserted its temporary dominion with the first warm day of the season. Small mounds of grime-stained snow melted away, leaving dark spots on the sidewalks as the only reminder of their existence; they would dry to nothingness soon enough.

"Hi, Cel," Anson said, welcoming her as she entered the café.

"Morning, Lina," Branson said as she stepped behind the counter.

Brothers, Anson and Branson owned the Roll and Role Gaming Café, an eatery and coffee shop dedicated to tabletop gaming. Their artisan coffees were on par with other upscale cafés in the city, their Hawaiian blend winning awards. The menu showcased an impressive selection of hot and cold sandwiches for breakfast, lunch, and dinner.

Celina put her purse – more of a courier bag than a purse – in a locker in the small backroom, and then joined Branson behind the counter, helping to fill coffee orders and make sandwiches while Anson delivered them to the customers sitting at tables. The brothers' natural moods were always pleasant and upbeat, though Anson was quick to fuss about situations he couldn't control, but they both had been cheerier these past few days. The necessary requirements to serve beer on the premises were almost complete. Branson was excited about enticing a more mature evening crowd while Anson liked the idea of charging eight dollars for a product that cost him two dollars.

After the morning rush calmed down, Celina took a moment to check her phone. A message in her email inbox from an address she didn't recognize sent a tremor rippling through her status quo. She usually flagged such emails as spam, but the subject line caught her eye – "your father." She gasped; a sudden pang of misery pinched her heart. Her adopted father and mother died in a car accident three years ago.

Images of her parents flickered through her mind – Mom with such a round face that she looked like she was smiling even when she frowned; Father's square jaw and short forehead made him look like he was frowning even when he smiled. She opened the email, but it wasn't about her adopted father, rather her birth father. She wanted to ignore it, forget it, move it to her spam folder, but the mention of her birth father caught her off guard, enough to muddle her. The sender claimed to have information as to who her biological father was and Celina read the email several times before deciding to reply.

After a few hours of serving sandwiches with names based on puns of popular tabletop games such as "Cheddars of Catan" and "Porkassone," Celina moved on to helping people browse the games for sale.

"Especially that guy over there," Branson whispered to her as he zipped by. "He's very cute."

Warmth bloomed within her cheeks. Branson was right – the man was handsome. At six feet tall and self-conscious about her height, coupled with her negative feelings about her strong nose, weak chin, and big lips she never mustered the confidence to flirt with men. If a man flirted with her, then she'd go along with the flow while mentally ticking through her "must have" list. First, he had to be tall. The customer in question had at least a few inches on her.

Flirting with customers went against her rules, though. But rules could change, right? In a few months she'd be twenty-nine, and then next year would start the metaphorical downhill slope. Never a better time to step outside one's comfort zone, right? And the "no flirting at work" rule was hers and hers alone. Anson never discouraged it and Branson overtly encouraged it.

After a few calming breaths – enough for the pink in her cheeks to subside – she approached the handsome customer. His jawline was angular and free from stubble, his chestnut brown hair short, but styled nicely. The wire-rim glasses gave him an intellectual look, something Celina hoped wasn't false advertising. "Hi. I'm Celina. Can I help you find anything?"

He turned to face her, smiling like a movie star, and officially became too handsome. Celina deemed him out of her league. No way he was single, and even if he was, she doubted he'd be interested in her. Guys like him probably had models to choose from, and beautiful women falling at his feet like tossed rose petals.

"Hi, Celina. I'm Robert. I'm… I'm sorry, but was that cheesy?"

"Was what cheesy?"

"Me. Well, me introducing myself. I've seen many internet articles and social media conversations about customers introducing themselves to the staff."

"Excuse me?" *What the hell is he talking about?*

Robert shrugged. "I've read instances where the people who work in retail say it's disingenuous or a lame attempt to endear oneself to the staff member hoping to get better deals."

"Does that make for good reading?"

He smiled. "No. It was click bait."

"Do you actually know of any retail workers who get annoyed by endearing customers?"

"No. No, I do not."

7

"Did you introduce yourself hoping for better deals that, one would assume, are reserved for my friends and family?"

"I did not. I introduced myself because it gave me a sense of hope that we might meet again after this interaction."

A blush prickled Celina's cheeks. She couldn't help wondering if his comment was for her, or for all retail staff. Her brown hair didn't touch her shoulders, but it was long enough to tuck behind her ear as she smiled and looked down. Then his shoes caught her attention.

Robert seemed too flashy for a businessman, yet too stylish for an artist. His cream-colored suit fit him perfectly, accentuating an athletic build. His shirt and tie shimmered in the light and were the same shade of forest green. And Celina couldn't stop looking at his shoes – snakeskin with a reticulated pattern in multiple shades of green, some patches matching his shirt and tie.

"Yeah, I know they're a bit much," Robert said as he pointed his toes inward and then back out.

"No. They're not too much. They're very nice."

"Most of my shoes are over the top. I'm embarrassed to say this, but that's thanks to my mother. She always said, 'Everyone sees you from the shoulders up, but if someone sees you all the way to your shoes, then they see the whole you.' Your shoes are nice, too, by the way."

Plain black flats. Celina tucked her hair again as she looked up into his face. Not knowing how to respond to such a ludicrous statement, she went back to, "So, I see you're looking at the games?"

Robert gestured to the shelf of dice games. "I am. I'm in town for my niece's birthday party and need a last-minute gift. It's either a dice game or a pine tree shaped air freshener from the gas station close to her parents' house."

Celina selected two games from the shelf. "As much as I'm sure no one could resist the alluring aroma of artificial pine, I doubt the fragrance would last more than a week. So, for the purpose of longevity, may I suggest this game?" Celina shook the square-boxed package. "Each player is a zombie, and the objective is to eat more brains than the other players while trying to avoid having your head blown off with a shotgun. Now, with *this* game here..." She presented him a rectangular game box. "You're transported back to the Wild West where each player is a gunslinger. If you don't mind the inappropriateness of anachronously stereotyping Native Americans, the players will have a great time shooting each other."

He scratched his chin. "I'm sure she'd view me as the cool uncle, but my niece is only eight."

Pushing down the pangs of embarrassment welling up inside her chest, she returned the boxes to the shelf and grabbed a simpler game with popular movie characters on the dice faces. "Well, this one will definitely keep you from being ostracized by your family. As long as she enjoys the movie franchise these characters are from, then she'll like it. It's a little like Yahtzee, but with more math."

Robert took the game and glanced at the enticing words on the back. "Corporate movie tie-in and educational. Perfect for an eight-year-old's birthday party. Now if I could only do something about my cousin who will undoubtedly drink too much."

Celina smiled, but not a full one. She always viewed her mouth as too big and felt like it emphasized the wrong parts of her face. "Unfortunately, I can't help with that."

"No worries. The good news is I'm heading home right after the party."

"Sometimes the best way to deal with drama is to avoid it." Normally she would have stopped there and disengaged. But something about him clouded her sense of judgment. Her brain told her she was reading too much into the interaction, but her heart suggested that she could construe a couple of his previous statements as flirtations. Hurrying the words out of her mouth before she changed her mind, she asked, "Where might home be?"

"Philly. I run an art gallery."

"Oh! I've always wanted to run up the Rocky Balboa steps."

"Well, who doesn't? My gallery is 'The 8th Street Gallery' and we showcase some pretty amazing artists. If you ever find yourself in the area, stop by."

9

"I will."

"Nice to meet you, Celina." He turned toward the register, then stopped. "Um, one more question before I go, one that I always ask when I'm visiting a different city. Other than this place, what's your favorite nearby restaurant?"

The question took her by surprise and she gave no thought when she answered, "It's called 'The Signpost.' A simple family place, almost like a diner. It's two blocks that way, and then one block left. I recommend the meatloaf. I'll probably eat dinner there tonight." Celina wanted to slap herself for adding that last part, feeling like she just threw herself at him. He offered that bright smile again and heat radiated within her from shoulder to shoulder. She wished he would leave now before she burst into flame from embarrassment.

With a slight bow, Robert said, "Sounds lovely. Enjoy the rest of your day."

"You, too," Celina said, tucking her hair behind her ear one more time as he aimed for the checkout. She begged herself not to watch, but couldn't take her eyes off him as he finished the transaction. He looked over his shoulder at her and smiled one last time before leaving.

Branson hurried over to her and asked a hundred questions in one breath. His eyes sparkled as she answered each one while replaying every moment in her mind. He never even hinted that Robert was out of her league and all but offered to buy her a train ticket to Philly. "He paid by card, so I got his full name and you can easily find him."

She waved him off and went back to work, chastising herself for getting all excited about a good-looking stranger she'd probably never see again, but couldn't stop feeling warm and high on endorphins for the rest of her shift. Until, right before leaving, she peeked at her emails again. The person who said they had information about her birth-father now claimed to be her sister. According to the email, they were separated at birth and should meet right away, today if possible.

Celina mashed her lips and sighed. Maybe the positive interaction with Robert emboldened her, maybe this mystery person's intrusion angered her, or maybe both emotions swirled together, prodding her to reply. And to meet. Had she been thinking more clearly, she would have suggested someplace other than The Signpost, but the restaurant lingered fresh in her mind. It was a public place and she wanted an end to this situation as soon as possible.

Now, perched at her regular spot at The Signpost, a corner booth by the window, Celina stewed, her mind racing in circles as she reread the email exchange on her phone. This person – her supposed *sister* – used far too many exclamation points. And she was late!

But then the door opened.

A woman walked in. Celina would have known her anywhere. Her sister. An identical twin.

She aimed for Celina, regarding her with the same face she saw every day, with minor differences. Hair a bit longer with a little more oomph to it. Bright eyes rimmed with subtle eye makeup. Lips a shade pinker. "Full" and "pillowy," were complimentary adjectives Celina never used to describe her own lips, but those words could be used to describe this woman's. A smile cracked at the corner of her twin's mouth. Then she smiled wide, revealing the biggest difference between them. Her smile was huge! She showed more teeth than Celina ever dared to expose

The woman plopped in the booth across the table and all but blew Celina through the back of the seat with her energy.

"Oh my God, look at you! This is amazing! I. Literally. Can't. Wrap my mind around this. Oh my God, this is crazy. Can you believe this? I can't believe this. I mean, really, this—"

"Stop!" The word came out sharper than Celina intended, but this woman was too sudden and too much. Too much to process.

After a few decompressing breaths, Celina stared into the woman's circle-wide eyes. "I'm sorry. This is… You're right. This is… freakish. I'm sorry that freakish is the only word I came up with, but…"

The woman's smile returned. Confident. Inviting. How did she turn her poise on like that?

"Hey, no problem," she said. "I'm as freaked out as you are." She shrugged. "I deal with being freaked out differently. I mean, how often does someone find out they have a secret mystery twin?"

Celina shook her head. "How did you find out about me?"

"Through research. I do a lot of research for work, and then when I found out about you, found out I had a sister, I tracked you down, jumped on the first train to the city and got a room at The Orchid."

"Tracked...? Research...? What were you researching? Why?"

Digging through her pants pocket, she added a chuckle to her words as she continued. "Oh my God, I'm so excited I forgot. I feel like a puppy about to piddle on the floor. I'm so sorry. My name is Caila. Caila Rappaport."

She withdrew a bold-red business card holder and whipped out a card.

Celina hesitated before accepting, only wanting to glance at it out of courtesy, but she snatched the card when she saw the similarity of their names. Funny how it hadn't occurred to her until she saw it in writing. "Caila is spelled with a 'C.'"

"It is," Caila said with the enthusiasm of a child on Christmas morning. "Crazy right? I'd say it's a twin thing, but that wouldn't make sense since we didn't choose our names. Maybe it's fate giving us a sign?"

"Or maybe we were named at birth before we were separated."

"That is a far more rational explanation. Despite my job, I sometimes get a little goofy with my theories."

Celina examined the next line. "Forensics Historian?"

Caila sat back in the booth, as if a bit more relaxed. "Yeah. I use modern methods and technology to analyze all kinds of data regarding cold cases and contested conclusions. Old cases. Like fifty plus years. But that's not my true passion, not why I'm here."

Anticipation desiccated Celina's tongue and she grabbed her glass of water and took a few gulps.

Caila leaned forward, elbows on the table, as if they were coconspirators sharing secrets. "I'm here because of our father."

Celina coughed water out of her nose. She grabbed her napkin and wiped the lower half of her face. "Our father?" she asked with a croak.

"Yes!"

Her smile nothing but teeth. How could she have that many teeth? *Do I have that many?*

"Okay, sorry. Let me back up. Like it says on my card, I'm a forensics historian, but my true passion is crypto forensics."

"Crypto…? Like Big Foot and the Loch Ness Monster?"

Caila giggled. "No. Everyone thinks that, but Big Foot and Nessie are cryptozoology. Crypto forensics is similar but deals with unexplained criminal cases that occurred outside the realm of logic and possibly even outside the realm of physics. Think about Jack the Ripper. Never solved, a billion theories, and elevated to a legendary status."

It didn't take Celina long to see where this was going. "Our… father? Our father and your crypto forensics are connected?"

"Yes!" Again, all those teeth. "I research mysterious figures, basically 'boogiemen' from different areas. I check out local legends and lore, trying to separate fact from fiction. One day, I thought, 'Hey, these events are twenty, thirty years old, so… What if these figures have children?' I started digging deeper into the lives and histories of these people and sure enough, I discovered a few of them do indeed have children. And then I discovered I was one of them. And you, too!"

"Whoa, whoa, whoa!" Celina held out her hands as if attempting to stop Caila from lunging across the table. "Are you actually saying that my birth father is some kind of crypto criminal?"

Caila's smile downshifted as her eyes narrowed. She looked at Celina as if she had suggested that a few ice cubes made up the Arctic Circle. "Celina, you have nooooo idea. He's far more than just a criminal. He's—"

The tinkling of a small piece of glass breaking.

The slop of a stone dropping into mud.

The wet splash of brains spraying across Celina's face.

Caila crumbled to the table; half her face still pretty, the other half a casserole of chunky meat, hair, bone. Her untethered eyeball, through a film of red slime, stared at Celina.

# CHAPTER 02

*March 24th, Las Vegas*

Victor Vegas woke and immediately raised her arms over her face, shielding her closed eyes from the angry and hurtful sun beams.

A bed. She lay on her back, unable to open her eyes due to the sharp glare, so she shifted onto her stomach.

Victor's arm dangled over the bed, her face smushed into a bare mattress. Silky sheets cocooned her feet and wadded under her naked body. They'd leave an indent along her chest and waist, possibly her hip as well. She smiled as the memory of last night's romp returned to her, but she couldn't seem to remember an important detail... "Is this my bed or yours?"

"Yours," a woman answered, voice as raspy as sandpaper against stone, her foul morning breath in Victor's ear.

"Cool. Get out."

"C'mon," the woman whined. "A few more minutes."

Victor turned to the other person in bed. Blonde. Naked as well. "Nope. Get out."

The blonde sat up in a huff and scowled down at Victor, muscles tensing along her gym-toned form. Her hair flat on one side, the other side reached for all ends of the universe while shadows of last night's mascara streaked her cheeks. Victor found it impossible to take this woman's ire seriously.

"Fine!" the blonde said. "You don't have to be such a bitch about it."

"I do. My name's Victor Vegas and they named this city after me, so I need to maintain a certain appearance."

Victoria Vargas was her legal name, but she didn't like it, it didn't do her any favors in life or career. If people made certain assumptions at the name Victor Vegas, then so be it. Those assumptions were better than the ones made at hearing Victoria Vargas or, God forbid, Vicky.

The woman swung her feet over the bed and ran her hand over her face, pausing on her left eye as if she needed to keep it from popping out. She glared over her shoulder at Victor.

"Bitch," the woman repeated.

Victor smirked. *No one gets my sense of humor.* She propped her head on her hand. "I prefer 'bastard' if you don't mind, especially since I don't know who my real parents are. But enough about my troubled and tortured past. I need to focus on my future, and you're not in it." *At least not yet.* "So, out you go. And take your brother with you."

A man's hand suddenly gripped the bed's edge, as if heroically saving himself from plummeting off a cliff. He pulled himself off the floor, wobbling as he stood. The man, as blond as his sister, shared a long glance with her. Faces softening, they turned away from each other at the same time; she stood from the bed while he collected his clothes. There were no hysterics from either him or her, no crying, no whimpers of, "Dear God, what have we done?" Even if Victor hadn't known them, their body language at the casino bar last night had strongly suggested that brother and sister were long-time lovers.

He was as devastatingly handsome as she was intoxicatingly beautiful and their faces held the mild contortion of disappointment from being hung-over. They'd probably blame the alcohol for what happened last night if they even talked about it at all. People always gave excuses for their behavior rather than finding reasons to support it. Pity. They made such a cute couple.

Lying on her side, Victor wiggled her fingers "goodbye" as the brother opened the door for his sister. He turned on his way out, pausing long enough to make his middle finger farewell meaningful.

Once the door slammed shut, Victor laughed. She shot her floor a cursory glance to make sure she wasn't about to step on any broken glass on her way to the bathroom. The maid service came today, so they'd take care of the mess of empty wine bottles, overturned nightstand, and crooked bed.

In the shower, her mind flowed like the warm waterfall running over her, splashing on the comment she made this morning about not knowing her real parents. That wasn't true – she didn't know her *birth* parents. Her adopted parents were her real parents, giving her a stable upbringing and affording her any opportunity she sought. They supported all her decisions and helped her earn a finance degree. Now that she was the top earning associate at Bouch & Becker Venture Capital, the largest venture capital firm in the state, she had repaid her parents tenfold. No want or desire went unmet while they enjoyed their lives in Hawaii.

Time to give them a call. Or a new car. Or both.

Today she decided on a charcoal gray three-piece suit with thin silver pinstripes. A black shirt to make her solid red tie pop. Ruby cufflinks and matching pocket square completed the ensemble. Feeling an old school look, she opted for a pair of white spats, the tips and short heels adding a touch of black. Perfect.

Victor knew very well what people in the office thought about her and what they said behind her back – she wanted to be a man. Not true. She loved being a woman. More than a few dresses in her closet hugged the curves of her 5'10" frame and caused the viewer's eye to drift to her cleavage. But the dresses were for fun, for nights out. The suits were for business, for her career. Of all the rumors about her, not one accused her of using her feminine wiles to advance her career. No man ever got accused of fucking his way to the top, and neither would she. Most women followed women's rules, dressing like women, thinking like women. Victor flipped the script. She loved beating men at their own game while creating her own rules. Especially when she needed to be ruthless.

However, she did allow herself a couple indulgences traditionally viewed as feminine. One being her long hair. Straight, its length flirted with the bottom of her neck. Her stylist colored it jet black, with two streaks of blood red starting at her hairline and running the entire length. When slicked back, as she often wore it, the red looked like horns. Her second nod to modern femininity – bright red lipstick. She had a wicked smile, a devil's smile as she had been told on numerous occasions, and she wanted to make sure people remembered it. She wanted to make sure it haunted their dreams.

Wallet, keys, cash, cell phone, lipstick in pant pockets. Fuck purses. On her way out the door, she texted her driver. Her chauffeur – a shorter woman in a black, double-breasted suit with a blue ponytail poking out from under the traditional chauffer hat – had the Rolls-Royce Phantom purring at the curb, door open. "Morning, Murphy."

"Good morning, Ma'am."

A gray-haired man wearing a lemon-yellow shirt drove by in a high-end piece of Italian machinery, convertible top down. Victor loved his incredulous frown and how he almost hit a parked car while staring at her. She raised a brow, amused, her lack of interest in high-end sports cars reinforced. A man drove high-end sports cars in Vegas either because he was old and advertising that he wanted to be a sugar daddy, or because he was young and over-compensating for a small penis. A woman drove high-end sports cars in this town either because her sugar daddy gave it to her, or she relished her status as a trophy for a man with a small penis. Victor had neither a penis nor the need for a sugar daddy, thus no desire for a high-end sports car.

Victor waited until Murphy pulled into traffic before asking from the back seat, "Any progress on the special project?"

"I should have more information for you within the hour, Ma'am."

"Excellent, thank you."

"Shall I explore other options for you regarding that matter?"

Murphy, an excellent chauffeur, possessed other skills that Victor tapped into once in a while.

"Not yet. Let's see if you're able to get the information we're looking for."

"Sounds like a plan."

End of their conversation, and Victor was grateful since her hangover started to assert itself. She was content to stare aimlessly out the window for the duration of the drive. At this hour in the morning the desert sun hung in a cloudless sky, muting the flashing casino lights. She smirked at the walks-of-shame on full display, and another hour would pass before the busses started dropping off out-of-towners with complimentary vouchers in hand at casino doorsteps. Owners and employees of the stores lining the side streets made their way into the shops, getting everything ready for the daily turn of the "closed" sign to "open."

The traffic was mostly commuters, but plenty of vacationers and gamblers rushed to start their day. Despite that, Murphy made great time as she pulled up to the offices of Bouch & Becker.

Less than two years old, the three-story complex sported the sleek curves of a race car. The sidewalks remained white with no algae in the front fountain. The first floor held cafés and boutique shops while the second floor contained offices. The third-floor apartments were so expensive that only the owners of the offices below could afford them. Victor had looked at them when they first opened, but found no value in what was being offered compared to the price.

Bouch & Becker's lobby bordered on ostentatious. Grays and whites styled with bold streaks of green colored everything. The walls, the furniture, the carpets, the paintings, the receptionist's desk. Green, gray, and white crushed stone lined the bottom of the hundred-gallon fish tank. The modern decor attracted younger entrepreneurs, and its flashy style gave them a sense of what they could have if Bouch & Becker invested in them. Victor understood the psychology behind the lavishness, but she didn't need to use it. She always let numbers do the talking. If that didn't work, then she'd dig into her devious playbook.

Strolling past the receptionist, a young man fresh out of college taking any job available so he could to get his foot in the door, Victor smiled at him. "Good morning, sweety. Love the tie. Brings out the blue in your eyes."

Just as he did every time she gave him a compliment, he blushed. "Thank you, Ms. Vargas."

Vargas. That had to change. If he still worked here by the end of the week, she'd correct him. No time for that now. She had a meeting to prepare for.

Unlike her luxury apartment, her office remained sparse. No personal knick-knacks, no framed pictures on her desk or bookcases, no plants, and the only wall hangings were two thirty-six-inch touch screen monitors. No need to include any part of herself in this office since she had designs for a different, bigger office. That could happen as soon as today. But she put that out of her mind to focus on her meeting with a company the firm planned to invest in. It was a done deal, the papers were going to be signed, but she wanted a refresher.

Then her phone buzzed.

A three-word text from Murphy: `We got it.`

# CHAPTER 03

*March 24th, New York*

Celina ran.

Less than a dozen other patrons were in the restaurant, but it seemed like a million. People screamed. They ran. Pushing and shoving. Panic rose all around her.

Celina ran.

Out. Out of the restaurant.

A red streak trailed along the sidewalk behind her.

Celina ran.

She had felt a splash when Caila's head exploded and she imagined herself splattered with blood, glops mixed in her hair, and dripping down her face.

The stale city air was too thin to fill her lungs, her breaths short and rapid. Acid bubbled up her throat and she swallowed hard to keep herself from throwing up.

*Move, just keeping moving.*

"HOME" flashed in her mind like a neon sign.

*Don't stop. Don't look back!*

One foot in front of the other. Faster. One block, then another.

No one looked at her or glanced her way as she weaved among the other people scurrying about. This was New York, though. A blood covered giantess was hardly enough of a sight to disrupt their myopia. Another block. Faster. Another. Sirens echoed off the buildings in the distance, getting closer. Another block.

*Two more, just two more.*

She made it! Home at last.

The brownstone was an indeterminate number of years old, but old enough for her grandparents to have lived in one of its apartments as young newlyweds.

Celina surprised herself by inserting her key in the door locks on the first try, considering how hard her hands shook. *Must be muscle memory*, she thought as she slammed the door closed and latched the five locks. Her body allowed her four long steps to the kitchenette sink before she vomited.

She turned on the faucet and cupped her shaking hands under the flow of cold water, then closed her eyes and splashed her face. The refreshing, cleansing, cool reality was short-lived when she opened her eyes and saw pink water swirling around the drain. With legs limp as overcooked pasta, she fought against collapsing to the floor, and a jolt of pain hit her shoulders as she caught herself.

The sight of Caila's blood brought back all the fear, confusion, and disgust. Celina wanted to crawl to her bed, get under the covers, and forget that she had a sister, one she had known for less than ten minutes. Forget the sight of her face exploding. But there was no forgetting. There was no running any farther than her apartment.

After a few deep breaths, she fumbled her way to the bathroom.

Water on, soap in hand, she bent over her sink and maniacally washed her face and neck. But the mirror told her it wasn't enough. No globs or chunks, just continual watery streaks of red along the right side of her hairline, ear, neck. A gurgle of disgust came from her stomach, echoing in her small bathroom.

Clothes off, shower on. Warm water hit her shivering body. The water helped calm her. Helped her think.

She should contact the police and explain everything, that she met with a stranger who turned out to be her long-lost twin on the verge of providing information about their birth father. Purely coincidental that he happened to be some kind of... of... how did Caila put it? Oh yes – a crypto forensics interest. And then Caila's head exploded.

Celina hugged herself when she started to shake again.

"No," she said, and clenched her fists and tightened her gut.

*No! Think.*

Caila's head couldn't have spontaneously exploded.

*Think.*

Glass. Celina remembered the sound of breaking glass right before the explosion of gore. Not a shatter, but more like a crackle. The sound came from the window by the booth, but it hadn't broken.

*Think.*

A hole? When Celina had jumped from the booth, she saw a hole in the glass.

*Did I? Or is my mind trying to fill in gaps?*

A bullet. A bullet made the hole in the glass and tore away half of Caila's head. That made no sense, but it was far more logical than spontaneous explosion.

She could have been shot.

*Okay, the police would certainly be there by now, investigating. I'll give them my statement and tell them what happened, and they can confirm whether or not she was shot.*

Celina felt moderately better now that she had decided on a plan of action. At least she stopped shaking enough to wonder if the police would allow her to claim Caila's belongings since they were her sister's. If they said, "no," because Caila hadn't listed her as a next of kin, then Celina could meet with the next of kin and ask more questions. That would be one way to find out more about her sister.

As Celina dressed, she ran through different scenarios about meeting the people in Caila's life, her thoughts interrupted when she eyed the bloody heap of clothing on her floor. She stuffed them in a black trash bag, then shoved that in another trash bag and so on until she had quadruple-bagged the entire mess. She'd deal with it later; right now, she needed a drink.

Though not much of a drinker, she had stored a few bottles of wine in the fridge for a cozy night in with a book. But this was no cozy night, and wine wouldn't cut it. A small conglomeration of harder stuff stood on top of her fridge, leftovers from friends and parties. Celina didn't know any of these bottles, but found one synonymous with elixir – whiskey. After one swig, she doubted the validity of this stuff being panacea as she coughed and shook her head. Thankfully, the sting in her throat and chest didn't last too long. But it allowed her to forget about her situation for a few seconds and it helped burn away the aftertaste of vomit.

She gulped another swig. It still stung, but she was prepared this time.

After one more swig, she replaced the cap and slid the bottle back where she found it. It wouldn't do her any good to smell like a distillery when she went to the restaurant to talk to the police.

She paced a few laps around the living room of her one-bedroom apartment, running through what she wanted to say and how to present the facts. The biggest issue would be explaining why she fled a crime scene. She had panicked. A person got shot right in front of her, less than five feet away. She'd seen her face burst, a woman who looked exactly like her. That was a valid reason to run away in a panic, right?

A thought struck her hard enough to stop her pacing, as if she'd been nailed to the floor.

*What if that bullet was meant for me?*

Impossible. Ludicrous idea. *Who would want to kill me?*

Her small group of friends and the occasional date did not qualify anyone as a possible murderer. But those were people *she* knew.

Caila was someone she didn't know, and she didn't know Caila's acquaintances, either. Or enemies. If someone had hunted Caila down, that meant others could hunt Celina down as well. But who? Who would want to? *Had they thought I was her?*

Another thought struck Celina, a good one, a freeing one. A proactive one.

*If she looks like me, then that means I look like her.*

Celina grabbed her jacket and ran out the door.

# CHAPTER 04

*March 24th, Frederick, MD*

High school was Hell, a penance that must be paid. At least this was how Orion Fogelberg felt. A few months over eighteen, he had lived a good, moral life. He listened to his parents for the most part, helped other people whenever he could, went to church now and again, studied to get good grades. He never cheated, rarely lied, and avoided nefarious thoughts. Sure, when a cute girl in a skirt bent over, he'd sneak a peek, but he still viewed her as a human being, not a prize or something to be hunted. So why did he have to suffer this punishment?

And, yes, he recognized "Hell" and "suffer" were terms too strong to describe his situation, but they were all he could come up with to define the mind-numbing monotony of coming to the same building day after day, sitting in the same chairs hour after hour. Droning teachers. Boring topics. Idiotic classmates. Orion got along with most in his age group but shared similar interests with only a few. Conversations about sportsball or celebrities held zero appeal. Then there were the complete assholes like Lance, the star quarterback waiting for Orion at his locker.

"So," Orion said as Lance struck a clichéd pose of huge arms crossed over huger chest. "How do I find myself so lucky to be graced by your scintillating awesomeness?" Orion knew he shouldn't provoke his nemesis, but he couldn't stop himself.

"Thanks to you, I got a 'D' on that pop quiz in math," Lance said with a growl.

Orion had known Lance was cheating off him, the beefy jerk as subtle as a brick through a window, so he performed the classic maneuver of penciling in the wrong answers. When Lance turned in his test, Orion erased the wrong answers and wrote the correct ones. "Interesting. I didn't realize I was holding your pencil for the quiz."

Lance gritted his teeth and his neck ligaments flared. Orion could hear the jock's muscles flex. He'd been beaten up by Lance a few times over the last four years, but not lately due to one reason, which Orion evoked by saying, "You don't want to jeopardize your scholarship, do you?"

Lance leaned down, his face uncomfortably close to Orion's, and said, "Just remember, if I fail any of my classes and lose my scholarship, that means I won't be going to OSU. I'll be staying around town. With you. So, next time, make sure your answers are right. I thought you people were supposed to be good at logic."

"Next time" meant the final, and it would be administered online, but if the dumb ass didn't already know that, Orion wasn't going to tell him. "When you say, 'You people,' I'm assuming you mean humans?"

Lance's wolf grin advertised that he thought himself clever. "Nah, I mean the chink in your armor."

Orion sighed. He had so many issues with that statement. First, he was Japanese, not Chinese. Actually, half Japanese, and if he wanted to be technical about it, he had mailed off a spit and hair sample to a DNA service and discovered he was 53.28% Japanese and 46.72% Eastern European. He wasn't entirely sure how the service had the technology to come up with freakishly precise percentages yet wasn't able to offer heritages more accurate than "Eastern European." Secondly, it twisted his gut that this moron thought his euphemism subtle enough to exonerate himself from the school's anti-bullying policies. Unfortunately, every policy had its loopholes – as a star athlete, Lance had a blank check for most aspects of high school life. Including being an asshole to anyone he deemed weak, such as Orion and his best friend, Brennan, on his way to join Orion at his locker.

As much as Brennan feared Lance, he never let it stop him from meeting up with Orion.

"Oh, look, your fag," Lance said, bringing his first two fingers to his lips, pantomiming smoking a cigarette. Orion always imagined Lance crushing a celebratory beer can against his forehead followed by nonstop rounds of fist bumps to his fellow football players after learning the derogatory word was also British slang for "cigarette."

"Oh, look, it's Phil," Brennan said.

Lance frowned and took a menacing step toward Brennan. "Yeah? What's that supposed to mean."

"Phil. Phil McCraken." Brennan licked his lips and then winked. "That's the name on your scholarship, right?"

Lance shoved Brennan against the lockers, then glanced around the busy hall to see if anyone noticed. Orion was sure everyone saw, but thanks to aggressive apathy, no one reacted. Another reason why Orion disliked his classmates. A bunch of cowards. Lance must have taken the apathy as a sign of good fortune because he mumbled, "Faggots. Both of you," and strutted away.

"You okay?" Orion asked Brennan as they started down the hall to their next set of classes. "That hit sounded hard."

Brennan shrugged. "I'm good. Like Lance, it was all sound, no substance. Plus, I'm in too good of a mood. I went on a date last night."

"Nice! Anyone I know?"

"Doubt it. He's a freshman at Towson University." Brennan spotlighted the last two words to imply sophistication.

Orion replied, "Oooooh, older man! I didn't realize you were into daddies, you grave robber."

"He's literally seven months older than me. You're just jealous."

"Maybe."

"What about Sophie from art class? I know you're shy, but you two get along."

"Yeah, but she's too goth. There's nothing wrong with tapping into one's dark side to enhance who you are, but she takes it to an extreme. Wouldn't surprise me if she raises zombies just by walking through a cemetery."

"Raising zombies is difficult. They eat a lot, never sleep, and don't make great pets. You can dress them up in cute little outfits, but they are *not* photogenic and if you can't post pics on all your social media accounts, then what's the point?"

Orion chuckled. "Maybe I want one for companionship?"

"Ugh. So, you'll have to buy one then, but make sure you get one that comes with papers. Don't want to get one from a backwoods zombie mill. My Uncle Zeb got busted for running an illegal zombie mill and he's now in county for six years."

Orion laughed. "Weirdo."

"None weirder. All right. Off to class. See you at lunch."

Orion found his next class, Psychology – a science credit with no lab time – just as mundane as any other non-art class. However, he was excited to get started on his new character, Zeb the zombie farmer.

The sketches started simple enough, a large man in overalls standing in front of a barn and facing a line of zombies. Orion enjoyed sketching to get the ideas and images floating around in his head on paper, but he loved the detail work. Details breathed life into his world. The rotting skin falling off one zombie's jawbone. The farmer picking mushrooms from another zombie's shoulder. One zombie only had nine fingers, the missing one in the ear of a different zombie. The black void of their eyes. Orion's hand moved in tight circles to make their eyes darker. Darker. The abyss within their skulls triggered something within him. A memory? Not quite. A dream he had? Maybe. If it were a dream, it tapped into feelings he couldn't articulate. Fear? Comfort? Was there such a feeling as finding comfort in fear? This elusive feeling moved out of range whenever he reached for it, blurring right before he could define it. What was it? What caused it? What—?

"*Orion!*"

He jolted, almost jumping out of his seat. Looking around to see who yelled for him, the voice unfamiliar, he began to wonder…

"Where am I?" he mouthed, disoriented. This wasn't Psychology class. This was the cafeteria. Which meant he not only blanked out for Psychology, but English as well.

"Hey. Whoa, that drawing looks intense."

Orion jumped again, but this time he saw who startled him. Brennan. He joined Orion at the lunch table. "Wow. You really need to cut back on your caffeine intake."

After one last look over each shoulder, Orion said, "Yeah, sorry. Just zoned out."

Zoned out was an understatement. Orion lost almost two full classes worth of time. And a mysterious voice snapped him out of his stupor. Rationality pointed to Brennan, but it didn't sound like him. Deeper. Colder.

"Okay, you have to tell me about this character," Brennan said as he pulled Orion's notebook from him.

"Ummm, you were the one who came up with him. It's—" Orion's voice disappeared when he saw what Brennan was looking at. Not Zeb and the zombies, but a different character stared back at him, its face stretched into a horrific rictus, razorblades for teeth, tight skin accentuating maniacally bulbous eyes. Fingers twisted into pernicious tips reached from the confines of the paper. The only accoutrements were a bent blue top hat and blue collared cape, the bottom finishing in jagged shreds. "—ummm. I... I've seen him in my dreams."

Brennan didn't blink, his breaths soft and shallow, his tone a reverent whisper. "This is amazing. Your foreshortening is perfect. It's like he's reaching for me."

"Yeah, cool. Thanks." Orion was pretty confident those words came out of his mouth, but he barely heard them, too distracted when Brennan flipped the page to another image of the character in perfect realism as if photographed rather than drawn. The eyes glossy, a film of ooze ready to drip from them. Goosebumps flowed along Orion's arms.

The voice that he had heard came from this man.

# CHAPTER 05

*March 24th, New York*

The Orchid Hotel harkened back to the days of yore; a big chunk of building splashed with art deco. Celina was relieved by the lack of doorman in front of the hand-carved wooden doors under the awning, since she had been standing across the street staring at it like a stalker for the past five minutes.

Celina needed the time to ready herself for what she had to do. She paced, controlled her breathing, played through a hundred different scenarios. Maybe she looked crazy, but she needed answers.

She had always been tall, hitting her current height at fifteen. From that moment until adulthood, she helped her friends get into rated-R movies by pretending to be older. Boys with excess cash paid her to buy nudie magazines for them. No one selling the movie tickets or magazines ever asked a six-foot girl with an earnest face for identification. *Just like I did back then, frown and act like I'm in a hurry*, she reminded herself as she crossed the street. But stopped before she entered the hotel.

Caila wouldn't frown.

Celina only knew her for half a conversation, but without a doubt, her sister never once frowned. Maybe her smile didn't always beam, but she never stopped smiling. Celina's cheeks hurt thinking about smiling for that long, but she needed to do this, so she readied herself to grin without grimacing.

Adding a bit of haste to her step, Celina entered the hotel and aimed for the front desk the way Caila had entered the restaurant. Confident. Excited. On a mission.

The front desk clerk wore a suit with a coordinated shirt and tie. Celina guessed him to be her senior by a decade or two, and unamused with the world in general by the way he typed furiously on the computer keyboard.

"Hi," Celina started, upset at how squeaky the word came out of her mouth. "I've been gone all day and just realized that I left my keycard in my room. I'm so sorry to ask, but may I have a new one?"

Maintaining an aggravated hunch over the keyboard, the clerk raised his eyes at her. "I'll need to see identification first."

Celina shrugged and arched her eyebrows, hoping to elicit a modicum of sympathy. "My name is Caila Rappaport, but I left my driver's license in my room."

"Room number?"

*Shit*! Celina hadn't thought of that. Her first instinct was to abort the mission. *No! Think!* "I'm really embarrassed to say this, but...." She pulled on the words like taffy, stretching them out to buy enough time for an idea to coalesce. "... but I travel so much that I literally forget my room number. It took me a half an hour of wandering around this area for me to remember which hotel I'm staying at."

The clerk looked up from the computer to address Celina with cross-armed scorn. "Look, Miss, you can't whisk in here and ask me to take you on your word for a room key—"

"Whoa!" from a younger man wearing the same color combination of suit, shirt, and tie. "Whoa, Milton. Let's take it down a notch. You remember Caila, right? You were with me yesterday when she checked in."

"I do remember Ms. Davenport. But something is off with her. Her hair is shorter. And she's wearing different clothes than when she left this morning."

Celina glanced to the door and judged how many steps it would take to sprint away. This man – Milton – saw through her shabby ruse. The other clerk – Tucker, according to his name tag – smiled at her while he continued to address Milton.

"I find it hard to believe that there could be anyone else in this world like Caila."

Caila. Not Ms. Davenport. Obviously, Caila had interacted with Tucker.

Celina tried to brighten her smile more. "Thank you."

Tucker put both hands on Milton's shoulders. "Tell you what, Milton. Why don't you take a break?" He guided the older man away from the counter. "I can handle this from here."

Milton pulled away from Tucker and stormed off in a huff, but not before muttering, "Oh, I bet you can."

Tucker pulled a new keycard from a drawer and tapped away on the computer. "Please forgive him. He's one of the million struggling mystery writers in the city, so everyone is a criminal with nefarious motives. He has seven unpublished novels, and he came to work complaining that the latest just got rejected for the tenth time."

*Keep smiling.* "We can all relate to frustration. I mean, I locked my key and driver's license in my room after all."

Tucker slid the card out of the reader and into a paper sleeve. He wrote the room number on the sleeve and handed it to her. When she reached for it, he clasped her hand with both of his. Celina gasped when he leaned close enough for her to smell a hint of mint on his breath. He whispered, "Any time. And I mean *any* time. I know you told me you're not in town for long, and I gotta be honest – I was walking funny for most of the day, but I'd be more than happy to meet up again. If you'd like to, that is."

The blush hit Celina so hard and so fast she swore her head was going to turn to ash. Of all the scenarios she took into consideration before walking into the hotel, being propositioned by a man – one her twin sister had sex with last night – was not one of them! Mind not fully in control of the situation, she gently slipped her hand from his and said, "Thank you. I'll think about it."

*I'll think about it?* she screamed at herself as she hurried to the elevator. *What kind of response was that?*

She kept her focus straight ahead until the elevator doors closed. Shaking, she looked at the key. Room 504.

Thank God for the slow elevator – it gave her time to recover.

Her plan almost failed thanks to an overly observant mystery-writing stickler for the rules, but she fooled the man who had more intimate knowledge. A handsome man. About an inch or two shorter than she, but his bright blue eyes made up for the height difference. Did her sister have sex with him *immediately* after arriving in the city? Sheesh. Just another question that she couldn't directly ask. And that little nugget of supposition opened another barrel of questions about Caila's life. Hopefully there would be a few answers in room 504.

The room was the size of Celina's apartment, maybe a little bigger. Everything looked newer, too. No water stains on the ceiling, no paint discoloration in the corners of the walls. It saddened her to see this room, designed to be a transitory stay, had homier décor, even if it lacked the knickknacks and art that made her apartment a home.

The bed was made. A small suitcase, zipped closed, sat on the ottoman in front of the armchair. On the floor next to the chair lay a pair of pants, top, panties, and bra, presumably what Caila had worn the night before. Nothing in the closet, nor in the dresser drawers. Caila's clothes remained in her suitcase, three days' worth by Celina's estimate. The bathroom counter remained just as sparse. A tube of lipstick. Eyeliner. Small compact with foundation. Toothbrush, toothpaste, floss. This made sense. Within a few minutes of knowing her sister, Celina imagined her not wanting to waste time with unnecessary formalities. There was no real need to unpack a suitcase and put away clothes in a hotel room, yet people did, Celina being one of them. Not Caila. Why waste time when you might need to pack at any moment? Why spend the night alone when you could have fun with the handsome desk clerk? Why spend money and effort on an elaborate beauty routine when all she needed was small touch of makeup? How could Caila have natural beauty but not Celina?

Celina looked at herself in the mirror. This face sat across from her less than an hour ago, yet it didn't. Caila's lipstick shade had been subtle, close enough to her natural coloring. The same with her eye shadow. Her eyeliner did nothing more than make her eye color pop. Yet, such minimal changes made their faces very different.

And Caila smiled more.

Celina hated the patronizing *you-should-smile-more*, but if someone owned a tool that made life easier, why not use it? She owned the same tool that helped her sister, but she didn't know how to use it. And so she smiled. The mirror reflected a woman similar to Caila, but the difference was like one between a match flame and a flashlight. How did Caila wield it? Bigger. Brighter. Celina thought about how she had smiled when she walked into the hotel lobby. She thought about Tucker. *There! That smile right there!*

*Now* she was looking at Caila.

Celina frowned and turned away from the mirror.

*Stupid!* She came here to learn more about her enigmatic twin sister, not about herself as if she were in an insipid afterschool special. Celina turned off the bathroom light and went back into the main room, to the desk.

She plopped in the chair and wondered if she'd get lucky with the laptop. A password prompt appeared on the screen when she tapped the space bar. Her sister probably stored all the answers she needed in this computer. Who was their father? Did other crypto-forensics figures also have children?

She'd take the laptop with her and try random words in the comfort of her own home. Most of her friends were nerds like her, and maybe one of them knew how to pick the lock of this treasure chest so she could access its riches.

Then her luck changed ever so slightly.

Next to the laptop sat a notepad, generic white sheets with blue lines. Caila's writing was different. Wild. Frenetic. Celina's was much more controlled, boring. Celina wasn't sure how this made her feel, but the writing told her Caila was a note taker, something they had in common, and that she must have been conducting research while waiting for their appointed meeting time.

Only one page of notes, and at the top Caila had written, "What if she says no?" Under that were two choices: "Find out where she lives. Go to where she works." A star by the second option.

Celina's social media accounts made it easy to find her work address. She often posted pictures of the newest games arriving at Roll and Role. At least one account offered accessibility to her email address. Zero reference to where she lived, though, and the lease remained under her maternal grand-mother's maiden name.

A line drawn by a heavy hand separated that section from the next. Two names. Two other people Caila must have been researching. The first name was Victor Vegas, and where Victor worked – Bouch & Becker – includ-ing a phone number and address, coincidentally enough in Las Vegas. The next name was Genocide Stone. At least Celina thought that was a name. Under it the words "Genocide & The Doomsdays. B-Sides bar, Chicago, next show the 26th."

The room phone rang, and Celina jumped from the chair.

Who could possibly know she was here? Maybe a family member checking on Caila? Another hook up she had wanted to meet? Someone else she contacted from her research list returning her call? If so, it might bring Celina one step closer to answers.

She answered the phone. "Hello?"

"Hey, Caila? It's me, Tucker. I wanted to give you a head's up... There are a couple cops on their way to your room. They came in asking if you stayed here and Milton gave them your room number. I don't know if you're in trouble, but... I just... I just wanted to let you know."

"Thank you," Celina whispered before gently replacing the receiver. She then ripped the first few sheets from the note pad and shoved them in her pocket. She snapped the laptop closed and slid out the door just as the eleva-tor dinged. The blue leg of a police uniform stepped out. Celina turned and started walking the other direction.

"Miss?"

Head down and heart pulverizing her ribs, she kept walking toward the stairway at the end of the hall.

"Miss?" A little more assertive this time.

*Just keep walking. They didn't see my face. They don't know I look like Caila. Five more steps. Three.*

"Ma'am!"

Celina tried opening the stairwell door enough to slip through, afraid that if she whipped it open, she'd make herself more suspicious, but it was heavier than she thought. The push bar hit her hip and she bounced off the jamb as she stumbled her way into the stairwell, aiming for the first step with no control of her feet. Grabbing the railing with both hands, she dropped the computer.

Many elements of the hotel made a visitor feel as if they stepped right into the 1930s. Not that stairwell, though. Its cinderblock walls were painted beige and on each floor a landing broke up two flights of stairs. But the stairs didn't touch, creating a gap all the way to the ground floor, where the laptop crashed.

As pieces of the shattered screen fell away, Celina stopped only long enough to snatch the computer. Clutching it to her chest and crying, she ran the entire way to her apartment. The tears didn't stop even after she slammed her door closed and slumped against it, sliding to the floor.

Twice tonight she came home shaking and in tears. She wanted to get back to the status quo, but someone had murdered her sister, and she had run from the police.

She pounded the floor and swore at herself for panicking, concerned at how bad it looked to leave the hotel room of a dead woman whom she looked like. Assuming anyone had actually seen her face. She had intended to go back to the restaurant after looking around Caila's hotel room, but she returned to her apartment because she panicked. If she hadn't wasted time fiddling with the computer, if she had snatched and dashed, then she would have left with a working laptop. Not now. Thanks to being clumsy – *always so damn clumsy!* – she destroyed the one thing that could have helped her get answers.

Maybe the computer could be repaired. An electronics repair shop sat on every other block. But she didn't have the password, the last four digits of Caila's social security number, her mother's maiden name, or *any* personal information about Caila.

Her room felt stifling hot even though the temperature read a comfortable 70 degrees, exactly where she had set it. She stood and took off her jacket, then shuffled far enough to collapse on her couch. Still too hot. And now she heard a scraping noise. Fast. Close by. Coming from…? Her. It was coming from her chest, her hard breathing, fast and raspy. *Control. Control it.*

Eyes closed, she forced herself to inhale deeply, then blow it out to a count of five. Again, and again.

Though the rasping subsided, she still felt antsy and discontent, uncomfortable in her own home, her own skin. The police had no idea who she was, but she feared they might burst through her door at any moment. *Control your breathing.*

She had to move. She got off her couch and paced in circles, wanting to keep walking. Out of her apartment. Out of the city. She needed help.

Who to contact? None of her friends would know what to do. A handful of them would panic just from listening to her story. Others would offer a place to stay, but they lived in the city with apartments just as small and confining.

She pulled out the paper with Caila's notes, her handwriting strange and wonderful. Celina suddenly felt linked to the two names on the paper more than any of the contacts in her cell phone. One of those names was in Las Vegas. To get back to the status quo, she'd have to go *very* far outside her comfort zone.

Celina grabbed a small bag from her closet and began to pack.

# CHAPTER 06

*March 24th, Las Vegas*

Victor was leaning back in the visitor's chair with her feet propped on the desk when Marshall Becker entered. Like every businessman in his sixties, he prospered around the middle and thinned everywhere else, his white hair a ring around the back of his head. His thick mustache curved around the edges of his mouth, the tips pointing downward to the draw attention to his jowls. They were extra floppy when he frowned, as he did right now, eliciting a smile from Victor. This was his office, and he was clearly not happy to see Victor in it.

"Mornin', Marshall," Victor said.

Marshall slammed the door, his face like that of a man ready for a colonoscopy, but by the time he dropped into the leather throne behind his desk, his expression softened. "What do you want, Victor?"

From his tone Victor figured he was weary of her brusqueness – "shenanigans" as he so often described it. "I'm here to talk about my promotion."

Marshall laughed. "You came here right out of college and been here six years. That's hardly enough experience for me to think of you as a partner."

She swung her legs off the desk and sat up. "Me not leaving since I got here shows that I'm loyal, and I've been the top performing associate all six years. My portfolio is more than double the next best associate, Johnson, who has been here ten years. Look, I'm not asking for my name to be on the letterhead yet. I just want the opportunity to buy in. Ten percent. It doesn't disrupt control, but it gets my foot in the door and sets me up to buy more whenever you and Bouch decide to float away on your golden parachutes."

"You are a damn near perfect associate, but I'm not seeing partner."

The conversation thus far had gone as if he were reading from a script Victor had typed. Time to drop the proverbial bomb with what her assistant-slash-chauffeur-slash-procurer of the illicit, Murphy, had discovered.

Victor pulled out her phone and tapped away at the screen until she found the video. She hit play and then slid her phone across Marshall's desk, right under his face. He looked down at the black and white video and his frown returned.

Bouch & Becker invested top dollar for their security system, so advanced that the partners forgot how to operate it, often forgot it was even on. The hi-def video clearly showed Marshall's pants down around his ankles with Ana's skirt—Stanley Bouch's executive assistance—up over her waist and her blouse off, her fake breasts jiggling with every thrust.

"See, Marshall, you're only looking at me as an associate, but I am capable of much more. For example, I suddenly and mysteriously received this video, but I possess the skills to find out how it ended up in my inbox and thusly prevent it from reaching the public."

"I assure you, this act was consensual."

"Never said it wasn't, but I'm confident your wife and children won't care. Plus, it's Stanley's secretary on Stanley's desk."

Marshall leaned closer to examine the footage, a look of surprise on his red face as if he forgot where he was at the time. He looked back up and huffed. "Blackmail? You feel the need to try blackmail?"

"Nope. Blackmail is a forced quid pro quo where one party threatens to quid the quo out of another party by sharing information the first party dug up about the second party. I didn't dig this up and I'm certainly not threatening to share it. I'm demonstrating my value. As I said, I will discover how this came into my inbox and make sure it never goes public. I'm more than an associate, Marshall. I'm a forward thinker who will propel this firm to the stars."

Becker rolled his eyes.

She expected that reaction. After all, she handed him a plate of shit and told him it was chocolate cake.

But she didn't expect his prompt response. "The Ashtons and the Plimptons. Get fifty-one percent of those two companies and you can buy ten percent of Bouch & Becker."

*Fuck.* Two family run businesses looking for a little extra capital from B&B. The Plimptons' company was a generational financial cluster-fuck of siblings, uncles, aunts, and cousins sticking their hands in the money-pot. Victor already had a meeting with the Ashtons today to sign paperwork to buy twenty-five percent of their company for the cash they needed.

Victor sat back. She stared at Marshall, trying to see directly into his brain and figure out where to take this negotiation.

Marshall smiled.

That pissed Victor off more than anything else.

He leaned forward and rested his elbows on his desk. Never taking his eyes of Victor's, he dismissively slid her phone back to her. "Takes balls to do what you just did, but that doesn't equate to how you can take Bouch & Becker Venture Capital to the next level. As you implied, I'll be out of here in less than a decade. If that video makes it to the public, then I leave a little early. The wife will divorce me, my kids will be pissed at me, and Bouch may never speak to me again. I lose a few million, but I got plenty to keep me living a good life. An inconvenience. You want to be partner? Prove you'd be good at it."

Victor felt like she got played. She overestimated his priorities. But he gave her an opportunity. Challenging, yes, but she liked a challenge. She stood and pocketed her phone, then extended her hand and said, "You don't live up to your end of the agreement and there will be Hell to pay."

Marshall stood as well and shook Victor's hand. "Get those two companies in our portfolio with controlling ownership, and I'll have the paperwork ready the next day."

Now, off to do the impossible.

\*

40

The offices of Sugar Fix, Incorporated offered little comfort for a company with fifty employees. Modest. Clean. A bit too cramped, but they were located right above manufacturing. If the Ashtons accepted the new offer Victor was going to propose, they'd either have to move the offices or move production. Would the owners view that as a positive or a negative?

Sitting alone in the conference room, Victor ran through all kinds of scenarios while she waited for the owners. She didn't feel the need to flip through paperwork; her exceptional staff perfectly updated the last second changes. Every branch of her decision tree depended on how the owners would react to seeing her. No more time to mull over a plan – the door opened, and the owners entered.

Jackson and Jaime Ashton, the siblings Victor woke up with this morning, the very ones she kicked out of her bedroom.

"Oh, for fuck's sake," Jackson said as he turned to leave.

"What...? What...? Why? Why are you here?" Jaime asked, pushing past her brother and hurrying to the conference table.

Victor assumed their reaction would be bad. A million smartass comments skittered through her mind, but they were pesky bugs and she stomped on them all. This was business.

"My name is Victor Vegas and I represent Bouch & Becker Venture Capital. I'm here to deliver the final paperwork."

Jackson stopped short of leaving the room, and then looked to the heavens. "This keeps getting better and better."

"That's your real name? When you said it last night, I thought it was some stupid made-up name."

If Jaime's words were acid, Victor would be a pool of hissing goo. "It's real enough, and last night has nothing to do with right now."

Jaime dropped into the wingback chair closest to Victor. "Did you know who we were last night?"

"Of course, she fucking knew," Jackson barked as he slammed the conference room door shut hard enough to rattle the tacky paintings on the wall. He marched over to the table and took the seat next to his sister. "Either it's a game for her, or she wants to twist the situation for her benefit." He snatched the lone folder on the table and flipped it open. After a few head shakes and grunts of disgust while paging through, he flipped back to the first page and showed his sister. "I knew it. I fucking knew it. The bitch wants fifty-one percent of our company. That's why Marshall Becker's not here. He tells us what we want to hear and then sends her to fuck us over."

Frown as deep as the Grand Canyon, Jaime grabbed the paperwork and read it over. "Unbelievable. We agreed to twenty-five percent. Now you're asking for control, and at the last second?"

"Bitch probably recorded us last night. You gonna threaten to expose our relationship?"

Jaime pulled her eyes away from the papers and the siblings glared at Victor while awaiting an answer.

Victor decided to forgo her standard, "I'm a bastard, not a bitch," comment. They already heard it once this morning and it would do no good now. Posture relaxed, but professional, tone even to encourage a sense of calm, Victor said, "Yes, I knew who you two were when I interacted with you for recon. We were having too much fun to let business interfere. No, I did not record anything. Yes, we want a controlling share, but that's because your company has an amazing product."

"Then be happy with twenty-five percent," Jackson said in snap, "and give us the cash so we can show the world how great our product is."

"I said amazing, not infallible. You two developed a system that creates a fast, simple, and delicious single serving dessert. Who doesn't want a perfectly baked cheesecake for one in less than ten minutes? Or a bakery quality blueberry muffin in five minutes? Problem is – once Green Mountain developed Keurig and the K-Cup, everyone developed a similar system for other products. Now there's a system that makes mixed drinks. Another system cooks whole meals. A countertop cooking system reads the bar code of a pre-packaged meal for perfect cook time. How long do you think it will take any one of these established companies to compete directly against yours?"

Jackson worked his jaw muscles, chewing on unspoken words.

Jaime still frowned, but at least she was capable of speaking. "We had plans to take the money from your investment to expand production. The whole plan was spelled out in the proposal that your company *agreed to.*"

"Yep. I saw it. It's a nice plan, but not realistic. By the time you found a new place and got ready to ramp up production, the Huns would be at the gates. Your competitors will be prepared to take their product to a larger market, relegating you to a regional market. You'll own these shiny new machines and not enough people to sell to. That's if you don't blow the rest of the money trying to tackle your competitors head-on."

Jaime's expression of ire melted away to expose the concern underneath. "And you're saying if we agree to your new terms, you'd get us national market share before our competitors?"

"Absolutely. Sign today and tomorrow we'll take you and your brother to look at new locations for production or offices or both. Next week we'll double your HR staff so they can prepare for the impending increase in line workers. Week after, we'll show you the delicate dance between advertising and production. We at Bouch & Becker Venture Capital don't care that you two are president and vice president."

"As long as we do everything you tell us to," Jackson said with a snarl.

"At least you know the rules of the game."

"Fuck it." Face reddening, Jackson grabbed the papers and signed on all the applicable lines. He slapped the pen on top of the forms, slid them to his sister, and stomped his way to the door. "Just fuck it all," he said as he left.

With quick movements, Jaime signed as well. When finished, she stood and slid the papers toward Victor. "Though I'm not as colloquial as my brother, I share his sentiment. I remember what you said this morning and you're absolutely right. You are a bastard. I'm sure you can see yourself out and return to whatever Hell-pit you came from, because I can't stand to be in the same room with you for one more second."

By the time Victor collected the papers and stood, Jaime was gone. That was fine with her because she couldn't stop smiling. One down, one to go.

# CHAPTER 07

*March 24th, Chicago*

The crowd at Club B-Sides whooped and hollered, chanted along with the lyrics while fists pumped in the air. Genocide Stone paused from singing and paced, absorbing the audience's energy. She loved being on the stage, loved the heat of the lights behind her while sweat poured from her in sheets, loved how the crowd loved her. Sure, out of only a hundred people, half came because they knew someone from the opening band, but they all knew her songs, they all jumped and screamed and banged their heads and pounded the air with their fists.

> *Another day of what you need*
> *Nothing left of me, who I used to be*
> *Too late, I know*
> *But now it's time I make you go*

Definitely a pumped crowd tonight. She'd have to remember to talk to Ven about the opening band after the set. Right now, he was too busy strumming his bass while Gen screamed at the crowd.

They all knew the lyrics and screamed along.

> *I'd rather go to Hell than stay with you*
> *Everything you say*
> *And all that you do*
> *I'll see you dead*
> *Than in my head*
> *I'd rather go to Hell than stay with you*

Gen and her band blasted the small crowd with the refrain accompanied by an up-tempo shift. As people thrashed, they screamed along, sweating and smiling and laughing. X upped the pace on the drums while Lucas's guitar screamed and howled as if throttling a banshee.

Gen leaned over, letting the fans in front of the stage touch her, worshipers seeking blessings from their god. They yelled along with her, faster and faster.

*I'd rather go to Hell than stay with you!*
*I'd rather go to Hell than stay with you!*
*I'd rather go to Hell than stay with you!*
*I'd rather go to Hell than stay with you!*
*I'd rather go to Hell than stay with you!*

Their crescendo ended with the three different instruments playing their own chaotic noise of orgasmic bliss. Hands extended toward her from the audience, Gen slapped each and every one of them. With the final seconds of cacophony from her band, Gen offered the parting words, "And your friends suck, too! They're next!"

The room in Club B-Sides went dark, and shouts and applause followed. After a few beats of silence, the club's glaring lights illuminated the ugliness and the audience's mass dispersal. Generic punk music flowed from the house speakers tucked in the corners of the ceiling.

A few people aimed for the exit, but most lingered by the bar and high-top tables. Stragglers hung around up front and gave encouraging shouts as Genocide and The Doomsdays walked off the stage. Gen and Lucas offered a few shouts back while giving the heavy metal devil-horns salute. The ever-stoic Ven just kept walking, eyes straight ahead. X, on the other hand, whooped as he left the stage to join the patrons in their festivities. Gen knew well enough that he was in search of getting drunk, high, and in the pants of a groupie or two.

"I don't like him," Ven grumbled as they entered the backroom. His long hair was so black it seemed to absorb the light.

The dusky room – large enough to serve as an office with plenty of space to move around the standard desk, couch, chairs, and two file cabinets – shrank anytime Ven's bulky form stepped inside. His surliness fit right in with the threadbare carpet, faded walls, and water-stained ceiling tiles.

Gen sat in the chair behind the desk and propped up her feet, her thick soled, knee-high boots next to a stack of papers. She ran her hands through her hair, platinum with a dozen random streaks of dark red, creating the image of blood flowing from the sun. Clumped with sweat, she lifted her hair off the back of her neck. "You don't like anyone, Venom."

Leaning against one of the file cabinets, Lucas smirked as he dragged his hand through his sweaty spiked blue hair. "There is truth to that statement, Ven. You don't like anyone."

"He's not part of the cluster," Ven said with a grumble.

Lucas looked at Gen and gestured to Ven. "He does make a valid argument."

Gen picked at the tangle of necklaces off her torn, sleeveless black tee shirt and started to separate them. "Jesus, pick a side, dude."

Lucas' smile grew, the lines chiseling his face in all the right places, turning him into a sculpture of masculinity. "My side is with the band, always."

"X isn't a part of the band, either," Ven said.

"You thinking about keeping him full time, Gen?" Lucas asked.

At first, she hadn't. They landed a handful of out-of-state gigs over a two-week period and needed a drummer. A friend of a friend recommended Xander, or X as he referred to himself. He was loud and prioritized finding a party above everything else, but he never missed a meeting, show time, or beat. After the last short tour, she wanted to put on a show for her home venue and had asked him to drum again tonight.

Her home venue. Gen still thought of this place as her favorite place to play, not able to wrap her head around the fact that she now owned it. It had been eight months since she signed the paperwork. Over time, she became more comfortable running it, but it nestled within two places of her heart. The business side of running a club took up one spot, but every time she saw the "Club B-Sides" sign when she walked through the front door, she felt like it burrowed into a dark disassociated spot in her heart, like the club belonged to someone else.

"How pissed at me would you be if I did keep him full time?" Gen asked.

"I'd accept it, but I would silently seethe," Ven answered.

"His drug problem doesn't bother you?" Lucas asked.

Gen shrugged. "Name a drummer who isn't on something? He partied every night for the last two weeks and we had zero problems with his performance. Long as he shows up when he's supposed to and keeps that shit out of my club, then I don't see the issue."

Lucas' smile faded into a look of seriousness Gen seldom saw. He gave a curt nod toward the computer on the desk. The monitor, divided into quadrants, displayed what the security cameras recorded in the club. In black and white the upper left corner showed X hanging out at the bar with two skinny young women in tight skirts, everyone with a drink in hand. X tilted his head for maximum exposure of his neck while one of the women pressed her thumb and forefinger against it. X winced, then smiled.

"Did we just see her shoot him up with latro?" Lucas whispered.

"Mother fucker!" Gen shouted. "Ven, tell Vinnie to kick those bitches out, then you bring that piece of shit back here."

Though Venom rarely smiled, his glee was that of a devil dragging the damned to Hell. When he swaggered out the office to track down Vinnie, defeat weighed heavy within Gen's chest.

"Guess we didn't get rid of it all," Lucas mumbled.

"Looks that way." Gen had put herself through a lot, lost even more, to rid the world of that damn drug. If not for latro, though, she never would have become owner of Club B-Sides, nor other properties. But she was in no mood to be blinded by confliction and silver linings. She had to look at the ugly world with twenty-twenty vision.

Ven gave X a shove as they entered the office, and he shut the door behind them.

Pulling up from a stumble, X frowned, yet still held a party smile and looked back at Ven. "Hey, hey, hey, what's that all about?" Still flushed from a night of drumming, his skin shimmered oddly as if he were coated with a thin layer of grease instead of sweat.

"I don't like you," Ven answered.

"No shit! Not entirely sure why. I'm fucking delightful! And that's no excuse to bust up the little party I had going on."

"Took this off one of the skanks," Ven said as he tossed a latro delivery pack onto Gen's desk. A crushed bulb of clear plastic the size of a nickel with two needles, each a quarter-inch long.

"They have names, you know. They're people, too, with hopes and dreams," X said, but shrank back when Ven glared at him.

"Where'd you get the latro?" Gen asked.

X smiled and held his hands out, spread wide. "That's what this is all about? That? That's not latro."

Gen eyed the deep burgundy discoloration of X's injection site from where she sat. "Stop with the bullshit, Xander. Where'd you get it?"

"It's not mine and it's not latro."

Gen stood; Lucas and Ven took an aggressive step closer to X. Sweat flowed through X's matted hair and down his face. Gen snickered – Ven and Lucas were intimidating, and X might be ready to shit himself.

She didn't know how it was possible, but his skin reddened another shade or two, a web-work of green veins surfacing. Latro had nasty side effects, but nothing like this. She never saw anything like this before. "Fine, it's not yours then it belongs to one of your skanks. Where'd she get the latro?"

"It's not fucking latro!" X's arms shook. Not like a slight tremble of fear, rather an uncontrollable quake. His eyes bulged, and his skin tightened from swelling.

"Where'd you get it?" Ven barked.

"I don't have to tell you shit!" X snapped back, spittle slicking his lips and chin. "You two boys worship the fucking ground she walks on, but I don't! You jump when she says jump, but I don't fucking have to! This is a temp gig for me and… you know what? I'm done. I'm fucking done with you three fucks."

A line of blood trickled from his nostril.

"Watch your tone," Lucas said. "You wanna quit the band? Fine. But you need to tell us where the latro came… Hey. What the fuck is wrong with you?"

"Shit!" Gen yelled. "I think he's ODing!"

"Never seen latro do this," Ven said as he pulled out his cell phone. "I'll call an ambulance."

"Maybe he was telling the truth," Lucas said. "Hey, X, calm down buddy. Take a deep breath and let's get you to the couch. Just—"

X's phlegm-filled gurgle cut Lucas off. Then a spasm hit him. His arms snapped in odd directions, crossing over each other, while his legs turned inward, his knees knocking together. His head cocked to the right while his jaw jutted to the left. And his body didn't stop swelling.

An overdose of latro could cause rigor mortis like paralysis, leaving the victim twisted in unnatural ways. But the swelling? The blood from his eyes, mouth, and ears? This was crazy, and something other than latro.

"We need an ambulance at Club B-Sides," Ven barked into his cell-phone, but then caught his breath when X's left eye popped out of his head.

A wet noise of garbled vowels came from X's mouth, the sounds of screaming underwater. As if by an invisible knife, the skin along his neck split open as did the flesh from shoulder to elbow, blood gushing from both openings followed by a foamy orange ooze.

"What. The. Fuck," Lucas whispered.

More gashes tore open along his flesh, the sudden bursts of blood staining his clothes dark red. Different hues of red and black globs flowed from under his shirt.

Gen shuddered as X's skin fell away in thick sheets, exposing parts of his skeleton still covered in sinewy meat, and his gelatinous organs. Swollen tongue wedged between his teeth, he finally fell to the floor. Slime-slicked flesh and bone lay in a thick pool of red, as if a blind god tried to make a human but quit the effort in a fit of frustration.

"Police," Ven spat into his phone, voice rough. "Ambulance and police at Club B-Sides."

Gen pulled out her cell phone. "Vinnie? Yeah, shut the place down. Get everyone out now, no need to settle tabs. I don't care what excuse you use. And find out where those skanks live! It's going to be a long night."

# CHAPTER 08

*March 25th, Las Vegas*

Victor meticulously separated the red streaks of hair from the black on the right side of her head and let them hang in front of her eye. Gently, she did the same thing to the red lock of hair on the left side. Through two crimson curtains of hair, she looked down at the forms on her desk. Instead of rose-colored glasses, she wanted to look at the world through blood red hair, hoping that'd help her see the numbers differently. Nope. Same as the last time she looked at them.

"Quit fucking around," she said, scolding herself as she sat up straight and slicked her hair back. So focused on landing the Plimptons, she had stayed in last night. With no form of usual hangover, she was jittery. But she needed to figure out a solid approach to this problem.

Plimpton Enterprises, Incorporated consisted of seven different shareholders, each shareholder a separate corporation owned by a different family member. Due to the poorly written bylaws of Plimptons Enterprises, the number of shares shifted annually based on the valuations of the companies holding the shares. Needless to say, each family member did their best to increase the value of their individual corporations, mostly by adding as many product lines and other businesses to their own portfolios. The seven relatives offered ten percent of Plimpton Enterprises to Bouch & Becker for cash and leadership expertise. Their desire for leadership expertise was bullshit – the Plimptons just wanted the cash.

Victor could turn Plimpton Enterprises into a gold mine, but she needed the right approach. She had been in her office for two hours, stewing. And nothing. She even thought about praying for an answer, but this was Sin City and no way her prayer would be heard over the billion prayers flowing from the casino floors every day. Then came a knock on her door. "Yeah?"

The receptionist poked his head in. "Ma'am? Someone is here to see you. She says she came all the way from New York."

An unannounced guest from the east coast? Interesting. "Send her in."

Awkwardly, the woman thanked the receptionist and stepped into the office. The answer to Victor's problem hit her like a lightning bolt. Easily six feet tall and wearing a casual green dress of thin material, the visitor fidgeted with the complimentary bottle of water that Bouch & Becker gave to all guests. As most people did when they first saw Victor, the woman did a double take. "Oh, hi. Sorry to bother you, but I'm looking for Victor Vegas?"

Victor stood and smiled, gesturing to the chair in front of her desk. "I'm Victor. Please, have a seat."

With downcast eyes and a sheepish smile, the woman accepted the invitation. "Sorry. I assumed you were a man?"

Victor returned to her leather chair. Instead of spouting any form of rhetoric, she simply said, "Most people do."

"I'm guessing it's short for Victoria?"

"Something like that." This wouldn't do. She needed this woman to be more than what she was presenting. Not only was she tall, but she also had a solid frame. If she put on ten more pounds of muscle, she might be able to whoop the ass of an average man. And Victor loved her face – if she let loose with a big smile, she'd be devastatingly radiant, but on the flip side, if she frowned, she'd give the observer fear sweats. Obviously, Victor didn't have the time to bulk her up, but she could do a lot with this raw material. "I go by Victor not to make people think I'm a man, nor do I want to be a man. I just use a man's rules."

The woman hadn't come to hear this, but she leaned forward enough to show intrigue. "Rules?"

"Yep. Twenty-five years into the twenty-first century and we, as a society, have come a long way, but men still have certain advantages because they follow a different set of rules than women."

"I'm sorry, but I'm not sure what you're talking about?"

"You're a perfect example of what I'm talking about. You've apologized three times in the two minutes. Manners are a necessity in society, but you literally did nothing wrong and yet still apologized. Your eyes went right to the floor as you walked from the door to the chair. Every sentence I've heard from you ended with the upswing of a question, almost like asking for permission to be heard. And I still don't know your name because you haven't introduced yourself. You haven't done that yet because you've been trained to wait for someone to ask you to validate yourself. Think of all the men in your life. Do any of them follow those rules? I'm not talking about the dude bros who bathe in toxic masculinity, and you don't seem like the kind of person who associates with those kinds of men anyway. I'm talking about the regular guys, the sensitive ones, the progressive ones, the nice ones, the ones who actually take other people's feelings into consideration. Sure, they might do a couple of the things you just did, but do you know any man who would have handled this situation exactly how you did?"

The woman's eyes widened at first, then she blinked rapidly, as if processing this new information and applying it to her views of the world. "Wow. I never realized I was following a set of rules. I always thought of my-self as—" She cut herself short and frowned.

Victor could almost hear the gears of this woman's mind grind through her thoughts.

The woman smiled and extended her hand to Victor. "Hi. I'm Celina Davenport."

Getting better. Victor reached across her desk and shook it. "Nice to meet you, Celina. I'm Victor Vegas. What can I do for you?"

"Well… I don't know for sure. I had the whole flight from New York to think about this, so I should be better prepared. There's a lot going on right now and… Oh my God, I'm rambling. Sorr—" Celina stopped herself and closed her eyes. After a deep breath, she opened her eyes and started again. "I know this is going to sound unbelievable, but I think we're connected some-how."

*Oh, Christ, we got a crazy one.* "I've heard some unbelievable pickup lines before, but this has got to be the wildest one yet."

Blushing, Celina sat straighter and waved her hands in front of her as if trying to erase her words. "No, no, no, no. Nothing like that, I swear."

This wasn't good – Celina seemed like she got flustered too easily. Clearly, she wasn't going to be a good enough actress for what Victor had in mind. But, still, Celina was workable. Victor only wanted her presence, and Celina didn't need to speak to be intimidating. Two hours until the meeting with the Plimptons. Could Victor *really* pull this off? *Yes. Yes, I can.*

Celina cleared her throat. "What I mean is – weird and scary things happened to me yesterday and I discovered I might be a part of something bigger. I came across your name and I wanted to talk to you and hear if anything like what happened to me happened to you and if there might be any commonality between us."

Could Victor spend two hours listening to crazy ass delusional conspiracy theories? The list of things she wouldn't do for career success continually shrunk. "Okay, I'll listen, *but* I need you to do something for me."

Celina looked concerned. "Do... what?"

"I have a big meeting in two hours. It's a world changer for me. If it goes well, I'll make it worth your while."

"A... a meeting? Like a business meeting? I... I... I work in a tabletop gaming themed café. Men rules or women rules, I don't think I'd be qualified for any kind of business meeting."

Victor stood and strode toward the door. She paused and gestured for Celina to follow. "Trust me, if you follow my lead, you'll be perfect. First, we need to get you into something more befitting the situation. While we're prepping, I'll tell you all about it and you can tell me all about the weird things that happened to you yesterday."

Eyes dropping downward, Celina looked as if Victor had stolen her lunch money. After a few moments of stunned silence, Celina shrugged her shoulders and stood. "Okay."

\*

"Stop fidgeting," Victor whispered sternly to Celina as they walked along the sidewalk toward the offices of Plimpton Enterprises, Incorporated.

Tugging at her light gray suit jacket, Celina replied, "I can't help it. I've never worn a suit before, let alone a men's suit. And these shoes feel... weird."

"That's what comfortable feels like. Another secret that men have kept from us – their dress shoes are way more comfortable than our heels."

Right after they had left Victor's office, she called Murphy. A quick drive to where Victor got most of her clothes and within an hour, they had Celina dressed in Armani and a pair of black Bottega Veneta Oxfords. People stared as they walked by, which made Victor happy with her fashion choices. Celina looked like a bona fide force of nature.

After Celina told her story, Victor didn't know what to make of her. There was a certain sweetness about her. Naiveté usually annoyed Victor, but Celina made it work. Even though she had so few experiences, she was receptive to learning, and Victor appreciated her willingness to try new things. But... did she really witness her twin sister getting shot in the head?

Victor's exposure to mental illness had been nil, so she didn't have a good measuring stick to compare Celina against. She always assumed there would be more signs of schizophrenia or disassociation than one crazy story. Then again, having known this woman for only two hours, Victor had convinced her to dress in a suit and take part in a wild business scheme. Now, Celina needed to keep her shit together and not spout off any more conspiracy, crypto forensics nonsense, and everything would be golden.

The receptionist of Plimpton Enterprises showed them to the conference room. They were the first ones to arrive, due to the arrogance of the seven family members.

"Perfect," Victor said as she opened her briefcase. She pulled out the contract and eight folders, each one containing her proposal. She handed one of the folders to Celina and then placed the other seven around the table. "The plan is simple. I'm going to yammer for a few minutes and then I'll give you a signal. All you have to do is say the numbers are shit. That's all. No matter what happens after that, you sit in silence."

"Okay," Celina said. She opened the folder, and after a few seconds, she squinted and cocked her head. Then frowned and turned the page. Did she actually understand what she was looking at? The hosts entered the room before Victor could ask her.

Victor had once known how the Plimptons were related to each other, but long since forgot. Cousins, uncles, aunts, and at least two sets of siblings among them. It didn't matter.

Boisterous, the family members chatted and laughed among themselves as they took their seats. This was their usual tactic – get their mark smiling and laughing along with them, make them feel like part of the family so too many questions weren't asked and red flags were ignored. Victor sat quietly until they were ready.

"Victor Vegas!" Dante called out joyously from the head of the table. He wore a golf shirt and kept his thick hair and beard as perfectly coiffed as a Greek statue. Straight teeth gleamed unnaturally white in his bright smile. "It's so very good to see you. I'm assuming you're here to become a shareholder in Plimpton Enterprises, Incorporated, which is great news. But I see you've brought a new friend for us to meet."

Just as Victor suspected. Dante glossed over the point of the meeting in an attempt to cut out negotiations and secure signatures on the dotted line. She planned to get the conversation back around soon enough, so she placated him by saying, "This is Monique Deveraux, a world renown financial analyst from France."

The lie was a risk, but she remained confident that none of the Plimptons would make the slightest attempt at any form of due diligence. There'd be no surprise moves from them.

However, a huge surprise arose when Celina blurted, "These numbers are shit."

Victor clenched her jaw to keep it from falling to the floor. When she cued Celina to say her line, she had hoped for some paraphrasing. And what kind of accent was that? Was she trying for Russian? But the statement wiped away Dante's smile and made everyone shift in their seats.

"Excuse me?" Dante asked.

"The bylaws make no sense," Celina continued in her weird new accent. "There is no consistency on how any of your businesses are valuated.

The intercompany transfers and loans to and from your businesses look like spider webs. I can see the need for a new proposal."

"New proposal?" Dante snapped, prompting everyone at the table to open their folders. After briefly looking over the papers, Dante yelled, "Fifty-one percent! This is preposterous!"

Before the harrumphs and grumbling got too loud, Victor said, "Every time you met with a representative of Bouch & Becker, you glossed over the numbers, hoping we would too. We felt unsettled by that, so I called in an expert."

"Her? Some woman we've never heard of? Why should we give a damn what she says?"

"Because I trust her enough to pay her a hundred thousand dollars for her opinion. And in case you missed the implication, she does not have a high opinion about the operation you and your family are running."

"Well, if you both think our numbers are shit, then I suggest you get the hell out."

Victor sighed. "Then what? Are you going to swindle some other venture capitalists? Hell, even if you got the money you wanted from us, then what's your plan after you and your family burn through it? I'm here right now because I see potential. The reason I want fifty-one percent is to get you past your own short-sightedness."

Seven alpha dogs barked at Victor all at once. Nothing she hadn't heard before. Insults, accusations, bluster. Once a majority of the red faces settled to shades of pink, Victor said, "None of you answered my question. What's your backup plan to my offer? Out of the forty-seven businesses in your combined portfolios, only twenty of them turn a profit, ten of them break even, and seventeen are dogs. You all need cash now, or else you wouldn't have come to Bouch & Becker. We say no and you go back to buying and selling businesses in order to maintain your lifestyles, but how long will that last? How long before the wells dry up? How long until you're all at each other's throats? I'm an only child from a stable family, so I can only imagine the family drama bullshit that happens behind closed doors. Now, consider what happens when I take my offer and walk away. The backstabbing. The lies. The alliances formed and broken."

Celina stared at her, but all other eyes furtively glanced elsewhere.

Victor had struck the nerves of the Plimpton family with a hammer, and then paused to let them marinate in guilt, anger, and fear of the monsters sitting around the table. Time to rescue them.

"I'm offering a different, better way to continue the lifestyle you've grown accustomed to. We get rid of your individual corporations and give all forty-seven businesses directly to Plimpton Enterprises, and restructure the bylaws. We'll liquidate the seventeen dogs and use that cash, along with the cash Bouch & Becker uses to buy the fifty-one percent of shares, to supercharge the other thirty businesses and take Plimpton Enterprises to the stars. You'll each get equal shares, so you can stop competing with each other, and focus on whichever aspects of the businesses you want to."

Victor tossed the contract into the middle of the table. "Basically, you leave behind the parts of running your businesses that you don't like and focus only on what you do like."

Celina cleared her throat and said, "This is a good deal. Your numbers are shit."

Victor glanced at Celina. She didn't know how far from reality this crazy woman sat, but she seemed to pick up what Victor put down.

With the cold quiet of a cemetery in winter, Dante was the first to sign. No debate or question as he slid the contract to the closest family member. Six more signatures and the contract returned to Victor.

*

After the meeting, Victor ushered Celina to the bar at the nearest hotel casino. She used the hotel's business services to fax the contract to Bouch & Becker, and then joined Celina at the bar for a celebratory drink. For the first time in her life, Victor's face hurt from smiling.

"It's not often I say these words, but *thank you*, Celina. I truly don't think I could have done this without you." Victor clanked her glass of Johnnie Walker Blue Label against Celina's glass of Sea Breeze.

After a sip, Celina smiled softly. "You're welcome. I was worried I would ruin everything."

"Not at all. I was surprised you understood what you were looking at."

"I do the books for the café where I work. During tax season, I help out a local accountant. Nothing too in-depth, but I understand the basics of bookkeeping. I didn't understand everything I looked at, but I could tell things were messy."

"That, they were. You did great. Not sure about the accent, though."

"You didn't like it? You said I was from France."

Victor almost spat out her whiskey, a slight burn working its way from her throat to her nose. "By way of Moscow, maybe."

"It wasn't good?"

"Oh, Sweety, the next movie night you have, choose French cinema and then try that accent again."

They shared a laugh as they took another drink. Looking nervous, Celina started, "So... about what we talked about earlier...?"

Victor sighed. "Let me have your phone. I'll give you my number."

Celina did as instructed. "So that we can talk about this?"

"No." Victor tapped away at Celina's phone, and then tapped away at her phone. She did what she needed to do in less than a minute and handed Celina's phone back to her. "So that I can pay you for your services. Check your bank balance."

Celina gasped and wobbled to the point of almost falling off her barstool. "You just gave me a hundred thousand dollars!"

"I did. I may be a bastard, but I'm not an asshole. This deal is worth tens of millions to my company and millions to me personally. You set me up for an obnoxiously luxurious future. I lied to the Plimpton shmucks in order to add millions to their bank accounts. No way I was going to use you or lie to you. You can go home knowing that at one point in your life you had a job that paid you fifty thousand bucks an hour."

"But, about the potential danger we're in—?"

"Celina, I'm going to stop you right there. I heard everything you said to me while clothes shopping, I really did. I feel awful about what you went through, but I don't see a connection at all between me and what happened to you. The only commonality we have is we're both adopted. I don't know anything about my birth parents, and I very much would rather never know. My life isn't in danger from anyone other than myself. And, no offense, the weirdest thing that has *ever* happened to me is meeting you."

She felt bad having to inform Celina that her puppy got hit by a car. Of course, she was the one in the driver's seat. Victor tapped away at her phone again and continued. "I'll have Murphy take you to the airport. With what you earned, you can fly anywhere in the world you'd like – back home, or to wherever the next name on your list lives, or to a tropical paradise."

Celina slouched, looking more pitiful and exaggerated because of her height. Then she set her jaw and sat straight, obviously using everything she had learned in the past two hours. She shook Victor's hand and said, "Thank you for listening to me. I'm *not* sorry for the experience."

She left without looking back.

"Neither am I. Hope you find what you're looking for," Victor mumbled, and went back to celebrating.

Her drinking in silence didn't last long. Someone occupied the barstool next to hers and said, "Sorry that your girlfriend left you."

Victor turned to the owner of the sultry voice and... *hot damn*! The woman was older by a decade, maybe even two, but smooth skin over toned muscles didn't give away her age. Rather, the look in her crystal blue eyes told Victor they had witnessed crazy shit over the years. The style of her long blonde hair framed a face that could improve the quality of any fashion magazine cover. Even the three faint scars running vertically over her left eye, from her forehead to cheek, made her sexier. With the low cut of her dress, Victor doubted people would even notice her face. Although, she was curious about the tattoo on the left side of the woman's chest – the name "Linda" written in script.

Victor smiled. "She wasn't my girlfriend. Whenever a girlfriend or boyfriend leaves me, there's usually more swearing and death threats."

"You sound like an exciting person to know."

"I have my moments."

"Don't we all?" The woman smiled, her grin more of a wolfish threat, like she was getting ready to devour. "Hi. I'm Dakota."

# CHAPTER 09

*March 25th, Los Angeles*

The hooker looked at Blaze and said, "Your hour is almost up. Do you at least wanna go to the men's room for a blow job?"

Sitting in the diner booth across from her, Blaze wiped his face one last time to make sure he cleaned away all the burger's grease. He tossed the napkin on his plate and offered a pliable smile, moldable like clay. As simply as changing the channel, his smile could make people feel smarter than him, or dumber; make them laugh or put them at ease. He even had a smile that made people feel creeped-the-fuck-out, like he was a demented circus clown on cocaine. The smile he gave the hooker was one that instilled confidence.

"Naah. I'm good for the night, sweetheart."

When they first met two months ago, she told him her name was Chelsea. This being their seventh dinner together, if Chelsea wasn't her real name, he'd surely know by now. He didn't like that she used her real name while she was hooking; he didn't want her to think that her identity and her job were the same thing. He never wanted her to think that.

She chuckled and shook her head. "I don't fuckin' get you, man."

"You're new in town and I take pride in my role as the welcoming committee."

"You pay full price for an hour, but all we do is eat an' talk. Why?"

"Look, this is a shitty town with shitty people. We all need friends. You're in a tough situation. Marcel ain't the worst pimp in the world, but he ain't the best either. Just wanna make sure you learn the things you need to know, like what triggers set him off, his daughter's birth date, shit like that. Did you learn any of that?"

"Yeah. Purse dogs really send him over the fuckin' edge. And his daughter's birthday is in September. The fourth, I'm pretty sure. Do I have to buy her a present?"

Blaze chuckled. He needed a little bit more info, and he shifted his smile to appear brotherly. "I doubt it. I mean, what would you get a six-year-old who you don't even know, right?"

"She'll be nine this year."

"Right, right, right. I knew that. So… Any acting gigs lined up?"

"I haven't been in L.A. long, but long enough to know that dream is dead."

Blaze rooted through the pockets of his jacket, a dull golden snake-skin blazer, and pulled out a business card with the name and phone number of a talent agent. Blaze got the guy's daughter out of a major drug bust without the police ever knowing she was there, so the bastard owed him big. Chelsea was worth this favor. "Here. Call this guy. He's a legit agent. You tell him Blaze sent you."

Chelsea's eyes widened as big as the empty plate on the table in front of her as she hurriedly took the card and shoved it into her bra. "Marcel's at the counter. Been here about ten minutes."

*Well, fuck.* "Yeah? No worries. We're good. He's probably checkin' to make sure I ain't tryin' to go past my hour. Here you go."

The diner was small, and Blaze would need to walk past Marcel to exit. He indiscreetly handed Chelsea a wad of cash so Marcel could see the transaction. He then tossed a couple twenties on the table behind the napkin holder so Marcel couldn't see the tip.

Blaze started toward the exit, and to no surprise, Marcel reached out and grabbed him by the arm. "Why does it piss me off that you pay my girls not to fuck them?"

Skin the color of mocha, he kept his head shorn of hair. The money needed for his shimmering blue suit worn over his black turtleneck made him stand out in this low-end diner, like a Monet painting in a garage sale. Although, his massiveness made him stand out anywhere except a gym.

Blaze used his conspiracy smile, sharing a joke no one else understood except the person he was talking to. "I get it, Marcel. It don't seem right and that makes you question my motives. You and I been here in this neighborhood long enough to know what it's like. Too much shit happens that's beyond our control, too much loss. I ain't got much control over nothin', but when I can control somethin', then I like to add a little light to the darkness. Know what I mean?"

"Not a fuckin' clue. But I know you deal in favors. And information."

"Psssh!" Blaze laughed as he deftly removed his arm from Marcel's grasp. "Information? From Chelsea? She's been here, what? Two months? Three? What the fuck could she possibly know? Look, I ain't denyin' I have a… proclivity of sorts… when it comes to quid-pro-quo, as rich fucks like to say. So, what do you want?"

"Nothin' from a fool like you."

"Come on. There's gotta be somethin' out there I can help with."

"Not unless you can get me a good deal on the new, limited-edition Mercedes that just came out."

"The one with the different driving modes? This is Los Angeles. Why the fuck do you need different driving modes to sit in fucking traffic?"

"This is Los Angeles. It's all about image."

Blaze laughed, a good one reserved for friends. It made Marcel crack a smile and shake his head. "No promises, Marcel, but I'll see what I can find."

"Next time you give one of my girls money, it better be after you've put your dick in her."

Blaze's smile shifted back to coconspirator as he backed toward the exit and flashed a peace sign. "My dick in your girls. I hear you loud and clear."

Glowing neon signs along the streets added to the muggy night air. His brain told him no heat or humidity came from neon lights, but his senses said otherwise. His brain also told him he shouldn't have a soft spot for hookers, but his heart said otherwise. Now, to get that new, limited-edition Mercedes… How many people did he know who could help him with that? A few, maybe more. If he gave one to Marcel, it should be enough to buy Chelsea's freedom. After all, he owed her a favor, even if she didn't know it.

Cell phone out and dialing Jerry's number as soon as he crossed the street, busy enough at this time of night to elicit a honk and a screech of tires from the car he ran in front of. Blaze ignored it and continued down the side-walk, phone to his ear.

"Jerry! Who do you love?"

"Fuck, man, did you get it?" His nasally voice slithered into Blaze's ear.

"I did. Marcel's daughter's birthday is September fourth, twenty fif-teen."

"You're a miracle worker, Blaze. Fuckin' miracle worker. Now I can—"

"Don't tell me anything else, Jerry!" Blaze assumed someone stumbled into Marcel's account and needed his daughter's birthday to get through security. But information was currency, and if he had too much, he'd spend it. He liked Jerry and would feel guilty about fucking him over for the right price. He had his own code of ethics, a bushido of sorts, and tried hard not to break it. "I honestly don't wanna know why you wanted it."

"Fair enough, my man, fair enough. So… you want a job?"

"Your jobs always put my ass in the line of fire, you fuck."

"Hey, this last job paid for your piece, remember?"

Blaze touched the left side of his ribs, where he holstered the Glock. The jacket hid the bulge, but his shirt kept people from looking at him too long. Red Hawaiian style shirt, covered with dozens of yellow emojis of various, ridiculous, facial expressions. People rarely wanted to stare at something obnoxious. Just in case, he kept the shirt unbuttoned halfway down his chest, wearing three gold chains of varying length, a three-inch shark's tooth, and a black rosary on full display. No one looked long enough to worry about if he carried a gun or not. "Yeah, yeah, yeah. What kind of job?"

"Easy distribution job."

"Distribution? Fuck you, Jerry. That means drugs or guns."

"Drugs. One called Iatro."

"God, no, Jerry. Never heard of it, don't wanna know about it. Anyone who needs distribution thinks they're some big shot drug lord. All ego, no brains."

"It's for Melissandra."

Blaze stopped in his tracks. "*The* Melissandra?"

"No, the *other* Melissandra. Of course, *the* Melissandra, ya dumb fuck! How many Melissandras do you know?"

Blaze knew her by reputation only. Up and coming organized crime boss, both ego and brains with a huge dose of fear thrown in for good measure. Blaze avoided dealing with people who possessed that quality mix, but having *her* owe him a favor? That could be new, limited-edition Mercedes-level favor. "I'm in, Jerry."

# CHAPTER 10

*March 25th, Las Vegas*

Three drinks in and Victor knew how the night would end with Dakota. Considering that the women were at a hotel casino bar, how else could the evening possibly go? The conversation flowed like champagne over silk, each sentence an enticement punctuated by a subtle shift closer to each other.

"So, Dakota," Victor started, and then sipped her drink. "What exactly does a Human Relations Adjuster do?"

"Just a fancy title for corporate talent scout."

"Mmmm. Sounds interesting."

"It can be. Probably not as interesting as venture capitalist."

"Only if you define 'interesting' as convincing whiney, rich brats – whom I'm smarter than – that I can help them become richer and whinier."

Dakota cocked her head. "So, you don't help mom-n-pop inventors bring their products to a bigger market."

"That does happen. Not as often as I would like. But due to a recent event, I might find myself in a position to do that more."

"You like helping the little guy?"

"I do. Everyone loves to cheer for the underdog, right? Well, I like helping them out, even if it means dealing with rich, whiney brats along the way. Sure, I like the stupid amounts of money that come with the job, but yes, my parents instilled *some* goodness in me."

Sullenness washed over Dakota's face as she turned her head toward her drink. She whispered, "Your parents...."

*Idiot*, Victor scolded herself. *Never bring up parents when trying to get laid! Bad, Victor, bad!* "Sorry, didn't mean to kill the mood."

Dakota looked back, the hunger in her eyes returned. "I should apologize. I just remembered it was my mother's birthday."

"No worries." Victor's eyes followed Dakota's fingers as they tucked a lock of hair behind her ear and then trailed along her neck. When they got close to the tattoo, Victor said, "Obviously, Linda is your mother. Am I right?"

Laughing, Dakota said, "Very, very not my mother. But Linda was a major influence in my life."

"Tattooed over your heart. Hell of a pedestal you put her on."

"She was a hell of an influence."

"But not as much as your mother. I mean, she named you Dakota after all."

"She did. I'm guessing yours named you Victoria, but you choose to go by Victor."

"You guess correctly."

"Is that because you hate your tits?"

"On the contrary, I love them, as does everyone else who has the pleasure of meeting them."

"Those lucky individuals."

Victor smirked and finished her drink. She set the empty glass on the bar, and asked, "Dakota… North or South?"

"Depends if you reciprocate or not."

Victor leapt from her barstool and planted a kiss on Dakota's lips. The mouth mauling didn't stop until they stumbled into Dakota's hotel room.

The number of scars Victor uncovered as she peeled away Dakota's flimsy dress should have raised red flags. Instead of heeding the obvious warnings, Victor explored the blemishes. All of them. Three gashes disrupted the perfectly smooth skin over her left ribs. A similar set of scars ran across her right thigh. Victor had never seen a bullet wound before but assumed the thumb-sized circles of imperfections all over Dakota's body were bullet scars. She counted eight as she kissed each and every one of them, in addition to another eleven scars of various shapes and sizes.

There were strange marks on the lower half of Dakota's left leg – teeth marks, maybe? What the hell had this woman done to get bitten by an animal that large? What did a Human Relations Adjuster *really* do? At the moment, Victor didn't care, her active thoughts giving way to the pleasures of Dakota's mouth, hands, lips, and fingers.

Victor enjoyed the way Dakota's muscles worked, like chugging steel under a layer of satin-smooth skin. Hours slipped away as the women altered between simultaneously pleasuring each and taking turns. Orgasms became uncountable, one blasting right into another. Victor's last one ended with a leg-shaking scream as she ripped part of the fitted sheet from the bed.

\*

"Wake up – but keep your eyes closed!"

*What the fuck?*

"She saw you twitch. Keep your eyes closed and don't move. Breathe slow and shallow."

*Why is a creepy version of my voice telling me what to do?*

"Because she's going to kill you."

*She? Dakota? Dakota is trying to kill me?*

"She will kill you if you don't listen."

*Okay, I'm listening.*

"Open your eyes… now."

Victor did as the voice instructed. She expected to see a woman standing over her, whispering in her ear. Instead, across the room, Dakota sat at the desk, tapping away at her laptop.

*Now what,* Victor thought.

No response.

*Okay, clearly, she fucked me stupid because I'm seeking instruction from a voice in my head.*

Victor wanted to get out of bed but closed her eyes and pretended to be asleep as soon as Dakota turned in her chair. She listened. The sound of the chair moving. Soft footsteps padding to the bathroom. The door closing.

Voice be damned, Victor popped up from the bed and hurried to the desk. She saw her face on the computer's screen.

*What. The. Literal. Hell?*

A thumbnail of her face was next to her name, Victoria "Victor Vegas" Vargas, among nineteen other faces and names, including Celina's. *No. No. No, no, no, no.*

Victor double clicked on Celina's name, the action taking her to another screen. She scrolled through a dozen pictures of Celina, some with friends, but most only of Celina. Once there were no more pictures to scroll through, she happened upon a dossier of information. Name: Celina Davenport. Address: Unknown. Works at: Roll & Role Café. Potential Danger Level: High. Birth Father:

"Move to your right! Now!"

Out of reflex, Victor did as the voice screamed into her mind, narrowly avoiding the massive hunting knife sinking into the desk.

"Turn! Right elbow to the back of her head!"

The creepy voice had saved her life, so Victor continued to follow its commands. Countless hours of martial arts classes kicked in, her spin fast and focused. She cupped her left hand around her right fist and put the force of both arms into the elbow shot to the back of Dakota's head. A puff of blonde hair. A sickening smack of skull hitting desk. Dakota dropped to the floor.

"Kill her!"

*What? No!*

"It's the only way to stop her."

*No!*

"Do it!"

"I'm not fucking killing her!" Victor yelled.

"Run."

Victor quickly dressed, shirt untucked and unbuttoned, shoelaces free, tie shoved into a pocket. *I'm going to take the computer.*

"No. There's a good chance that she'd be able to track it."

*Fuck. Okay, I'll create a dummy email account and email everything I can to myself.*

"No time. She's waking up. Kill her."

Dakota moaned and started to stir.

*I'm not a murderer!* Victor clicked back to the screen with the names and faces and took a picture of it with her phone. She then smashed the laptop against the corner of the desk.

"That did little good. Undoubtedly, she has other means to access the information."

*No shit. I was hoping that it'd be shocking enough to make you go away.*

"Very well."

Victor hurried down the stairs and onto the sidewalk. The sun had set, but with all the lights flashing on the buildings and cascading along the canopies over the street, it could have been any time of day, and time didn't matter here in Vegas. People flowed by, some in a hurry, but most whooping and laughing, not caring that they paid a tithing to the gambling churches of statistics.

Victor pulled out her phone and dialed. Murphy picked up in two rings. "Hey, sorry to call at such a shitty hour, but someone tried to kill me. I have no idea why, only that she had my name and picture on her computer. She said her name is Dakota, but that probably wasn't her real name and— I just thought of something. I'll call you back and I'll probably need to get to the airport."

Victor hung up and dialed another number. After a few rings, a tentative, "Hello?" came from the other end.

"Celina? You were right. I'll tell you all about it when I meet up with you. Where are you?"

"Chicago."

"On my way."

A five-hour flight. Plenty of time for Victor to mull over what the hell just happened.

# CHAPTER 11

*March 26th, Chicago*

Celina's flight from Las Vegas to Chicago was mind-numbing.

She wasn't sure if she had been awake or asleep for most of it, lingering in that bizarre limbo between consciousness and the abyss, being neither and both. If not for zoning out, she would have obsessed over what had happened in Vegas, how that Victor woman had dismissed her. Now in Chicago, she pulled the notepaper out of her pocket and reread it.

Genocide Stone. Genocide & The Doomsdays. B-Sides bar, Chicago, next show the 26th.

Still in her new suit, she made her way through the airport to the car services area while requesting a pick-up with a share-a-ride app. At two in the morning, the airport was nearly empty. A skeleton crew of security and custodians were on duty while the small crowd disembarking consisted of a dozen or so travelers, but enough people stared and Celina blushed when *The Imperial March* started to play from her pants.

How did that ringtone make its way onto her cellphone? The caller ID, "The most awesome person you ever met," made the experience more confusing and embarrassing. Just to make the song stop, she answered. "Hello?"

"Celina? You were right. I'll tell you all about it when I meet up with you. Where are you?"

"Chicago," she answered. It took a beat, but she recognized Victor's voice. *Did she say I was right?*

"On my way."

"Okay."

"Wait. You didn't make contact with anyone else yet, did you?"

"No. I just got off the plane."

"Good. I'll have Murphy get us a room at the Ritz. Stay there and be careful. I'll see you soon."

"Okay," Celina said, but wasn't sure if Victor had heard her or not before she hung up.

Celina's interactions with Victor left her head spinning like she had slammed back ten shots of vodka. But she did as instructed and sure enough, a room waited for Celina Davenport when she arrived at downtown Chicago's Ritz-Carlton. Make that a 1,500 square foot, two-bedroom suite. Jaw to the floor, Celina stood in the doorway and stared. "Can't be my room," she said under her breath. There was a mix up. A miscommunication. A mistake. She didn't belong here, and she thought if she crossed the threshold, the room would somehow reject her, spit her out like unsavory food. She started to feel like a fool for standing in the hallway for so long and decided to enter. After all, the key card *had* opened the door, so if it was a mistake, it was on them for giving her the wrong key card.

After making sure the door was locked, she took in the enormity of the place, free to gawk like a rube in closed door privacy. She turned on lights, sat in all the different chairs, opened cabinets.

Two bathrooms. Signs posted on the tub's ledge offered bubble service, a massage, and a facial. Warm, damp washcloths sat in a pyramid on the counter. Luxury brand toiletries. Robe and matching slippers in the closets. Individually wrapped chocolates on the beds. She rarely traveled, and she had never stayed in a place this extravagant, easily twice the size of her apartment, and possibly even bigger than the small house in the small neighborhood outside New York City where she grew up.

Celina ate a chocolate, and made a mental note to swipe all the little shampoo and shower gel bottles before leaving. She then pulled out her phone and took pictures but stopped herself before posting anything to social media. Victor had sounded… off. Scared? Angry? Upset? Celina didn't know Victor well enough but the sound of her voice said *something* had happened to her. No, best not to post to social media right now.

Paranoia started to creep inside of her like intrepid insects, exploring and looking for her weakest parts. The parts that wanted nothing more than go back to the airport and take the first flight back to New York, to her apartment, to her bed where she could hide.

No! No hiding. No letting fear win. A shower. A warm shower would wash away the fear and make her feel better.

She had packed a night shirt in her carryon, along with a few changes of clothes and necessary toiletries. After the perfect blend of temperature and pressure from the shower melted her muscles like butter, a cotton shirt seemed like sandpaper, so she opted for the impossibly soft hotel robe.

Celina slid onto the couch and looked around the room. How could Victor afford this? How could Victor afford... *Oh my God!* Celina remembered that she was now a hundred thousand dollars richer! Too focused on being shooed away like an annoying child and too distraught over Victor's phone call, the ramifications of the money transfer hadn't sunk in until now.

Celina worked her bottom lip with her teeth as she lounged deeper into the couch. She had fun in the business meeting. Like a scene from a movie, she pretended to be someone else for a few minutes, playing the part well enough to get paid a hundred thousand dollars! No. Other than a fake accent – apparently a bad one – she hadn't pretended to be someone else. She wore different clothes, something she normally wouldn't wear, but befitting the situation. She spoke with confidence. Sure, Victor did most of the talking and sealed the deal, but Celina helped. Contributed. Now, she felt empowered, and she was a hundred thousand dollars richer!

Thoughts of investing the money turned into fantasies of going on extravagant spending sprees. The fantasies of wealth turned into dreams of power. Being physically strong enough to fight a bear. Dreams of strength turned into nightmares of teeth, claws, and blood. Then the devil's face in front of hers. No, too pretty to be the devil.

"Victor?"

# CHAPTER 12

*March 26th, Frederick, Maryland*

The school hallway was empty, Orion the only occupant. It was unusual, but not unheard of. Once or twice earlier in the year he caught the timing perfectly, where he stood at his locker completely alone. Unfortunately, that kind of timing often meant he was late for class. Was he late right now? Which class did he need to go to? What time was it?

Those questions slipped from his mind as if they had never been formed. He simply went about the task of spinning the correct combination to his locker. A shadow darker than midnight approached from behind and it loomed across the bank of lockers. Startled, Orion spun around to see Lance. *Great. Just what I need.*

But something was different with Lance. He was more ominous than usual. Bigger? Taller even? "Lance, we don't have time for this."

Lance continued to approach, not saying a word, not acknowledging what Orion had said.

Lance's enlarged muscles swelled. Orion thought it was an optical illusion at first, but sure enough, Lance's veins protruded through his shirt as it stretched tighter. The football player's oppressive breath washed over him like that of an angry dragon's. Eyes glowing red, Lance snarled.

Flattening himself against the lockers, Orion didn't know what to do other than try and shrink out of the behemoth's way. He had never seen Lance like this before, something beyond human as the seams of his shirt split from his expanding body. Orion thought of the only thing that might save him. "Don't want to jeopardize your scholarship, do you? If you beat on me, I'll go to the principal. I'll… I'll… I'll go to the cops!"

"Open up!" someone said. Orion recognized it as the creepy voice from two days ago.

Lance kept walking closer.

"Open up," the dark, scratchy voice repeated.

"Who are you?" Orion asked.

Every step Lance took, Orion's heart doubled in speed, threatening to break his ribs with every pounding thump.

"Open up!"

"What do you mean?" Orion shouted, then realized his hand still clutched the latch of his locker. The only thing to "open up" was his locker.

As soon as the latch clicked, the door flung open, smashing Orion's hand against the neighboring locker, and a swirling flash of blue burst forth. It shot across the hall and hovered behind Lance.

Orion blinked a few times to register the familiar vision. A face with a rictus, razor blades instead of teeth. A crumpled blue stovepipe hat sat on top of his head, beneath it a gaunt figure with the gnarled skin of an unwrapped mummy. His collared blue cape with tattered edges flowed as if a breeze passed through the hallway. Orion was familiar with this... man? ... monster? ... spirit? He knew him well even though he had only known him for two days. This character took up pages and pages of his sketch book.

What did Orion name him last night? Bigby? Yeah, that's right. Bigby.

Orion's twisted creation opened his mouth, the darkness within made more abysmal by the ring of gleaming silver razor blades, and then closed his mouth on Lance's head, the metal crunching through his skull. With a twist of his neck, Bigby tore away the top of Lance's head, flinging blood and brains across Orion's face. Globs of crimson yolk oozed from the chalice of Lance's head. His eyeballs slid down his cheeks and slopped to the floor.

Orion's bladder let loose, and his stomach churned. Every muscle in his body quivered so hard that he wasn't sure if he vomited or not. Bigby smiled at him and said, "When I told you to open up, I didn't mean your locker..."

Lance's quasi-decapitated corpse slumped to the floor and Bigby floated closer to Orion. Reaching out his hand, he continued, "... I meant you!"

As Bigby rushed at him, Orion jolted awake.

Sitting up in his bed, he ran his hands through his sweat-soaked hair. The alarm on his nightstand buzzed and he lunged off the other side of the bed. Panting on the floor, he felt foolish for being so afraid, but what he saw, how he reacted, seemed so real. On the verge of embarrassment, he grabbed at the crotch of his pajama pants. Dry. He sighed with relief, thankful he hadn't reverted back to being a kindergartener.

By the time he took his shower, he was smiling and excited to start his day. Sure, the nightmare had been intense, but the cool character he created had bit the brains out of his nemesis. What a great way to start the morning, and he couldn't wait to tell Brennan.

At the dining room table, Mom and Dad nodded to him as he entered the room while Aika served breakfast. He didn't know how to think of Aika. When he was younger, she was the live-in nanny. He hadn't needed a babysitter for years, yet she still lived with them and did all the cooking and cleaning. The term "servant" seemed so archaic, and not entirely accurate since his parents paid her a good salary with benefits. "Maid" seemed rude. In his mind, she was part of the family.

And he was convinced that she was his birth mother. Orion had no proof other than the fact that she was Japanese and cagey about her past. Born and raised in Japan until she was twenty, she had come to the United States for vague "opportunities." For two weeks twice a year, she'd return home and always brought back a souvenir of some sort for him. Whenever he caught her in a rare nostalgic mood, Orion encouraged her to talk about Japan.

On more than one occasion over the course of his lifetime, he thought that maybe he was the product of an affair between his father and Aika. However, his parents never fought, and his mother loved Aika. He didn't think a wife would stay with her cheating husband, or share a household with his former lover. Even if his mom could bring herself to do that, no way would she be able to keep the resentment from manifesting. She'd have to achieve a Stepford Wife level of psychosis and his mother didn't exhibit any of the signs. Plus, his DNA test said, "Eastern European" which excluded both of his adoptive parents. Mom *and* Dad were tragically blond with incomprehensibly blue eyes, picture perfect Scandinavian stereotypes.

"Good morning, Son," Dad said, bright white smile ready to sell. As a mega-successful real estate agent, he was always ready to sell. Mom worked as his business partner, also mega-successful, always ready to sell, and just as smiley.

"'Mornin', Dad."

Orion's stomach rumbled, and he chuckled at his breakfast plate. Two sunny side up eggs for the eyes, strips of bacon angled inward for angry eyebrows. Breakfast potatoes for the nose and smile. Aika strategically placed a few potatoes to create fangs while drizzles of ketchup simulated dripping blood. A half wall separated the dining room from the kitchen and Orion winked a thank you at Aika. Doing the dishes at the sink, Aika replied with a smirk and returned the wink. She understood him, what he liked, and what made him smile. More reason to believe she was his birth mother.

"Get a good night sleep?" Mom asked. Even though she was a fierce salesperson, she tapped into the holistic nature of the world. A good night's sleep meant everything to her.

Orion dug into his breakfast, piercing both yolks so the yellow ran into the potatoes. "Yep, other than the intense monster nightmare right before I woke up. He's a cool new character I'm working on. Razor blade teeth and crazy top hat."

Metal clanged against metal from the kitchen, capturing everyone's attention. Standing in front of the sink, Aika held up a pan and said, "Sorry. This slipped while I was washing it."

Everyone had a good laugh, but Aika's reaction bothered Orion. Even though she smiled, worry registered in her eyes. He should've thought more about it, but breakfast had energized him and he was too excited about sharing his nightmare with Brennan.

Orion arrived at his locker at his usual time, and at first he thought Brennan was late. Then his heart sunk when Brennan didn't eventually show. He texted, where r u?

He received an instant reply. Not feeling well. Won't be in today.

That sucked. Deflated, Orion rooted through his locker to find his sketch book and his Literature book for his first couple of classes.

Something hit against the lockers, and he jumped, defensive, ready to face Lance's berating. With a cringe, he turned to three other football players farther down the bank of lockers. And they were… crying? One of them gurgled a sob and punched the lockers, his fist raddling the entire bank. The other two paced in tight circles, fists clenched and blubbering. A small group of students gathered around them, half of them crying as well. What the hell was happening?

The football players looked beyond pissed, especially if they were moved to tears. Not wanting to take any chances of incurring their wrath, Orion gently shut his locker and headed the opposite direction. Most of the other students along the hallways also looked upset and stunned as they whispered among themselves.

Art was his first class of the day, and he approached Sophie right outside the art room. "Hey. What's going on? Everyone seems weirded out and I saw three football players crying."

"You don't know?" Sophie asked. "You didn't hear?"

"No. Literally got to school five minutes ago."

"It's Lance. He died in his sleep last night."

Orion's fingers and toes went cold, and his stomach lurched. He wondered if it was too early to go to the nurse's office.

# CHAPTER 13

*March 26th, Chicago*

Never in a million years did Victor think she would need to flee Las Vegas from a one-night stand – a hottie named Dakota – who literally wanted to kill her.

"Care to explain the sudden desire to go to Chicago?" Murphy asked as she took the first-class seat next to Victor.

"Give me a minute and I'll explain. When the flight attendant comes by, order champagne."

Before turning her phone to airplane mode, she texted the picture she took of Dakota's computer screen to Murphy. She sent the picture to Celina, too, as well as a text explaining what had happened and how she got it, and then checked her emails. Marshall had come through with his promise.

The paperwork that would make her a partner was in her inbox. She squeezed Murphy's hand and did a quick shimmying dance of joy in her seat. She downloaded the file, inserted her e-signature, then sent the signed paper-work back.

For the first half of the flight, she filled Murphy in about the good news and the bad news. She was a bit disheartened at Murphy's nonchalant reaction after she shared that her most recent sexcapade tried to kill her. At least Murphy was supportive and asked questions. The second half of the flight was spent in dreamland, the champagne taking the place of adrenaline.

Once they landed, Victor calculated the time zone math and when she realized the office was open, she dialed the main number. As soon as the receptionist answered, she cheerfully said, "Hey it's Victor. Is Becker in? I wanted to call him directly, but he would have ignored me."

"He's in his office. I'll patch you through, but before I do, I want to let you know a woman came by the office as soon as we opened, looking for you. She didn't leave her name or contact information, even though I asked."

*Fuck*! Good mood ruined. Keeping her tone light, Victor said, "A pretty blonde? Probably late forties even though she looks mid-thirties? Light scar on her face?"

"That's her."

Victor chuckled even though she wanted to scream. "Heh. Just a mistake I made after I drank six or seven other mistakes. You know what I mean, right?"

Victor heard him blush through the phone as he stammered, "I... umm... Let me... let me transfer you to Mr. Becker."

After a few seconds of a poor rendition of *The Girl from Ipanema*, Marshall lethargically asked, "Do I even want to know where you are?"

"Miami." Victor winked at Murphy. She wasn't thrilled about lying to Marshall, but better no one else knew the truth, especially with a murderous one-night stand sniffing around her place of employment.

"Celebrating already?" he asked.

"Working. Got a lead I'm following."

"Well, you should be celebrating, Victor. You pulled off one helluva miracle."

"Two miracles, actually. Did you receive my signed paperwork?"

"I did. Congratulations. I'm beyond impressed that you did it within two days, but I knew you could. I appreciate that you play by a different set of rules. I wish more women would."

"Yeah? Like Bouch's secretary?"

"Ha, ha, fuck you."

Victor enjoyed the awkward silence, savoring the pause in conversation while Marshall gathered himself. Finally, he asked, "So... about that video...?"

"Don't worry, Partner. It's deleted."

"Victor, don't forget I kept my end of the deal. I kept my promise."

"Yes, you did, Partner. I promise, the video is gone, Partner."

"Is this what I have to look forward to from now on?"

"You better believe it, Partner."

"Jesus Christ." A soft click and the line went dead.

Victor laughed and thought about calling her parents, but it was too early, Hawaii five hours behind Chicago.

A car met her and Murphy at O'Hare International and drove them straight to the Ritz.

Murphy trailing behind her with the luggage, Victor threw the suite door open and stormed in with her arms raised in victory. "You are now looking at a partner in Bouch & Becker Venture Capital!"

Celina bolted upright on the couch. Her robe was closed, but she cinched it tight. Had she slept the night away on the couch? "What time is it?"

"Little after ten. You okay?"

"I'm sure she had a rough night, boss," Murphy said, dropping the two bags in the middle of the main room. She tossed her chauffer hat on the counter between the kitchenette and living room as she ran her fingers through her long, blue hair.

"Yeah," Celina said. "Yeah, just a nightmare. Can't remember it."

"Okay." Victor looked around. "It's kind of funny that you're in a suite in the Ritz, but you chose to sleep on the couch."

Murphy pulled her hair into a ponytail, her muscles testing the limits of her suit jacket. Celina eyed the statuesque woman.

"This is my manservant, Murphy," Victor said.

Murphy shot Victor a flat brow-look of annoyance. Victor rolled her eyes and said, "Sorry. That wasn't very sensitive of me. I meant to refer to Murphy as my henchman."

Murphy's turn to roll her eyes.

"Henchman?" Celina asked.

"You know, my faithful sidekick who does the leg work for my villainous plans of mustache-twirling world domination."

"Villainous? You've been nothing but nice to me."

"Ugh, I was joking! Yes, I'm nice! I'm a fucking angel, which makes me being a villain with a henchman funny. If you had a sense of humor, you would have realized it was a joke."

"I have a sense of humor," Celina said.

"I have yet to see it. You have no idea how to be funny."

"I can be funny."

"Sweety, you're as funny as a funeral clown."

Celina stood and removed the cell phone from her robe's pocket, then said, "Imagine walking into a bar with an orderly group of people waiting to hit you. That's the punch line."

Murphy laughed.

Victor closed her eyes and pinched the bridge of her nose. "Jesus Christ. Do not encourage this behavior."

"It's funny because it could be true," Murphy said. "In fact, I'm a little surprised it hasn't happened to you yet."

"I know how jokes work! I— You know what? Never mind. I didn't hurry my ass to Chicago to get roasted at open mic night. We got work to do."

Worry skittered across Celina's face, but she still managed a smile. "Congratulations on your promotion."

"I couldn't have done this without you, so I'm going to show my love through gastronomical excess. All meals are on my tab throughout this process, whatever that may entail."

"Okay..." Celina said.

But by the way her voice trailed off and how her eyes went to the cell phone in her hands, Victor realized her celebration was to be short-lived. Time to deal with... whatever this was.

"So, I got the picture you sent," Celina said, incredulousness etched all over her face. "But I'm still trying to wrap my mind around why you would have sex with someone who wanted to kill you."

Victor regretted including that information in her text. "At the time, I didn't know she was going to try to kill me."

"Are you sure?"

"Yes, I'm sure! Why even ask that?"

"In the limited amount of time that I've known you, it seems like something you would do. Plus, Murphy implied it sounds like something you would do."

84

Victor snarled at Murphy. "I play dangerous games, but nothing that dangerous."

"What about that guy you met at The Luxor two years ago?" Murphy asked.

"One time! That was one time! I was young and stupid and there was no way I believed he would— You know what? None of anyone's business but my own!"

"Until you had me beat him up for you."

Victor massaged her temples. "Okay, tell me we have something else to discuss now that I've made the biggest career move of my life?"

"I researched the woman named Genocide Stone while you slept on the plane," Murphy said as she sat at the table built for eight. Victor and Celina joined her.

"Genocide?" Victor asked. "Is that her real name?"

"Maybe, maybe not. Genocide and the Doomsdays came onto the scene about four years ago, starting local and moving to a little more regional. A ton of lineup changes. Active social media accounts, but focused on their music. Their favorite venue is Club B-Sides, been playing there regularly for three years now."

"They're playing there tonight," Celina said. "So, I'm going to go."

"You?" Victor asked.

"Ummm… Yes? It was my idea to come here and meet her."

"You want to go to a rowdy club to meet the singer of a punk band?" Victor asked.

"No, but I'm willing to do whatever is necessary."

Victor smiled at that, believing her words.

Murphy tapped away at her cell phone.

Within a few seconds, Victor received Murphy's text. A dozen pictures of Genocide, various poses, and expressions. A few of her on stage, a few more partying, a few more in promotional poses from a professional photographer. One last picture at the end made Victor squint. A black and white headshot of a teenage girl wearing a unique blend of anger, apathy, and pain.

"Those are pictures taken from Genocide's social media pages," Murphy said. "Except the last one. It's of a girl named Jennifer Faustino. She would have been fourteen in that picture. Birth parents unknown, bounced from foster home to foster home, never adopted. Once she turned eighteen, she disappeared."

"I see a resemblance," Victor said. "We think Genocide is Jennifer?"

"We do. What makes *that* interesting is almost two years ago, Jennifer Faustino took ownership of Club B-Sides."

"Well, that is certainly interesting."

"And coincidental," Celina added. "She's so young. Do you know how she bought it?"

"This is where things become even *more* interesting. It was purchased for one dollar. I just started digging into it, but it seems like it was sold by a conglomerate of unknown ownership."

"I think we moved beyond interesting into the realm of fuckery," Victor said. "If Genocide is Jennifer, how old is she now?"

"Twenty-two or twenty-three," Murphy answered.

"Not much younger than Celina and me, unknown birth parents like Celina and me. Weird connections, but I have no idea how that translates to why someone is trying to kill us. Anything else?"

"I know someone else on the list," Celina said, voice soft, as if she were afraid to be heard.

"Whoa," Murphy and Victor said at the same time. "Who?"

Celina turned her phone for everyone to see, and enlarged the picture of a handsome man in wire rim glasses. "Him. Robert Harrington."

"Damn, girl! How do you know him?" Victor asked.

If Celina's cheeks reddened any more, the suite would have caught fire. "I... ummm... I actually don't *know* him, know him. I just met him once. A couple days ago, he came into the café where I work."

Victor turned to give Celina her full attention. "Oh yeah? Must have been one hell of a meeting."

"He was looking for... he said he was looking for a game for his niece's birthday. Then we... chatted."

"Chatted, huh? Was it regular chatting? Or sexy chatting?"

"Don't be a dick," Murphy said.

"What? You can tease me about my sex life, but I can't tease anyone else about theirs? You're lucky you don't talk much, or I'd find out who you like to spend time with under the sheets. I'm sure there are stories that would make the hair on my toes curl."

Murphy chuckled. "You better believe it. But I don't talk much because the information you always ask me to find comes from people who talk more than they should."

"Okay, well, let's do that. You work your magic to get people to say more than they should and let's see if we can learn more about the people on this list, starting with this Robert guy."

"I like this plan," Murphy said. "Anything else?"

"There is one avenue we haven't strolled down yet – Caila. Celina, have you thought about investigating her? Visiting where she lives? Talking to her friends and family?"

Celina pocketed her phone, cinched her robe again, and slouched as if trying to hide by shrinking into herself. "I... I have. I assumed police would be at her place for a while, and I'm not sure how people would react to me asking about Caila when I look exactly like her."

Victor reached out and placed her hand on Celina's forearm. "What you're saying makes sense. We have plenty of names on this list. We'll find one who knows something about who's trying to kill us and why. How about Murphy finds Caila's address and then you determine what to do with it when you're ready?"

Celina sat straighter. "Thank you. I... I would like that."

Victor stood and clapped. "Excellent! We have a plan. In the meantime, Celina and I have some shopping to do. After breakfast, of course."

"We do?" Celina asked.

"We do."

"I brought a couple things to change into with me."

"I'm joining you tonight and despite the fact that we'll be the hottest women there, neither of us have the right outfits to go to a heavy metal bar."

Chicago wasn't Victor's town, and someone was trying to kill her, but by God nothing was going to stop her celebration of becoming a partner.

# CHAPTER 14

*March 26th, Chicago*

Celina and Victor hurried along the bustling sidewalk, the sweet-spot when those quitting their day converged with those starting their night. The air still felt unseasonably warm, but once the sun finally went down, a chill would be oncoming.

Celina fidgeted with the bottom of her skirt, nervous fingers running along the hem. A slight tug only added a half inch of coverage, but any extra length made her feel more comfortable. The skirt rode up after four or five steps, back to its starting position, and she yanked at it again. She had never worn a skirt so short in her life. Too short!

"Stop fidgeting," Victor hissed from beside her. "People will stare."

"If you didn't want people to stare, then you shouldn't have put me in such a short skirt and three-inch heels. I look like a hooker the Jolly Green Giant called for!"

Victor laughed. "Okay. I change my mind. You are funny."

"I'm serious. I feel like I'm the tallest person in the city."

"Quit being so dramatic. The Bulls are this city's basketball team, so there are at least five people taller than you."

"Victor!"

"Calm down. No one thinks you're a hooker. If you were wearing red stilettos, then maybe, but not black, studded, wedge booties."

"I don't know why you made me wear them."

"Because they go great with the skirt."

Celina sighed. Okay, she had to agree – the black leather skirt with a row of silver studs running along either side matched the shoes. However, the skirt and shoes did *not* belong on her. Nor the white tee shirt with a black anarchy symbol. Nor the multiple silver studded, leather wrist bands on her left arm. Nor the two skull rings on her right hand. Nor the earrings, silver crosses made from skulls.

89

Victor rocked her black leather pants and red lace top. Her black lace choker was wide enough to cover her entire neck, and she donned red fingerless laced gloves up to her elbows. Her black boots looked army issued, except for the red lace covering them. Her single element of makeup – red lipstick.

Celina pulled on her hem again. "I don't know why I agreed to wear this skirt."

"Jesus, woman! Legs! Have you never seen your legs? If I'm gonna get us laid tonight, I need my wing-woman showing off what she's got."

Celina stopped in her tracks. The fire burning in her cheeks chased away all fear of a chilly evening. "Wait, what? You *can't* be serious! What about the mission?"

A few paces in front of Celina, Victor put her hands on her hips and looked to the sky, either silently venting her frustration or asking a deity for strength. After a huff, she turned and took Celina's hands. "Please stop calling it a mission. We're not in some secret, paramilitary organization. And don't worry – we absolutely will talk to Genocide. We will do our best to introduce ourselves and explain why we want to talk to her in a sane, rational way. However, no one has truly acknowledged my good news about becoming partner. I want to celebrate! If it weren't for you, then I would have no good news, so I'd love, love, love it if you would celebrate with me."

A slight tremble rippled through Celina's body, her reaction to the anxiety that accompanied trying new things. "Okay."

"Good. I get that you're uncomfortable, but you absolutely own the retro look. Trust me, you look great, and don't forget how amazing you were the last time I made you play dress-up."

Again, Victor was right. Celina lived and loved the status quo, but she knew that wasn't a recipe for growth. Caila had given Celina a glimpse into another world while Victor acted as a willing escort into it. As uncomfortable as she felt, Celina appreciated the effort, happy with the beautician Victor had taken her to, and how she used subtle bronze and copper hues with her make-up. Her lips, shinier than ever, reminded her of Caila's lips.

Her smile looked like Caila's smile. Without a doubt, Caila would've traipsed into Club B-Sides with no hesitation. "Thank you. Let's do this."

Victor kept hold of Celina's hand as they walked the last block to the club. The closer they got, the more comfortable Celina felt. She almost giggled, no longer out of place by the proliferation of skulls, tattoos, spikes, leather, and mohawks. Dressed in a way so contrary to what she was used to, she fit right in.

Victor paid the cover charge for both of them and aimed for the bar. Still holding Celina's hand, she navigated them through the crowd. Celina had been in night clubs tighter packed than this, but she admired how Victor charged forth, pushing past people as if they were merely speed bumps. She never interacted with anyone while shouldering her way through the club, let alone acknowledged their existence. After every knock or jostle, Celina swallowed down so many apologies that her gut started to burn. But why say "sorry" when nothing happened to Victor after all the nudging and toe-stepping? The heavens didn't collapse on her. The Earth didn't crack open and swallow her. No one even got mad.

"Here you go, Sweety," Victor said, handing Celina a bottle of Miller Light.

Adrenaline must alter the taste buds, because Celina had never enjoyed beer, but this tasted palatable, almost good. Maybe it was the setting? Or the company?

Leaning against the bar, Victor was scanning the room. A wide, no-frills space. The front half held nothing except the stage. The back half had a few four-seat tables and a half dozen high-top tables.

Celina wasn't sure what Victor was looking for – Genocide or a bedroom dance partner. At first, she worked her jaw to the point of pain, upset about Victor not taking this seriously. For God's sake, she had an up close and personal encounter with the person trying to kill them. But the more Celina mulled it over, she realized Victor *was* taking it seriously, this predicament as well as the rest of her life. The woman escaped a near death situation, yet still followed up with becoming a partner in her company. Amazing!

Celina tapped Victor's shoulder. "Hey!"

When she got Victor's attention, she clanked bottles. "Congratulations on your becoming partner."

Almost girlish, Victor's smile warmed Celina. "Thank you."

Celina clanked bottles again. "I think it's awesome, you dominating a man's game and beating them with their own rules. I don't know if I said it enough yet but thank you for paying me to help you. You really didn't have to."

This time Victor clanked her bottle against Celina's and took a long pull from it. "You thanked me plenty. I will say this, though – women generally follow a few rules that I follow as well, like paying you what you deserve. Men make such a big deal about their ethics when they actually have any. A code, they usually call it. A few super douchey guys will go so far as to call it their bushido, going out of their way to pat their own backs whenever they exhibit a rare moment of honesty. Women don't need to do that shit and if they feel the need to label it, they call it being a decent person."

"Well, I truly believe you're a decent person."

"Fuck right I am! And I'm really glad you think that, because I'm going to make you do something you don't want to do."

Whatever sense of empowerment Celina had built up within herself suddenly crumbled, leaving behind cold and jagged chunks of paranoia. "What?"

"Talk to that bouncer over there."

Victor pointed toward the door where a muscled man in a "Security" tee shirt three sizes too small sat on a stool, thumbing his cell phone.

"I don't want to get laid by him! He's not my type!" Celina said, her voice squeaking.

Victor draped her arm on Celina's shoulder and laughed. "Calm down. I'm not sending you over there in an attempt to bed him. There's nothing wrong with being an introvert, but you'll never get everything you want in life by sitting back and waiting for it. Sometimes you need to interact with other people, and sometimes you need to be the initiator. So, go over there and ask him about Genocide, if she's here and if you can talk to her before the show. Keep it simple and don't be creepy, and do not mention that you think someone's trying to kill her."

Celina frowned and started toward the bouncer. *Creepy? She's the one dressing me like a hooker and telling me to go talk to bouncers.*

Flustered by Victor's comment, she didn't think too far ahead, so when she found herself standing in front of the bouncer all she could say was, "Hey."

The bouncer glanced up, but then a did a wide-eyed double take as he sat straighter, puffing out his chest. "Hey to you."

"Hey." Feeling stupid for repeating herself, she charged forth. "Is Genocide here yet?"

He shrugged his hefty shoulders. "The show starts in about two hours."

"I know, but I was wondering if I could talk to her now."

The bouncer's face went slack as if disappointed. "Sorry, but you can't."

"It's important."

He smirked. "It always is."

"But...." Celina realized that he thought of her as just another groupie. She had to tell him the truth. Victor would disapprove, but she couldn't think of any other way. "Her life could be in danger."

The bouncer frowned. "By you?"

Celina didn't like the way he shifted in his seat. "No! No, no, no, not by me."

"Then who?"

"I... I don't know."

The bouncer signed, his frown deeper. Pointing as he spoke, he said, "Look, either go enjoy the show and wait to see if she wants to party afterwards like everyone else, or have me escort you outside like I do with rowdy, drunk people."

"Okay... Sorry. I'll just... sorry." Head down, Celina retreated. She aimed for the bar even though she wanted to leave the club, the city, the situation. But why? She'd done nothing wrong, yet apologized and scurried away because of an awkward conversation that no one else had witnessed with a person she'd never see again.

She met Victor with a sigh, and before she could tumble too much further down that emotional rabbit hole, Victor asked, "How'd it go?"

"He wouldn't let me see her."

"No worries. C'mon."

Victor took Celina by the hand again and they moved away from the bar to the closest high-top table where three men and a woman were enjoying a round of frilly drinks.

Victor inserted herself in their conversation with, "Hey, wassup?" After smiles and responses from everyone at the table, she continued. "I'm Victor and this is my cousin, Svetlana. She's from Russia and speaks very little English. We're from out of town and this place looked awesome. Are you familiar with the band tonight?"

They were locals and had seen Genocide and the Doomsdays a few times but didn't know anyone in the band. After a few more minutes of conversation, Victor and Celina moved on to a different group of people and gave the same spiel.

Celina spoke with her Russian accent whenever someone addressed her. After a few more interactions with others, Celina learned that no one was close with anyone from the band, but those who had at least met them stated that Genocide and Lucas, the guitarist, seemed personable and quick to converse about any topic while Ven, the bassist, was less so, almost brooding.

Celina wanted to keep talking to a pair of brothers, one was her height even in these ridiculous heels. He was cute and nice. Then she got a little nervous talking with a trio of other women while Victor overtly flirted with one of them. Even though the woman flirted back, Victor and Celina moved on to another group of people, a small party of five. With a beer-full of confidence after the last hour of meeting people,  she wanted to talk to the handsome man in the group, flirt with him if the circumstances warranted. Heartbeat increasing, she approached, excited when the man looked at her and smiled.

Walking closer, she mentally prepared herself to say, "Hey, wassup?" She could do this. She *wanted* to do this.

Then a hand clamped down on her shoulder.

She stopped and brought her knees together to control her bladder. The big door man she had talked to earlier had Victor by her arm as well. Fist clenched, Victor took a firm stance. A lump formed in Celina's throat, suddenly worried that she was about to get into her first fight ever. And that it would hurt.

Victor visibly relaxed when the bouncer said, "Come with me. Genocide wants to see you."

# CHAPTER 15

*March 26th, Chicago*

The dark hallway smelled of urine and vomit. As a member of a band who frequented dive bars, Genocide was familiar with the smells. The fact that she smelled them in the hallway of this apartment building was not surprising, just sad.

Gen led the way, Lucas and Ven in tow. Hands in the pockets of her coat – faded beige leather, edged with white fur – she ran her fingers over the contents. They were grim, but necessary if the impending situation played out like she thought it might.

Apartment 405, the number five missing and only a shadow. Again, not a surprise. She always instructed her bartenders to card anyone who looked under sixty, and to use the I.D. scanner. It was faster than trying to do math, and the customer's pertinent information was saved to a database. *Never know when you need to track down a dirt bag.*

Gen pounded on the door. Of course, if the girl she was looking for used a stolen ID – the computer also filtered out the fakes – then this excursion would all be for nothing. Judging from the dazed, "Fuck off," that came from inside, Gen felt confident this was the right place.

Gen replied, "Either open the door or I'm kicking it in."

After the scuff of shuffling feet, three locks clicked open. A pallid, greasy forehead and blood shot eyes aligned within the door crack. "The fuck you want?" a girl's voice asked.

"This the skank?" Gen asked Lucas and Ven.

"Yep," they said in unison.

The door started to close, but Ven reached from behind Gen and elbowed his way in with little effort, shoving the girl aside in the process.

Gen strolled into the apartment, as disgusting as she imagined it would be. Empty pizza boxes piled in the corners, thread bare furniture, paint peeling from the walls. The smell of burnt plastic told Gen that the girl's taste in drugs went all the way to crack. "Do you know who we are?"

"Yeah, I know who you are," the girl snapped. Arms wrapped around her own waist, she trembled, and Gen doubted it was from fear. "You're the band from that shitty club."

"Well, I own that shitty club and we kicked you out of it two nights ago. Remember why?"

" 'Cause you suck?"

"Close. It's because you broke our rules. We don't have many." As Gen spoke, she moved closer while the girl backed away. "No puking or pissing anywhere other than the restrooms, pay your tab, don't be a dick, no drugs. You broke three of those rules. The one that pisses us off enough to come to your shitty apartment is the 'no drugs' rule. Where'd you get the latro?"

"Fuck you." Stumbling, the girl fell onto the couch.

Gen lorded over her. "Remember the guy you were partying with at my shitty club? He OD'd. In the club. So not only did I have to find a fill-in drummer for our gig tonight, but I had to spend all day yesterday dealing with the cops, cleaning up the mess, and tracking your filthy ass down."

"Sorry that he OD'd," the girl said dryly. "But it's not my fault."

Gen stuck her hands into both coat pockets, shaking the contents. "You don't understand. It wasn't a regular OD with convulsions and trouble breathing. He swelled up like a fucking balloon, and then his skin split and ripped, melting off his body as his bones broke and his liquified guts and muscles ran all over the floor like soup. Don't believe me? Here's what's left of him." Gen tossed half of X's lower jaw, a dozen teeth, and a few chunks of bone onto the girl's lap.

The girl gasped and swatted the bones away as she jumped from the seat of the couch. "Fuck!"

"Exactly. Where'd you get the latro?"

"It wasn't latro. Well… not exactly."

"Explain."

Lucas and Ven grabbed the girl by the shoulders.

Speaking faster, she said, "It was latro but it was mixed with a new drug one been around only a month or so from what I hear and it's called rec."

Gen pulled out her cell phone and held it up for the girl to see the screen. "Tell your dealer someone wants to buy a metric shit ton of that shit and to meet us at this address. Then get dressed, 'cause we're going for a walk."

\*

The girl had lost her attitude the moment Gen threw X's bones on her. Been cooperative ever since.

"I like your coat," the girl mumbled.

Gen wasn't sure if the girl meant it, or if she was trying to ingratiate herself. Didn't matter either way. Gen didn't care enough about the girl to remember her name, and she sure as hell wasn't going to become friendly with her no matter how much the girl liked her style.

"Two blocks to go," Gen said.

They had briskly walked five blocks already, and judging by the girl's wheezing, this was the most exercise she'd gotten in a long while.

"Okay. Yeah, okay, I know where we are," The girl said, sounding relieved. She looked around at the line of condemned row homes leading to the abandoned warehouse two blocks away – their destination. She then did a full three-sixty without breaking pace or falling over. "So, umm... where's the big guy?"

"Disappeared a couple blocks ago. You should pay attention more."

"Yeah, I guess."

Once they got to the warehouse, the girl was even kind enough to confirm that the lone figure standing in the parking lot was her dealer. "That's him. His name's—"

"Don't care," Gen said, cutting her off. The conversation would only last a couple minutes, no need to waste energy on names that didn't matter.

The dealer approached with his arms wide as if ready to give a hug. Wearing the smile of a car salesman, he said, "Hey, Hanna!" The girl's name. Then he chuckled. "Good to see you so soon. You didn't tell me your friends were so gorgeous. So, you're looking for—"

"Not here," Gen snapped as she hurried past him.

Lucas slowed and gestured for Hanna and her dealer to follow Gen.

She led everyone around the warehouse, walking tight along its siding, stopping by a ramshackle open doorway into the darkened building, the door long gone.

"All right, yeah, you're right," the dealer said, still cheery. "Much better. A little more secluded for us to discuss our business—"

"Who's your supplier?" Gen asked. She and Lucas converged on him, and he retreated toward the doorway.

"Whoa, whoa, whoa. That's privileged information. I can assure you, though, that the quality of goods is the best, if that's what's concerning—"

"Last chance. Who's your supplier and where can I find them?"

The dealer dropped his smile and lifted his shirt to reveal the handle of a gun sticking out from his pants. "Look. I don't know what game you're playing, blondie, but—"

Gen heard enough and shoved him into the warehouse, then smirked, relishing what was coming next.

After the slap of skin on concrete, the dealer yelled, "Mother fuc—"

Following the script her mind had developed, a distorted hiss cut off the dealer. Then he yelled, "Oh God! Oh Goooooood!" His screams raised to incomprehensible shrieks, then faded after a scuffle. Hanna's eyes widened, wondering, but Gen knew it was the sound of his body being dragged away.

Leaning against the building, Gen said to the girl, "You can run away in terror now."

The girl wasted no time doing what Gen suggested.

"We expecting a good crowd tonight?" Lucas asked, picking at his fingernails.

"Weather's been unseasonably warm. Not warm enough for picnics and shit, but warm enough to get people out of their apartments. Usually means good crowd."

"Good. Good."

After another minute or so of silence, Ven emerged from the warehouse, pulling his shirt on over his head.

"Got a name?" Gen asked.

Ven flipped his hair, and the trio started their journey back to the club. "Name and address."

"Do we think the info is good?" Lucas asked.

"He was too scared to lie."

"Well, I know what we're doing tomorrow," Gen said. "Let's get back to the club and put on a good show."

\*

"Those two have been asking for you," Vinnie said. He found Gen the moment she got back to the club. "They seem a little... odd. Not your typical groupies."

Gen breezed through the crowd with her doorman – shaved head, muscular. She had personally picked out his overly small "Security" tee shirt, knowing it'd make him appear intimidating. Plenty of people to play for, but not so packed as to call attention from the fire marshal.

Reaching the center of the club, they stopped, and Vinnie pointed out two women. "The tall one said your life might be in danger. The one with the red streaks in her hair was less dramatic but asked every bartender how to meet you. Want me to kick them out?"

Gen almost laughed. Then she suddenly felt a kinship toward them. They were different. They even smelled differently than all the other patrons. "No. Bring them to my office."

# CHAPTER 16

*March 26th, Chicago*

The stained carpet was too thin to muffle the rat-a-tat-tat tapping of Celina's boot heel. She folded her hands together and rested them on her thighs to make herself stop jackhammering the floor.

"No need to be nervous," Victor said with a certain level of mirth in her voice. "I can take him."

The "him" of the statement was Ven, the band's bassist. Victor and Celina learned his name while Vinnie the bouncer escorted them to Gen's office.

Ven leaned against the wall with his arms crossed over his chest. Glowering. The strong angles of his face made him handsome; the frown made him frightening. "Doubt it," he said.

Legs crossed and hands folded behind her head, Victor slouched in the chair next to Celina. Grinning, she tilted her head toward her. "My spin instructor at the gym I go to says I'm the most enthusiastic student in class. Trust me, I can take this guy."

Celina knew Victor was downplaying her abilities. During their conversation while they had been clothes shopping, Victor listed all the martial arts she had taken. Celina believed her, but doubted she could truly take this man, six feet tall and nicely muscled. She didn't know much about fighting, but the cramped quarters of the office gave Victor a distinct disadvantage.

Ven didn't reply to Victor this time, simply stared at her with dark brown eyes. Something about him made Celina nervous. Well, more nervous than sitting in the back office of a heavy metal bar while waiting for a woman whom people called Genocide. It was his eyes – definitely his eyes that made the tiny hairs on the back of her neck stand on end. Did he have two pupils in each eye?

Celina almost jumped out of her skin when Genocide entered the office with a man behind her. Since he had spiky blue hair, Celina assumed him to be Lucas, the guitarist.

Genocide took the seat behind the desk and propped up her feet. Dozens of tiny spikes on her knee high, platform boots glimmered from the lone, unadorned bulb in the ceiling. "So, I hear you two ladies are looking for me?"

Victor shifted in her seat, sitting more attentive. "We sure are. But we were hoping for girl-time."

"Not if you're threatening to hurt me."

Celina had hung around Victor long enough to know that she found Genocide attractive. Celina found her unnerving. Not because of her aggressive image, but something... more primal, a form of danger that a caveman would sense. She squinted, focusing on Genocide's blue eyes. Did she have two pupils in each eye? She blinked and the double pupils were back to one. *Must be the lighting in this room.*

Victor leaned forward; a predator ready to pounce. "I may threaten to do a lot of things to you, but hurting you isn't one of them."

Gen chuckled. "I like men more often than women, but I do like women. *You* are not my type of woman."

"Honey, I'm everyone's type of woman."

"Victor," Celina whispered. "You're straying off topic."

In a sarcastic faux-whisper, Victor replied, "Thank you, Jiminy Cricket, but I'm trying to wish upon a star here."

Lucas laughed and Genocide rolled her eyes. Ven didn't move, not even a slight twitch.

"Fine," Genocide said. "You guys go find the new drummer and make sure he's good to go in an hour."

"You got it, boss," Lucas said as he left.

As Ven followed, Victor blew him a kiss. "Guess I'll have to kick your ass later."

"Doubt it," he replied as he shut the door behind him.

"So," Genocide said. "You gonna keep trying to get in my pants, or are you gonna tell me why my life is in danger?"

"We think someone might be trying to kill you," Celina said as she pulled out her phone and displayed the picture of faces and names. "Because someone is trying to kill us."

Genocide snatched the phone from her. "Sucks to be you."

Elbows on knees, tone all business, Victor said, "We're serious. I'm Victor and this is Celina. Someone shot her sister in the head while they were at dinner. I met the woman trying to kill us at a bar and barely got away from her."

"After they had sex," Celina added.

Eyebrows knitting, Victor turned to Celina. "Do you really have to?"

"It adds to the story."

"First of all, it doesn't. Second of all, the sex was implied."

"Actually, it wasn't," Genocide said. "People meet in my bar all the time and don't have sex."

Victor crushed her eyes closed and scrubbed her fingers through her hair while growling. She slicked her hair back and continued, "Okay, I met a woman at a bar, and by some not so crazy coincidence we went back to her room, fucked all night, and then she tried to kill me."

Genocide dropped her feet to the floor and handed Celina's phone back. "Look, the murder of your sister is truly messed up." She then addressed Victor, "But someone trying to kill you before, after, or during sex? I'm surprised that you're surprised. I kinda want to kill you myself and *not* have sex with you." She leaned back to address both women. "I honestly can't see why you think these events are related. And I still have no idea in hell why you're trying to involve me."

"The picture on her phone," Victor said. "I took that picture from my one-night-stand's computer. She has a whole portfolio on each person."

"That's how you found me?"

"No. I didn't have time to click on each name. During my harrowing escape from death, I only had time to take the picture."

"But my sister knew how to find you," Celina said. "The night she died, she had tracked me down because she's involved in crypto forensics. She studies urban legend level killers, like modern day Jack the Rippers. She told me our father was someone like that. She had my name, Victor's name, and your name. All three of us are on the same list of names that someone had, the same someone who tried to kill Victor. I think that's more than coincidence."

"So why would Victor's poor choice in sex partners want to kill us?"

"Don't know," Victor answered. "Two things the three of us have in common – we're close in age, and we don't know our birth parents."

Genocide sat forward, and a slight frown started to form. "Who says I don't know my birth parents?"

"You're a product of this country's foster care system, Jennifer," Victor said.

"Genocide," she corrected.

"Naah. Genocide Faustino just doesn't sound right."

Genocide froze. Her frown deepened.

Goose bumps broke out on Celina, and she felt the need to defuse the situation. "What I think Victor's trying to say is we found your real name and learned about your childhood in less than a day. How much more do you think someone could find if they're actively hunting you?"

Genocide frightened Celina. Victor had scared her, too, when they first met, but that stemmed from anxiety and the fear of trying something new, a consequence of breaking the status-quo in order to restore it. But Genocide agitated the shadowy thoughts and feelings lurking deep within the pits of Celina's soul. Every time Genocide shifted in her seat, Celina felt the need to shift the opposite direction. A slight ease came to her heightened emotions when Genocide asked, "What do you want from me?"

"Help us find out who's trying to kill us," Celina answered. "Help us track down the other names on this list to find out why."

Genocide laughed, and for some reason this shot Celina's anxiety through the roof. "You can't be serious."

Victor shrugged. "Why not?"

"As much as I truly appreciate a girl-power team up, I don't think I'm gonna get involved with this. My father died before I was born and even though my mother wasn't around when I was a kid, she and I reunited a couple years ago, so I know exactly who she was. Even if I was connected like you're suggesting, I simply don't have time to drop everything and track down a bunch of strangers. I have plenty of my own personal drama, beyond my band and successful bar."

Celina didn't like the smug look of playing a trump card that washed over Victor's face.

"My name is Victor Vegas not because I like the town, but because I own it. You own Vegas by winning big pots from big gambles, and I've won enough to lead a life of excess. My money could blow past the top of Maslow's pyramid. Just like a shark knows another shark, money knows money, and you got it, sweetheart. You got it. I can smell it on you. Your ratty office and shitty furniture may as well be sitting on top of an underground volcano of cash. I'm confident that you own more than this bar, Jennifer."

"Time for you two to leave."

Ice slid down Celina's spine from the tone of Genocide's voice. She jumped out of her chair when the office door opened.

Victor laughed at her. "Drama queen."

Lucas and Ven entered.

Genocide stood. Taking Victor by the arm, Celina escorted her toward the door, desperate to leave.

Lucas offered them a bright smile and waved goodbye with his fingertips while Ven stood chill and cool like there was nothing in this world deserving of his concern.

As Victor walked pass Ven, she glided her fingers over his cheek. "Can't wait to throw down with you."

Unflinching, he said, "Doubt it."

*

The text from Murphy came right after Celina and Victor exited Club B-Sides, a request to meet them at an address seven blocks away, but she didn't specify what the address had to do with anything. During their walk, they reviewed their meeting with Genocide.

"What a bitch," Victor said once they crossed the street.

Celina didn't agree with the assessment. She didn't understand Victor's point of view, but she understood the motivation. Victor remained an alpha in all aspects of her life, professional and personal, work and play. When presented with an obstacle, Victor plowed her way through it; this much Celina had learned. But what would she do when she found an obstacle she couldn't overcome? Butt heads with another alpha? Celina tried to appeal to Victor's sensibilities. "I'm sure she'll come around."

"If she doesn't wind up dead first."

"She seems… capable. If we can get another person or two on the list to help us, then it will be easier to get her – and others – to figure out who's trying to kill us and why. Murphy found Caila's address and sent it to me while we were in the bar, so we have that option, too. Don't forget, you said, 'No,' to me at first."

"Yeah, but you came across like a delusional conspiracy nut. I, on the other hand, presented our case logically, like a rational person."

One thing Celina had learned from Victor was how comfortable men's shoes were compared to women's – right now the balls of her feet throbbed from walking along the city sidewalks. She also learned the benefits of standing up for herself, something she wanted to work on, even if it was to Victor. "You take that back! My message delivery was perfectly calm and rational. And what did you do when I gave you that information? You dressed me in a suit to perpetrate a zillion dollar business ruse."

Celina didn't like how hurried her words came, but they had the desired effect. Victor threw her hands in the air and huffed. "Fine! When you put it that way, it does make me sound a tad less than rational and there's no denying my love of ruses."

"I accept your apology."

106

Victor shot Celina an incredulous look as if she dreamed up her own point B to get from point A to point C.

After another block in silence, Victor mumbled, "God, Gen and her bandmates gave me the creeps."

Celina nodded, relieved she wasn't alone in that feeling. "Me, too!"

"It felt like there was a snake crawling up my leg the whole time."

"Or bugs. Like bugs were skittering all over my skin."

"I don't get it. All three of them were hot. No way I should have been so skeeved out being in room with three gorgeous people."

"I… uhh… Yeah, what you said."

"I can honestly say I've never felt that way before. And…." Victor looked around, and pulled out her phone to double check the address. "Where the fuck are we going?"

The two- and three-story buildings had given way to row homes. The night exerted its dominion as the number of working streetlights dwindled, the few lit porch lights not enough to chase the darkness away. They continued in silence, following Victor's phone's GPS.

A few more row homes, only one unit with lights on. Celina would never venture through a neighborhood like this at night back home, but she felt safe with Victor. Not only did she believe Victor could handle herself in a bad situation, but her presence made Celina feel stronger, confident.

They stopped and looked around, Celina shivering. "Is this the right place?"

An abandoned convenience store. A simple thirty foot by thirty-foot cinderblock box with plywood over the doors and windows. Graffiti covered the building, simple tags from bored locals, nothing artistic. Knee high weeds poked from the cracks in the parking lot, the space big enough to accommodate half a dozen vehicles. One streetlight had been assigned to keep the area lit, but it flickered and buzzed.

Victor mumbled, "Why does she want to meet us here?"

Celina moved closer to Victor in an attempt to leech off her strength. Almost arm to arm, she looked over Victor's shoulder as she texted: Where r u???

A faint lion's roar sounded like it came from the building. Victor whispered, "That's Murphy's text tone."

She tapped her phone, calling Murphy's number. *The Imperial March* played.

Victor and Celina followed the music around the building, the flickering streetlight a poor guide. The music rang louder as they turned the corner. Celina wanted to hold Victor's hand, but her hands were busy – one holding her phone, the other clenched in a fist. The dim streetlight barely illuminated brush and a couple small trees. Celina activated her cell phone's flashlight.

The light beamed in Murphy's face, eyeless and distended in a scream. Arms and legs spread wide, she hung displayed on a spider's web, the web's strands shimmering any time the streetlight flashed. Her torso's skin had been stripped away to expose an empty cavity, wet and glistening.

Legs giving out, Celina dropped to her hands and knees and vomited. Her world started to go black.

# CHAPTER 17

*March 26th, Los Angeles*

Blaze lit his third cigarette, cussing under his breath. It'd taken twenty minutes since meeting up with Jerry to walk to the warehouse. After a deep inhale to calm his nerves, he blew two columns of smoke from his nostrils and said, "An abandoned warehouse. Why does it *always* have to be an abandoned warehouse, Jerry?"

"You answered your own question," Jerry said. "I mean, the reason is in the name, don't ya think? 'Abandoned warehouse' implies no other human involvement."

No other human involvement. Blaze wasn't confident in that statement. Eyes were on them the moment they stepped foot inside. They were being watched. It might just be rats and roaches and spiders, but the racks of dusty metal shelves and the dark second floor concourse running along the perimeter created plenty of hiding places. Hiding places meant potential ambush.

Blaze's loose definition of a friend, Jerry, had offered him this mystery job last night after Chelsea provided him with the Marcel information. Less than twenty-four hours later and now Blaze felt nothing but regret. Fear, too. He thought about leaving and telling Jerry he was on his own, but Jerry's voice had held a slight warble. He couldn't leave Jerry high-and-dry like that, so he panned the light from his cellphone across the warehouse floor as they walked. "It's just so cliché nowadays. Whatever happened to the good old days when back-alley transactions happened over a dinner at some fine dining establishment? Not in a dark and dirty abandoned warehouse."

"Jesus, Blaze. There are like a hundred things wrong with what you just said. First, again, you answered your own question. 'Old days' mean days of yore, bygone, in the past because they don't fit in the present and the future don't want them. Second, they made deals in dirty places back then, too. Like you said – back alleys. Just as dirty and nasty as abandoned warehouses. Third, only rich mafia bosses meet over dinner in fine dining establishments. Just in case our lack of money, respect, or underlings didn't tip you off, we aren't mafia bosses. And since you clearly don't know your history, those old-days mafia bosses always got shot up at dinner in the fine dining establishments."

"Damn, Jerry. You've always been a little… what's that fancy word I'm looking for? Pedantic. Yeah, that's it. You've always been pedantic, but now you're being super pedantic. You got pedantic 'roid rage or somethin'."

Jerry lowered his voice to a whisper, but it still quivered, fear seeping from him in the form of words. "This place creeps me the fuck out."

"Then why'd you agree to meet Melissandra here?" Blaze whispered back. His mother had taught him that voices carried in Hell.

"I didn't. She changed the meeting place on me. We were gonna meet at Rosella's, that four-star Italian place right outside Hollywood."

Blaze flicked ash from his cigarette. "You're a real piece of work, Jerry. I'm going to assume that you called me after she changed meeting venues."

"I needed some muscle."

Blaze laughed. "You got a distorted view of the world if you think I'm the 'muscle' in any crew. If you would have told me you needed that, I would have gotten Big Lou. He'd be perfect for this right now."

Blaze, though not a tall man, clocked in at an average five foot ten. Jerry was almost half a foot shorter. Blaze was thinner, though. Not skin and bone, like the drug addicts he sometimes dealt with, but no one ever mistook him for an athlete. People usually thought he was a musician, but that assessment came from his self-described impeccable style and bad boy looks. With the way Jerry's belly pushed against the blue Polo shirt tucked into his khaki cotton slacks, it was no wonder Jerry had often been mistaken for a comic book shop owner or electronics store clerk. A shaggy beard and overgrown bowl cut completed his intended look.

People *always* made assumptions about looks, and Jerry exploited the hell out of that. No one ever suspected Jerry's involvement in a shootout, even though, undoubtedly, he'd started it. He'd also be the only one to survive.

"I figured your mouth could get me outta any trouble I might find myself in. Plus, you got your new gun, right?" Jerry asked.

"I do. Are you carrying?"

"I got three on me."

Where the hell he hid them was beyond Blaze's comprehension, but asking at a time like this would be stupid.

Jerry reached behind his back when a clang of metal against the cement floor rang from the back of the warehouse. Blaze reached for his gun as well, but then the clang sounded like something rolling along the floor toward them. Instead of his gun, Blaze aimed his cell phone light on a rolling fifty-five-gallon drum.

Jerry remained tense, looking like he might draw his gun and shoot first, ask questions as he ran away. Blaze opted to fake a level of confidence, and he stopped the barrel with his foot. He cocked his head and glanced at its open end. Empty. Jerry twitched again as a motor grinded to life. A string of light bulbs dangling from the ceiling flickered on, illuminating a small portion of the warehouse enough to spotlight their hostess, Melissandra.

"Greetings, gentlemen."

Blaze was confused. Her reputation instilled a tremble in the speaker's voice when uttering her name, and he expected a scary looking woman in a business suit, not a gorgeous redhead dressed like a dominatrix.

"What the fuck am I even looking at?" Blaze whispered from the corner of his mouth. "Is she trying to be some sort of super villain?"

"Yeah," Jerry moaned. "Her superpower is the ability to send all the blood in my body to my crotch in under one second."

"You're a piece of work, Jerry. A real piece of work."

But her undeniable sexuality was a weapon unto itself. She sauntered toward them, the stiletto heels of her thigh-high leather boots clacking against the floor in time with the swing of her hips. Her black pants and top, leather or vinyl – Blaze couldn't tell which – gleamed in the dull light. The red corset, tight across her waist, emphasized her hourglass figure. When she approached, Blaze understood the sense of unease when people talked about her – she had two different sized pupils, one much larger and blacker than the other. He'd never seen anything like it in his life. And this woman reeked of fucking crazy, like it was her favorite perfume.

Fear played Blaze's spine like a harp, and he wanted *nothing* more than to run the hell out of this warehouse. He would have rather dealt with an ugly woman in a business suit, or a hundred pimps like Marcel, anything other this level of crazy.

She eyed Blaze. "So, Jerry, I see you got me a driver."

Blaze glanced at Jerry. "A driver, huh?"

Jerry shrugged, his gaze stuck on Melissandra like a horny freshman's in awe of a hot new teacher.

His friend now rendered useless, Blaze faced Melissandra and summoned more fake confidence. "What am I driving?"

"A van small enough to go unnoticed, but large enough to fit six of those drums and make it to Chicago."

"What will be in the drums?"

"That isn't—" Melissandra cut herself short and reeled back, as if her proximity to Blaze suddenly offended her. The tone in her voice changed, from whimsical and salacious to clipped and pained. "There's something about you…"

Glistening red lips twitched as if peeling from her face to expose her teeth. Mouth opening slightly, she stepped in close. *Oh man those eyes.* Blaze reared back, thinking she might bite him, but she inhaled instead, breathing him in. "I don't know if I want to kill you or fuck you…"

"I certainly know which choice I'd prefer if given a vote."

Melissandra circled him, much more in control of her voice now. "You're different. I feel a certain kinship with you, yet adversarial."

Yep. Fucking crazy. Blaze wondered how many other times she had used this tactic. It was an interesting power move, a bold way to throw the other person off guard. He repeated, "What will be in the drums?"

Melissandra continued pacing around him, and he imagined the skin of his neck blistering from her hot breath. She faced him and stared deeply into his eyes. Her smile made his stomach flip-flop. "That isn't important."

"It absolutely is," Blaze said, shifting his stance so he wouldn't piss himself. Waves of instability rolled off this woman, but he had to say his peace, even though it might get him killed. "Barrels imply liquid. Liquid implies chemicals. Chemicals can be explosive. If I'm driving explosives halfway across the country, I need to make sure your van has shocks that will make me feel like I'm riding a cloud to Heaven. If not, I will, of course, alter my price."

Her eyes widened, as did her smile. Her pupils seemed to dance, and Blaze's skin crawled. "I will supply you a good van. I assure you, Mr. Blaze, you won't be hauling explosives. And your pay is fifty thousand."

"Just call me Blaze. One word, kind of like 'Melissandra.' And fifty thousand isn't what I had in mind. Let's say ten thousand."

"What the fuck?" fell out of Jerry's mouth.

Melissandra frowned, yet her smile remained, a pernicious halo around teeth ready to tear his throat out at any second. "You certainly are interesting, just-Blaze-one-word. Care to elaborate?"

"Sure. I want you to stash ten thousand cash in the trunk of one of those new, limited-edition Mercedes that just came out."

"The one with the different driving modes? This is Los Angeles. Why do you need different driving modes to sit in traffic?"

"This is Los Angeles. It's all about image."

"It's a hundred-thousand-dollar car."

"I'm hauling chemicals. If they're not explosive, then they're going to be used for drugs. 330 gallons of chemicals makes a looooooooot of drugs."

Melissandra stepped closer, her face mere inches from Blaze's, close enough to make him wonder if she were going to kiss him or eat him. "That's very bold of you, Blaze, negotiating with a woman as dangerous as me."

"It's very bold of you to come alone to meet two men in a warehouse."

"Who ever said I was alone?" She turned so abruptly that the ends of her long hair brushed across Blaze's cheek. Boot heels clacked as she walked away. The lights flicked off, and Jerry ran. The darkness hissed and clicked, stirring like a creature awakening from a slumber. Not one creature. Many.

"We have a deal, Blaze." Melissandra's voice rode along the blackness. "Be here, ready to drive, in twenty-four hours."

Blaze took off behind Jerry, the two of them sprinting back the way they came. They hit the side street and ran side by side until they reached the main drag. They didn't stop there, but branched off and ran in different directions.

Shaking and wheezing, Blaze ran ten more blocks to his apartment. As soon as he crashed through his door, he snapped all the locks shut and turned on every light.

In the fetal position on his couch, he snuggled with his gun. It didn't make him feel any safer.

# CHAPTER 18

*March 27th, I-90, outside Cleveland*

Victor slouched in her seat and stared out the bus's window. She tapped her phone for the time. After midnight. Yearning for sleep, she couldn't. Too upset.

Celina stared down at her phone, scrolling and tapping, the whole bus trip spent researching Caila's apartment and address.

Panicked from what – and whom – they had found behind the abandoned convenience store, they decided not to go back to the hotel. Instead, they headed straight to the bus station and paid cash for two tickets to Philadelphia to find Robert.

After fleeing the scene, they locked themselves in a stall in the bus station women's room. They cried, they freaked-the-fuck-out, they hugged, they planned. Going to meet Robert was the best option they had.

Right after they had hopped on the bus, about a third full with empty-eyed travelers, Celina started to research Caila's address. Earlier in the day, it was sent to her from....

Victor couldn't even think *her* name or else she'd start crying again. She went back to blankly staring out the window, at the black landscape beyond, speckled by random lights. The darkness moved by the window, moved on its own and twisted, molding itself into a shape. A face. Murphy's dead face.

Tears fell silently down her cheek. Victor shook her head and turned away from the window to the dim interior lights and bobbing heads of riders blessed by sleep.

Celina's phone buzzed. A text. Making no effort to angle her phone away for privacy, Victor easily read the screen, a friend explaining her level of drunkenness and asking about Las Vegas. Celina replied, fingers tapping a story. She wrote that she attended a tabletop gaming convention and had a good time and great food.

"It's not nice to lie to your friends," Victor mumbled.

Celina shrugged. "It's not entirely a lie. As weird and as short as my stay was, I did have a good time in Vegas."

Victor chuckled. "You're welcome." After a few seconds of silence, she continued, "I never thought of you as the kind of girl with friends who drunk texted."

Celina turned to Victor. "Not the kind of girl? What do you mean by that?"

"Well, you know, you're kind of mousey."

"Mousey?"

"Yeah. Shy. Awkward. Gangly. Afraid. Uptight."

"You make me sound like a hermit. Yes, I'm introverted. And sometimes afraid. It doesn't stop me from living. Doesn't stop me from trying new things. Having a routine doesn't mean I'm uptight, it just means I like parts of my life a certain way. And I'm six feet tall! I can't help but be gangly."

"If you hadn't noticed from all the way up there, I'm only a few inches shorter than you and no one calls me gangly."

Still wearing the same slutty outfit she'd worn to Club B-Sides, Celina shifted in her seat and tugged at her skirt as if she might get it to her knees this time. She couldn't even stretch the skirt halfway down her thighs.

Crossing her arms over her chest, Celina huffed. "Those extra few inches make all the difference. You'd be uncoordinated, too, if you were this tall." She turned away from Victor and muttered, "You said I have nice legs."

Victor pursed her lips and raised her brow. She then released a pent-up sigh of emotions – frustration, anger, sadness. More than that, she was frightened and didn't know what to do. Well, one thing she shouldn't have done was take it out on the other person who knew what she was going through. "You do have nice legs. Okay, maybe 'mousey' wasn't the right word. It's just that when I looked at your social media accounts, none of them had more than a hundred contacts. I assumed none of them were the drunk-texting type."

"We drink, you know. And have fun and go out and party. Not crazy, champagne, orgy parties like you do, but that doesn't mean I don't know how to have fun."

"Crazy, champagne, orgy—? Good God, woman, what you think of me."

"See? Doesn't feel good to be judged unfairly, Mister 'I own Vegas, I am Vegas, I eat, breathe, and fuck Vegas.'"

Celina had dropped her voice lower to mock Victor. Victor stared at Celina, surprised by her gall. Then she laughed.

Celina snorted, then joined her laughter. After they stopped giggling, Celina squirmed on the seat to adjust her skirt again, and said, "I don't have many contacts on my social media accounts because they are all actually people I know, like, and associate with. True friends. I care about each one of them. I've been lying because I don't want to worry them. I checked your social media accounts, too. You have hundreds and hundreds of contacts, but I haven't seen you text or call anyone. Are you close with at least a few of them? Enough that they'd want to know where you are?"

"No. Well, I'm close enough to—" Victor caught herself in time, stopped herself from saying Murphy's name. Too late. Thinking her name conjured how Victor last saw her. Trussed up between the trees. Mutilated and desecrated. Her eyes open. *Oh, God, her eyes were gone!*

"Do you want to talk about it yet?" Celina asked, her voice almost as soothing as a salve.

"No." The word flew out of Victor's mouth. She worked her jaw muscles, as if chewing other words that wished to be heard.

"You know," Celina started. Already, Victor didn't like her tone, one that sounded like she was about to make a point and it was going to be a good one, too. "There is one rule men follow that I think is stupid; the rule that disallows them from talking about their feelings. You know which rule I'm talking about? The rule where they can't share their feelings? I mean, you play the game of life using men's rules, so I was wondering if—"

"Okay, okay, I'll talk. God, you're annoying. You wield annoyance like a sword."

Turning with a wince on the cheap fabric bus seat, Celina stared at Victor with hurt and anger. Most people in Victor's life looked at her that way, which might explain her lack of friends. Except for Murphy. She never took crap from Victor and Victor loved her for it. Now she was gone. "I don't like talking about my feelings because I hate to cry. I hate the burning in my eyes and the weird sting behind my nose; hate that it never solves anything, never amounts to anything productive. The phrase, 'A good cry,' is pure garbage. There's nothing good about crying. I cried more in the bus station bathroom than I had the past five years combined."

Victor wiped away her tears before they fell from her face and took a deep breath, her bottom lip quivering. She slapped a hand over her chin. "I hate this quiver, too. What feelings do you want me to share? That I miss her already? That I'm pissed off she's gone? That I'm freaked out about how she died? That I'm angry at myself for being so scared that I ran away and left her there? What do you want me to say?"

A head from the aisle over raised and turned toward them. Victor sneered and the nosy passenger went back to minding their own business.

Celina took Victor's hand and whispered, "Keep going. You're doing great."

"Ugh."

"How did you meet her?"

What a stupid question. She'd just told Celina she didn't want to talk about Murphy, let alone how they met. But that memory felt like a warm blanket on a cold night. Okay, maybe it was a great question. "We met right after college. We went on a date."

"Am I seriously the only woman you know that you haven't had sex with?"

Victor tightened her lips and flattened her brow. "She and I never had sex. It was one date. I can go on dates with people and not have sex with them, you know."

"I actually did not know."

"Well, now you do."

"Was it a bad date?"

Victor swallowed down her initial anger at Celina, but she held such an honesty in her eyes. She cared, and was actually interested in what Victor had to say. The only other one who looked at Victor like that was Murphy. "No. I mean, obviously, it wasn't a great date. Somewhere along the night – a simple dinner at a nice restaurant – we started clicking in a different way. We stopped trying to be bedroom partners and started figuring out how to be business partners."

"Did you two start a business together?"

"Not officially. She went into the army right after high school and spent time with Special Forces. She didn't have the patience for numbers, but she loved to get her hands dirty. I'm the complete opposite. There was no info that she couldn't find. She was also infinitely patient, since she willingly put up with me."

Victor wiped at her tears again and dropped her hands to her lap. It felt like her bones turned to smoke and the seat wanted to absorb her. She wanted to disappear.

Celina wouldn't let her, and grabbed both of Victor's hands.

Victor hated how tired she sounded from trying not to cry, but she felt safe enough to mumble, "She was like a sister to me."

After a moment of silence, Celina squeezed Victor's hands. "We've known each other for only a few days, but I'm your sister now. That is, if you want me."

"I would like that very much. And the sister thing goes for you too, since you only knew yours for all of five minutes."

"I would like that, too. Or are you my brother now?" Celina smiled, her face impish and sweet at the same time.

Victor leaned to the side and rested her head on Celina's shoulder. "No, you jerk, but I love that you get me."

"That's what sisters do," Celina replied, resting her cheek on Victor's head.

Even though the road noise was rhythmic, almost soothing, Victor still couldn't sleep. One thought kept stomping around her mind, knocking things over. She didn't want to verbalize it, make it more real than it already was. She didn't want to test Celina's fealty so soon, but... "I'm scared."

Celina tensed.

Victor knew very well that Celina was never the strong one, never the one who had to carry someone on her back through the fire.

Tentatively, as if trying out a suggestion, Celina said, "We'll figure this out. We'll find who's trying to kill us.

"I don't know, Celina. I feel like this goes beyond that."

"What do you mean?"

"Did you get a good look at the scene, or were you too busy puking?"

"Too busy puking," Celina answered, her voice small and ashamed.

"No, don't feel bad. I was almost puking alongside of you. What I meant was – did you see how she was hanging."

Celina sat up. "Not really. I remember it didn't seem natural. I mean, there was *nothing* natural about it, but... Was she hanging from ropes?"

"She wasn't. She was caught in a spider web."

Celina frowned. "A spider web? *That* big? How? What does that mean?"

"I don't know. I feel like we might be dealing with something not human. That's why I'm afraid."

They spent the rest of the trip awake and in silence.

# CHAPTER 19

*March 27th, Frederick, Maryland*

At the end of school yesterday the principal held an impromptu memorial for Lance. Yes, Orion felt sad and a little freaked out that a school-mate, a kid his age, died in his sleep. Brain aneurism, whatever that was.

Orion's parents carved out time right after he returned home to talk about it. His father even shared a story about a boy in his school who died while riding his motorcycle drunk and how confusing it was to deal with feelings of sympathy as well as the anger toward him for being so stupid. Orion listened patiently and said everything he thought his parents wanted to hear so he could go to his room and work on Bigby. He appreciated their effort and the story, but he just couldn't muster the emotions to feel *bad* about the situation.

He held a level of sympathy for Lance's family. He'd love to think that if Lance were still alive, he'd would have received a future epiphany that would have opened his eyes and made him change his ways, but Lance had been a shitty teenager and all signs pointed to him being a shittier adult. Was the world a better place now that he was gone? Maybe. Orion couldn't bring himself to think otherwise.

After his parents' talk, Orion spent the rest of the night drawing more of Bigby, a superhero of the dreamscape. A badass one, with a blue top hat and cape and a wicked smile of razor blade teeth. Brennan was going to love this!

Despite going to bed later than usual, Orion woke up a half hour be-fore his alarm went off, which *never* happened. He came downstairs for breakfast to a table set for one. Mom and Dad had to go into the office early, something about closing a big deal. Whatever. He wanted to eat and run any-way. Pancakes and bacon today. But no hovering Aika. Orion wolfed down his meal in silence, worrying. It was unlike her not to be around the kitchen during breakfast.

He finished, placed his plates in the sink, and debated about heading off to school. No, it wasn't right to leave without saying goodbye to anyone.

Aika's voice floated in from the living room, soft and hurried. Whispering. She sounded upset, so Orion peeked around the corner to see if he could help her with anything. On her cell phone, Aika paced in a tight circle, one arm around her waist as if hugging herself, speaking Japanese far too quickly for Orion's limited, self-taught vocabulary. Though, he gleaned that something had happened and she didn't know what to do. She stopped pacing when she noticed Orion, said one last thing, and then hung up. "Orion, good morning. I didn't hear you come down the stairs. Did you eat breakfast?"

"Yeah. Delish as always. Thanks. Is everything okay? Sorry, didn't mean to eavesdrop."

Aika looked at her phone as if she had forgotten she was holding it, then back to Orion. For a second, she looked guilty, then she shook her head as if snapping out of a daydream and gave him a warm smile. "I apologize if I made you worry. My aunt in Japan isn't doing well."

"Oh. Sorry to hear that. I'm sure my parents will give you time off if you need to head back home."

Aika ushered Orion to the dining room, her hand on his back felt maternal. "Your parents are very kind and generous, so I'm sure they would. There's more than just that, but no need to concern yourself."

"But—"

"How did you sleep last night?"

"Oh… Umm… Good. Really good."

"Any more wild dreams?"

"No. But last night after school, I worked on developing my character, Bigby, that I told everyone about. A superhero of the dreamscape."

Aika shivered and looked away. She whispered, "I think the A/C is set too cold."

Orion grabbed his backpack and looked at Aika. She seemed sad, almost scared. Again, her face snapped to a smile when she noticed his attention. "Your superhero sounds exciting. Have a great day in school."

Orion felt bad. Aika must have been really concerned about her aunt. But her situation faded from his mind when he got to his locker and no Brennan. Dude where r u? U in school today?

Brennan's reply: YES! Just running late

So frustrating! Orion had to wait three classes before he could catch up with Brennan at lunch. The wall clock's hands moved like fingernails over a chalkboard, but Orion endured and hurried to the cafeteria as soon as class let out. But when he entered, he became confused. And concerned.

At a table of twelve, Brennan held court, accepting adulations from the eleven others sitting around him. He still looked ill, like the sickness had taken over and become a part of his personality. His skin seemed wrong, unshowered, oily, and a shade or two paler. Eyes wide and hair sticking out in jagged angles, he looked like a maniacal anime character. So, why was everyone enraptured by his presence?

Orion walked closer, and noticed that everyone at the table was reading a comic book? It sure appeared that way. He sat beside his best friend for the first time in two days and said, "Hey. Did you start a comic book reading group?"

Something was wrong. Brennan glared at him as if he were a piece of meat to devour. It took a few seconds for Brennan to even express recognition. "Hey! It's been a minute." He handed Orion a comic book, the same issue everyone else held. "Here. This is what I was working on yesterday and this morning."

Twelve pages. Full color. Almost photorealism artwork. Printed from his home printer. All about Bigby.

"What the hell?" Orion asked as he flipped through the pages. The story was about a group of high school students bullied by a football player. Then Bigby appeared. In four pages of graphic detail, he shredded the football player. First, he ripped the player's arms and legs off, blood and muscle and bone flying across the pages. He then gleefully tore into the player's torso, sending guts and organs all over the place. The evisceration ended with a full-page image of Bigby biting into a human heart with his razor blade teeth.

"Awesome, right?" Brennan asked.

"Hell yeah!" one of the other students said. "Can't wait for more."

"This is just a promotional printed copy. I'm developing it into a web comic."

"Dude," Orion whispered to Brennan. "The unnamed football character looks exactly like Lance."

"Thank you. I'm pretty proud of how well I did with that."

"No, I mean, don't you think it's a little insensitive?"

Orion shifted, more than a bit nervous when Brennan turned his full attention to him. His maniacal glare didn't diminish, but twisted from happy to angry. "Insensitive? To whom? The people who loved and supported that shit-head's reign of terror? Fuck them for creating such a fucking monster. Don't tell me you actually miss him. Look at everyone at this table. Lance tormented each and every one of us. If they see Lance in my comic book, then I've delivered catharsis. If anyone else sees Lance in my comic, then they're openly admitting he was an abuser."

Upon gulping down his fear, Orion took a second look. A few of the panels called to Orion – the way Bigby smiled. The way Bigby flowed from out of the protagonist's locker. The way Bigby hovered menacingly behind the football player. The way Bigby *smiled*. Those very images played in his dream two nights ago. "How did you get these images?"

Mirth returned to Brennan's wicked smile. He leaned in close enough for Orion to smell that he had gone over a day without brushing his teeth. "I saw them in a dream. In fact," he leaned even closer to whisper, "I think I killed Lance."

"Wait... what?"

"My dream didn't happen like in my comic. Lance had me cornered against your locker. Then I heard a voice, a scary voice, say, 'I need to find the one who can free me.' It was obvious what I had to do. I opened your locker and freed Bigby. But he didn't kill Lance like in my comic. He bit off the top of his head. How did Lance die? Aneurysm. A fucking brain aneurysm. Right where Bigby bit him in my dream."

*Impossible. How could he have almost the same dream I did?* Only difference, in Brennan's dream, Bigby was talking to him about Orion.

"I don't know, Brennan. It seems like you're inviting trouble."

"Hey, I'm an artist. Artists use their characters to hold a mirror up to the world."

"Your character? I drew Bigby first."

The smile disappeared altogether, the residue a terrifying scowl on Brennan's face. "You said you drew him from a character I created."

"I was talking about Zeb and the zombies."

"You didn't show me any lame ass character named Zeb and you didn't show me any fucking zombies. You showed me Bigby and said that he was my character."

"I was trying to show you Zeb and —"

Brennan's face reddened with anger. "Don't try to take my character from me, Orion. Don't be fucking lame." His voice got louder. Kids at the table stopped talking and looked over at Brennan. "You know, I thought about inviting you to participate with me in this, in *my* character, but now that you're being a dick, forget it. In fact, don't even fucking try to draw him again. If I see one image of him created by your hand, I'll sue. I'll fucking sue you! Or worse... I'll send Bigby after you."

A few smirks of camaraderie formed among the spectators. Orion wanted to explain, to talk it out, but this scene was becoming a kangaroo court. His best friend stole his idea and Orion had no way of getting it back. This was a setup. An ambush. The longer he stayed, the worse things would get. Before anyone pulled out a cell phone to record his humiliation, he got up and walked away. Brennan said something that Orion couldn't hear, but laughter followed. He wiped away a tear as he left the lunchroom.

During his next class, Orion googled dream gods, and liked the sound of Icelus. That's who he was now. A dream god since he created Bigby, since he was the one who killed Lance in a dream. He was the one who controlled Bigby, not Brennan.

For the rest of the day, Orion drew pictures of Bigby eating Brennan.

# CHAPTER 20

*March 27th, Philadelphia*

Celina exhaled and ran her hands over her dress, shooing away wrinkles that didn't exist.

"It's okay, you'll do fine," Victor said. The merriment in her voice implied she wanted to tease Celina, and showed great restraint. "If he doesn't trip over himself when he sees you, then he's stupid."

"It's not *that*." It was totally *that*.

They stood outside the 8th Street Art Gallery and *that* was what she was hoping would happen when she saw Robert again. She felt like a delusional stalker, showing up unannounced because she misread their exchange from a few days ago. But she wasn't here for *that*. She needed to warn him that his name was on a woman's mysterious list, a woman who seemingly wanted all those names dead. *Okay, which sounds worse, being hopelessly romantic or aggressively paranoid?* "It just feels... weird that we had a nice day."

Victor laughed. "What's weird is your definition of nice day."

They arrived in the city around 6:00 in the morning. Unable to sleep on the bus, they first found a hotel. Nothing as upscale as The Ritz Carlton in Chicago, but nice. Not nice enough to waive the early check-in fee, even though Victor paid by cash, but nicer than any place Celina would have stayed had she been traveling by herself. They slept until 1:00 and then went shopping.

Due to faint the aroma of lingering sweat and smoke on their day-old clothes, despite a shower, they received quite a few not-so-subtle sideways glances when they entered the boutique. Thankfully, Victor allowed Celina to pick her own outfit this time. A blue-gray sundress and flats. It wasn't the right season for the ensemble, but she craved comfort from the material playing against her shins when she walked. Victor opted for a light grey suit and black turtleneck, because, "It makes me feel like an art snob." She ditched the boots and found another pair of spats. "Spats are fucking timeless."

126

They had a nice lunch – and it was *nice* no matter Victor's sarcasm. Victor was quieter than usual, undoubtedly upset about Murphy. She and Celina decided to share a few childhood stories at first to see if any common threads dangled for a killer to pull, but that turned into a sharing of whimsical tales from their youth. Victor said she had always known she had a sense for business. No surprise, she had been a bit of a hellion as a preteen and bartered for less severe punishments whenever she got caught.

"We've been awake for only four hours," Celina said. "In that time, we bought clothes and had great conversation over a delicious lunch. I call that a nice day." She couldn't articulate why, but she found comfort in shopping and meals, in a safe place in a world full of danger. "Although... I feel weird. Like we're doing something two people should not do when they're hunted."

Victor grabbed Celina's hand. "There's nothing wrong with having a nice time, no matter the circumstances. We have no idea what's going on, only a handful of facts to piece together, and we're not even sure if they truly go together. We've examined them so extensively that it'd be a waste of time to look at them again. We need more information and more opinions from a different source. And if you end up having sex with that source, then extra double bonus for you."

Celina's cheeks exploded with warmth. "What? I don't... I mean that's not why we're here."

"It's not the primary reason why we're here, but I love making you blush." Victor opened the gallery's glass door and guided Celina through.

No one glanced at Celina as she stumbled in. She calmed the fire within her cheeks by hurrying to the closest display and perusing the first few pieces.

The gallery had been open for a couple hours and geared up to serve wine and cheese for the featured artist's showing. The room itself was a giant square, no permanent interior walls. Temporary and moveable walls created a labyrinth, taking the customer on a journey via the artwork. A few glass cases lined the perimeter walls, displaying jewelry and smaller sculptures.

Many of the paintings were abstract and colorful, but not aloof, inviting enough catharsis even if the observer didn't catch the metaphors the artist had meant to convey. At the very least, Celina could say, "Oh, that's interesting," without lying.

A handful of attendees were older than she and Victor, a few might have been their age, and the ones lingering around the display cases looked much younger. She whispered to Victor, "This place knows how to draw a young crowd."

"Doesn't hurt that Temple University is nearby," Victor whispered back. "Half of them are probably here for free snacks and booze. I'd bet most of them are gawking at the display cases because the jewelry and artsy knick-knacks are all they can afford."

Celina glanced toward one of the cases that Victor nodded to, and her breath hitched. Robert.

He was pulling an ornate necklace from the case for a customer. He looked exactly as she had remembered. Same chestnut brown hair, same wire rim glasses, same matinee idol smile. He even wore the same cream suit, his shirt and tie a shimmering black.

Victor hooked her arm in Celina's and steered toward Robert. "You can't eat if you don't hunt."

By the time Robert finished with the customer and started to close the case, they stood close enough to catch his attention. He did a double take. "Celina?" he asked, eyes wide.

"Hi! Yes. Hi!" Celina hated how unhinged she sounded. Judging by the way Victor delivered a subtle pinch, she assumed that her newest friend thought the same thing. "How did your niece like her birthday present?"

Robert smiled. "My niece? Well, I have to commend your customer satisfaction skills if you came all the way from New York to follow up with our transaction. But my niece loved it."

"Glad to hear. I'm assuming no one tried to kick you out of the family?"

"For giving the game to my niece? No. For standing up to my mouthy, racist, drunk uncle? Yes. Of course, the only person who tried to kick me out was the same mouthy, racist, drunk uncle."

"Drunk uncle," Victor chuckled. "Drunkle."

Celina blushed. "Oh, I'm sorry. Robert, this is my friend Victor Vegas." Not making introductions fast enough was hardly worth of an apology, but she couldn't stop herself and suddenly felt judged – and lacking – by Victor's eyes. "Victor, this is Robert...?"

Celina froze. Her creepy stalker alarm went off, and she pretended not to know his last name. Okay yes, she remembered his last name from the list and from when he had paid for the game, but she didn't want to appear eager or obvious.

"Harrington. Robert Harrington." Victor released Celina to shake Robert's hand. He continued, "Nice to meet you. I'm the proprietor of this establishment, so I want to make sure everyone enjoys themselves and the art. In fact..."

He turned his attention back to the case and pulled out a bracelet. A set of three concentric silver circles with a chalky white crystal the size of Celina's fingernail in the center. The crystal sparkled with dozens of scarlet micro-fractures, web-like over the entirety of the crystal. The red of the cracks reminded her of blood. Flashes of Murphy hanging from a spider web, dripping blood, popped into Celina's mind. She did a quick head shake to get rid of them.

The black elastic band fit perfectly over Victor's wrist alongside the two bracelets she still wore from the previous night: a silver studded black leather strip and a circle of silver skulls. Admiring Robert's addition, Victor said, "Thank you."

"You're welcome. I noticed your other bracelets and thought it went perfectly with them. I love your shoes by the way. Spats are timeless."

"God damn right they are. Love yours, too. Snakeskin?"

"Alligator," he said.

Celina regretted her shoe choice, feeling like she had brought a muffin to a cake decorating contest. She regretted her whole ensemble. From now on, she would let Victor dress her.

Robert dipped into the case again, procuring a necklace. He held it up to Celina. A pendent dangled from the simple black leather band – a silver triangle, curved like a shield, with a center crystal similar to the one on Victor's wrist. Opaque white with scarlet-stained cracks.

"This is perfect for you," Robert said. Holding the necklace with both hands, he nodded toward her, gesturing for permission to put it on her. She responded by tilting her head, allowing him to slip it around her neck. Tingles burst up her arms and flowed to wherever his fingers grazed her skin, warmth radiating like ripples in a pond.

"Looks great. And the necklace is nice, too."

Celina felt her cheeks blush as she ran her hands through her hair to untangle it from the necklace. The pendant rested on her chest, the sundress cut low enough to expose a hint of cleavage. "Thank you. You didn't have to give us anything."

"True. But I really love these pieces." Robert raised his hand and exposed his shirt's cufflinks. They sparkled with the same crystals. "I'd hate to let them go to college kids."

"I don't blame you," Victor said.

"So, what do I owe the pleasure? Assuming you're not just here to ask about my recent purchase from Roll and Role Café."

Celina inhaled. This was it, time to send him running away screaming. "Someone is trying to kill Victor and me. We don't know who or why. But we discovered a list of people that includes us... and you. We've been contacting people on the list to figure out why we're on it."

Robert smirked and cocked his head, seemingly incredulous, and ready to laugh at the joke's punch line. "Someone is trying to kill you?"

Victor leaned in. "She sounds like a raving mad lunatic. Hell, I didn't believe her until a psycho woman tried to kill me. In fact, that's how I found the list."

Robert stopped smiling, disbelief shining in his eyes. He probably regretted giving them gifts. "How did you get a list of names from a woman who tried to kill you?"

"They had sex," Celina said.

Running both hands through her hair, almost pulling it out along the way, Victor mumbled, "Jesus Christ, why? Do you have Asperger's? Have you ever been tested for your lack of social cue comprehension? After we leave here, I want to take you to a testing facility."

Celina gave Victor her cat-who-ate-the-canary grin and said, "It's not the primary reason, but I love making you blush."

Victor's upper lip rippled as she snarled and bared her teeth.

Robert glanced around the room and stepped back. "I might be more scared of you two than any potential killer."

Victor sighed. "For the love of— Okay, let's get back to the potential psychopath hunting us down."

"Have you contacted anyone else on the list?" Robert asked.

Celina pulled out her phone and displayed the image of twenty people. She pointed to Genocide. "So far, just her. She's a singer for a punk band in Chicago."

"How did that go?"

"Not well. She didn't want anything to do with us."

Robert gave Victor a smirk. "Why? Did you sleep with her, too?"

"Ha ha," Victor said, tone flat as she glared at Celina.

"Made you blush," Celina said, tickled that Robert joined in the ribbing.

"Not blushing," Victor growled. "It's lava. Lava rising from the center of my murder core."

"Well, *that* I believe," Robert said. "But the whole 'someone is trying to kill us' thing is…"

"Crazy," Celina said, finishing his sentence. "I know how it sounds, and I know how *this* is going to sound…" Celina took a deep breath. "My identical twin sister, who I never knew existed, met up with me a few days ago to tell me about our birth father. While we were talking, someone shot her in the head."

Robert's eyes widened and his face paled. "That's awful."

"And while we were in Chicago…" Celina's words trailed away, uncertain if this was her story to tell. She looked to Victor.

She accepted Celina's invitation to finish the story. "A good friend of mine was murdered. Brutally murdered."

"Wow. Wow, wow, wow," Robert muttered gazing downward, arms crossed, chin resting in his hand. "That's… This is… Wow. Okay. What you're saying does sound ludicrous. But I believe you. I truly don't know how I could be connected to this, but I believe you when you say someone is trying to kill you. Since my name is on the same list as your names, then I'd be a fool not to be concerned." He rolled his shoulder. "So, what do we think the next step should be?"

"We've been debating that," Victor said. "And when I say, 'Debating,' I really mean, 'Celina knows I'm right, but won't admit it.'"

Robert turned to Celina for an explanation. She didn't want to talk about it but had no choice now that Victor let the cat out of the bag. "My sister." Celina cleared her throat to keep her voice from cracking. "My sister lives… lived… in Morgantown, West Virginia. Since she seems to be a part of this – who knows what to call this mess – Victor thinks it'd be a good idea to visit her apartment and see what we find. I, on the other hand, want to track down another name on the list."

"Is that what you really want to do?" he asked.

Celina sighed. A million thoughts about the situation, about what could go wrong, about how exhausting it was to traipse all over the country, about how scared she felt, about how much she'd rather converse about anything else with Robert than this. "No, I think Victor's right. I think I would really like to know more about my sister."

Robert handed Celina his business card. "Okay, then we're off to Morgantown. My staff can handle the rest of the show tonight. I'll go home to pack a small bag while you two find us a flight to Morgantown. If nothing's available, then Pittsburgh should be close enough. My cellphone number is on my card. Text me where and when to meet. I still have a million questions, but we can discuss the details on the plane."

"Okay," Celina said. "Thank you for believing us."

Robert smiled as he turned to walk away. "I'm not entirely sure what I believe, but I know what you believe. Right now, that's enough. Talk to you soon."

"Bye," Celina whispered as he walked away. She turned toward the exit, and Victor hit her with a wicked, wicked smile. "What?"

"All signs point to you getting laid in the near future."

Celina could have lit a candle from the blaze within her cheeks.

# CHAPTER 21

*March 27th, Chicago*

Genocide stood with Ven and Lucas across the street from an abandoned car dealership. This was not the place she expected to find a drug supplier. "Are you sure this is the right address?" Gen asked.

"The girl's drug dealer was too scared to lie," Ven replied.

"I'm guessing there is no way we can ask the drug dealer again?"

"No, we cannot."

Gen squinted, looking for any signs of activity across the street. "Seems exposed."

Lucas took a long, final drag from his cigarette. He flicked it away and exhaled a thick plume of smoke. "Car dealership kind of makes sense. Lots of space for a lab, if that's what they got going on. They can drive cars and small trucks right inside. Makes packing and delivering easier."

"And the windows are all blacked out," Ven added.

"Surprised the place still has windows at all," Gen said.

Lucas pointed to the graffiti scrawled all over the building. Most of it consisted of single-colored markings made from spray paint, sloppy pictures, or nonsensical words, and then a large, multi-colored RAGE! "I'm sure that's a code telling the denizens of the underground to stay away."

"Yeah, you might be right. The open lot makes for a great line of sight, so we're not sneaking inside. No trees or whatnot to hide behind and nowhere to run for cover. They'll see us as soon as we step foot on the parking lot."

Lucas clapped his hands and rubbed them together, a wide smile across his face. "Who's ready for an ambush?"

"Pretend I made an equally infantile reply to your infantile question," Ven mumbled. Hands in the pockets of his black, leather jacket, he started across the street.

"Let's go be infantile," Lucas said as he and Gen followed.

If Gen was honest with herself, she hated the idea of an ambush. Drug makers or not, whoever was in that building could easily post a sniper. The waning daylight was probably the only thing keeping them alive right now. The few cars driving by offered plenty of potential witnesses, and if this was a drug warehouse, they'd take no unnecessary chances to attract unwanted attention.

The front doors were locked, of course. Ven broke open the lock with enough finesse not to break the glass doors.

Sure enough, it was an ambush.

Gen and Lucas put their hands up at shoulder level, in response to the guns pointed at their heads. Eyes half shut as if he were ready to fall asleep, Ven kept his hands by his sides. "We're unarmed," Gen said. "No need to go crazy."

"Seriously, we didn't think you three would be so fucking stupid," said a thin man with a shaved head and facial tattoos, thick scar on his cheek. "We saw you lookin' at us from across the street, lookin' like you was gonna be stupid and come over. I said to Snip, 'Hey, look at them stupid fucks lookin' at us, lookin' like they're gonna come over. They can't be that stupid, right?' Ain't that right, Snip?"

"Right. And I said you looked stupid enough to come over." Snip brushed his long black hair off his tattooed face, a couple the same as the thin man's: an M on their lower jaws, black tear drops dripping from their eyes. Gen had no idea why he went by Snip. No sign of a knife, no reference to knives or scissors in any of the tattoos running up and down his arms. Not that she'd lose sleep over it. "Shoulda bet that you would be stupid."

The others chuckled. Five men in total, each with a gun, formed a semi-circle around Gen and her bandmates. "Hey," one of the other men said, tattoos of red diamonds over his eyes. "I know who they are. They're that band that plays at that club on the other side of town."

"Yeah?" Thin Man asked. "They any good?"

Diamond shrugged. "Yeah. I like 'em."

Thin Man smiled. Two teeth missing. One tooth gold. The rest stained yellow. "Heh. Maybe they came here to play special for us." A dry tongue scraped across drier lips. "You here to give us something special?"

Gen slowly lowered her arms. She wanted to laugh at these assholes, but figured her patronization should wait a moment or two longer. She took a step forward, then another, weighing their reactions. No one seemed too trigger happy, so she strode between Thin Man and Snip, trying to get a better look at the set up. It was definitely a drug lab, and the ingredients smelled as she expected. She caught a whiff of latent new-car smell, and something else she couldn't quite identify. "Maybe we came inside to see what you got going on, and make a business deal."

Thin Man's gun followed Gen, keeping his aim trained on her head. His smile disappeared. "Ain't got no business with you unless the boss says so. And the boss didn't say so."

"Who's your boss?"

Thin Man answered by cocking the hammer.

Okay, so now she knew who the leader was of this little band of idiots. Fortunately, this was going exactly how Gen thought. Thin man kept his back toward everyone else, exactly what Gen wanted. "Okay, boys. They want to do this the messy way."

Ven and Lucas began to take off their jackets, shirtless underneath.

"Yo," Snip said with a wave of his gun. "What the hell you doing?"

Boots untied, they slipped off easily. By the time they unzipped their pants, the other four drug makers shared confused looks with each other.

"Tito?" Snip asked Thin man. "Did... did you order us male strippers?"

"What the fuck are you—?" Tito cut himself short when Ven's and Lucas' pants hit the floor. Unencumbered by clothing, Ven and Lucas changed.

Transformed.

Into their true selves.

Each of their arms split into two, each leg as well. Necks disappearing, their heads merged with their chests to form their cephalothorax while their torsos ballooned into abdomens. Jaws snapped and shifted. Ven's chelicerae grew larger than Lucas'. Ven wasn't much for bragging or trying to one-up anyone, but in this case, he made an exception whenever he needed to put Lucas in his place. Ven's black exoskeleton outshined Lucas' brown. But neither had the red hourglass, a feature reserved for the females of the species.

No shots were fired; in shock, the gunmen froze. One's bladder let loose, a familiar smell in these situations. Clearly, they had never seen human-sized spiders before. The only reason all five hadn't pissed themselves or gotten a single shot off was because they hadn't the time, owing to Ven and Lucas' speed.

Ven wasted no time with the two drug makers closest to him, driving his two front legs through their chests.

Lucas sunk his fangs into Diamond and sprayed webbing all over Snip. Diamond screamed and gurgled, his body going rigid while he convulsed. Soldier straight, his body shook, but didn't swell like X's had. No popping eyes, no splitting skin. In less than a minute, the spasming stopped, the venom making short work of him. Lucas then turned his attention to Snip. As he approached, the drug maker screamed loudly despite being muffled by webbing. With an eye roll, Snip quieted and went limp. Dead.

Heart attack, Gen assumed.

That left Tito. "What the fuck?" he mumbled, his reaction deadened from wide-eyed shock. Gen grabbed his arm with the gun and bent it back. A twist of his wrist and he dropped the weapon. Gen planted her foot, applied the proper leverage, and shoved Tito to the floor. He tried to scrabble away, the effort futile due to his broken wrist. Cowering on the floor, spittle sprayed from his quivering lips as he whimpered.

Gen crouched down and grabbed two fistfuls of Tito's shirt. With little effort, she pulled him back to his feet and released him. His legs shook hard enough for her to wonder how much longer he'd remain standing. Eyes wide to the point of bulging, he stared at the two spiders lurking behind Gen. "What are you? What the fuck are you?"

"Well, Tito, what we are is irrelevant at the moment. What matters is what *you* are. Right now, you're our tour guide."

Tito held his injured arm close to his chest, his breaths ragged, shaky inhales and quick burst exhales. She patted his cheek to get his attention. "Hey, Tito. Show me your operation."

Tito nodded. "Yeah. Yeah, okay, I can do that."

The lab was an assembly line. They stored raw material in a couple of the sales offices and set up the production process in the show room. The final product was boxed and stored in other sales offices. Lucas' theory of vehicles pulling in to be loaded proved correct. But Gen was more interested in the raw material.

Empty containers littered the corner of the one office like discarded beer cans. They reeked of latro's main ingredient. She held the can in front of Tito and asked, "These contained raw material?"

"Yes," Tito answered, nodding. "That's how the raw goods get shipped to us."

"Shipped? From where?"

"Los Angeles."

"L.A.? Who's your supplier?"

"I don't know."

Gen sneered and clenched her fists, crushing the can. Tio held up his good hand and backed away. Judging by the panic in his voice, he told the truth. "I don't know! I don't! All I know is there's a big shipment in two days, in the morning, but it's different."

"Different how?"

"I was told that this shop is gonna get upgraded. We get the raw liquids sent to us in those small containers and then we make the latro. I was told we're getting the source. The source of the liquids, the main ingredient."

This disturbed Gen for many reasons. The source only came from one place. Who in Los Angeles had access to it? "You were told? How are you contacted?"

Tito reached in his back pocket and pulled out his phone. Hand shaking, he tried to hand it to Gen. "Text. All texts. Take a look, you'll see."

Gen ignored his offering and went back to examining the sales offices -turned-supply rooms. Black paint on the dealership windows kept out most of the sun's rays, making it difficult to see everything. A string of incandescent bulbs along with a few hoods of florescent lights lit the center of the showroom, but the rest of the drug lab was cast in shadows, some of the far corners as dark as midnight. The corners where Lucas and Ven disappeared to explore.

The lab was set up to make two different drugs. One row of equipment filled tables for the latro, one row for rec. Gen was concerned about the latro, but wanted to know more about the rec. What was the main ingredient? One last sales office to search.

The room she investigated by herself had a desk, a couple of chairs, a file cabinet, all collecting dust. However, boxes took over half the room. Each box held hundreds of empty plastic bulbs, each tipped with two small needles. "I see the delivery bulbs for both latro and rec. I see evidence of the latro ingredients, but I don't see anything for rec. That's made here, too, right?"

"It is," Tito said from outside the room. "But the ingredients are sourced locally."

"Locally?" This suddenly got worse.

"Yeah. Next shipment is three days from now."

"Two days for the latro ingredients, three days for the rec ingredients. Is that right?" Gen asked as she exited the office.

She was greeted by the opening of a gun barrel. "Yeah, but it ain't gonna do you no good."

Gen's time in the office had been long enough for Tito to find a gun. She hoped she could have fostered a level of loyalty, no matter how temporary, through fear. But the moment she turned her back, Tito tried to take advantage instead of trying to run. Stupid. Guess he forgot about Ven and Lucas.

Two sets of fangs sank into his shoulders from behind. The gun clattered to the floor as they dragged him into the shadows. The screaming didn't last long.

Gen strolled over to the set of chemistry equipment. A few half-filled delivery bulbs were strewn about. Faulty fills tossed aside. She smelled the venom in the beakers, but... what kind was it?

139

Ven and Lucas strolled out from the shadows in their human forms. Swaths of red streaked Ven's chest. Lucas was clean but used the back of his hand to wipe blood from his mouth.

"I can't believe you turned your back on him," Ven snapped.

Gen shrugged. "No big deal. I knew you two would rescue me."

Ven grumbled to himself as he and Lucas dressed. Lucas made a mocking face behind Ven. Gen smiled.

Lucas slid on his boots, and asked, "Were you able to get enough info?"

"Everything I needed from him. I'll return in two days."

"Alone?"

"Yep. I need you two to do a little leg work." She dropped a full bulb in Lucas' palm. "This is rec. It's made the same way as latro, except with different venom."

"Different venom? Does that mean what I think it means?"

"There's another cluster of spiders around."

"Fuck."

Gen agreed one hundred percent with Lucas' assessment of the situation.

# CHAPTER 22

*March 27th, Los Angeles*

Blaze tapped his match book on the diner's table while bouncing his knee. He paused to check his phone for the millionth time in the past hour. Still no response. Back to tapping his matchbook and knee.

"Jesus, dude, you're gonna put a hole in the table," Jerry said from the other side of the diner booth, a wad of half-chewed burger distending his cheek.

"Where is he, Jerry?" Blaze asked, and texted, where the fuk r u?

"Don't know. I don't know Big Lou like you do. I barely know him at all. We met once at the Club Diablo scam."

Ah, the scam. Despite anxiety running through him like mice behind the walls of a condemned building, Blaze afforded himself a chuckle at the memory. Two years ago, he and Jerry ran into Big Lou outside Club Diablo, a trendy hotspot for young, rich douchebags who couldn't tell how watered down the overpriced drinks were. A group of four approached Blaze, Jerry, and Big Lou and asked if they were the doormen. Blaze lied, giving them a nod and charging a twenty-dollar cover charge, each. Four hundred dollars later, they took off for a strip club, leaving a line of twenty people waiting for the doors to open to a club that wasn't set to turn on their lights for another three hours. If Blaze recalled correctly, the cash bought him a couple lap dances, Jerry passed out on the bar, and Big Lou went home with one of the strippers. Good times!

"Maybe he's getting laid?" Tulip said. She sat next to Blaze in the diner's booth. She had just finished a big plate of pancakes with a side of bacon. Nothing beat breakfast for dinner. After running the last strawberry across the syrup slicked plate, she tossed it in her mouth and shrugged. "No meeting more important than getting laid."

"She's not wrong," Jerry added as he chewed the last of his burger.

"Yeah, but he ain't one to no-show," Blaze said. "Not Big Lou."

Blaze had known Big Lou for over two decades now, met when they were kids. Lou and his mother moved into the same building that Blaze and his mother lived in. The apartment building, a shithole that collected hard-luck stories, housed residents who struggled through life until they died. Lou was a big kid who grew into a seven-foot-tall monster of a man. Big Lou always said his mom felt compelled to move to L.A., almost like she had been called here. Blaze didn't know about all that, but Big Lou was a good guy. In a town that discouraged true friendship, Blaze came close to calling Big Lou a friend and meaning it. He was also the perfect muscle whenever a project needed it. Like this one.

Tulip shrugged again. "Just a thought."

Turning her attention back to her plate, her eyes saddened as if remembering a friend who passed away. The moment was fleeting; she perked up and kissed Blaze on the cheek, her lips sticky, her breath smelling like bacon and strawberries. "Thanks for dinner. I love pancakes. Is there *anything…* else… I could do for you? To you?"

Blaze returned the gesture, a simple kiss on her cheek. "No, gorgeous. I just wanted to see how you've been."

Jerry cleared his throat. "If you got three minutes left…" He trailed off, the implication punctuating his sentence.

Blaze scowled. "Come on, Jerry. Have some fuckin' class, will ya?"

"What? You're not using the services you paid for, so I figure I'd offer."

Blaze glanced at Tulip. "She gave me more than I paid for."

"You're a sweety, Blaze. See you around."

After Tulip left the diner, Jerry wiped his mouth and tossed his napkin on the plate. "I don't get you, man. It's like you're taking a car to an engine shop for them to wash the windows."

As Blaze typed another text to Big Lou, he said, "Just trying to do a little good in this world."

"You buy hookers dinner and not have sex with them. That makes no God damn sense."

Frustrated, Blaze slapped his phone down on the table and leaned in, resting his weight on his elbows. Despite Big Lou not showing up for the job and Jerry busting his chops, he still smiled. "You can get everything you want in this world with the right smile," his mom always said. He'd been thinking of her a lot lately, and he didn't know why.

"Name one profession in this world worse than being a prostitute?" Blaze asked.

Jerry rolled his eyes. "I don't know. How about cleaning pigpens? Yeah, that's gotta suck. Shoveling pig shit all day."

"Well, the pig shit shovelers at least know where the shit's coming from and where it's going. A prostitute doesn't know when or where it's coming from, and she always has to take it. And before you make some smart -ass remark about getting fucked no matter what job you have, just remember that in most jobs, you can fuck back, and if you can't, you got a boss who won't slap you around."

Jerry held up his hands as a form of surrender. "All right, all right. Jesus, dude. You got a weird crusade and all I'm saying is I don't understand it, and I don't know why you're always buying them dinner."

"Nobody helps nobody without some gettin' somethin' for them-selves," was another thing his mom would say. Still didn't know why he was thinking about her so much.

Blaze's smile grew wider. "Like I said, I'm just trying to do some good. And this time, *you* bought her dinner, because you're paying for this meal, unless you're joining me tonight."

"Sorry, brother, you know I can't. I got another meeting I'm about to be late for."

"But you had enough time to proposition Tulip?"

Jerry stood and tossed a few twenties on the table. "Like the lady said – there's no meeting more important than getting laid."

Jerry headed toward the door, and Blaze called out to his back, "How about a meeting where your friend could get killed."

"We're not friends, Blaze," Jerry replied as he exited.

Ignoring the other patrons staring at him, Blaze texted Big Lou again.

*

Blaze wasn't smiling. The warehouse made his nerves twist beneath his skin. Gooseflesh along his arms. Hairs on the back of his neck stood straight. This part of the neighborhood sucked to begin with, and Blaze had to traverse it alone. Where the fuck was Big Lou?

Yesterday, Blaze had talked to him, told him about the job. Drive a van to Chicago, unload six barrels, drive back. Sounded simple enough, but the simplest of plans often wound up as the most complicated. Especially when his muscle didn't show up.

If it was a true drop-and-go delivery job, then Blaze had no need for muscle. He didn't know what Chicago held for him, but if the recipient was also a part of Melissandra's network, then he didn't expect a problem. No one dared to fuck with her. He wanted Big Lou for this moment right now, for Melissandra herself. The last time Blaze stepped foot in this warehouse, he had nightmares about creepy-crawly things lurking in shadows. Sure, he felt like a sissy for wanting a seven-foot-tall bruiser to walk into a scary warehouse with him, but no other human being would feel differently.

*Show no emotion.* Blaze sauntered into the warehouse and lit a cigarette. Flicking away the spent match, he was happy it wasn't completely dark, like last time. Lights, strung together in clumps, lit the middle of the warehouse. Of course, that meant more shadows, more dark beings watching his saunter turn into a trot. Eyes forward, he smoked his cigarette faster.

The van was parked in the middle of the space, the star of the stage under the spotlight, the grill facing Blaze. Figures bustled behind the van, but Blaze couldn't make out details – a few men loading fifty-five-gallon drums into the back. By the time he made it to the back of the van, the men had finished and scurried into the shadows. Blaze caught glimpses of them. They were shaped like men but didn't move right, something off about them. His triggered survival instinct yelled at him to get the fuck out of there. He ignored the warning and looked into the back of the van.

As promised, six metal drums, three strapped to the left wall, three to the right. At least Melissandra kept her promise about that. Satisfied that there were no other packages – especially the kind with blinking lights or a timer attached – Blaze shut the right door. The left door shut on its own.

Melissandra.

Not wearing the same over-the-top attire as last time, she eyed Blaze like a piece of meat. She still wore shiny black leather and thigh high boots, but she looked more like a stripper than a super villain. Her eyelids fluttered as she inhaled deeply and stepped closer.

No pretense this time about implied kinship. She didn't need to articulate it; he felt it as well. Like meeting a stranger and somehow knowing they were cousins by blood.

Melissandra reached for his face, and Blaze willed her to touch him, his skin begging for her caress. Electricity popped from his cheek where her fingers made contact. But her fingertips felt gloved, as if mimicking the texture of skin. Like they weren't hers.

Lips moving closer to his mouth, her heavy breath heated his face like nothing he had ever felt before. It held no aroma, but he couldn't help thinking of raw steak when she spoke. "What is it that makes me want to devour you, metaphorically and literally."

"I've been told I have a nice smile."

"You're not smiling."

Blaze looked into her funky, misshapen pupils and smiled. A wicked one, an inappropriate one, the kind that happened when the visual of a burning church slipped into his mind while masturbating. A smile that was wrong.

Melissandra released him and stepped back. The mask of sexual predator fell away, exposing an expression of stunned anger. Continuing to back away, she said, "Keys are in the van, address too. It's an abandoned car dealership. Drive in, drop off the barrels, and drive back."

Surprised by her sudden change in attitude, Blaze wasn't about to ask questions or push his luck, so he kept his mouth shut. Offering a slight nod of acknowledgement, he hopped in the driver's side and shut the door. Again, as promised, the keys were in the ignition and the address was on a sheet of paper stuck to the steering wheel. The interior had a new car smell.

Blaze drove out of the warehouse, daring not to look back.

# CHAPTER 23

*March 28th, Morgantown*

The flight from Philly was brief, but long enough to provide Robert with the necessary details. Victor wanted to hold some information back, that was how good negotiating was done, but Celina rambled on and on. What upset Victor, though, was how Robert's story differed from theirs. He said he knew his birth parents, and his father was still alive. Not adopted like Victor, Celina, and Gen. No pictures on his phone, but he swore that he was a spitting image of his father, with his mother's eyes.

On their way to Caila's apartment building, they thought about devising a clever ruse with Celina pretending to be her sister to get the manager to unlock the apartment, but when Victor saw the old door with its single lock, she devised a new plan.

They dashed to into the local hardware store for a small flathead screwdriver. Thanks to teenage hellion days, all she needed was a screwdriver and a paperclip, which she kindly asked the cashier for. The lock didn't stand a chance.

After straightening the paperclip, Victor used the screwdriver to crimp the very tip. She drove the screwdriver head into the doorknob-lock, then inserted the bent paperclip on top of it. Turning the screwdriver as the ersatz key, she raked the paperclip's tip across the pins of the lock. Victor's hamstrings started to burn. She'd been crouching for well over ten minutes now. *Fucking locks*.

"I thought there'd be yellow police tape all over the place," Celina said.

"Only if it were a crime scene," Robert replied. "No doubt the police had been here, but they probably spent the day searching her apartment and then left. I'm sure they've taken her computer and any other electronic devices that stored any kind of data."

"Oh. Makes sense."

147

There it was again. The awkward silence. Celina's man-game was weak. Since she didn't know what to say to Robert, she aimed her focus on Victor. Like a weight on her shoulders, Victor felt Celina's gaze, heavy and desperate.

After a few more minutes, Victor looked over her shoulder. As expected, Celina was staring down at her with those big, deer-like eyes. "May I help you?"

Celina was the portrait of discomfort. Hands folded together, thumbs fidgeted with each other. Victor heard a million thoughts crashing around inside Celina's head. "Ummm... Is this one of those situations where the real world is different than the movies?"

Naiveté could be exasperating. Dipping into the well of patience she never knew she had until meeting this woman, Victor said, "Yes. This is absolutely one of those situations where the real world is different than the movies. The people in the movies can pick locks instantly because no one wants to watch someone jiggle a bent paper clip for twenty minu—"

The lock clicked and the screwdriver turned. Victor stood and opened the door an inch or so. She stepped away and gestured to Celina. "Up to you now. Your choice to open it the rest of the way, or we all go home. Of course, if you make the wrong choice, I'll shove you inside anyway."

Celina opened the door. After a few deep breaths, she stepped in, Victor and Robert following behind her.

Sunshine lit the apartment, even with the blinds closed. A nicely sized living room. The kitchen was too small for any form of table, but there was a dining nook for that. A couch, loveseat, and armchair – all matching in style – fit well in the living room, spacious enough to accommodate a desk in the corner without anything feeling cramped.

"I'll snoop around out here if you two want to check the bedroom," Victor said.

"Sounds like a plan," Robert replied.

The blush of Celina's cheeks spoke for her as she followed Robert into the bedroom.

*That girl is too fun to play with*, Victor thought while heading for the kitchen. She had no idea what to look for, but the photos on the refrigerator caught her eye. Tacky, yet oddly quaint. A dozen small pictures, mostly of Caila with friends, and a few of her with an older woman. Victor studied the pictures, scrutinizing Caila. The only noticeable difference between the sisters was their radiance. Like looking at the sun with and without sunglasses, not only could Victor see the glow, but she felt it. Caila used her smile like a battering ram. However, one picture of Caila captured only a small smile, one of contentment while hugging the older woman.

The woman looked grandmotherly, thinning white hair and a great number of wrinkles. Adopted mother maybe? Victor took the photo from under the silly pineapple magnet and flipped it over. Blank. No date, no names. If Celina and Robert didn't find anything more conclusive, Victor would float the theory that this woman was Caila's mother.

Victor held the photo closer to her face. She had never met identical twins before, so she wasn't certain how nature would allow them to be truly identical. They shared such a unique face, something beautiful, yet potentially frightening.

What if there was no twin?

Celina had a heart of gold, but what if she had been lying this whole time, and there was no Caila? Would Celina's motivations be something other than nefarious? A psychotic break? Split personality? No way Celina would do this on purpose. If not on purpose, then what?

Victor shook her head and put the picture back on the fridge. She and Celina had kept track of the murder investigation in New York. The police identified the victim as Caila Rappaport, and Victor had seen Celina's bank account information and driver's license. Plus, the name on the computer screen of the potential killer – *who you had sex with by the way* – read, Celina Davenport.

Potential killer. Being hunted. Twins. Murder.

Maybe this was getting to Victor, and now she was succumbing to paranoia? Or maybe she was being forced to think about something she hadn't thought about in years – her own birth parents.

Every once in a while, when she was a little girl still answering to the name Victoria, she'd become curious about her birth parents. A stray fantasy would flit through her head with her as a princess from an exotic land, and she had to remain a secret for some silly reason or another. Who hadn't fantasized about being undiscovered royalty? She'd eventually come back to reality because, well, her reality was pretty great. Middle class parents who were nothing but love, smiles, and encouragement. Honestly, that was always better than having a king and queen for a father and mother. As royalty, how many insipid rules would she have had to follow? And they'd never have enough time for her! As she got older, she assumed that her birth parents were drunk teenagers who hooked up at a party without ever learning each other's names. But then how did that make a case for someone trying to kill her? And why had she held a conversation with a voice in her head?

If she was hearing voices, it might mean she was crazy. But crazy or not, that voice was the only reason she was alive. She hadn't heard the voice since her Kungfu fight with Dakota, so maybe she wasn't crazy. Or maybe just part-time crazy?

*Hello?* she asked the ether. *Anybody there?*

Nothing. No response.

*Would the voice that helped me escape my walk-of-shame from Hell the other day please stand up?*

More nothing.

Victor looked around to make sure neither Celina nor Robert was within ear shot, and then whispered, "Hello? Voice?"

The nothingness that answered her seemed louder than the previous nothingness.

*Okay, now I'm just being stupid,* she thought as she walked over to the desk.

Clearly, the police had been here – they left behind the laptop's power cord and Caila's phone charger. They didn't do a thorough job, though, and she found Caila's appointment book buried under loose papers in the second drawer.

Victor flipped through to the day Celina had said she met her sister. Sure enough, scribbled in black ink over three days were the words, "Go to NYC! Find Celina!"

Victor pulled out her phone and found one of Celina's social media pages. She cross-referenced some posts with the same dates in the planner. Many of them overlapped, including a few days labeled, "Mama!" in the planner. Mama came up a lot in the planner, at least four times a month. There was only one reason for that...

"Guys!" Victor called out as she headed to the bedroom. "Caila's mother is still alive. She visits her a few times a month."

Celina and Robert both sat on the bed as awkwardly as Victor imagined she'd find them. Each on one side, a leg draped over the edge, while they paged through a photo album centered on the bed.

"Interesting," Robert said. "We've seen a lot of pictures of Caila and her mother, but we weren't sure if she was still alive." He flipped to a page with four photos of Caila and the same old woman from the photos on the refrigerator.

"Great news," Victor said. "This means we can contact her, ask her a billion questions about what's going on."

"Okay," Celina said. "Now we need to keep digging to find out how to contact her."

"It might be easier than we think," Robert said. He pointed to one of the photos. Caila with her wheelchair-bound mother on a manicured lawn, framed by perfectly groomed bushes. In the background, a red brick building displayed the words, "Acorn Creek Manor Estates."

Victor typed the name into her phone. "Found the place, and it's pretty close by. But contacting Mom might be more difficult. Apparently, Acorn Creek Manor Estates is an assisted living facility."

"Oh," Celina said. "Can't we just call and ask for her?"

"Sure, but we don't know the status of her mental faculties. How's she going to react when we call her on the phone, asking questions about her dead daughter?"

"Good point. I guess we have to go see her in person."

"Not we. You."

Celina's brows furrowed. Her confusion lasted a minute until the implication sank in. "What? No. No. No, I can't. No."

"You can. I've been dressing you up and making you pretend to be other people all week. Look here – you have a whole closet of clothes that will fit you. All you have to do is pretend to be your sister."

"My sister I barely met! I don't know her. I don't know who she is. I can't pretend to be her to *her mother*, the person who probably knows her the best!"

"Her mother is like a hundred years old and in an assisted living facility. One can assume her faculties are not the highest functioning."

"Victor!"

"Okay, okay, that was crass, but that doesn't mean I'm wrong. Robert, help me out here."

Celina turned to Robert, a plea for support written across her face.

Robert looked away, not siding with either of them.

Celina shook her head, abandoned by her perceived ally.

"You have a chance to learn something about who you are and about your birth parents, Celina. I would kill for that opportunity." Victor lied, but sometimes the ends justified the means. The old woman had answers, and Victor wanted them, needed them.

Avoiding eye contact with Celina, Robert added, "You don't have to do this Celina. We can stay here and continue to go through Caila's things."

His words went against what Victor had said, but his tone set her up. And she took it. "We certainly could, Celina, but what are we going to find? The police took her electronic devices and that's probably how she kept track of her research. Unless you think she has secret research journals hidden somewhere…"

Victor didn't need to finish her sentence.

With a trembling hand, Celina wiped away a tear. "Sometimes I really hate when you're right."

Sometimes Victor hated that, too.

# CHAPTER 24

*March 28th, Frederick, MD*

Orion took a deep breath. This was going to suck, but he was an adult, and needed to act like one. Even if Brennan didn't want to. Orion rarely met up with Brennan before school, but it wasn't unusual. One neighborhood over, Brennan lived in a house just as upper-middle class as Orion's.

They had known each other since kindergarten, way too long to let one misunderstanding tarnish their friendship. Obviously, Brennan hadn't been feeling well, and hadn't been in the right frame of mind. Even if he wasn't sick, he was certainly sleep deprived, which could mess up the human brain just as badly. No reason they couldn't work together, share the credit for Bigby and any wicked stories they'd come up with. This project should be fun, not divisive! They'd collaborated before, and they would again. So, Orion decided to apologize, even though he did nothing wrong.

One more deep breath and Orion knocked on the door.

Brennan's father answered wearing an ankle-length black robe. He took a slurp from his steaming mug of coffee. "Oh, hi, Orion. Getting an early start on the day, I see."

"Hi, Mr. Dorsey. Yeah, I guess so. Is Brennan awake yet?"

"You bet. He hasn't gotten much sleep these past couple of days. He created a character that he's super excited about and that's kept him working nonstop on a comic. Come on in."

Orion had the foresight to imagine a scenario like this, but it still chafed him to hear Bigby being referred to as Brennan's. *Let it go,* he reminded himself. *Think about the bigger picture.* "Thank you."

Orion slowly took the stairs. *Is this carpeting new? How long has it been since I actually visited him? Over a month. Maybe I am a bad friend?* At the closed bedroom door, Orion pressed his ear against it. No music, only the slight rustle of paper. Another deep breath and Orion gently knocked.

"Be down for breakfast in a minute, Mom." Brennan words were clipped but patient. That patience might soon be lost.

"It's… ummm… it's me."

Silence. The air chilled around him.

"Come in."

Seated in his desk chair with the posture and pose of the scorned party, Brennan greeted Orion with a laser-beam glare. He crossed his arms.

Orion expected as much. "Hey. I… ummm… I wanted to come by and apologize for yesterday."

"Mm-hmm," Brennan answered, obviously wanting more.

"You're excited by this character. I am, too. I guess I got carried away because I was around when… you… came up with the idea. I'd like to work on it with you. We've worked on some pretty amazing stuff together before, and this idea is the best one yet. You and I make a great team."

Brennan sighed; his posture relaxed but kept the sour look of biting a lemon peel, and he watched Orion with a dubious eye. "You're right. We do make a great team." More judgement, but his tone softened. "Want to see what I've been working on?"

Orion smiled. Brennan did not seem quite back to normal, but definitely much closer than he was yesterday, which made for a good start. "Oh, hell yeah!"

Brennan's expression softened as he scooted his chair back, an invitation for Orion to view the two computer monitors and open sketchbook. Various pens and pencils of all different colors were scattered about the dozens of loose sheets of paper, images of Bigby slaughtering and eating Lance. "Whoa. Bigby's razor blade teeth… They've sliced through those body parts with so much blood that I gotta check my feet and make sure I'm not standing in any that spilled from the desk. These are amazing. As always."

"I know."

"So, you have a great deal of Bigby taking care of Lance… or a Lance-like character… are we going to move on to what happens next?"

With an eye roll, Brennan tensed his body and huffed. "Jesus, Orion!"

Feeling like he was tiptoeing through an eggshell coated minefield, Orion stepped back and held out his hands. "Sorry. I'm sorry. What... what did I say?"

"You've been here *literally* less than a minute and already you're trying to take over."

"Take over? I just wanted to know what happens next for Bigby."

"Whatever comes next is whatever comes next! I'm not done with this storyline yet. Whenever I am, then I'll figure out what comes next. Whatever it will be is not for you to say."

"Sorry! I was just curious."

"Curious. Right. Jealous. You reek of jealousy, Orion. You're jealous that Bigby talks to me and not you."

Of all the nastiness Brennan spewed, that statement made Orion clench his fists. He didn't know why; it just did. "He talks to *me*. He visits *my* dreams."

"Really? Really, Orion? Did you kill Lance? No! I don't think so! I did. I killed Lance. I summoned Bigby and he and I killed Lance together. Me, not you."

With no one else around to worry about, Orion focused on his emotions – anger, fear, frustration, confusion—without caring what anyone else might think. The feeling that stood out the most, though, was sorrow. Sadness swept through Orion as he realized his friend lost himself  in delusion and pain. "Brennan, listen to me. You are sleep deprived, like an unhealthy level of sleep deprived."

One of the computer screens behind Brennan flickered.

"I get plenty of sleep, you fucking moron! That's how Bigby talks to me! That's where Bigby and I killed Lance! In my sleep!"

Fingers reached from out of the monitor, spindly and spider-like. Once free from the confines of the screen, they curled around the edges of the monitor for leverage, and pulled. Bigby's crumpled top hat bent as it scraped along the top of the monitor's edge, and then snapped back into place once his head popped through. He looked around the room, then smiled – gnarled lips stretching over two rows of razor blades – when he set his hungry eyes on Brennan.

"Brennan, please don't call me a Moron. You know I hate that."

"Fuck you, moron! Fuck you!"

"Please! Please listen to me! You need to stop. You need to… you need to… wake up!"

With a cartoonish shimmy, Bigby pulled himself the rest of the way out. Noiselessly, he floated behind Brennan.

Face reddened, spittle sprayed from Brennan's mouth as he yelled, "Don't tell me to wake up! I am awake!"

"Bigby is behind you."

Brennan's expression changed. For the first time today, Brennan looked sane, calm. "I know. I summoned him."

That couldn't be right. Not with the feelings that Orion had the last time he conjured Bigby. Not with the way Bigby looked down upon Brennan with hunger in his eyes. Orion had the connection to Bigby. "Brennan, please, please, please believe me. You did *not* summon him."

"I did! I fucking did! I've had it with your bullshit, Orion! I summoned him because you keep trying to take, take, take. I'm done with you! We're in your dream and now that I've summoned Bigby, we're going to kill you. Bigby is mine! He's mine! I'll show you. Bigby! Kill!"

Bigby smiled, the corners of his mouth stretching upward, past his ears, past his temples, disappearing under his top hat. Bone thin fingers reached forward, toward Orion. Had he been wrong this whole time? Did Bigby truly belong to Brennan? Were they in his dream and not Brennan's?

No.

Gurgling laughter filled the air, like coughed phlegm splattering against the walls. Bigby reached down and jammed the tips of his fingers into Brennan's chest.

"Bigby, no!" Orion screamed, his words lost within Brennan's screams.

Bigby spread his hands apart, opening Brennan's chest like a wet, red shirt. Free from their confines, the cord of intestines spiraled to the floor. Like a bloodied messiah upon a macabre crucifix, Bigby spread his arms wide. Strings of glistening meat and flimsy swaths of skin dangled between the two sets of ribs in his hands. A shaky breath escaped his mouth, the ecstasy of release, when he tilted his head back as if to offer thanks to Heaven.

This couldn't be a dream. It just couldn't. Orion smelled the offal; felt the heat and humidity sticking to his skin. His stomach lurched and he wrapped his arms around his waist. This never happened in a dream before, never, no matter how bad the nightmare.

Tears streamed down Brennan's distorted face, from pain and disbelief, as he looked down at his opened insides. With palsy-stricken hands, he grabbed his own beating heart and held it out for Orion. His lungs acted like bellows as he spoke, blood spilling over his chin. "How? How... did this... happen?"

Orion couldn't answer. He didn't know. He could only watch impotently as Bigby lurched over top of Brennan to sink his razor teeth into the heart.

Orion shot up in his bed, awake, sweat-drenched and crying. He sat still for a moment, waiting for reality to sink in.

Holy crap, what a nightmare. Thankfully it was only that. But... So was the gory encounter between Bigby and Lance. No!

Wearing only a tee shirt and a pair of shorts, Orion dashed from his room, down the stairs. His parents and Aika, in their robes, sat around the dining room table, stunned as he ran through.

"Orion? You all right, honey?" his mother asked. "We heard you fussing. Were you having a nightmare?"

"Brennan!" he yelled as he sprinted past them and out the door.

The early morning sky remained gray with enough light for Orion to see his way through the yards between his house and Brennan's. He ran in bare feet as fast as he could through the slick, dew covered grass. He fell. No time to worry about it, no time to hurt, ignore the throbbing shoulder. *Run. Keep running.*

Hard enough to shake the closest windows, Orion pounded on Brennan's front door. He didn't care. He kept pounding, pounding, pounding until Brennan's father whipped open the door. "Orion? What the hell are—?"

"Sorry!" Orion yelled as he pushed past and ran up the stairs.

Brennan's door.

He didn't bother to knock.

He flung it open and rushed inside.

# CHAPTER 25

*March 28th, Morgantown*

*Breathe. Just breathe.* Celina tugged at the bottom of her cardigan as she approached the main entrance to Acorn Creek Manor Estates. *Stop fidgeting! Caila wouldn't fidget.*

Celina ran her hands over the comfortably warm white cardigan one last time. It fit nicely. It was an odd feeling to be wearing a dead woman's clothes, but as Victor had so eloquently put it, "Jesus, Celina, it's not like Caila actually died in these clothes." She was right, and so was Robert in suggesting that Celina dress the same way as a recent picture of Caila with her mother. Thin cotton khaki pants, green top, white cardigan. A touch of makeup, especially the shiny lipstick that Caila wore in all the pictures, and Celina was good to go. Except for one more thing. "As distasteful as this sounds, you need to smile more," Robert had said.

*Smile. Just keep smiling.*

The doors slid open, and Celina aimed for the front desk. Through research of the photos and the notes Caila had scribbled throughout her planner, Celina deduced that Caila's mother, Estelle, lived in room 406, but this was an assisted care facility, so she still had to sign in. As she wrote Caila's name in the opened book, the woman behind the receptionist did a double take, her mouth slowly gawping open. "You…? But…?"

Eyes wide, smile bright, Celina did her best Caila impression. "I know, right? I probably should have called first, but I just got back from clearing up that mess. Just a case of mistaken identity."

Unblinking and staring at Celina, the woman picked up the phone receiver. "Wow! Okay, that's… I'm going to call Estelle and let her know you're not… well, that you're on your way to see her."

Celina waved her hand. "Oh, please don't! I'd rather her hear that from me. I'm going to head in now, okay?"

"Yeah. Yeah, okay. Good... good to see you." The receptionist re-turned the receiver to the cradle and watched Celina walk around the desk and into the hallway.

Aiming for the nearest elevators, Celina squeezed her fists to keep her hands from shaking.

*That was the easy part*, she reminded herself. Now, for the moment of truth. Rather, the moment of pure lies.

Room 406. A quick knock on the door and, "It's open," said the wom-an's voice from the other side.

Using her smile like a knight would use a lance in a joust, Celina poked her head in. "Hi, Mama." After an hour of reading the notes on the back of the photos and throughout the scrapbooks, she had deduced "Mama" was how Caila referred to Estelle.

The room was small, like a college dorm room, with bed, couch, arm-chair, television, desk, small refrigerator. Two doors – one for the closet, one for the bathroom. Estelle sat in her wheelchair, close to the window. Celina assumed the older woman had been whiling her time away with the happen-ings of the world outside, judging by the way Estelle was angled.

A lethargy to her gaze, Estelle wheeled around to see who came into her room. A milky sheen coated her eyes, but it didn't hinder the intensity of her stare. She started to shake. "A ghost! You're a ghost!"

Estelle's panic exposed the scared little girl within Celina who want-ed to run. *Be Caila. You can be her for a few minutes. Smile.* Celina forced a smile on her face, large enough for her anxiety to hide behind, and glided over to Estelle.

Another thing she had noticed in the photos; the way mother and daughter held hands. In most of the pictures of them posing together, Caila held Estelle's hand with her left and rested the fingertips of her right hand on the back of Estelle's hand.

Taking the chair next to Estelle, Celina reached for her hand and took it into hers. As tenderly as she would with her own mother, she stroked the back of the old woman's hand with her fingertips. "Not a ghost, Mama. See? It's me. It's Caila."

Breath shaky, Estelle looked between Celina's face and her hand, again and again. Eyes as wide as a spooked horse, Estelle asked, "Caila? Caila, my girl. Is that you?"

"It is, Mama."

"You don't look… right."

"If you show fear, she'll be afraid. Be confident." Victor's words.

Celina pushed forward with her bright smile, the one she had never been comfortable with. "You're just startled. See? It's me."

"But… but they said you was dead."

"A mistake, Mama. A terrible mix-up, is all."

"But… but how? The policemen, they said you was… was *shot* in New York City. They asked me if I knew who would want to do that to you, and awful, awful questions about if you gambled or took drugs." Even though her whole body quaked and tears streamed over her cheeks, Estelle gave a triumphant smile. "But I knew they wasn't right. I knew that wasn't you. I told them policemen that they got the wrong girl, because my Caila don't gamble or do drugs! I told them that my girl don't live in New York City, and got no business being there."

A swarm of bees stung the sensitive spot behind Celina's eyes, the spot that so desperately wanted to cry. *Just keep up the act, and you won't break the heart of this nice old woman.* "It was a misunderstanding, all right. But…" She took a deep breath. "I really was in New York city. I met someone we need to talk about."

Estelle stopped shaking, but her face drew a look of concern. "Who? Who did you meet?"

*This is it. Stay smiling, be brief and direct.* "The girl I met – the girl who the police mistook for me – said she was my sister. My twin sister."

Estelle pulled her hand from Celina. Not a harsh or sudden movement, but slow, as if she didn't deserve to be held. She wheeled her chair away and angled herself back to looking out the window. She clenched her jaw so tightly that the muscles below her ears bulged. Silence.

"We need to talk about my birth parents, Mama."

"Nothin' to talk about."

Celina couldn't imagine Caila being stern with anyone, let alone Estelle. But Caila was human, and humans had a wide range of emotions, no matter how hard they tried to control them. Caila must have gotten frustrated, angry, terse with her mother.

Celina let her smile fade, just a little, and spoke with more authority. "Mama, I met a woman claiming to be my sister. She looked exactly like me. I am not a child anymore, Mama, and I think I have a right to know where I came from. You will always be my mother, and that will never change, but I need to know about my past."

"Your real mother is dead," Estelle said hurriedly as if throwing the words out of her mouth.

"You are my *real* mother. I told you that will never change. But… My birth mother is dead?"

Estelle stifled a cry and brought her hand to her mouth in an effort to keep from talking, but she nodded.

Celina pressed on. "And my birth father?"

"He's the reason she's dead."

"My birth father killed my birth mother? How? On purpose or by accident?"

Estelle let out a sob and looked to the Heavens. She closed her eyes and shook her head.

"Mama, please. I have a right to know." Celina didn't know what else to say, and her words cut into her own heart just as painfully as they stabbed Estelle's. "I have a right."

Estelle let out a holler as if waking from a nightmare, her breathing hard and heavy. After a few seconds, she shifted in her seat and straightened herself as best the hunch in her back would allow. Eyes set on something far away outside the window. "You're right." She had resolve in her voice. "My girl, you're right. I will tell you, but I gotta warn you – you ain't gonna like what I say."

Celina leaned forward in her chair, her heartbeat pounding in her throat, thankful Estelle wasn't looking at her or the hunger on her face. Summoning a conscious effort to keep her tone even, she said, "It's okay, Mama. It's okay."

"Your Papa... No. I won't even call him that, 'cause he was a *monster*. When your mother was sixteen, she and two of her friends spent a weekend at a lake. Just a few girls spendin' summer as it was meant to be spent. Her one friend's name was Betsy Barberry. I don't remember the other girl's name, but I remember Betsy Barberry, 'cause it always tickled me to say her name. Then that monster... Zebadiah Seeley... took them. He took all three of them girls to a barn in the woods and... and... did unspeakable things. One of the girls escaped and got the other two out as well. The cops found Zebadiah and took that monster away."

Celina's mouth went dry, her lips pasted closed. Caila had been right about their father, but there had to be more to him or else he wouldn't have been a part of her crypto forensics investigation. Celina had more questions about this Zebadiah Seeley but Estelle moved on.

"Your mother's name was Montana Whittaker. She was my sister's granddaughter. My niece and her husband were raised right, maybe too right, in that they wouldn't let Montana... Well, Montana didn't want to come to term, and her parents wouldn't listen to such notions. They all but locked her up in that house of theirs, only going out to see the doctor to make sure she and the twins she was carrying were healthy. Doctor never asked her how she was *feeling*, though."

Estelle tapped her finger against her forehead and Celina understood perfectly, and with fear, where the story was headed. The old woman folded her hands together and rested them on her lap. "Obviously, she carried you girls to term. But that was it. I figure nine months of carrying you girls was nine months of remembering, reliving what that monster, Zebadiah, did to her. Well, I ain't no headshrinker, but I can tell you *that* would have an effect. I can also tell you she blamed her parents, because she took their lives right before taking her own."

Estelle paused to wipe away her tears and probably to collect her thoughts. She then sat a bit straighter with clarity in her voice. "I'm the last of our kin, but I didn't want to be. I was an old woman already back then, so I couldn't take care of two babies. But I needed to keep at least one of you. There was this nice couple from my community whose husband got a new job, and they were moving away. They had trouble conceiving, and even more trouble adopting. So, I made the choice. I kept you as my own and gave your sister to them. I did my research and asked all kinds of questions, made sure they were a good, loving, caring couple."

Celina smiled. Despite the horrible journey, the ending made her think of her parents, the laughter, the love, the good times. Then the words just slipped out: "They were." Celina held her breath, hoping and praying the old woman's hearing was as frail as the rest of her body.

It wasn't.

Estelle shifted in her wheelchair, her expression growing dark as storm clouds formed behind her eyes. With a voice far more sinister, "Now why would you say that?"

Celina squirmed in her chair, suddenly finding it hard and uncomfortable. Her smile wavered. "No reason, Mama. You made the right decision in giving away my sister, and you wouldn't have given her to a bad family."

Scowling as if someone had raided her garden, Estelle wheeled from the window and closer to Celina.

"Don't call me that. Don't you dare call me that."

"But, Mama—"

"I said don't!" Estelle yelled hard enough to make Celia jump in her seat. "You're not my daughter! You're the other one."

As if every lie she said had turned to stone in her guts, Celina couldn't move from her chair, weighed down by guilt as the old woman continued to malign her. "I looked into your eyes when you were born, and I saw *your father* there! Caila had the spark of her mother, but you… you look exactly like my Caila but there's only *darkness*. You were just like your father. I knew what was inside you, even as a baby. I knew I had to send you away because you're *evil!*"

That last word turned the key to all the locks keeping Celina chained to her seat. Able to stand, she moved behind the chair, using it as a barrier between her and the screeching old woman. She couldn't defend herself from the attacks, couldn't speak against the accusations thrown at her. She could only shake her head like a child while Estelle yelled louder and gripped the arms of her wheelchair so tightly the whole thing shook and squeaked after every statement. "You're the devil, 'cause your father's the devil! Your father killed your mother! And you killed your sister! You killed my girl! My Caila is dead because of you! You killed her! You killed her!"

"I'm sorry," slipped through Celina's lips, though she doubted Estelle heard her, or that it would have mattered if she did. The barrier holding back her tears had been breached, the flood of emotions overwhelming it. Celina cried as she backed out of the room. She escaped into the hallway, and shut the door.

Still, she heard Estelle sobbing, "You killed her! You killed her!"

Through the blur of tears, Celina ran all the way out of the building, hating herself for what she had done.

# CHAPTER 26

*March 28th, Morgantown*

"Where the hell did you say you were?"

Victor almost laughed at Marshall's question. She didn't blame him for needing her to confirm her prior statement. A few days ago, she wouldn't have believed it herself. Hell, she was living it and still wasn't sure she believed her own words. "You heard me. I'm in West Virginia."

Silence. Again, she wanted to laugh at the images forming in her head of him slouched in his chair, face crunched, working his temples with his fingers.

Finally, he said, "Are you really waiting for me to ask why?"

"Yep. This has been the highlight of my day and I'm going to savor it."

"By making me regret that I made you a partner, all but proving it was a bad idea. You lost your fucking mind as soon as the ink dried on the paperwork? Miami, I can understand. Philly, too. But West fucking Virginia?"

"Are you really waiting for me to explain the obvious? Fine. Untapped Potential."

"Christ in Hell, Victor, you're really reaching this time."

"Seriously, Marshall, do I need to remind you that our fancy office building is in a city that started off as a desert? Las Vegas is an *entire city* built on the success of finding untapped potential. Our portfolio is filled with young and hungry upstarts who are more than happy to move their base of operations to wherever we tell them. Right now, as full as our portfolio is, Bouch & Becker's liquidity exceeds a couple million. That kind of money could buy half this state. We find the right development company, one environmentally focused because this state is nothing but fucking trees, and we could start our own mini-Vegas."

"What are the odds of that happening?"

"Like ten percent."

"For fuck's sake, Victor…"

"Hey, our next logical step is to become players on the national field. We can't do that unless we visit different parts of the nation. To the best of my knowledge your ass has a codependent, and often abusive, relationship with your chair. And don't get me started about Bouch. The last time he looked for new investments outside of Vegas was before Hoover had a dam. So, quit busting my balls and let me do what I need to do."

The good thing about old men was their lack of stamina. Marshall waved the white flag in the form of a sigh. "Just make us some money."

"It's all I know how to do. Bye."

Victor tossed her phone onto the hotel suite's coffee table, desperately wanting to take her frustrations out by slamming it. Instead, she scrubbed her fingers through her hair. She hated waiting and wanted to be at Acorn Creek Manor Estates, but everyone agreed that Celina needed to go by herself. She had pretended to be other people well enough, but Victor had aided her by dressing her up and all but feeding her lines to say. Would Celina be good enough to get the info they needed from Caila's mother? Victor hoped so. Small town life made her soul itch.

"Trouble at home?" Robert asked from the desk.

The suite had two rooms, a tiny kitchenette, and a main room with a couch, coffee table, television, desk, and armchair comfortable enough for Victor to claim as her own. She worked her fingers through her hair again to tame the mess she made. "Nothing I can't handle. I'm just wondering how Celina is doing."

"Me, too. I'm beginning to doubt the wisdom of letting her go by herself. I must confess, I'm more than a little worried about her being alone while someone's out there trying to kill us."

"If our would-be assassin followed us, then she knows where we are right now, and she'd be after the easy picking, two-for-one special sitting in this hotel room."

Robert chuckled. "Well, now that you made me realize we're in more danger than Celina, I'm no longer so worried about her."

There. Right, there – the way he used subtle self-deprecation and disarming charm to make himself more affable, to make everyone around him comfortable, made Victor quite uncomfortable.

*Quit being so jaded,* she scolded herself. Was she so used to swimming with sharks that she had a hard time seeing any other kind of fish? Maybe that was it. Or maybe the fact that she had no true friends was starting to bother her.

During the down time when Victor wasn't dressing her up and making her pretend she was someone else, Celina kept in touch with her friends, even Anson and Branson. Not because they were her employers, but because she genuinely cared about them. Sure, Celina had to be vague and tell half-truths, but she didn't want anyone to worry about her. Victor didn't have anyone like that in her life, other than her parents, and she had always felt that the distance between her and them was for their benefit. Fire had many uses, but if one got too close, one got burned. Victor always worried about burning her parents.

Was that happening right now with Robert? Here was an opportunity to make a new friend, a real connection with another person. Was she so cynical that she fought against it? That didn't seem right, though. She had a ferocious sense of protection with Celina and an uncategorizable feeling when she was around. But with Robert? She wasn't sure. She liked him, but she remained wary, the same feeling she had about petting a cat. She wanted to give herself over, but those little balls of demon fur could slice through her skin at any second. She didn't want to think this way, but couldn't stop herself from asking, "Are you sure no one has made an attempt on your life recently?"

"I think I would have noticed."

"You certainly seem like someone is hunting you, the way you dropped everything and came with us."

Robert had been giving most of his attention to his phone, but when Victor verbally poked him, he stopped and looked up. Victor studied his face, looked into his eyes, watched for tics or twitches to reveal any secrets. After all, she couldn't be a prominent businesswoman in a city full of poker players without knowing how to read people.

He remained unflappable. "This is going to sound like a pick-up line lacking all form of creativity, and I have never been one to employ duplicity, but I feel a connection of sorts with you two. Like we're ants from the same colony."

"I would have gone with wolves from the same pack, but I know what you mean. I know the feeling. But… ants? You couldn't come up with a better metaphor? You run an art gallery and you compare us to insects."

Smile spreading across his face, Robert reclined in his chair. "As faithfully as I pay tithing to the temple of Minerva, beseeching her graceful touch, alas, she has yet to bless me with divinity."

Victor chuckled. "So, you're saying you love art, but have no talent for it."

"No matter how many classes I take, everything I do looks like stick figures drawn with crayons."

"Well, I was in your gallery for only a few minutes, but from what I saw, you at least have good taste in art." Victor held up her hand and pointed to the bracelet on her wrist. "And handmade jewelry."

"Thank you. I do appreciate the compliment."

No signs of lying, not even the slightest hint of deceit. Victor hadn't lied either; she meant what she said about feeling a connection. It was an unusual feeling, small and barely perceptible. But that connection was there with Celina, not Robert. Something told her that she and Celina – even Genocide – differed from everyone else in the world. She didn't know in what way, and that worried her. More information was needed. Pointing at Robert's phone, she asked, "So… find anything on the kid?"

"We were correct in our assumption – there's only one Orion Fogelberg."

After Celina left, Victor and Robert read over the list of names and determined that Orion was the best candidate to look at next. A young man with Eastern Asian features and a Western European last name shouldn't be difficult to find.

They were right.

"Yeah, I came to the same conclusion. Lives in Maryland. On the other side of Maryland, but drivable."

Robert added, "I agree. What I found odd, though, is a student at the same school died a couple days ago from an aneurism. A football player."

Victor shrugged. "Obviously got hit in the head too many times."

"Be that as it may, that's still very young. Young enough to make my anxiety rev."

"Almost everything within the past few days has revved my anxiety, too." And the way Celina burst into the room let Victor know the feeling wasn't going to ease up any time soon.

Victor and Robert leapt up and ran over to Celina as tears flowed over her ashen face. She ran to the kitchenette and grabbed a glass from the cabinet. Hands shaking, she gulped down tap water.

"What happened?" Victor asked.

Celina slammed the glass down so hard that Victor wondered how it didn't break. "She said my father was a monster, and she called me the devil!" She stared at her hands as if they acted on their own, then brought them to her mouth, her chin trembling. In a surprised whisper, she repeated, "She called me the devil."

Slowly, calmly, Robert approached Celina like a zookeeper would a wounded lion. "It's okay, Celina. You were very brave to enter uncertain territory like that. Go ahead and take a breath. Have some more water. When you're ready, tell us what happened."

Nodding, Celina wiped away her tears and then took another drink. Angry that the old woman had upset her friend, Victor stewed. She should have insisted that she had gone along, knowing that Celina didn't have the fortitude for this. With all the softness and empathy she could muster, Victor asked, "So… what happened?"

Hugging herself, Celina dropped on the couch, but stood as if immediately struck by discomfort. She paced in a circle a few times, then stopped and stared out the window. "Your plan worked. She thought I was Caila. At first."

"Did she give you anything to work with? A name?"

"Yes!" Celina snapped. Victor jerked back as if Celina had taken a swing at her. "Yes, she gave me names. My mother's name was Montana Whitaker. She's dead. My father's name was Zebadiah Seeley. He's dead, too. And he was a monster. He raped my mother when she was sixteen."

Robert and Victor gasped simultaneously.

Celina wiped her nose with the back of her hand and continued. "He raped my teenaged mother and two of her friends while they vacationed by a lake. The one girl's name is Betsy Barberry. I don't know what happened to her or the other girl, but my mother... my sixteen-year-old mother was forced to give birth to me and my sister, and then she killed her parents before killing herself."

"Jesus," Victor whispered. Of all the different forks she had taken while traipsing down the paths of daydream and fantasy whenever she thought of her birth parents, Victor never imagined one so horrible. If that happened to Celina's parents, then what terrible scenarios existed behind Victor's birth parents? Trying to get her mind out of the forming quagmire, Victor asked, "Then what happened next?"

Celina scowled; Victor didn't think she could do that. "What happened next? I fucked up your plan, that's what happened next!"

"My plan? We came up with it together."

"No we did not. You came up with the plan, and you bullied me into thinking it was a good plan."

It was Victor's turn to frown. "Hey, you went along with it."

"Like you gave me a choice! Ever since I met you, you've been dressing me up like a dancing monkey and making me into someone I'm not."

"I didn't know anything about you when we first met."

"And you didn't bother to find out anything about me until your life was in danger. You used me. You saw an easy mark and used me for your needs."

"Of course, I did! You showed up at my office babbling like a lunatic; no way I was going to listen."

"I tried warning you that someone out there was trying to kill us!"

"Well, you did a shitty job and yet, I came along anyway. And came up with plans. I came up with the plan for you to meet Estelle, because you didn't have one."

"Well, you did a shitty job at that!"

"You're upset that a crazy old lady called you the devil, but you got the information we were looking for!"

Celina's face changed from pale white to cheeks as bright pink as her eyes. "I *crushed* an elderly woman today, Victor! How are you not getting this?" More tears flowed. "This woman lost her daughter. She's not crazy, she's in pain. I came into her life... *me*, not you... and told her... *insisted* to her that I was her dead daughter. Who does that? A monster. The devil. She wasn't wrong, Victor! I must be pretty fucking soulless to allow you to push me into this."

"We had no other choice."

"There is always another choice!"

"Sometimes there really isn't."

"There is *always* another choice. Here, let me demonstrate. This is my choice on what to do right now."

Fists clenched, Celina stormed from the hotel room and slammed the door behind her.

Staring at the closed door, Victor whispered, "What the fuck just happened?"

# CHAPTER 27

*March 28th, Morgantown*

The bar was small and dark, tucked among all kinds of downtown store fronts. Celina wiped a bar napkin under each eye to mop the residual tears. She couldn't tell any more if she was crying or not. Fucking Victor.

It wasn't all her fault, though. Celina was enlightened enough to know that it proverbially took two to tango. She was mad at Victor for forcing her to do something she didn't want to do, something she had known would be wrong. But Celina didn't say, "No." Had she even tried?

On her second rum and Coke, she had a hard time recalling how hard she tried to fight Victor. Why hadn't she fought harder? Because she didn't want to.

Victor possessed so much strength that it seeped into Celina when she got close enough. Strength by osmosis. A silly concept, but, God, that was how she felt. Like she could do anything. Why? Because not only was she immediately strong enough to attempt whatever Victor told her to, she was strong enough to succeed. Just like she succeeded at learning about her birth parents.

As far back as she could remember, a day hadn't gone by when she didn't feel like a victim or a monster. Most times, both. Now she knew why.

"Hey, sweety, you seem pretty down. How 'bout I cheer you up?" a man asked from the barstool next to her. She should have expected that – this bar seemed like a place for lonely men.

"Not tonight, thank you," she said, then took a sip from her glass.

"No? You're not even going to give me a chance?"

Celina gave him side-eye to get a better look and figure out the best way to handle him. He wasn't sitting in the stool, instead leaning against the bar with a beer bottle in his hand. He was attractive enough in a blurred vision kind of way, and she heard Victor say, "Why not?"

Not tonight, though. She wanted to wallow in self-pity and self-loathing, and she couldn't do that while conversing with someone else. He was short. Five-eight, maybe even five-seven. She knew exactly how to get rid of him, and she didn't even need to say a word. All she had to do was stand.

"Oh!" His eyes widened as if afraid. Voice quivering, he retreated. "I, uh, I see you, umm, you want to be by yourself tonight."

Worked every time. Before she sat back down, she realized that her fists were clenched, and she was frowning. No wonder he was scared. She was a monster, after all.

It took one last slug to get to the bottom of the glass and she signaled to the bartender that she'd like another. Sighing, it was time for the self-pity portion of the night. And time to learn more about her father. After a sip from her third drink, she pulled out her phone and typed "Zebadiah Seeley" into the search bar.

At first, the popular searches showed only facts reported from a local news station. He raped three young women in 1995 and went to prison after police killed his father in a shootout. But Celina kept digging, kept clicking on links reserved for people like her sister, people who followed unusual stories of the macabre. Entire websites devoted to crypto forensics, but some theories and opinions skewed into supernatural, too outrageous for Celina to believe. It was easy to understand how people made the leap in logic that a rapist was also a murderer, but to believe that he was something other than human? Even after ordering her fourth drink and as her heart raced faster with every post, every article, she still managed to separate fact from opinion, no matter how fervent the presenters of the opinions. No matter how easy it would be to believe that he was the devil reincarnate.

It had been well over a decade since the last post about Zebadiah Seeley, but many conspiracy theorists pointed to an article written back in 2006, by a writer named Xora Salazar. It was for a counter-culture online magazine, an exposé about Zebadiah Seeley. The magazine folded shortly after they published the article about his killing spree in the year 2000. Celina took another swig.

The more she read, the more she wanted to believe the whackos posting their crazy theories, until she finally found Xora's article. The world around her dissolved, hissing away into black nothingness. There was only her phone in her hands and the drink in front of her. Was it drink number four? Five? From the corner of her eye, she saw an old woman sit next to her, a crooked and withered crone from Shakespearean plays. Too afraid it might be Estelle and too engrossed by the story of her father, Celina willfully ignored the old woman, took another drink, and kept reading.

Zebadiah had been released from prison in 2000. Xora uncovered the dirty prison warden who was ordered by a dirty judge to release the monster back into the wild. Zebadiah promptly returned home and to the barn where he had held the kidnapped girls.

*Where he held my mother.*

Six people had been vacationing in a nearby beach house, and they crossed paths with Zebadiah. Police found his decapitated body in the burned beach house while the partially eaten remains of four of the vacationers were found nearby. They discovered a fifth vacationer's body, molested, and broken. Her name was Dakota. *I think I've heard that name recently? Haven't I? Can't remember.* The sixth vacationer was unnamed and never found. The article, part one of two, said the follow-up would reveal the sixth vacationer and an exclusive interview.

There never was a part two.

Celina continued to scroll and research the incident of the lake house, and everyone involved.

*Is this a new drink? Or still my last one? Where did the creepy old woman go?* Didn't matter. Celina needed to understand what the hell happened. She went back to the crypto-forensics website as a starting point, set on not believing anything unless verified from more than one source. The owner of the lake house disappeared a year after the incident. One of the vacationers was an undercover DEA agent. Xora went missing shortly after the article was published.

Everyone involved was dead or missing.

Celina turned off her phone, afraid she might be next, afraid she had stirred up ghosts who wished to remain in the afterlife. The room started to spin.

The bar was darker, her peripheral vision closing in on her. How much did she have to drink? She dropped cash on the bar top and aimed for the door. Was she drunk? Or did that guy spike her drinks? Sweating profusely, she needed to leave.

The cold air felt good, slapping her cheeks. Deep breaths. She needed a little more to clear the fog from her head. Wait. The fog wasn't in her head. Along the street, fog flowed like spilled milk. The nearby river had a nice riverwalk, a well-lit path to stroll along and clear her head.

She didn't know the exact time, and it never occurred to her to check her phone, but it was late enough to keep most people inside. The fog continued to encroach, and she crossed the street in a hurry to escape it. The road sloped downward, making it easier to run toward the water. A bit more than a block and she found herself closer to the water, walking through a small parking lot next to a scenic overlook. She felt better, but she couldn't escape the fog.

Rolling pillows of white escorted a wall of gray moving toward her. Had the fog followed her? *Is there someone inside the fog?* Celina squinted, trying to get a better look. The shadow seemed small and moved like an old person, like the stoop-shouldered old woman at the bar. Did Celina forget something, and was the woman trying to return it to her? No. She had her phone in her hand, still not thinking to use it, too mesmerized by the old forest witch from country folklore. Then clear as day, the figure shifted, changed, stood straight.

A woman.

No longer the old woman from the bar.

Blonde, physically fit, and maybe late forties if Celina had to guess. Her black clothes and boots looked like tactical gear that special ops soldiers wore in video games. She strode closer, a murderous look upon her face. The front of her outfit was unzipped to her cleavage, and Celina saw a tattoo. It was one word over the woman's heart. A name. Linda. *Why do I know that name?*

A dull light shined, fighting its way through the fog. Not one light, but two. Headlights. A grill with a Mercedes symbol approached behind the woman, and it showed no signs of slowing down. It was going to hit her! Celina reached out, but before she could call to the woman, a thought – a voice maybe? – told Celina that *this* woman wanted to kill *her*. She reigned in her hands and held her breath, anticipating a collision. But the car passed through the blonde woman as easily as it did the fog.

A mirage. The woman who had been following Celina turned into gray mist and dissipated as the fog gave way to the car. It drove closer and stopped. Victor and Robert hopped out and ran to Celina. Grabbing her by the shoulders, Victor looked worried. "Celina? Are you okay?"

"The woman disappeared."

"What woman?"

"The one you hit with your car. You came through the fog and hit her with your car, but she disappeared. I think... I think she's the woman trying to kill us. Blonde. The word 'Linda' tattooed on her."

Victor's head turned on a swivel as she gave the surrounding area a wide scrutiny. "Celina, sweety, that's exactly how I described her to you, but she's not here. There is no woman, and there is no fog. Are you okay? Are you drunk?"

Celina blinked. Stars twinkled along the crystal-clear sky. No fog. Her cheeks tingled, her vision a bit blurred around the edges, her mind not as fast as she wished. "I might be. You came looking for me?"

"It's dangerous to be out by yourself at night."

"I'm from New York. I can handle Morgantown."

"We are intelligent and progressive women. Our kind is not welcome in West Virginia."

"Victor! That is untrue, and you know it."

"Untrue? Don't forget, the movie Deliverance is set in West Virginia."

"Actually, it was set in Georgia," Robert said.

Victor rolled her eyes. "Georgia, West Virginia, same thing."

"Now you're being unreasonable and… and mean."

Victor squeezed Celina's shoulders. Brows crinkled, Victor bit her lip, and then took a deep breath. "You're right. I'm worried and taking my frustrations out on the state of West Virginia. I just don't want you walking into any spider webs."

Her statement confused Celina, her brain a bit slogged with alcohol. After seeing the concern in Victor's eyes, she caught on – Victor was worried she'd end up like Murphy, and even though they shared a lot with Robert, there was still plenty they hadn't. Celina cracked the code. "Thank you."

"And I'm sorry if I made you feel like I pushed you to talk to Estelle. I didn't think of how she would feel, and how it would make you feel. I don't know what's happening in the big picture and I'm scared. I saw Estelle as a source of answers, not as a person who lost a daughter."

Celina had a couple more tears left, but they weren't from sadness. "Thank you. I'm sorry, too. I took my frustrations out on you, and that wasn't right. I need to own up to my own actions. Forgive me?"

Victor hugged Celina, and she returned the gesture. Victor mumbled, "Of course, you big dope."

"You broke your rule again. Twice."

"How?"

"You apologized and expressed your feelings. Men don't do that."

"Jesus Christ, I hate you."

"You love me."

"I do."

After they separated, Celina wiped her thumb under her eyes and turned to Robert. "Sorry I was being so dramatic earlier."

With a smile, he opened the passenger door and gestured for Celina to get in. "Nothing to apologize for. You had to navigate through difficult emotions. I'm happy you're okay."

Celina wobbled her way to the car and flopped into the passenger seat. As Robert got in the back, Victor took the driver seat. "Now that all the mushiness is out of the way, we're going to visit another person on the list."

"Where?"

"Maryland."

# CHAPTER 28

*March 29th, Frederick, MD*

Sitting at the dining room table with his parents and Aika, Orion finally stopped crying. Not because the pain subsided, but because his eyes had given all they could. Despite being joint-achingly tired, his chest burned with grief, a fire he believed would never be extinguished. He'd been awake for thirty straight hours, starting with the discovery of his best friend. Dead. Heart attack was the best guess from the EMT who got there five minutes after the 911 call.

Heart attack. What eighteen-year-old kid has a heart attack? The EMTs didn't know the truth – no one did except for Orion – so they came up with theories to fill in the missing information, asked Brennan's parents a billion questions, and then pulled Orion aside to ask him a billion more.

"Was he on drugs?"

"No."

"It could be recreational or prescribed medications."

"No drugs."

"Was he under a lot of stress?"

"No more than any outcast forced to go to public school."

"Had he been acting irrational or not like himself recently?"

Orion paused – that was enough of an answer.

"In what ways has he been acting irrational or not like himself?"

"He's an artist and he's been working on a comic book."

"Were there tight deadlines? Other pressures?"

"No. He just became really obsessed with it. Worked on it day and night. He wasn't getting a lot of sleep."

"Was he using any recreational or prescribed medications to aid in staying awake."

"No."

Orion went back to one-word answers when he realized that he wasn't being heard.

His parents arrived shortly after the EMTs. After the questions, they took Orion back home. They had questions as well, but Orion didn't answer them, didn't speak. Trapped in his own thoughts, he didn't want to be around anyone else anymore.

His parents gave him the latitude to lock himself in his room to cry.

An hour, two, maybe three. Orion wasn't sure how long. He closed his eyes and whispered, "Why'd you do it?"

No answer.

"Come on, Bigby." Orion kept his voice low.

No answer.

"Tell me why you did it." Orion pounded his bed, demanding answers. "Tell me, tell me, tell me."

Still no answer.

"Fucker," he mumbled as he moved to his drawing desk.

Using his favorite set of colored pencils, the ones only for the illustrations in his professional portfolio, he got to drawing. More time slipped by, and he took as much as he needed. He wanted to get it right, make the image perfect. Every line for the twisted face, the shading in the eyes, the right shade of blue for the hat and cape. Bigby.

"Tell me why you did it," Orion asked his illustration.

Nothing.

"Fuck you. How about that? Is that how I summon you? Anger? Fear? Well, I got it all, so fuck you, tell me."

Nothing.

Tears splashed on the paper, smudging the colors with every drop.

Not a realistic enough picture. Orion grabbed his computer tablet and his favorite stylus. It'd take longer than freehand, but it didn't matter. He had created Bigby, but had no control over him. Other than God and Dr. Frankenstein, no other creator had lost control of their creations. Orion couldn't accept that he had lost control of his. He made Bigby, he had to be able to control him.

Perfect colors. Shading on point. No stray lines. By the time Orion finished, the image on his screen looked like a photograph. Pride and disgust played through him as he decided this was his best work. "How about now? Are you ready to talk to me now?"

Nothing.

"Come on, you fuck, come on," Orion growled, teeth grinding so hard his temples hurt. More tears. "Come on, tell me."

Nothing.

Sleep. Bigby came to him in dreams. Bigby killed in dreams. Maybe that was the only way to communicate with him. Orion had watched a few videos and listened to a couple podcasts about lucid dreaming, about entire cultures dedicated to the craft. The concept was awesome, so he should be able to do it. After all, he had been in control of his actions in his dreams lately. Hadn't he?

A knock on the door. "Son? How about you come on down for breakfast?"

Breakfast? What was Dad talking about? Orion wiped his nose with a sleeve and checked the time; a little after 11:30 a.m. Thirty hours. He'd been up thirty hours and hadn't even noticed. This was some kind of record for him. He'd look up the world record later to see if he even came close.

"Yeah, I'll be right down."

No food on the table, just three sad faces waiting for him, like the funeral was in a few minutes. Dad was the first to talk, swallowing hard before he asked, "How are you feeling, Son?"

Orion stared blankly. Did his dad just ask such a stupid question?

Dad shook his head. "Sorry. That was a dumb question. I... we all know how you're feeling. What I meant to say was, you can talk to us any time you want."

Orion nodded. "Okay. Thanks." He then glanced at Aika even though he still addressed his father. "You mentioned breakfast?"

"Yep. Sorry," Dad said. "On its way. Pancakes and bacon?"

"Sounds good."

As quiet as a whisper, Aika got up from the table and glided into the kitchen.

After a minute of silence, Dad cleared his throat and continued, "Yesterday morning, you ran from the house, right to Brennan's like you knew he was in trouble. Your mother and I... Well, we were wondering – how did you know?"

Orion traced a pattern in the polished wood grain of the dining room table with his finger and shrugged his shoulders. "I just knew."

"Did he call you?"

"No."

"Send you a text?"

"No."

"An email, or any other communication?"

"No."

"Then how did you know?"

"I just knew."

"Son, you need to tell us."

Orion had been staring off into space for most of the conversation, replaying the worst scene in the movie of his life over and over again. His father's voice sounded like he was talking from the other end of a mile long tunnel. Orion answered the questions as if reading words from a book. But his father's last statement was pointed and stern, as if he were mere inches from Orion, shifting from parent to interrogator.

"Dad?"

"Honey, you're scaring him," Mom said as she put a hand on Dad's.

He pulled away and folded his hands together. Bringing them to his chin, he said, "This is—" He stopped himself, frowning, yet his eyes were as big as plates. Orion had rarely seen him angry, and never scared, but now he looked like he was both. He huffed and then turned away in his chair.

Mom closed her eyes and inhaled through her nose, then exhaled a shaky breath over pursed lips. With tears in the corner of her eyes, she gave a forced smile. Orion felt fear coming off her in waves, and frustration radiating from his father. *Am I dying of cancer?* Orion wondered. *Brain cancer, and that's why my dreams have been intense?*

"Sweety?" Mom started. "We know you're in a lot of pain over losing your best friend, and we know you're not in a good place to talk about it yet, but... We really do love you and want to help you, and we believe the best thing to do is talk about it. Tell us how you knew Brennan was in trouble. No matter how strange or how much like a made-up story it might sound like, I promise we will listen."

"Even if you'll think I'm crazy?"

"I promise we won't."

"Dad?"

After a quick thumb swipe under each eye, Dad straightened his posture and turned to face Orion. "I'm sorry if I made things tense and uncomfortable, son. My emotions got the better of me. No matter what you say, we won't think you're crazy."

"Promise?"

"Promise."

Orion felt like he was being setup – neither of his parents made him feel comfortable. He put his proverbial toe in the water with, "A dream."

"A dream," Dad repeated.

Mom gulped down a sob. "Did you have a dream that Brennan was in trouble, or was there more to it?"

Dad didn't laugh or belittle Orion for saying it was a dream, so he added a little more. "I dreamed I was there. That I saw it happen."

"It? You mean Brennan's heart attack?"

"Not exactly. It... It all started with a character I made." Orion wanted to stop there, but his mouth took over. He told his parents everything. The more he spoke, the better he started to feel, so he kept talking. The drawings of Bigby. The dream with Lance. The argument with Brennan. The details of the dream where Bigby killed Brennan. He stopped himself before telling them that he thought he could control Bigby. That he wanted to control Bigby.

Anyone who ever said, "talking makes things better," was right. As the words left his body, they took weight with them. He felt lighter.

But Mom was crying now; silent tears streamed over her cheeks and quivering chin. Had they lied to him about thinking he was crazy? Maybe she was crying because they had to call men with straightjackets to take him away?

"I want to make sure I understand what you're saying," Dad said. "You go into other people's dreams?"

A sour ball formed in his gut, usually reserved for whenever he got caught doing something he shouldn't have. There was no back peddling now, no way to lie his way out of this, so he swallowed the acid back down his throat and said, "Yes, that's what I said. I know it sounds crazy and I know it sounds like I'm making it up and letting my imagination get the better of me, but I swear each time it felt real."

"Were you able to affect change?"

"Affect change?"

"Could you control things? Make Lance or Brennan do things?"

"I... don't know. Maybe? I was interacting with them. I didn't really know I was in their dreams until Bigby showed up."

"The man with the top hat and cape, right?"

Dad turned to Mom with a look of desperation in his eyes, like he was asking her if he could buy a new boat. "You heard that, right? He couldn't *control* things in their dreams."

Mom shook her head. "He said he wasn't sure. He said, 'maybe.'"

"Maybe's not the same thing as yes. We can spin this. We can tell *him* that Orion can't control anything when he goes into someone's dreams. Hell, we don't even have to tell him that Orion can go into people's dreams."

Orion felt like he was no longer at the dining room table in his house. He was at a movie theater watching his parents turn into other people on a screen. "Mom? Dad? Who is 'him?' What are you talking about?"

"Do you really think we could pull that off?" Mom asked, her tone implying that Dad was talking nonsense. "He'll find out. He always finds out about these things. We knew this day was coming."

"We did, and I've been planning. I've got cash, and we can run."

"Run?" Orion yelled, his voice cracking. "Run where? Run from who? What are you two talking about?"

Mom's face turned red, cheeks shimmering with tears. "Are you serious?"

"We lie to him for as long as we can. We'll save up more money and establish different identities—"

"What the fuck?" Orion slapped the table with his hands. "What are you talking about? Tell me! Tell me tell me tell me!"

Mom turned in her seat to address Orion, but suddenly screamed out in pain.

From the knife in her side.

Thrown by Aika.

# CHAPTER 29

*March 29th, Frederick, MD*

Outside the hotel, Victor leaned against the wall, resting the back of her head on the painted stone. Her breakfast swirled and gurgled in her stomach. The outdoor air cooled the emotions steaming inside of her. Spring had taken hold, but once in a while, winter liked to remind everyone that it'd return in nine months. Today was one of those days; chillier than expected with the bright morning sun and cloudless sky.

She didn't want to make the phone call.

Last night, Celia told Victor and Robert about her half-drunken research and the horrifying information she had uncovered regarding her father. It was easy to understand why Celina's crazy great-aunt Estelle thought of Zebadiah as the devil. Then she passed out in the passenger seat of the Mercedes Victor had rented. Robert researched from the backseat for the entire three-hour drive. He found the prison records of Zebadiah, including mugshot. Celina got her height, mouth, and jawline from him. Since Montana Whittaker was a minor when these terrible things happened to her, there were no photos of her related to the news articles about Zebadiah. However, Robert discovered a weird, niche website that served as a database for high school yearbooks, and found her junior year picture. Barely more than half Celina's age, Montana's eyes, ears, nose complimented her daughter. Same with her smile, the big bright one Caila had used in all her pictures.

Victor, Robert, and Celina had found a nice hotel when they rolled into town for a few hours sleep. Over breakfast, Victor and Robert told Celina what they had found. She didn't want to see any pictures of her father. Ugly fucker – who could blame her? But she cried when she looked at the immortalized, angelic picture of her mother.

Robert wiped toast crumbs from his mouth. "I also researched Betsy Barberry."

They found a Louis Barberry on the list of names and faces marked for death, his face the perfect unholy blend of Zebadiah and Betsy. That could not be coincidence. Robert continued, "I found her photo from the same yearbook as Montana, and an apartment in Los Angeles under Betsy's name."

"I have a half-brother?" Celina said.

"It seems that way."

"Oh, wow! So, Los Angeles after we visit Orion?"

Robert's smile was reassuring. "Absolutely."

"Okay. So...? What do we know about Orion?"

Victor slurped from her coffee. "I'm confident that Orion belongs to our 'being adopted' club. As successful real estate agents, pictures of his parents' pretty faces were easy to find, and I practically heard their Swedish accents from my phone screen. Orion's southeastern Asian features didn't seem to fit their bloodline, so he has to be adopted."

"Maybe a child from a previous relationship?" Robert suggested.

"Regardless," said Victor, "It means one of his parents could be the wild card linking us all together."

"Except for me. I'm still the odd man out."

As much as Victor liked Robert, she didn't buy it when he said he knew everything about his "normal, dull, middle class" parents. He was hiding something, but what and why?

Victor stood and tossed her napkin on the table. "All right, let's go ruin a kid's day. I'll meet you two at the car. Gotta make a phone call."

Now, staring at her cellphone while leaning against the hotel's wall, she dreaded this call. *It's so early over there*, she told herself. *Shut up, you know they're awake.* She took a deep sigh, and pressed "call."

After two rings the smiling faces of her mother and father appeared, both squeezed shoulder to shoulder to fit on the screen. Her father greeted her first. "Hey, sweety!"

"Hey, guys. How are you doing?"

"Great," Mom replied. "How are you?"

"Good. Is everything okay with you two? Has anything... weird happened lately?"

Her parents frowned and then turned to glance at each other.

Mom shrugged. "No. Not that we can recall. Are you okay? You look nervous."

This was that moment she never thought about as a kid, so she had never prepared for it. "I... ummm... I was wondering if you... could tell me about my birth parents."

"Oh," Mom said. She looked to Dad, then back to Victor with sad eyes, maybe pity. Mom continued, "We absolutely would if we could. You were adopted anonymously through a church called... What was it called?"

"The Shepherd of Heaven's Gift," Dad answered. "They were a huge, mega-church back in the mid-nineties. Expanding into big cities, had television shows, all kinds of stuff. Then, they disappeared. Rumors of financial corruption. Your mother and I actually tried to look them up when you graduated high school, just in case you ever asked about your birth parents, but the church doesn't exist anymore."

"Hunh," Victor said with a grunt. She was happy that she hadn't upset her parents – nothing broke her heart more than making her mom cry – but she couldn't hide her disappointment.

"Victor? Are you okay?" Mom asked. "You seem on edge, more than usual. Any reason why you're thinking about your birth parents?"

Victor ran a hand through her hair. "Yeah, I'm okay. Nothing to worry about. One of my new friends is adopted and she just learned about her birth parents. Got me thinking about mine."

"New friend?" Dad asked.

"Yeah, she's really nice. A good spirit."

Mom smiled and raised her eyebrows. "Oh yeah?"

Celina and Robert exited the hotel and waved to Victor as they walked to the car. Victor chuckled and when they were out of earshot, said, "It's not like that, Mom. She is awesome, but nothing more than a really good friend."

"Did you hear that?" Mom asked Dad.

"I did," he replied. "Victor has a really good friend. Finally, after twenty-eight years."

Victor frowned. "What in God's name are you talking about? I have plenty of friends."

Mom took a deep breath. "Oh, Sweety, you don't have friends, you have associates, comrades, pals, buddies. Even as a child, you used the word 'friend' like you used the words 'shirt, pants, shoes.' You were an independent spirit so it never bothered me, but you never had a true friend with any kind of emotional connection. You went through several phases when you were younger, trying to find your identity, especially through high school. The longest was the athletic phase – track, volleyball, martial arts – but I knew your heart didn't belong there; the rebellious teen phase was exhausting; God help me there was even a short-lived popular phase; your grades were always stellar, but the all-academic phase seemed ultimately unfulfilling; the MMA phase was entertaining, but not a lifestyle; the goth phase was tragic and only for attention. And then finally, right before selecting a college, you discovered the stock market, and instantly learned your vocation."

Mom was right. A group of people came with each of Victor's phases, some she liked, none she hated, most just supporting characters in her story. When she moved onto the next phase, she moved onto the next group of people. No malice toward those she left behind, just a simple fade away. Except the popular girls. They were bitches. But at no time in her life had she made a true connection, developing neither the need nor desire to be needed.

"Okay, okay, okay. You made your point. No need to psychoanalyze the high school me. The adult me has friends now."

"Is she there now?" Mom asked.

"Yeah."

"Turn the phone around! I want to see her."

"Oh my God, no!"

"Victor, turn the phone around."

"Mom, stop. I'm gonna call the governor and tell him you two are from Mexico."

"We've been citizens since before you were born," Dad said. "And we look more Hawaiian than half the people on this island. God damn tourists. Clogging the streets and driving up food prices!"

"See what you did, Victor? You're getting your father all wound up. Now, quick, just turn the phone around."

"Jesus Christ!" Victor shouted. She approached the rental and turned the phone toward Celina and Robert as they opened the car doors. "Here! Here they are! My friends! Friends, the insane people waving to you are my parents."

Both Celina and Robert smiled and waved. Celina displayed her big smile, the bright smile, and she wasn't faking it or forcing it.

About ten feet from the car, Victor stopped walking and turned the phone around to see the goofy grins of her waving parents. "There. Happy?"

"Hey, if she doesn't want to date you, the young man you're with is rather handsome."

"Mom! No!"

"Just sayin', Sweety."

"Okay, gotta go now. Love. Bye."

Victor pocketed her phone and harrumphed into the driver seat. She started the car, barely waiting for everyone else to shut their doors before squealing away.

"Did your mother say something about me?" Robert asked from the backseat.

"Yeah, she said she could smell your patchouli through the phone."

Fistful of shirt up to his nose, he sniffed. "Wait... I don't wear patchouli."

"Your parents seem so sweet," Celina said as she clicked on her seatbelt.

"They are. Why wouldn't they be?"

"Well... it's... well, sometimes you can be ... snarly." Celina curled her fingers into pantomime claws while rippling her lips in a silent growl.

"Snarly? You think I'm snarly?"

"If not snarly, then most definitely surly," Robert said.

"I am neither snarly nor surly."

"You have a great propensity to be either and/or both."

"The fuck I do!"

Celina continued to swipe pseudo-claws at Victor. "See? You're becoming snarly right now."

"It's true," Robert added. "In fact, you're becoming snarly while arguing how unsurly you are."

Victor tossed her head back. "Jesus Christ! Are we there yet?"

"We haven't even left the hotel parking lot," Robert said.

"So snarly," Celina whispered, turning her attention to her phone. "GPS says Orion's house is about ten minutes away."

The car sat at the stop sign, blinker on and waiting for the GPS to tell her where to turn. "Okay, so do we know what we're going to say when we get there?" Victor asked with a snarl.

*Ha! That shut them up.* However, Victor had no answer either.

As she drove along with the directions, her hopes of not only learning more about Orion, but simply being able to talk to him faded. Mini-mansions lined both sides of the neighborhood street, their oppressive size acting as a palisade. Unwelcoming message received loud and clear – no one came here who didn't belong.

Victor sped into the expansive driveway as if it was hers, then killed the ignition. "Fuck it, we belong. Okay team, Robert does the talking from here on out."

"Me?" Robert asked.

"But we don't have a plan," Celina said.

"Exactly why Robert does the talking. If we need to negotiate with the real estate agent parents for any reason, then I'll step in. Celina, you can't lead the way and barf your crazy all over the place. Robert is the poster child for affability and he thinks quickly on his feet."

"Ummm...?" Robert replied.

"See? He's fucking unstoppable." Victor cracked her knuckles. "Okay, let's go act like raving mad lunatics."

Celina and Robert leaned against the car seats, both bug-eyed and a bit pale. Celina gawked at the house and whispered, "I don't think that's really a plan."

"If you have something better, then I'm all ears."

Celina turned to Robert, and he raised his brow and shrugged. In awkward silence, they exited the car.

Robert approached the front door and mumbled, "Here's hoping I learned something from my improvisation class."

As his finger aimed for the doorbell, a scream emanated from the house, followed by a crash. No longer worried about a plan, or etiquette, Victor pushed passed Robert and tried the doorhandle. Unlocked. She flung it open and charged inside.

# CHAPTER 30

*March 29th, Chicago*

Genocide pulled a Marlboro out of her pack and placed it on the lab table. Her third one of the morning. It was rare for her to smoke before noon, let alone three, but she found the smells of the drug lab unbearable.

She tucked the pack back into the designated coat pocket and pulled out her lyrics pen, the one with such a fine tip that it drew lines as thin as eyelashes. With a practiced hand, she took her time writing on the cigarette, "When I say I love you, I'm telling you the truth, but lying to myself." Pen back in its pocket, she lit up.

Nerves discontent, she stood and walked a lap inside the dealership. This was her third lap, one for each cigarette. She didn't plan for it, but she developed a pattern: sit for a bit, get bored, have a smoke while walking around, get disgusted by what she saw, sit back down to calm herself. Each time she lit a cigarette she thought about using the match to burn the place to the ground. It needed to be destroyed. Not yet though.

Tito had said the delivery would arrive "sometime" this morning, not that drug mules were known for punching a time clock. The driver would expect a functioning lab, so she had to leave it intact a while longer.

Cigarette gone, she strolled over to an empty canister of raw material used for making rec. Canister close to her nose, she took a deep breath. Spider venom, obviously just by the smell of it. A burn in the back of her sinuses, a familiar smell. But which species? Latro came from black widow venom, this she knew from painful experience. She learned about other spiders mostly from internet searches. She couldn't place this particular odor, though, nor could she separate it from the other smells in the building, especially her recent cigarette. *God, I need another one already*, she thought as she set the canister down and returned to her chair.

She leaned back and put her feet on the table, fingers folded together behind her head to keep from reaching for the pack. The folding chair was flimsy and none of the tables looked sturdy enough to hold Girl Scout cookies, let alone chemicals and equipment. Gen's stomach grumbled, an uncomfortable blend of hunger and nausea. The smells were getting to her. *Focus.* This was her chance to discover the supplier's identity, especially since yesterday was a bust.

Interviews. She spent most of yesterday interviewing new drummers. Of course, yesterday almost ended with her needing to find another guitarist and bassist, Ven and Lucas both acting like asses.

"Do you participate in the use of recreational drugs?" and "Do you know what rec is?" were literally the only two questions Ven asked each candidate. Even though Lucas asked pertinent questions, he threw off the interview's flow with stupid nonsense like, "How many groupies have you banged in one night?" or "How many shots can you handle before you involuntarily shit yourself?"

"You're both fired," Gen had said after the last drummer left.

Lucas laughed and Ven glowered.

She continued, "As much as neither of you seem to care, we need a drummer before we can perform again."

"What about the drummer from last night?" Lucas asked.

"He's a friend of a friend who's in another band. He lives four hours away, so it's a no go."

Ven paced the office. "We should be investigating the rec."

"We know the supplier is sending a delivery tomorrow, and I'll be there for that. Fucking up the band isn't going to help."

"That's the supply side. I'm talking about the distribution. The five idiots we ate aren't the ones moving it on the street level."

"He's got a point," Lucas said.

Gen grabbed a stack of papers from her desk – she didn't care if they were bills or receipts – and threw them at Lucas. The hit sounded substantial when they exploded like a blown dandelion puff against his head. "And you! What the fuck were those fuckwad questions?"

Lucas shook his head and then checked his hair with his fingers. "Damn, Gen, the pretty face! You and Ven were as fun as angry morticians. Not the band's vibe under regular circumstances."

She put her hands on her forehead. "Shit. Pisses me off to admit it, but you're right."

Ven didn't seem to lighten up, though, and asked, "Am I needed here at the club tonight?"

"No."

He pocketed a few blubs of rec and headed for the door. "See you tomorrow."

That was twelve hours ago.

Feet still on the lab table, Gen rubbed her face, tired from not getting enough sleep as the pressure of her needs weighed upon the airiness of her wants. She wanted to keep the club successful, but needed to spend more time with her inherited businesses, which she hadn't been keeping up with. She wanted to focus on her band, but needed to think about her cluster. Maybe Ven was right about prioritizing this rec situation?

As if they knew she was thinking about them, her phone buzzed. First a text from Lucas: Warning Ven's in a mood. Followed by a call from Ven.

Gen propped her phone against a glass container with rubber tubes coming out of it. "What's up, Ven?"

He held his phone close to his scowling face and growled. "Been out all night."

"I can tell from the bags under your eyes."

"That's something Lucas would say."

"No need to insult me. I've been smelling black widow venom among other chemicals for over an hour now."

Ven gave her a nostril flaring grunt.

"Did your work pay off?" Gen asked.

"Got a name. Melissandra."

Cold apprehension ran up Gen's spine. Should she be afraid? If so, why. She'd never heard that name before, but felt like she should've. Her mouth started to form the word, but she stopped herself, as if saying the name would give that person more power. "Is it a woman's name?"

"It is."

"Did you learn anything about her?"

"She's the one sending the shipment."

"So, she's in LA? How confident are you with your source?"

"There was another layer between the idiots we ate and her. I ate that layer about an hour ago."

"Good to know. I'll—"

A knock against the metal bay door cut her off.

"—have to get back to you. The shipment is here. Get some rest. And Ven? Thank you."

Ven nodded and her screen went black.

Gen pushed down her anxiety; it would do her no good. She wanted another cigarette, but she pushed that feeling away as well, and strode over to the bay door. One last cleansing breath and she pressed the button to open the door.

# CHAPTER 31

*March 29th, Frederick, MD*

Celina's guts twisted as she rushed into Orion's house. On the list of wrong acts, breaking into someone's home was close to the top. Yes, they heard a scream and then crashing noises, but that could have been anything, like someone falling off a stool, or dropping a large pan onto other pans. These things happen all the time. But the second she heard that noise, Victor ran in, Robert right behind her. Celina had no other option than to follow.

She had seen plenty of pictures of Orion and his parents – Conner and Madison – from their social media accounts, so Celina knew what they looked like. She imagined their faces contorted in shock and horror when three people suddenly barged into their house. But when Celina and company turned the corner from the expansive living room to the dining area – another massive room with a table large enough to seat eight and a chef's kitchen on the other side of a half wall – Celina's mind took a snapshot, an image she would never forget.

Orion sat at the head of the table, his mother stood in front of him with her left arm extended protectively and her right hand holding the knife sticking out of her waist!

In the dining room, Orion's father was fighting with a smaller woman. Black hair in a ponytail, the woman wore the cold expression of a grim reaper. She slashed at Conner with a knife. He dodged her attacks, using the half wall to his advantage. He attempted to strike back with quick hand jabs, but she moved too fast.

"Aika!" Orion cried. "Aika! Stop! Aika, stop! What are you doing? Mom? What's happening? What's happening?"

Madison remained silent, continuing to shield her son while watching the fight unfold. Her other hand pressed near her gory wound, and she grimaced in pain.

"What the fuck is going on?" Victor yelled.

Neither Conner nor the woman he fought – Aika, Celina presumed – acknowledged the presence of strangers; the slightest break in concentration could prove deadly.

Madison pivoted around Orion to face the intruders. Celina winced as Madison pulled the knife from her side – fresh blood soaking her shirt – and wielded it, ready to fend off the trio in her dining room. "Are you with Aika?"

"What the fuck is an Aika?" Victor asked.

"No," Celina answered Madison. "We're here to help Orion."

"Who are you? How do you know my son?"

Celina stepped forward, her hands out in supplication. "We think we're being hunted." She pointed to Victor and continued. "She and I have been attacked and found a list of names and faces that the woman hunting us had. All three of us are on the list, and so is Orion."

"Mom?" Orion's voice quivered as tears streamed down his face. He shook as he looked from his father to the trio of strangers. "What's going on? Who's hunting me? Why is Aika trying to kill us?"

The intensity of Madison's glare diminished. She clutched the knife defensively, but her body language relaxed the slightest bit as she squeezed her wound. Celina wasn't sure if Madison was beginning to trust her, or if she was succumbing to the blood loss.

"The woman hunting you... Is that her?" Madison asked, jerking her head toward the fight in progress.

"No," Victor said. "Blonde bitch, about my height, fifteen to twenty years older."

Skin paling, Madison dropped onto the nearest chair. "Jesus Christ, Calista is after you." Sweat dripping from her face, she pointed her knife toward a hallway. "Closet at the end of the hall. Grab the ace bandages and a towel." She then pointed the knife toward the fight. "Keep my husband alive and we'll tell you all we know."

Victor removed her jacket and rolled up her sleeves. To Celina, "I bet you have the least amount of experience compared to myself and Mr. Tall and Muscular, so I think you're nominated to help Madison."

Celina wasted no time – she gave Victor a quick nod and ran down the hall. The linen closest was bigger than either closet in her apartment. Towel, two rolls of ace bandages, and she ran back to Madison.

With her non-blood-covered hand, Madison stroked Orion's cheek as he whimpered. She kept saying, "It's okay. It's okay, I'll explain everything when this is over…"

Celina handed what she had to Madison and crouched in between her and Orion, Madison lifting her shirt to reveal her wound. Celina put her hand on Orion's shoulder.

He pulled away. "Who are you?"

At least he didn't see the raw gash in his mother's side. At first glance, it didn't look wide, the knife being one found in any kitchen, but from the blood flow, she knew the wound was deep. She hoped none of Madison's organs had been punctured.

Madison pressed the towel to the wound and wrapped the ace bandage around her waist.

Victor and Robert circled outside the fight between Conner and Aika. Robert snuck into the kitchen and grabbed two knives. Victor prowled the dining room perimeter with her fists clenched. Aika moved like water, flowing over and around the half wall to strike at Conner and dodge his attacks.

Celina's impossible new job – distract Orion from the kitchen commotion and from Madison's gore. She began talking to him. "My name is Celina Davenport. My friends and I are here to help you. One of them… the woman… her name is Victor… she and I are both adopted. We think there's some kind of connection. That's why we came to visit you."

"You think Aika is trying to kill us because of my birth parents?" Orion asked. "I… I sometimes thought *she* was my birth mother."

"She's not your birth mother, sweety," Madison said, her voice nurturing, soothing, despite tending to her knife wound. "But the woman Celina is talking about, the one after her and her friends… It seems like she's after you as well, because of your birth father."

"Except for Robert," Celina said. "He said he grew up with boring, normal, middle-class parents."

As cold as a tombstone in December, Madison's tone changed. "If he is on the list, then his parents are *far* from normal."

Celina stared at Madison as she cinched the ace tight. Madison then stood and hobbled toward the hallway.

"Mom?" Orion called out. "Mom! Where are you going?"

"To end this, Sweety. I'll be right back."

Celina reached out to put a comforting hand on Orion's shoulder but thought better of it. "It'll be okay. It'll be okay." She wasn't entirely sure she believed her own words, no matter how many times she repeated them.

Aika jumped over the half wall into the kitchen, and Robert lunged with the knives as if they were fencing. Without so much as a minor break in her fight with Connor, she snatched both knives from Robert. A quick spin, her elbow connected with Robert's forehead. A knife swipe followed, barely missing him as he fell backward and away from her. Slumped against the cabinets on the floor, he was no longer an immediate threat.

"Hey, bitch, don't forget about me!" Victor yelled, lifting a dining room chair and throwing it when Aika jumped back into the dining room. A quick sidestep and the chair clattered against the wall. But Victor garnered Aika's attention.

Victor's speed impressed Celina. She blocked Aika's strikes with her forearms, and even threw a few punches. None connected, though, not fast enough.

Aika faked a punch and when Victor went to block, she received a foot to her gut.

"Bitch," Victor coughed out as she doubled over.

Aika turned back toward Conner. He held the chair Victor had thrown with the chairback over his head, seat in front of his face like a shield, its four legs outward as he deflected Aika's kicks to his chest. She jumped and used both feet to land a kick on the chair's support bar, the seat bashing him in the nose. Stunned, he dropped the chair. With only a tap of her foot on the floor, Aika spun the chair, gabbed its cracked support bar and broke it free, which she launched at Robert. It narrowly missed his face and clanged into the kitchen sink.

Aika gave the chair another quick spin and sat in it as it slid toward Victor. Another punch to Victor's gut dropped her to her knees.

"Fucker," Victor managed to mumble.

With Victor out of the fight, Aika slid the chair back toward Conner with a push. Halfway to him, she leapt from it and flipped it over her back, throwing it at him. He was large enough to absorb the hit and grab ahold of it, wasting no time to swing it at Aika. She ducked and it shattered against the half wall.

Conner had missed, but he used the broken chair legs as weapons. Aika dodged one and blocked the other with her forearm. She shook out her forearm – the hit must have hurt. Conner advanced and she retreated. She dodged his blows while edging toward the place settings on the dining room table. She grabbed two plates to protect her forearms, the China solid enough to absorb Connor's blows.

From the kitchen, Robert came running with a heavy cast iron pan held high, aiming for her head. Aika ducked, the pan connecting with the table and cracking the wood.

Celia winced, imagining the damage it could have done if it had connected with Aika's head.

Aika tossed one of the plates at Robert like a porcelain Frisbee. It slammed into his chest and with a grunt, he collapsed to his knees. Aika spun, hopped onto and off the dining room table, and smashed the other plate over Conner's head, dropping him to the floor.

Aika turned to face Orion.

"Aika, please! Please stop! Please don't!"

Celina tensed so tightly that her stomach threatened to vomit. This woman wanted to kill Orion for some reason, and Celina couldn't stop her. She had zero skills as a fighter. Victor had participated in and won MMA contests, yet wasn't able to lay a hand on Aika, so what hope did Celina have of stopping her, or even slowing her down?

But Aika had only incapacitated Victor and Robert. Maybe she wasn't a mindless killing machine? Maybe she could be reasoned with? Orion's pleas made Aika hesitate, and it was obvious that she held some form of connection with him.

Celina stood and took a tentative step forward, hands out, fingers splayed, to show she was no threat. "You don't have to do this."

"I do," Aika said, staring at Orion. "He's too dangerous to live."

"What does that mean?" Orion cried. "Please, tell me what I did. What did I do?"

"It's what's inside of you."

With the dark eyes of a shark, Aika continued toward Orion. Celina moved herself between them, shielding him the way his mother had. From his chair, he reached out and hugged Celina's waist, yelling, "No! There's nothing inside me! There's nothing inside me!"

*This is how I'm going to die*, Celina thought, with nothing left to do but close her eyes and beg God for a quick death.

A small crack of thunder and someone grunted.

Celina opened her eyes.

Aika held both hands against her waist, crimson soaking through her shirt and over her pants.

Madison stood in the hallway, holding a smoking gun.

Celina's skin prickled, adrenaline flooding her body, but helpless when Aika surged one final time.

She pushed Celina aside to get to Orion. Dropping to her knees, she reached out with her bloodied hands.

Orion opened his mouth to scream, soundless after Aika sharply tapped behind his ears. Orion wilted, his head falling back and his body slumping in the chair. Blood pumping from her wound, Aika collapsed on Orion's lap and closed her eyes.

# CHAPTER 32

*March 29th, Frederick, MD*

"Hello?" Orion called out. His voice didn't echo through the endless black like it should have. "Anybody here? Where am I?"

A dream. This felt like a dream. Dark, but he saw his hands, body, and feet when he looked down, but nothing else. Just pure black.

"Kill her!" a raspy voice said. It came from everywhere and it made Orion's skin itch. "She tried to kill us."

Orion stumbled forward and searched the darkness. "Bigby? Is that you? Where are you? Where am I?"

"Inside your head." A different voice this time. A woman's voice. Aika. "Inside your dreamscape."

Orion pinched his knees together to keep from wetting himself. He barely heard his own voice when he whispered, "Aika?"

The blackness retreated as Aika walked forward as if the darkness burned at her touch. She looked exactly as he last saw her – hair pulled back, blood soaking the bottom half of her shirt, cold eyes. "Yes, Orion."

The last thing he remembered was Aika getting shot and then lunging for him, reaching for his head. "I'm dreaming?"

"Yes. I needed to render you unconscious so I could move my existence into your mind. My body is dying, but inside here, I can still end this."

Eyes stinging more than when his favorite comic book writer died, Orion cried. "Why? Please just tell me why you want to kill me."

A sword, a ninjato, materialized in her hand. "I don't want to, Orion. I have to."

"Why?" He screamed.

"Kill her!" Bigby called out again, his voice closer.

"Because of him," Aika said.

"Because of Bigby? I don't understand. Please tell me! You owe me an explanation."

Aika stood about ten feet from Orion. A tear escaped her eye, rolling over her stone, expressionless face. "Your father. He had the ability to invade people's dreams. He could change them. He was a god in the dreamscape, and he could kill anyone with a single thought. So can you, with Bigby."

Aika raised her sword. With one slice his head would no longer be attached to his body, but Orion couldn't move. He saw the woman who had been a part of his life, raising him and shaping him into who he was today. He no longer saw the ninja sword, just her dark soulful eyes, and another tear sliding over her cheeks.

An abrupt scene appeared over their heads as if they were in a theater and a movie played on the ceiling. A younger Aika singing to two-year-old Orion. Both of them sat on the grass and his chubby cheeks gave way to a huge smile while he clapped with uncoordinated hands. Another scene ran beside the one playing, one of Aika with Orion as a toddler sharing an ice cream cone. Then a third scene of her reading a picture book to him. Another scene of happiness and warmth played out along the others, then another appeared, and another. Even though he was terrified of dying, as soon as a good memory hit his mind, it played out like a GIF on the walls and ceiling of the dreamscape.

Aika trembled and cried. Her chin and mouth quivered. "Please don't make this harder than it has to be."

"I can stop Bigby," Orion said. "I can control him."

"You can't. Your father couldn't, and neither can you."

"My father—?"

A shriek of anger and hatred filled the area. The scenes of Orion's memories shattered like glass as Bigby burst through them. Claws out and glistening like knives, razor teeth gnashing, he flew at Aika. He missed, Aika spinning out of the way.

Tattered blue cape flapping behind him, Bigby circled around and attacked again.

Aika slashed her sword while dropping to the ground on her back. She sliced his chest, but his clawed fingers cut her arm.

"It's just a dream. It's just a dream," Orion whispered. He knew it was much more than that, but he lied to himself for the sake of his own sanity, to justify the impossible. No way his nanny was trying to kill him. No way a nightmare creature was trying to protect him. Yet the two fought right in front of him.

The shattered pieces of glass around his feet continued to playback his memories. Though fractured and scattered about, he could tell which ones were which. He saw Aika's love for him and knew in his heart what she had told him was true. Bigby was evil, and he needed to be stopped.

Both Aika and Bigby bled. However, their wounds affected them differently. Aika's right arm shook with the sword as she pressed her left hand against her open wounds. Cascades of crimson liquid flowed from Bigby as he flew around, but he showed no signs of slowing. Bigby rushed toward Aika, his mouth stretching open in impossible ways, wide enough to bite his target in half. If he were to reach her.

"Bigby, stop!" Orion yelled. The creature halted, his head lurching backward as if his neck had been yanked by a leash. After a few seconds, Bigby began to struggle, desperately reaching for Aika, each tug a stab between Orion's temples, but he continued to think, *Hold on to Bigby, just hold on.*

"Kill her or she kills you!" Bigby screeched.

This was true. Orion hadn't been an adult for very long. He thought adulthood was complaining about taxes, getting upset at the news, and regretting decisions made during youth. But staring at a literal nightmare, he realized that adults dealt with one nightmare after another. In order to deal with this nightmare, he had to make the best choice from shitty options, and do the right thing. Orion accepted his fate. "Okay, Aika, do it."

Limping toward Orion, her arm dangled, the tip of her sword skimming across the ground. The closer she came, the more she cried, tears dropping from her chin by the time she stood before Orion. Her voice cracked when she asked, "Are you ready?"

Orion didn't even try to speak, his throat too constricted by emotion. He nodded.

Aika stood straight and wrapped her fingers around the ninjato's hilt. Her nose crinkled and she winced in pain as she raised her sword.

Orion thought about closing his eyes, but when he looked into Aika's, he felt comforted.

Her shoulders tensed and her arms flexed.

"Aika?" A woman's voice warbled from beyond the blackness. "Aika, is that you?"

Aika lowered her weapon and looked around. "Impossible," she whispered. "Senpai?"

"Yes, Aika! It's me." The woman's voice was clearer, followed by the rattle of metal. With no other warning, ten hook-tipped chains shot out from deep within the darkness, each one sinking into Bigby. Not hooks. Because of Orion's love of ninja lore, he knew what dug into Bigby were kusarigama. "Bigby escaped my cage. Help me return him."

Aika smiled and dropped her sword. Both her hands cupped Orion's cheeks. "When I hit Bigby, let him go."

"What is happening? Who is the other woman?"

Aika gave no answers. She turned away from Orion and eyed Bigby. From either anger or pain, Aika screamed as her fingers turned into metal spikes. Even though she had a limp in her step, she ran to Bigby and jammed all ten of her fingers into his chest. "Let go, Orion! Let go!"

Orion released his hold on Bigby. The chains retracted into the nothingness, snapping Bigby and Aika away with them. From the same spot in the darkness, a pin prick of light shined. It widened as if a train were barreling toward him. No, as if he were in a tunnel rushing toward escape. Bigger, brighter, until...

"Mom? Dad?"

Back in his dining room, his parents looked down on him with tear-filled eyes and smiles of sudden relief. Still in a chair, he sat up. Celina and her two friends sighed with relief. Both of his parents hugged him while his dad muttered, "Thank God, oh thank God."

"Aika," Orion said. "Where's Aika?"

"She's dead," Mom said. "She won't try to hurt you anymore."

"She wasn't trying to hurt me. Well... yes, she was trying to kill me, but only to stop Bigby. But when she knocked me out, she went inside my mind... my 'dreamscape' she called it. That's where Bigby lived. Then another woman was there – Aika called her Senpai. I didn't see her, but she and Aika stopped Bigby, put him in a cage. I think Senpai was my mother."

Dad exhaled slowly. Orion was stunned by the number of bruises on him. "Son... Your mother and I are going to tell you the truth. It'll be difficult to believe, but we have to tell you. Your birth mother is dead. We were there when she passed away, the day you were born. We don't know who Aika's Senpai is, but we are very glad Bigby is no longer a problem."

"No longer...? You knew about him?"

"Sort of. Well, we knew about the potential for a monster like him. See, Son..." Dad paused to run his hand over his face, something he always did when he was about to deliver bad news like the death of a pet or relative. "God, this is hard. Orion, your mother and I were assigned to adopt you. The man we work for knows about what your father was capable of. Every few months, we delivered a progress report to him. You showed zero signs of going into other people's dreams, until recently."

Orion's eyes burned again, but no tears. He was far, far too angry, too mortified to cry. "I'm... an... *assignment*?"

"No," Mom stepped in. "No, you haven't been since day one. After holding you, feeding you, and watching you sleep for the first time... you became our son. We didn't care about our employer; we didn't care about his motivations. We never had to engage with him other than tell him you displayed no signs of interacting in other people's dreams. In fact..." Mom trailed off as she glanced at Dad.

Dad understood her unspoken message. "Give me a minute, be right back," and hurried down the hallway.

Orion wanted to run away from these strangers posing as his parents. These people had lied to him his entire life. His birth father could go into other people's dreams. His real mother died from childbirth. Bigby was evil, but a part of his family legacy. The woman inside his head was a part of him somehow. And Aika was connected to it as well.

His so-called mother kneeling in front of him had hidden all that information from Orion. Yes, she cared for him, took him on vacations, healed his wounds, gave him a comfortable life. He had a multitude of good memories, but so what. They were all part of an "assignment." They were as fake as her smile on the real estate brochures she handed out to everyone she came in contact with. Orion didn't know this woman, and he wanted to get away from her.

Dad came back with a large duffle bag and Orion's computer bag. As he unzipped the duffle bag, he crouched down next to Mom... No, Madison. The duffle bag bulged with clothes, sneakers, toiletries. On top sat a plastic envelope which Conner pulled out and opened to display the documents inside. "This is a go-bag. Your mom and I packed it in case something like this happened. Inside this envelope is a new identity for you. There is also a debit card and information on how to access a bank account set up under your new name." Conner gestured to the three people behind him and continued. "You need to go with them. While you were fighting Bigby, they explained why they're here, why they wanted to meet you."

"Stop! This is too surreal! What the literal fuck?"

Madison took a deep breath and ran her hand over the lower half of her face. "Their names are on a kill list, and so is yours. The person who made that list is named Calista Lindquist." She glanced back to the trio, and they nodded. "They're heading to Los Angeles. They agreed to take you to the airport. When you get there, go anywhere you'd like. You have a new identity, a new life. Make it everything you want it to be."

"What about the man you work for?"

Conner and Madison both looked at Aika's body lying on the dining room floor. "We'll take care of that. This morning, we were talking about running away together, but plans change. This will work. We'll make it work. We'll stay here and deliver a cover story to make sure you're safe."

"Who is this *man*? Who do you work for?"

Conner chuckled. "We're not telling you, because you or one of our new friends will research him. It might not be tomorrow or next week, but there'll come a day when you can't help yourself from typing his name into a search bar. As soon as you do, he'll know you're alive, and he'll find you."

"But you gave us Calista's name?" Celina said.

"Don't bother searching for her, either. She's very good at this, and she all but scrubbed her name from existence. We're hoping she'll buy our cover story too."

Cover story. Assignment. Airport. New identity. Orion flipped through the documents in the envelope and pulled out his new driver's license. "John O. Miller."

"The 'O' is for Orion," Madison said, tears pooling in her eyes. "You can still go by 'Orion.'"

Orion's anger waned. This was still his house, his life. They were still his parents and they were helping him live. They had set him up with a clean slate. A new beginning. Kids his age were going to college, moving out of their parents' home. Most of the kids in his class would be starting a new journey all on their own in the upcoming three or so months. Leaving home with nothing but a bagful of clothes. If they could do it, so could he.

Orion stood. "Okay."

# CHAPTER 33

*March 29th, Chicago*

Blaze pulled the van into the parking lot of the car dealership, the exact address Melissandra had given him. It was mid-afternoon daylight, so he could make out every detail of graffiti should he choose to inspect that closely. He kept his distance, though, and pulled out his phone.

Jerry picked up after two rings. "Are you there? Please tell me you're there."

"I'm here, all right. It's creepy as hell."

"Creepy? You're at a car dealership in the middle of the day."

"That's why it's so friggin' creepy! Not a single car on this entire football field of weed speckled asphalt and all the windows have been painted black. It's like a post-apocalyptic wasteland."

"Well, you certainly paint one hell of a picture."

"Yeah. And I haven't heard from Big Lou in two days. You heard anything?"

"Dude, I told you I don't know the guy. I'm not one of your hookers who will do anything for a dinner."

"Don't get nasty. I've been in a van for a day and a half."

"Well, my ass is on the line with Melissandra, too. Your success is my success. You fail and skip town, my ass is dead."

"I'm not skippin' town. I told you I'm here."

"Good!"

"Good!"

"Now, go knock on the door and deliver the barrels."

"Fine!" Blaze hung up and tossed his phone on the passenger seat, which bounced to the floor. Last time he was going to do any kind of job that involved driving!

*Just nerves,* he reminded himself as he guided the van to the bay doors. Jerry was right; he had a personal stake in this job as well. Deliver the barrels and go.

He thought about honking, but that'd be too loud. The streets weren't busy, and probably no one would spare a glance in his direction if they heard the horn, but he'd rather not take the risk. A quick hop out of the van and he pounded on the metal bay door. Back in the driver seat, he lit a cigarette and tossed the empty pack on the passenger side floor, the graveyard of fast food bags and wrappers.

The bay door opened, and he pulled in.

Blackened windows kept most of the afternoon sun from peeking inside. A string of bulbs hung here and there, and a few hoods of fluorescents offered light, but he turned his headlights on anyway. Blaze liked this job less and less. Until he was finally greeted.

A blonde stepped into the van's light. Mostly blonde. A few streaks of red ran through her platinum locks, the same shade of red as her jacket. Too many buckles to be practical, long sleeved and short-waisted with tails touching the ankles of her thigh high boots. Black mini skirt with silver spikes forming an "X" in the front completed the look. Blaze smiled and mumbled, "Long live rock and roll, sweetheart."

The woman gestured for him to drive deeper into the dealership and make a right onto the showroom floor. Once he made the turn, his suspicions about a drug lab were confirmed. Long tables topped with colorful liquids and glass contraptions he hadn't seen since high school chemistry lab. Black hoses ran from Bunsen burners to propane tanks on the floor. He expected to see workers along the assembly line, but as far as he could tell, the blonde was the only person in the building. This didn't sit well. *Just smile, drop off the barrels, and get the hell outta here.*

He put the van in park and took a moment to admire the woman in his side view mirror as she approached. *Okay, maybe find out what she's doing later, but then get the hell outta here.*

Blaze hopped out of the van, mile wide smile on his face. "Hey there, beautiful. Got a bunch of barrels for you."

"Beautiful? You talk to all the drug lords like that?" Her raspy voice had a perpetual day-after-drinking-and-smoking sandiness to it.

Blaze offered a slight bow with his palms out, an unspoken apology as she walked toward him. "I wasn't expecting someone so gorgeous."

"You don't have gorgeous women where you're from?"

"Oh, sweetheart, where I'm from, being gorgeous is deadly."

"That's a hell of a way to describe Los Angeles."

"You've heard of the place?"

Then it hit him – the same hair-standing, skin-prickling sensation he experienced with Melissandra. She, too, must have felt it, as she suddenly stopped in her tracks. She growled and squinted at him as if he had accidentally stepped on her toes. Squirmy thoughts of Melissandra twisted through his head, and he wondered if he'd have to face the same insanity from this woman. After all, the only other drug lord who dressed this ridiculously was Melissandra. He cut the silent tension, and said, "Name's Blaze. And you are?"

"Not interested."

"Come on. It'll take a few minutes to unload the van and then I'll be outta here. Just feel more comfortable knowing who I'm dealing with."

Sneering, she gave a reluctant, "Genocide," and moved to the back of the van.

"Got a dolly?" Blaze asked.

Genocide opened the van doors and pulled out the ramp. She nodded toward one of the offices. "Should be one in there."

Blaze unloaded the six barrels in silence, hot from her laser beam gaze boring holes through his soul, but every time he looked at her, she was staring at the barrels. After putting the dolly back where he found it, he returned to the van patting his hands together as if clapping away dust. "All right, all done." He thought about asking what she was doing later, but it'd be like a fox flirting with a wolf. He rarely played it safe, but the chill in the air let him know he should seek a warmer climate. "I'm gonna head out now. I'll tell Melissandra you send your love."

Genocide looked up. "Melissandra?"

"The one who sent me." Stupid. Blaze felt stupid. Information was currency and he accidentally dropped his wallet into the sewer. *Fuck!*

The signs were all there, right in front of him and flashing in neon, yet he missed them all. A lab this big wouldn't be guarded by a lone individual, especially with a shipment coming. The process wasn't running either. There were plenty of chemicals, but not a single burner burned, no part of the assembly line was active. Was Genocide a cop? Was he about to get pinched?

Strolling over to him with her hands in her pockets, Genocide locked eyes with Blaze, and his legs turned to stone. He kept his hands visible, palms out and shoulder height.

"Who's Melissandra?" she asked.

Blaze gave a knowing smile, one that showed he was on her side, on the same team. "She's who sent me. A player in L.A., but I don't work for her. This was just a contract gig. I don't know what's in the barrels, and I don't care what you do with them."

With one of the drums between them, Genocide looked deep into his eyes, weighing him, measuring him. Her stare added fifty pounds of anxiety to his gut. "You don't know what's in the drums?"

"She didn't pay me to ask questions."

"Let's see if you're telling the truth." Genocide kicked the drum over, top facing away from them. It hit the ground with a clang, and the lid popped off. Thick, milky liquid splashed out in a gush. A black spider with a body over three feet long and legs curled tightly to its frame glided out.

"What the fuck?" Blaze shrieked as he jumped away. He backed into one of the other drums and yelled as he reached out to keep it upright.

For the first time in his life, he felt out of control. There had been plenty of times when he'd been afraid, or found himself in dangerous situations, yet he always walked away unscathed. But no amount of smiling or smooth talking or negotiating would exorcize the memory of a human sized spider sliding out of a fifty-five-gallon drum. "What is that?" he screamed again. "Is there one of those in each barrel?"

"Huh," Genocide grunted. "Looks like you're telling the truth."

"Well, look at this. A two for one special." A woman's voice came from the direction Blaze had entered, a blonde with her hair pulled back into a ponytail and dressed in a black tactical outfit. Gun holster on each thigh, a utility belt with pouches, and at least one knife visible. She was pointing a gun at them, her smile wicked enough to challenge one of Blaze's when he's at his most devious. Now was not one of those times. He was too scared to think about mustering a smile of any kind, and the barrel in front of him offered no protection. Knowing what was inside made him think of it as more of a detriment.

Genocide stood next to him, close to the manufacturing table, the van behind both of them. Too far to make a break for it, but close enough that it made a viable escape option with a proper distraction.

"Who the fuck are you?" Genocide snapped.

Blaze admired her courage, but it made him uneasy. There was more to her than bravery, her reaction to giant spiders and guns pointed at her was similar to stepping in a puddle on rainy day. Blaze had faced the wrong end of a gun barrel before, but it still frightened him every time. Arms trembling, adrenaline touching the wrong parts of his insides, he displayed his hands, fingers spread wide.

"I'm your death," the blonde with the gun replied while she made her way toward the table where the final product was piled. Small, single dose plastic bulbs with two tiny needles sticking out. Careful not to prick herself, she took one. "Interesting." She dropped it back onto the pile and gestured with her head toward the table. "So, what are all these pretty colored liquids for?"

"Fuck you," Genocide replied.

"You couldn't survive the ride. Hell, you're not going to survive this, but I'm going to give you choices. Choice one; tell me what I want to know, and I kill you quickly. Choice two; well… I'm the kind of girl who rips the wings off flies, so just imagine what I'd do to you."

"You don't scare me."

214

The blonde stuck out her bottom lip, an exaggerated pout. She lowered her gaze to her gun and jerked her head back as if she'd never seen it before. "Well, would you look at that. Silly me, I'm using the wrong gun."

Her weapon now trained on Blaze, she pulled a second gun from her holster. She pointed it at Genocide and said, "*This* is the one I'll use on you, the one that has the tranq darts. There are *plenty* of them, enough to knock you out. And you will *not* be happy when you wake up. Scared yet?"

Genocide's jaw muscles flexed as she chewed on her words to figure out which response held the most flavor. "It's a drug called latro. It's made from black widow venom."

"No matter how many spiders I kill, there always seems to be more. But it does explain the dead bug on the floor."

It didn't explain anything else, though, like why the size of the thing didn't freak out either woman. Or why the blonde with the gun was here in the first place. Her first words were "two for one special." Why did Blaze's twisting guts tell him that he was one of the two? He had to get out of there.

The barrel.

As much as he didn't want to touch it, he stood close enough to bring his right knee to it. The blonde had her gun trained at his chest, but she focused more on Genocide and the drugs. The barrel was heavy, but with luck on his side, he lifted it a couple inches without it rolling on him. He shifted his left foot under the barrel. It hurt, but he kept working on it, right knee against it, left foot sneaking under it a little at a time while the blonde threatened Genocide. *Slow. Careful.* He lowered his hands until they hovered close to the top of the barrel. He was ready, all he needed was the opportunity.

"Well, that's a fucked-up drug," the blonde said, her eyes going to the table.

Now! Blaze lifted the edge of the barrel with his left foot, pushed it over with his hands, and launched himself toward the van.

A splashing sound followed by a gunshot.

As Blaze had hoped, she shot the spider. Another gun shot and the sound of metal smashing into concrete rang out from behind him. He dove and slid across the floor to get behind the van. Scrabbling to his feet, he ran to the passenger door. Time to get out of here!

"Hey!" the crazy blonde yelled. "Come on out, or your girlfriend's brains will be outside of her head!"

Blaze peeked around the van enough to see Genocide on her knees, the blonde pointing both guns at her head. Genocide laughed. "You're shit out of luck. I don't know him; he doesn't know me. He doesn't know what's going on here anyway."

Blaze had no idea what the hell was happening, but he knew bullets go through skulls with great efficiency, and Genocide's pretty head was worth saving. He couldn't leave her. Why not? She's fucking scary! No. It wasn't right.

Blondie had a gun, but Blaze had one, too.

Gun drawn, he aimed at one of the propane tanks, praying Genocide would survive the explosion. He squeezed the trigger.

No explosion, but the bullet pierced the tank and launched it like a rocket toward Blondie. It didn't hit her, but distracted her enough to duck and turn around. Genocide took full advantage and rushed Blondie. Blaze was certain no one could move that fast, but Genocide disarmed Blondie then punched her hard enough to lift her off her feet and send her onto one of the tables.

Following the momentum, Blondie rolled off the table and landed on her feet. Genocide charged but stopped short when Blondie flipped the table.

"Quit fucking around and let's go!" Blaze yelled from the van's driver seat.

Not needing to be told twice, Genocide turned and ran, jumping into the passenger seat right as Blaze hit the gas pedal. A quick look in the side mirror – Blondie gave no chase, simply dusted herself off and looked around.

He swallowed hard as the van shot across the vacant parking lot. Tires squealed when he hit the first turn. "Doesn't seem like she's gonna follow us."

"Take me to Melissandra," Genocide ordered.

"You don't want that, trust me. First of all, she's in Los Angeles."

Genocide glared at him. "I said take me to Melissandra."

"Fine. Your funeral, though."

Blaze couldn't help but think he was actually driving to his.

# CHAPTER 34

*March 29th, Baltimore*

The car ride to the airport was quiet, Celina in the back seat with Orion, the occasional sniffle breaking the silence as he stared out the window. She did well with silence when she was alone; with other people around, the longer and louder the silence grew, the faster her heart raced, and the more she needed it to end. "Victor and I are adopted as well. I can't remember if I mentioned that or not."

A sniffle. "You did. Thank you. Did you find anything awful about your birthparents?"

She nodded. "My birth father was a monster. He raped and killed young women."

"Jesus Christ," came from the driver seat. Victor's angry eyes burned holes in the rearview mirror. "I'm going to buy you a filter for your birthday."

Celina knew she should have phrased her answer to Orion differently, but her need to end the awkward silence superseded proper decorum. Plus, it seemed to help Orion.

He turned toward her, his face no longer scrunched with sadness. "Really? That's... Did... Is that what happened to your birth mother?"

"He kidnapped her and two of her friends and held them captive for a few days. They escaped and he went to prison. My mother gave birth to my sister and me, then killed her parents, and then herself."

"Oh my God!" Victor snapped. "Robert, can you please tell her to stop acting weird."

"She's not being weird," Robert replied from the passenger seat. "She's just being honest without sugarcoating everything."

"Well, *you're* weird if you don't think she's acting weird," Victor mumbled.

"Whoa," Orion said. "That's pretty intense. Are you okay?"

There was a sweetness to Orion. However he might feel about his adopted parents at the moment, they at least taught him empathy. "It's been a lot to process, but I'm working through it. That's why we're going to Los Angeles. We think we can track down a man who might be my half-brother."

Orion leaned forward, clutching his duffle bag on his lap. "How about you, Victor? Have you learned anything about your birth parents?"

Victor kept her eyes on the road. Right when Celina cleared her throat to speak, Victor said, "Nothing useful. My parents said they adopted me through a mega church that doesn't exist anymore."

"Oh. Okay." Orion sounded disappointed, probably hoping for a connection to another person in the car.

"We learned that Victor's parents are very nice," Robert said.

"No, you didn't," Victor snapped.

Celina couldn't help but laugh. "We did, and they are."

"You saw them on a phone screen for three seconds! You know nothing about them."

"I could immediately tell that they were amazing."

"Ha! Little do you know they like to kick puppies for fun and profit. You want to know their favorite baking ingredient? Kittens!"

A short giggle escaped from Orion.

Celina winked at him. "I don't believe any of that, Victor. Your parents are lovely people."

Victor grunted and then looked into the rearview mirror at Orion. "How about you, kid? When your ninja nanny put you into a sleepy time nap, what did you see?"

Orion shared with them everything he saw, including Bigby, and that Aika had told him his father had killed people by going into their dreams. Silence occupied the car for the rest of the trip, as tangible as if another passenger rode in the car. After Orion's story, Celina welcomed it.

The airport. The worst part of living in a city crammed into one place. Crowds. Lines. Rudeness. Becoming so monomaniacal with egocentric purpose that a person forgot about the other inhabitants. Celina did her best to ignore the worst humanity had to offer and focused on Orion. Her heart broke for him.

Computer bag strap over his shoulder, he stood in front of the departures board clutching his duffle bag with both hands. He had the means to go anywhere, do anything, but he slouched with the wide-eyed gaze of a lost child. At eighteen years old, this had to be overwhelming. Hell, Celina would be thirty soon enough and *she* was overwhelmed. Not from the airport, but from everything that recently happened.

Merely five days ago, her deepest desire was for her tomorrow to happen exactly like her yesterday. Satisfaction came from curling up under her favorite blanket, or drinking her favorite tea, or watching her favorite movie. For Celina, comfort came in the expected. Whenever she felt the need to be impetuous, she visited a new restaurant or club with her friends, played a different game during game night, went on the rare date. Even then, a lot of known factors remained. These past five days? Pure unknown.

After getting violently shoved outside it, her comfort zone was so far away she wondered if she'd ever find it again. She had learned more about her birth parents than she cared to, yet couldn't stop from wanting to find out more. Thus, the whole reason they were about to board a plane to Los Angeles, after Orion figured out where he wanted to go.

Standing far enough away to give him privacy, Robert, Victor, and Celina watched the poor kid stare at the departures board in a gape-mouthed stupor. Victor elbowed Celina and said, "I bet he's gonna pick my town."

"Vegas?" Celina asked.

"Yep. He's an eighteen-year-old boy with access to money. He's going to the land of booze, gambling, and brothels."

"He would need to be twenty-one to do any of that."

"Oh, he probably doesn't know that," Victor said with a smirk.

"Well he is absolutely not going to do that. He's eighteen and scared and confused."

"He still has a dick and that's absolutely what he uses for spiritual guidance. Back me up on this, Robert."

Robert chuckled. "Not only do I refuse to add any credence to your statement, but I will pretend you never even said it. Contrary to popular opinion, men do have hearts, and if he follows his, he might choose Japan."

Victor rolled her eyes. "He doesn't even know how to buy a plane ticket. There's no way he's going to a foreign country where he doesn't know the language."

"Sometimes the best way to learn a topic is to dive into it. What happened earlier stirred up a lot of questions about his birth mother. He might want to connect with her by going to where she was from. You remember the conversation on the way here."

Lowering her voice, Victor replied, "Yeah, I remember. It was creepy as fuck."

Celina remembered as well.

"You're both wrong," Celina said with a smile. "He's going to choose to come with us."

"Oh, God, that'd be awful. We'll just tell him, 'no,' if he asks," Victor said.

"Why?"

"I didn't sign up to be a babysitter."

"We wouldn't be babysitting. He is an adult, after all."

Victor ran her hands through her hair and turned to Robert. Voice gruff with agitation, she said, "Do I even need to ask?"

Robert shrugged. "I don't see an issue with it. If his name is on the list, then he has as much right as we do to try to figure out why."

"You always take her side."

"If you ever say the right thing, then I'll take your side."

"I'm going to buy your art gallery and fire you."

"I'd love to see you try."

Victor wasn't looking at him, but Celina saw something in Robert's eyes. His tone was playful, but the spark of anger and defiance went beyond what was called for. Nothing in the nature of Victor's statement suggested she was serious, so why the aggressive expression? Did he view the gallery as so sacred that he considered joking about it taboo?

The fire in Robert's eyes extinguished as Orion ambled back to the group. Robert asked, "So, what have you decided?"

Shifting from one foot to the other, Orion mumbled, "I'd like to go to Los Angeles with you guys."

Victor leaned into Celina's ear and angrily whispered, "You're a bad luck charm."

"He'll be fine," Celina whispered back.

"What made you decide to come with us?" Robert asked.

Orion looked up, his eyes wide and hopeful. "We all have something in common, right? I mean, our names are all on a list for *some* reason, right? Celina and I have birth fathers who are monsters. That might not necessarily be the connection, since we don't know anything about Victor's birth parents, and yours are normal, but whatever the reason why this Calista person is hunting us, then we need to stick together and help whoever else is on the list. Right?"

Robert put his arm around Orion's shoulders. "Sounds like a good reason to me."

Victor huffed and looked to the heavens. "Fine."

"Well, I'm happy you decided to join us," Celina said.

Victor started to walk to the check-in counter. "The next flight to L.A. is in three hours. Plenty of time to get tickets. If first class is available, my treat."

Celina and Robert followed, but Orion didn't move. "I... ummm... I get plane sick."

"No you don't," Victor said, flat-browed and tone terse.

"I do. Last year, we went to Disney in Florida. I puked the whole way."

"Are you sure you weren't sick because you were going to Florida?"

"I puked so much I had to borrow puke bags from other passengers."

"Borrow? Did you just say, 'borrow?'"

"Not borrow. You know what I mean." His tongue shot from his mouth as he pantomimed the act of vomiting.

"Jesus Christ, kid, I know what you mean."

"It's okay," Robert said. "I get plane sick, too."

Victor frowned as her jaw dropped. "We sat next to each other on a plane from Philly to Pittsburgh and then another to Morgantown."

"Those were short trips. Anything longer and I'm puking my guts out." He then nodded toward Orion, showing that his act was for the kid's benefit.

Orion faked heaving again, with retching noises.

Victor ground the heels of her hands into her eyes. "Oh my God, kid, I get it!"

"It's okay, we'll rent a car and drive," Celina said.

"You do realize it's a day and half from here to L.A., and that's driving nonstop."

Celina shrugged. "We'll take turns driving. It'll be a nice bit of downtime."

Victor put her hands in her pockets and started to trudge toward the car rental counter. "Come on, let's go rent us a car."

Orion's face lit up as he followed Victor. "Road trip!"

"It's not a road trip."

"We're taking a trip. On roads."

"I understand that, but the term 'road trip' implies fun. Being stuck in a car for over thirty-six hours is not fun."

"Celina said it was good downtime."

"There's a difference between fun and downtime."

"Then what do you like to do for fun?"

"I'll call this a road trip if you promise to shut up."

Robert gave Celina a half bow and extended an arm toward Victor and Orion's direction. "Shall we join them? If for no other reason than to make sure Victor doesn't eat young Orion?"

Celina curtsied. "I believe we should."

She appreciated Robert's easy-going ways. For the most part, he kept silent unless spoken to or had something important to say. He did everything necessary to help Orion through his difficult time. But Madison's words kept haunting her. "If he is on the list, then his parents are *far* from normal."

# CHAPTER 35

*March 29th, Nebraska*

The diner was exactly what Blaze needed after eight hours driving in stone cold silence with only one stop to gas up and hit the restroom. He considered himself a people person, and being in close confines with someone whose only conversation was a grunt of approval four hours ago when he said, "I'm going to pull over here to get gas and take a leak," was torturous. But a diner provided an opportunity to talk. And this was his kind of diner.

Open twenty-four seven, smoking still allowed inside, cup of coffee less than two bucks, and nothing but truck drivers and outcasts. Sure, he and Gen got some side-eye glances when they walked in and took a booth in the back. Don't often see a wildly attired nuclear blonde with blood red streaks in her hair accompanying a man with a knowing smile and a gold hued, snakeskin jacket. The stares didn't bother Blaze and judging by the look of pure disdain on Gen's face, they didn't affect her either.

Gen ordered a burger, rare, while Blaze went with a stack of pancakes with strawberry syrup and a side of bacon. He had a craving ever since Tulip ordered that a couple nights ago. He thought about her, and then wondered how the new girl, Chelsea, was doing. He needed to help her out of her situation. First, he needed to help himself out of his.

Smiling, he lit a smoke. "So—?"

"Nope," Gen cut him off as she pulled a pack of cigarettes and a pen from a pocket inside her jacket.

Blaze chuckled. "Nope? Nope what?"

"Nope to this. Nope to conversation. Nope to us using this moment to understand each other. Nope to you trying to get into my pants." Gen tapped a cigarette from the pack and set it on the table.

"That's not what this is about."

"So, you do not want to get into my pants?"

Blaze couldn't stop his mouth. "Well, I didn't say that..."

"Nope."

"Hey, I was joking. Just trying to lighten the mood."

"Nope."

"Look, we have another day or more of driving. You gotta give me something. I really can't handle the silence. I have a lot of questions about what happened at the dealership, and I'm sure you want to know everything you can about Melissandra. You need me to get you to her."

"I'm sure I could find her without your help."

"You didn't know who she was until you met me."

Gen's jaw muscles worked while she wrote on her cigarette. Blaze thought she was crazy to try, but the tip of the pen was so fine she seemed to have no issues.

"What's that you're writing?"

"You love me every time I leave, hate me every time I don't," she mumbled. When finished, she returned the pen, lit her cigarette, and took a pull. Through a cloud of smoke, she asked, "What do you want to know?"

The food came and Blaze started by pouring strawberry syrup over his pancakes. "Genocide. Let's start with that. What's your real name?"

"Genocide is real enough."

"Come on."

"Okay, Blaze, you tell me your real, legal, full name."

"Blaze Stanford is my real, legal, full name."

Gen laughed. "Your real name is Blaze? Was your mom a stripper?"

"Only when she had to be. She mostly stuck with hooking."

*What the hell?* Blaze rarely told anyone the truth about his mother. He'd always use some euphemism like "she did this and that" or "odd jobs when she could." What was it about Genocide that made him go against his nature?

Gen's laughter faded into a sick chuckle accompanied by a head shake. "You're serious, aren't you?"

"As serious as the heart attack this bacon will give me."

Gen looked out the window, the pull on her cigarette long and worrisome. Blaze could tell she was arguing with herself. Maybe she felt the same urge to be honest with him as he was with her. She finished the cigarette in a hurry and dropped the butt in the little tin ashtray. Diving into her burger, she said between bites, "Shouldn't take a genius to figure out my real name is Jennifer."

That was the opening Blaze needed. "Jennifer. Nice to meet you."

Gen grunted and rolled her eyes while she took another bite.

"So, you write on your cigarette before smoking it. Something you always do?"

Wiping her fingers on the cheap napkin, Gen squinted at Blaze, sizing him up, still debating with herself. After a few seconds of chewing on his soul the way she chewed her burger, she swallowed and said, "I'm a singer in a band. Instead of writing lyrics in a notebook or whatever, I write them on my cigarettes."

Blaze nodded. "I get it. If they're worthy of being a part of your song, then you absorb them, make them a part of you."

Barely noticeable and it could have easily been mistaken for a mere twitch of her lips, Blaze had made her smile. "Yeah, something like that."

He thought about asking more personal questions but didn't want to push his luck. Two personal facts in a row were a good start. "At the risk of ruining the moment... I gotta ask – what was in the barrels?"

"You saw what was in the barrels."

Blaze's stomach gurgled. He focused on the sweetness of the pancakes to help push the unpleasant memories aside. "I did, but I can't wrap my brain around it." He was going to mention that she didn't seem fazed at all by the barrels' contents, but he was afraid she'd view that as a challenge. A bit more passivity was in order. "I've never seen spiders so large."

Gen's shoulders tensed and she spoke to her burger. "They're a special breed, not ones found in textbooks or the internet. But they're hunted for their venom. Obviously, the dealership was a drug lab. I don't like drugs being sold in my neighborhood."

"Neighborhood watch. I get it. You follow a lead to the dealership, learn there's a shipment coming in, so you set up a little ambush. That about sum it up?"

Gen finished her burger and sat back against the cracked and torn booth seat. She tossed her used napkin on her plate and glared at Blaze. "You got it."

"So, the blonde with the gun. Was she in charge of the lab?"

Looking out the window, Gen looked… confused. "No. She had nothing to do with the lab. But… This is going to sound unbelievable."

"I think we're well beyond the land of the believable."

"A couple days ago, two women came into my club and told me someone was trying to kill them. A blonde woman."

"Well, that seems a bit more than coincidence. Why did they come to you?"

"They showed me a list they'd taken from the woman trying to kill them with names and faces. Theirs were on it and so was mine."

*Two for one special.* That was what the gun-toting Blondie had said, like she was looking for Blaze as well as Gen. "Didn't happen to see my pretty face on that list, did you?"

"No. I glanced at the list and told the women to fuck off."

"No interest in hearing what they had to say?"

"I heard what they said. They wanted me to drop everything and go on some crusade with them to find everyone else on that list."

"Really?"

Blaze had pushed too hard. Gen's tone went back to clipped. "Look, two whack jobs come into my office saying someone is trying to kill me because that same someone is trying to kill them. There's no way I believed that. They were raving lunatics at best, probably con artists trying an elaborate scam. Now, enough about the list. Start telling me what you know about Melissandra."

It was a demand, laced with a threat. If Blaze had made a connection with her, it was a tenuous one at best. He finished his meal and reeled in his smile, showing he took her seriously, but left enough of a grin to let her know they were allies. "I don't know much about her. She's a new player in the city, getting bigger and doing it quickly. I met her twice, and both times she creeped the fuck out of me, like she's the kind of person who enjoys the screams of her victims as she kills them. My buddy, Jerry, set up the gig. She offered me a stupid amount of money to make the delivery but didn't tell me what I was hauling. Unfortunately, that's all I got."

The waitress dropped off the check with a pen, leaving without asking if they'd like anything else. Gen took a moment to mull over what Blaze had told her. "Do you have direct contact with her, or is it just Jerry?"

"Just Jerry."

Gen held out her hand and said, "Give me the keys. I'll drive for a bit while you contact Jerry. Tell him the drop was a success."

"I love this plan." Blaze handed the keys to her and grinned wide. For the first time since meeting her, she smiled back.

"I'll take care of the check." Blaze stood from the booth and fished around in his pocket, stalling until Gen exited the diner. He paid with cash and gave a nice tip despite the nearly non-existent service. Double checking to make sure Gen hadn't come back, Blaze took a cigarette from his pack and grabbed the pen. With sloppy and jagged letters, he wrote one word on it.

Genocide.

# CHAPTER 36

*March 31st, Los Angeles*

Another diner. When Gen and Blaze had stopped to eat at their third one somewhere before they left Utah, she asked him, "Don't you know of any other places to eat?"

Blaze waxed poetically about diners being the true windows into the soul of society. There's nothing made up or manufactured about the people in a diner. No one ever spent an hour preparing or dressing up to go to a diner. They might end up at a diner after going to a place they had spent an hour preparing and getting dressed up for. In those places, people were fake, actors playing a part, or else they wouldn't need to prepare or get dressed up. At a diner, people removed the masks and costumes, and could be themselves.

Of course, five hours prior he told a story – one of his many stories – about his mother waitressing at a diner and bringing home unsold baked good. It didn't take a psychologist to figure out that he liked her earning money as a waitress rather than as a prostitute. He obviously felt a sense of security in diners and overly romanticized the feelings he had from when he was younger. Though, Gen liked the line about masks and costumes, so she wrote it on a cigarette and remembered it ten hours and two more diners later.

"This one's different," Blaze said as he slid into the booth. "This is my home diner."

"Good to know," Gen replied. She sat across the table from him, as she had each time in all the other five diners. "Will we be meeting Jerry here?"

"Yeah. He'll be late and say inappropriate things, but he'll be here."

From what Blaze had told her about him, she probably wasn't going to like him, though Blaze admitted he was an acquired taste, if he didn't get spat out first.

229

Gen knew a lot about Blaze – he flapped his gums during their ride – and she felt like she knew the few people he referred to as friends. Gen had quietly listened to Blaze's stories about Big Lou, the person he had known the longest. Seemed like the gentle-giant type unless he got pissed off. Blaze used him as muscle for a lot of his jobs – he told plenty of those stories as well. And he was worried about Big Lou.

Even though Blaze shared quite a few details – one of the few people he knew to graduate high school; didn't do drugs because his mom OD'd, but would sometimes peddle them if there was a need to do so; had a one-bedroom apartment and paid no rent since he did odd jobs for his dirt-bag landlord – Gen still didn't know what to make of him.

Chicago streets had plenty of fast talkers who used their words to line their pockets or barter with information. None as flashy as Blaze, and his motives seemed a bit... different. Just like any other con man, his disarming charm certainly made those around him feel like the only people in the world, the only ones who mattered. But his currency of choice was favors. He owed a favor to get a favor, and he always paid his debts. From his stories, sometimes the favors weren't necessarily for his benefit. That detail intrigued Gen.

The drive with him was nowhere near as awful as she had expected. Sure, his voice shooed away the silence more than she would have preferred, but he remained quiet while she slept and smelled much better than her band when they went on tour. Though, he did slip in, "One stall or two?" when they stopped at a truck stop that offered showers. He laughed when she replied with a middle finger.

There was something about him, an aroma that existed right on the border of memory, the same sensation from when those two head-cases visited her. What were their names? Right, Victor and Celina.

One of Blaze's stories held more details about his meetings with Melissandra. During each meeting, the crime queen had commented to Blaze about how different he was, how she could sense something special about him. Obviously, *Melissandra* was different as well, but in what way?

Blaze talked to kill time, not to brag about himself or try to impress Gen. He'd ask her questions, a few of which she answered. She kept her personal topics to her band or to the club. Muted stories. She shared a few tales about Club B-Sides, but never told him that she owned it. She let him know her latest drummer OD'd but left out the part about his body swelling to the point of splitting open with his insides oozing out. And she remained evasive about the spiders.

"So, are those things native to America?"

"I don't know."

"What country did they come from?"

"I don't know."

"Have you ever seen a live one before? That must be fucking freaky as hell."

"No."

"Where the hell did Melissandra get them?"

"I don't know. That's what I want to find out."

"Fair enough."

They arrived in his home diner to wait for his friend Jerry. After they ordered, she pulled out a cigarette and her special pen. *I have death in my veins; when I'm cut, I bleed devils.*

Blaze craned his neck to get a better look. "That's a good one. I like that."

"Thanks." She appreciated his comment. But not the shadow looming over the table, too oppressive to be the waitress. A large black man in a shimmering gray suit and matching tie. A small scar ran along his cheek.

He spun one of his seven gold rings while he spoke. "Glad to see you taking someone else's girl out to dinner."

"Sorry, Marcel, she's not a working girl."

Gen glared at the pimp, the look in her eye letting him know that she had killed before and she'd do it again.

Marcel smirked. "Nah, she ain't." Whatever hint of a smile he had disappeared as he turned his attention back to Blaze. "Chelsea says you have an appointment with her tomorrow. Just want to make sure you know the rules."

Gen learned all about Blaze's proclivities toward renting prostitutes, but instead of spending any time doing what a man usually did with hookers, he'd treat them to a meal. He also mentioned one of the pimps didn't like it, some kind of weird power play. She assumed Marcel was the pimp in question, and the frightened looking girl with the black eye cowering at the counter was Chelsea.

Most people would be intimidated by Marcel's presence, but Blaze smirked. "No worries, Marcel. I know your rules."

Marcel clenched his fists so tightly that his knuckles cracked. "Ya know, I don't like your tone."

"Hey, Marcel. Looks like Chelsea needs to talk," came a voice near Marcel. A pudgy man who stood to Marcel's shoulder. He wore a dark blue collared shirt and khaki pants.

Gen thought she was about to witness a murder, but Marcel's face dropped the confrontational grimace. Chelsea most certainly did not look like she needed to talk, but Marcel got the message. "Sure, Jerry." He sucked his teeth and glared at Blaze for a moment before walking away. "I'm done with this fool anyway."

*What the hell did I just witness*? A pimp over six feet tall with the stature of a football player retreated from I/T support?

Blaze laughed. "Thanks for the save, Jerry."

"No problem." Jerry slid into the booth next to Gen and wiggled his eyebrows. "And who is this lucky lady of the night?"

Genocide raised a brow back at him.

Jerry slid out of the seat and spun onto the seat next to Blaze. "Looks like you got a feisty one."

"She's not a hooker, Jerry." He eyed Gen with a smile that implied, "Sorry about my friend." Gen rolled her eyes in response.

The food arrived and Jerry attacked Blaze's plate before the waitress set it on the table. She rolled her eyes as well and went about her business without a word.

"Not a hooker? Okay, then an aspiring actress," Jerry said while shoveling fries into his face. "That, I can help with. I can get you in some movies. You wanna be in movies?"

"None that you would watch," Gen answered.

"Oh shit, she's *very* feisty. I like her."

"Did you set up a meeting with Melissandra?"

Jerry had a few fries primed to go into mouth but halted at Gen's question. He dropped the fries on Blaze's plate and wiped his fingers on a napkin. "I did."

"I'm assuming the same creepy warehouse," Blaze said. "What time?"

Jerry looked at his watch. "Three hours."

"Great! In the meantime, the three of us—"

"I gotta stop you there, Blaze." Ever since appearing out of nowhere, Jerry wore an expression of ignorant confidence, like he hadn't known he should be afraid of Marcel. But now, he looked away, worried. "I'm leaving town."

"What? Why? When?" Blaze asked. In the short time Gen had known Blaze, this was one of the few times he didn't smile. It was off-putting, like seeing someone with beautiful hair take off a wig.

"You forgot 'how' and 'where,' but as for 'when'...." Jerry stood and wiped his hands on his pants.

"Whoa!" Blaze reeled back as if Jerry had reached out to strike him. "Now? You're saying you're leaving home right this instant?"

"Dude, Melissandra is a nightmare. My ear is to the street, and the street is fucking terrified of her. And fuck this 'home.' L.A. is just a city and there's cities all over this big, fat-ass, beautiful country. The only differences are denizen accents and pizza type preferences. Don't tell me you wouldn't ditch your shitty apartment for a better location."

"But—"

Jerry frowned and waved his hand as if erasing Blaze's words. "Nah, nah, nah. Nope. No. Get out of town, Blaze. If you're missing Big Lou, go get him, and get a house in the suburbs with a white picket fence. I'd suggest you skip the meeting with Melissandra and run away. I'm outta here. Bye, Blaze."

Jerry didn't stick around for Blaze to offer a farewell.

Staring at Jerry's exit, Blaze mashed his lips as he contemplated his associate's words. Then his smile returned, though Gen felt it was fake. "Well, now that he's gone, it's just the two of us. Since we have plenty of time before the meeting, I wanna swing by Big Lou's place. Don't worry, it's only a few blocks away, and he's a real nice guy. Much nicer than Jerry."

"Okay," Gen said. She wanted to focus more on Melissandra, but not after what she just witnessed – a man with a reputation so psychotic that he caused a monstrous pimp to back away just decided to leave the city he lived in because of Melissandra.

Heading over to Big Lou's place suddenly felt like a good idea.

# CHAPTER 37

*March 31st, Los Angeles*

Victor pulled up to the curb and immediately regretted not first stopping at the local car rental place and swapping out the Mercedes for a shittier car. "This car is totally getting stolen."

"You got insurance, right?" Orion asked as if insurance would protect them from the dangers that lurked within the burgeoning shadows. "My dad always said to get insurance."

"Yeah, kid, I got insurance. And at least three ride-share apps on my phone for when we need to get back to the hotel."

They had made it into Los Angeles two hours ago. Victor demanded – since she was driving and financing their adventure – that they find a hotel first. After a quick freshen up and a bite to eat at a nearby restaurant, they decided that even though twilight tightened its grip on the sky, it was still early enough to pay Louis Barberry a visit. Had Victor and friends known he lived in such a bad part of town then they might have thought differently.

No bars or restaurants nearby drew any kind of crowd, but plenty of people milled about. Blue tarps flowed like plastic water on both sides of the street from corner to corner, housing for the homeless.

Once upon a time, the apartment building Victor and company approached was new and modern. Dull graffiti, the multihued words reaching high enough to touch the art deco archways, covered the once cream-colored stucco. As they made their way to the steps – cracked stone with chunks missing – Robert said to Victor, "If you'd like, I could stay with the car."

The homeless shuffled about, talking with each other or sitting alone and staring off a million miles away. Victor's heart broke. She sighed. "No one here is going to steal this car."

"I've never seen homeless people before," Orion whispered, summing up his background and lifestyle with that sentence.

"Don't blow what your parents gave to you, or else this is your future." At the moment, that was all the sage advice Victor could offer.

Wall sconces meant to look like old time streetlamps lit the hallway. Only half the bulbs worked. The stairs creaked as they ascended. Victor wasn't sure if this place had an elevator, but even if it did, there was no way in hell she would take it. Four more floors of stained, torn carpet and peeling wallpaper. Music or loud televisions, crying kids, and loud arguments emanated from behind doors. Louis' apartment was at the end of the hallway, the apartment number scraped into the door's paint.

Huddled around his door, the members of the quartet stared at Celina. Victor placed a hand on her shoulder and gave a supportive squeeze. If roles were reversed, if the only thing separating her from a potential sibling was a closed door, she'd be a mixed-up ball of emotions. Excitement. Confusion. Fear. Too many questions to ask, with every answer leading to more questions. Would Louis be as excited to meet Celina as she was to meet him? Victor hoped so, or else she'd have to punch him.

Celina folded her hands together, then unfolded them, shaking them out. "I'm nervous. I don't know why I'm nervous."

"It's okay," Victor said. "I'd be nervous, too."

"You? Really?"

"Really."

"I'd be nervous, too," Orion whispered.

"I as well," Robert added with a nod.

Celina worked her bottom lip, her eyes meeting everyone else's one by one, and balled her fist, ready to knock at the door. "Okay. Okay, I'm going to do this. Here we go. This is me potentially meeting my half-brother."

She knocked softly.

The door, unlocked and unlatched, creaked open on its own, but only slightly.

*Fuck*, Victor thought. *This isn't good.*

Keeping her fist tight, Celina drew her arms close to her body. Glancing at everyone for advice, she whispered, "What should we do?"

Victor stepped forward and pushed the door open farther, revealing an apartment as tiny and grimy as she had imagined. "Hello?"

Celia grabbed Victor's arm and tugged. "We can't just walk in."

"Something's not right about this, and we need to check it out."

Victor entered the small living room, and wrinkled her nose. The odor went beyond the general funk of a single man living by himself in a run-down apartment. She could see into the bedroom on the left, and the kitchen-ette separated by a half wall to the right. She called out again, "Hello?"

No answer.

Like a tour guide for disappointment, Victor led the way to the bedroom, hand over her eyes and fingers splayed, ready for a jump scare. But after a heartbeat or two, she dropped her hand and looked into the messy room of a person who no longer cared. "Doesn't seem like he's here."

"It smells so bad," Orion mumbled.

"The stench of despair, kid." Victor didn't want to tell him the raw meat and fecal smells came from rot. She had one last place to check.

She strode toward the kitchenette, to peek behind the half wall, long enough to obscure a dead body. "Ah, shit."

Louis lay on the floor in a small puddle of his own gore, his skin a shade of exsanguinated blue-white, with a circular fist-sized hole in his chest. His tongue hung out from his drooping jaw, his cloudy eyes still open. "Stop!" Victor yelled, palm raised. "Don't—"

Too late. Everyone saw it.

Orion turned away and vomited his dinner on the threadbare living room carpet. Robert rubbed the kid's back while leading him away from the kitchenette.

Celina covered her mouth and squeezed her eyes shut. "No! No, no, no, no, no...."

Victor's guts twisted as well, but she willed them to behave as she examined the scene. In an open robe and tighty-whities, he lay stiff with rigor mortis. Dead for a while, but she couldn't tell for how long. His horrid skin color presumably came from blood loss, the hole in his chest too big and too round to be a bullet hole. On the topic of blood – where was it? This place should be covered in red from a wound this size.

Victor had seen enough, but something else caught her eye – a sheet of paper resting on his thigh. Holding her breath, she snatched it off his leg and read it. "You misfits are next. Love, Calista."

"Mother fucker," Victor whispered through her teeth.

"What?" Celina asked, her skin pallid, and tinted green at her cheeks. "What did you find?"

Orion had stopped vomiting, but his clammy skin made his brown eyes darker. Robert still kept the kid from collapsing with a hand under his arm, and he, too, shared a similar look of concern.

Victor held up the message for everyone to see. "Calista got to Louis before us."

"Oh, God, she knows where we are. She knows where we are," Orion sobbed as his knees buckled. Robert caught him and said, "She doesn't, Orion. She's just trying to scare us."

"It's working," he squeaked.

"Okay, what the fuck is going on here?" Wearing a snakeskin jacket the color of dull gold, a man with mussed and spikey blond hair stood in the doorway pointing a handgun at Victor. He swung his aim to Celina, then Orion, and then Robert. Gun back at Victor, he said, "Where's Big Lou and why are you in his apartment?"

"Seriously?" came from a voice in the hall. Then she entered the room – a blonde woman with red streaks in her hair. "What the fuck is happening right now?"

Genocide.

Victor grumbled under her breath. "You?"

Genocide frowned. "You? Fuck's sake, what are you doing here?" Before anyone had a chance to answer, she turned to her partner and said, "You can put the gun away, Blaze. These two women are the ones I told you about." She eyed Robert who stood protectively by Orion, the kid leaning over with his hands on his knees. "But I don't know who those guys are."

Orion looked up with a line of drool dangling from his bottom lip, and said, "I'm Orion. Wait. Are you Genocide from Genocide and The Doomsdays?"

"I am."

"Love your music." Orion then hiccupped and lowered his head to dry heave.

Blaze laughed as he tucked his gun into an inside jacket pocket. "If all your fans react that way to your music, I can't wait to see you perform."

"Sorry," Orion said as he stood and wiped his mouth with the back of his hand.

Victor didn't like the way Blaze smiled at her. Or maybe she did? That weird feeling again, the one she got when she had first met everyone else in the room, except Robert. This Blaze guy was one of 'them,' whatever that truly meant. It was his smile, that tipping point between blissful intoxication and a stomach-mangling vomit session like what Orion just experienced.

Blaze knew it, too, knew how to use his smile like a weapon or a drug. "Hey."

"Not even if your dick was as gold as your jacket."

Blaze shook his head and turned to Celina. "Hey."

Before Celina opened her mouth to reply, Victor grabbed her arm and pulled her away, inserting herself between the two of them. "Not her either."

Blaze shrugged and turned to Orion. "Wassup, kid?"

Robert crossed his arms and moved to block Orion from Blaze.

Now that the wild card seemed to be under control, Victor asked Gen, "So...? Long way from Chicago."

"Blaze and I are investigating something. But..." she crossed her arms and looked away, as if wondering how much she should share and how to phrase it. She turned back to Victor with her scowl. "Our interests might be more aligned than I originally suspected. We were attacked by your blonde friend in Chicago."

"Wait," Blaze said to Victor. "You know that blonde chick?"

"Apparently, they slept together," Gen said.

Victor turned to Celina and swatted her shoulder. "I can't believe you!"

"Ow! Why are you mad at me?" Celina asked.

"Because you got her doing it now."

Blaze chuckled and said to Victor, "I don't blame you. Blondie is hot."

"She is?" Orion asked with youthful ignorance.

"Gorgeous," Blaze answered.

"Oh my God! Everyone stop talking!" Victor said. Needing to regain control of the situation, she went back to an earlier question. "So why are you two here?"

Blaze stepped forward, leading with his smile. Looking around, he said, "This is my friend's place. Big Lou. I haven't heard from him for days. He isn't around, is he?"

Though Victor didn't like him on first impression, a cold wave of pity swept through her. Having recently lost a friend, she wouldn't wish those feelings on anyone, even a potential sleaze ball like Blaze. Taking a step away from the kitchenette, she said. "Your friend is... here. He's... I'm sorry... Just be prepared."

Blaze's smile faded more and more with every step closer. It disappeared by the time he rounded the half wall. He crouched, and put his palm over his nose and mouth. "Aaaah, fuck, man! What did you get yourself into, Louie? What the fuck did you do?"

Victor handed the note to Genocide. "Our mutual friend's name is Calista Lindquist. Louis Barberry was on her list. The same list you and I are on."

"We're all on it," Celina said, holding out her phone. She had pulled up the list and pointed to Blaze. "Even Blaze Stanford."

"Wait, what?" Blaze stood and frowned as he took Celina's phone. "This list is real and I'm on it." He handed Celina's phone back to her. To Gen, he asked, "Do you think Melissandra is involved?"

"Who's Melissandra?" four people asked simultaneously.

Genocide crossed her arms and glared at Blaze. "Well, I guess it's story time. Do we happen to have a better place to go, or should we hang out in the apartment with the rotting corpse?"

Blaze winced.

"We got a room at Covington Towers. We can meet there," Victor said.

"We probably left all kinds of evidence for the cops," Orion said, looking at the pile of evidence he had left on the floor.

"And fucked up the evidence they'd need to investigate this," Gen said, looking at the note in Victor's hand.

"Doubt it'd make a difference," said Blaze. "Not around here, anyway, not with these cops."

Celina was the first to leave, then Robert with a hand on Orion's back. As Gen sauntered out in silence, Victor followed her, lingering, watching Blaze. He went to the coffee table, to a telephone, an old landline that apparently still worked. He dialed 911, dropped the receiver on the couch, and Victor hurried out hoping he didn't notice her watching him.

Blaze joined them in the grimy apartment hallway and shut the door.

# CHAPTER 38

*March 31st, Los Angeles*

The tension in the hotel room reminded Celina of the time she went to a concert and the band was an hour late. The air was heavy and hard to breathe. People pressed too close together. Frustration and confusion surged against everyone's chests, made worse by the glaring lack of answers.

Everyone in the hotel displayed some form of tension. Well, everyone except Blaze, who propped his feet up on the coffee table, a beer in his hand. And a slight smile on his face, like something reminded him of a joke he once heard.

The hotel was not the fanciest the city had to offer, but better than most. Another two-bedroom suite with fully functioning kitchenette. Thanks to a quick stop at the convenience store on the corner of the block, they had stocked the refrigerator with energy drinks and milk for the two boxes of cereal Orion wanted. Robert sat in the armchair of the spacious common room, his air of regality transforming it into a throne. Genocide stood by the open window, smoking a cigarette she had just written on. Victor sat at a small table with Orion and Celina.

Celina respected Victor's inner strength, but more than that, she admired Victor's deep love within her snarly exterior for those she deemed worthy. Victor protected those she loved, and she made it clear that she wanted to keep Blaze away from Orion and Celina.

Though she agreed with Victor – there was something unnerving about Blaze – she didn't consider him dangerous. His boyish, impish face implied he was always looking for fun, but that didn't make him evil. He smiled a lot and in a variety of ways, but Celina thought she understood his feelings, because right now, she felt his pain even though Blaze wasn't showing it. He just lost his best friend, violently, and found himself in a situation where he couldn't mourn. Instead of crying or yelling, he smiled and joked his way through the stories he told about how he met Genocide. The only time his smile faded was when Orion shared his recent experience with Aika.

Genocide, on the other hand, never smiled. Celina didn't trust her. She obviously withheld information, but so did she and Victor. Celina shared one more time what had happened to Caila, but let Victor take it from there. Victor deleted the part about Murphy, but reiterated, "Yes, I had sex with the woman who is trying to kill us. I did *not* know she was a murder death machine."

"Was it at least good?" Blaze asked.

"I'm the best, so yes it was good." Of course, Victor stared at Genocide when she said that. Celina didn't like Genocide. There was something about her. Well, there was *something* about everyone in this room. Except Robert.

Celina got a weird tickle in the back of her skull when she first met everyone, like she could actually feel her brain trying to find a memory from a few vague details. Like she knew something she didn't know she knew. Like she had met everyone in a previous life.

Except Robert.

When they had first met, she felt the tingle of flirtatious excitement, not familiarity. Since then, the tingle faded. The more people she met from the list, the more Robert didn't belong.

"Why are any of us on the list?" Celina asked after everyone shared their story of how they got here.

"No friggin' clue," Victor said. "I only know that Calista wants to kill everyone on it."

"I think it has something to do with our parents," Orion said absentmindedly as he drew in his sketch book. He paused and looked up. All eyes were on him. "I mean, it must be, right? My father could go into people's dreams and kill them. Celina's dad killed people. Maybe Calista is killing the children of killers?"

Blaze chuckled and took a swig of beer. "My mom was a good woman. Poor. Worked hard. She did this and that, odd jobs when she could." He gave Gen a subtle glance. Her posture relaxed and her expression softened.

"But it wouldn't surprise me if my old man was a murderer. I never met the guy and when my mom was alive, she never talked about him. Ever. I don't even know his name."

Orion pointed to Victor. "You don't know anything about your birth parents." He then pointed to Genocide. "And you're also adopted."

Through a stream of smoke, Genocide said, "Sorry, kid. I met my birth mom, and there's no doubt in my mind she would have told me if my father was some sort of monster."

Celina didn't believe a word Genocide said, the little voice in the back of her mind screaming, "She's hiding something."

But what about Robert?

"Your theory about us being progeny of devils is very compelling, Orion," Robert said. "But as I said before, I grew up with both my parents, and neither were capable of *harming* another human being let alone taking a life."

If Robert was lying, he was a pro. But why lie? Why hinder the investigation? Maybe he was telling the truth, and Celina was paranoid. "So, now what?"

Genocide flicked her cigarette butt out the window and blew one last puff of smoke. "Now Blaze and I meet Melissandra. C'mon Blaze, let's go."

Blaze placed his empty beer bottle on the coffee table and followed Genocide toward the door.

With her hands up and palms out, Victor moved to block their egress. "Whoa, whoa, whoa. You said our interests were aligned after Calista attacked you two."

"They are," Genocide said. "After we deal with Melissandra, we'll come back and figure out what to do next about this Calista problem."

Orion fidgeted with the corner of his sketch pad, a look of panic in his eyes. "We can't split up."

"The kid's right," Victor said. "We're coming with you."

"No," Genocide replied.

Blaze inched closer to Genocide and kept his voice low, but Celina overheard him say, "It's not a bad idea. We don't know what we're walking into and Melissandra has people working for her. We could use the numbers."

Ants skittered down Celina's spine when Genocide smiled. "Don't worry. I can take care of Melissandra's people."

"No doubt in my mind," Victor said. "But a metric shit-ton of things could go wrong."

"No."

"Look, I know you don't like me – I have no idea why, because I'm charming as fuck – but you must admit, we're similar. Strong, independent, rich, blah, blah, blah. Neither of us like to accept help. A feeling of vulnerability comes with that. I get it, but we didn't get to be strong, independent, rich, blah, blah, blah all by ourselves. Whether we want to admit it or not, we accepted help throughout our lives. Accept our help now."

Genocide's expression was puckered, lemon-biting sour. "Ugh, God, it's like you ate fortune cookies and greeting cards and then barfed them on me. Fine, come along, but no more of that kind of talk."

"Deal."

"Not the kid," Blaze said.

"What?" Orion asked. "Why not?"

"Come on, man, have you ever had a gun pointed at you? Have you ever been in a fight? Before a couple hours ago, have you ever even been to the bad part of town? Any town?"

Orion dropped his gaze and slouched in his chair.

"Plus, Calista left a note for us," Blaze said, walking to the window where Genocide had perched. He peeked out, looked around, then shut the window and drew the curtains. "Assume she knows at least one of us is in town. We don't know where she is or who she's targeting or when. It's not a good idea to make her job easier by putting all her targets in one place."

"Makes sense," Victor said. "Celina can stay here with Orion."

Even though they were headed into a dangerous situation, Celina didn't like being left out, and the feeling of abandonment percolated behind her chest. "What? Why?"

"Because I don't trust this eighteen-year-old embodiment of bad decisions by himself in this expensive suite. *I'm* not staying, and judging how Robert handled himself against crazy ninja nanny, he'd be useful in a fight."

"Which is why I'll stay with Orion," Robert said. He turned to Celina. "Not that you couldn't handle yourself in a bad situation, but if, God forbid, Calista shows up here, who would you prefer to keep Orion safe?"

Orion reminded Celina of the friends she had when she was his age, and a younger version of the friends she had now. Reserved, unsure of himself, but content. He wanted to learn about life, but at his own pace, just like Celina. And his father was a monster, just like hers. Fiercely protective of him, she wanted to stay, but Robert's words rang true. He'd do a better job protecting Orion should Calista make an appearance.

"You're right." Frowning, she glared at Victor. "I'm coming with you."

"Fine! But first..." Victor grabbed Orion's phone and added her phone number as "Most Awesome Person Ever."

Orion immediately texted, `Plz pik up more Red Bull.`

"Jesus Christ, kid," Victor muttered.

"Need to have some fun," he mumbled.

"Dude, you have plenty of blank pages in your sketch book, so spend the next few hours ... hey, is that me?"

Celina looked over Orion's shoulder. Yes, without a doubt, Victor was the subject of Orion's drawing. More curvaceous than in reality, Victor sported two devil horns. Her forked tongue wriggled from her mouth while she lasciviously ogled Genocide who was on stage and surrounded by flame.

Real life Victor rolled her eyes and aimed for the door. "You're funny, kid."

Celina chuckled, then whispered to Orion, "Did you happen to draw me?"

A hint of pink touched Orion's cheeks as he flipped through a few pages. Even though it was only a sketch, he stopped at a clear image of Celina, fists on hips and wearing a cape. A superhero. "Really?"

"You tried to protect me from Aika."

The sweet spot behind her cheeks stung as she pushed away the urge to cry. No one had ever viewed her as a hero, not even herself. "Thank you."

Celina followed Victor, Genocide, and Blaze out the door. Time to be super.

# CHAPTER 39

*March 31st, Los Angeles*

"We should go after them," Orion said, cracking into his third Red Bull.

"Sorry, Orion, we're not going after them," Robert replied. "Want to pass the time with some television?"

"Naah. I'm good. Thank you."

Everyone else had left a few minutes ago, but it felt like hours. Might have been the excess caffeine, or the frustration of not being where he thought he should be. It didn't sit well, stirred up his guts like boiling soup. Again, it might have been the energy drinks.

Orion went back to a self-portrait, his face behind a set of bars. Like Bigby. He fought with his hand to keep from drawing the monster ever since the bastard killed his best friend. But was Bigby Orion's father? Or did his birth father have Bigby in his head too? And who was the woman in his dreamscape who called to Aika? His mother, maybe? Who else could it have been? His sleep since then had been black, peaceful, and dreamless. He couldn't have been happier about that!

"Who are Conner and Madison and what do they know?" Orion wrote on the last page of his sketch book, the page where he kept his notes. Slouching in his chair, he swigged from his can and contemplated that question. He pulled out his phone and readied the internet search. He didn't bother to type in their names; article after article about how amazing they were as real estate agents would appear.

What else could he search for? His parents had warned him not to research Calista Lindquist, and purposely withheld who they worked for so he couldn't research that name either. However, they didn't say he couldn't research himself.

He typed his name, and then almost dropped his phone.

He was dead.

According to the article in his town's newspaper, about two hours after he had left his house, his nanny kidnapped him, then lost control of her car and drove over an embankment. The kidnapping ended in a fire and two corpses: Aika, and him.

A tremor started in his hands and worked its way up his arms. He shivered as if it was twenty below zero, yet sweat poured down his head.

His parents – no, Conner and Madison – said they'd take care of everything, and they certainly made good on their promise. Then realization punched him in the gut. "Hey Robert, we gotta go."

"Orion, please, we—"

"No, listen to me. I'm dead."

Orion had never been the best at conveying his thoughts. His mom, *Madison*, had once told him his brain worked so fast that he was onto a second thought before he could express his first.

Robert put down his phone and turned his full attention to Orion. Robert had been patient with him ever since they met, good at helping him accurately express himself. "What exactly do you mean by that statement? Does it have anything to do with why you're shaking?"

"I'm dead, and yes. I mean…" Orion took a deep breath and held out his phone, displaying the news article reporting his demise. One more inhale, exhale, and his tremble slowed. "Conner and Madison faked my death."

"That is intense, I agree, but they said they were going to do that."

"There were *two* bodies. Aika's and *mine*."

"Okay, that's a little more—"

"Where'd they get the second body? Where'd they get the *me* of the pair? They could have done something like go to a morgue, or whatever, and bought a dead body, but the news said the accident happened two hours after I left, not enough time to go to a morgue, so that means… that means they were already prepared? How could they have known the future? They couldn't, so then they killed someone around my age and height and weight and features. How could they do that?"

The sting behind his nose and cheeks started halfway through his rambling, and by the time he took another deep breath, the tears started flowing.

Robert inhaled deeply, gesturing with his hand for Orion to do the same, and then exhaled. Again and again, still waving his hand like an orchestra conductor to guide Orion through the process. It helped. Matching Robert breath for breath, Orion eventually calmed.

"Okay," Robert said. "First of all, we do not know what they did, and we absolutely cannot guess. Maybe they paid the right people to fake the right reports. Second, we should stay here and let our friends do what they need to do."

"If I was next on Calista's list, then she'll think I'm dead and move on to someone else. I'm not very good at math, but even I know that means the odds are it's one of the other four."

Robert worked his jaw muscles. "Maybe not. There are a lot of names on that list. She could be after me next."

"Then what good is it to be sitting ducks? You were pretty awesome against Aika, but she still beat you and Victor and Conner and Madison. It took a bullet to stop her. Calista is at least that good, if not better. If she comes after you with just me to help defend you, there's no way to stop her."

"My goal isn't to stop her, it's to buy you enough time to escape."

"I'm not a kid!" Orion closed his eyes, immediately recognizing that his intense outburst had nullified his words. *Deep breaths. Calm down. Try again.* He opened his eyes and repeated, "I'm not a kid. I can legally make my own decisions. There are other individuals my age signing with the armed services, making the same choices about life and death."

"Which is why you'd need to run if Calista shows up."

"Which is why you'll die. And I can't imagine outrunning her, so then I'll die. And then all she'd have to do is wait around for the others to come back and kill them, and that's if they don't die doing whatever it is they're doing. If there's a chance that Calista is coming here, no matter how slim, then let's not be here."

Robert looked away. He had a similar frown to Conner's whenever Orion made an argument good enough to make him think. Robert shook his head and turned back. "I'll admit, you might be right, but we don't know where they're going."

*Damn it!* Orion hadn't thought about that. Maybe he could text Victor? No, that was stupid. What would he say? `Are you dead yet? If not where r u? On our way!` If only it were that easy... "Wait! I have an idea."

Orion tapped away on his phone, checking different URLs and social media posts. He whittled the suggestions down, tossing out the useless ideas while mining for the right ones. "Found it!" As he waited for the download to finish, he explained. "My pare... Conner and Madison, put a tracking app on my phone in case of an emergency. I read about a mod to the app that can reverse track any phone number. I just installed it aaaaaaaaaand... It worked! I found Victor's phone."

A look of disbelief washed over Robert's face – Orion saw that look plenty of times from Conner. But then Robert smiled. "Impressive, Orion. Nicely done. Now, one last time... Are you sure you want to do this?"

"Yes!"

Robert stood and snatched the keys to the rental car from the table where Victor had left them. "Okay then. Let's go."

# CHAPTER 40

*March 31st, Los Angeles*

Blaze guided the van into through warehouse's open doors. He had no idea what this building was once used for, but he assumed the design was meant to accommodate filling vehicles much larger than the one he drove. The center's configuration opened to the second floor, and a few hoppers connected to extra wide catwalks.

An audible gulp came from behind him. Celina. The poor girl was not cutout for this. No one truly was; people like Blaze learned how to deal, accept, adapt. Although, Genocide might have been born from the darkness they drove into.

"It's okay. We got this," Victor said to Celina. "We circled the block four times to check things out, and there's nothing more harmless than a few sleeping homeless people. Let Blaze and Genocide do the talking, and we'll be out of here before you know it."

Celina's height made her an imposing woman, but far from intimidating. Too bad she wasn't more of a bruiser like her half-brother. None of them looked at Big Lou's dead body longer than they had to, and death had changed his face, so they couldn't see the resemblance. It was there. The same long jawline. Similar mouths and eyes. Big Lou was quick to get in the mix when shit hit the fan, but that wasn't his default setting. Any other city in the world and he might have been a kind person. Los Angeles? Not a chance. "Big Lou would have liked you."

Celina's breath hitched. "You think so?"

"I know so. After we get out of here, I'll tell you all about him."

In the rearview mirror, Celina nodded, much calmer now.

Blaze sighed. "Yeah, he absolutely would have liked you."

Like the last time Blaze was here, a light came from the end of the warehouse, only a few strings of bulbs, but bright enough to see Melissandra. It unnerved him how she stood there with her hands behind her back.

Blaze kept the van moving forward, but slowed enough that if any-one wanted to, they could open the doors and hop out safely. It also allowed him to look out the windows and check the mirrors, hoping to see in between the shelves stretching all the way to the second floor, or into the dark corners. Shadows. Nothing but shadows and fear. Were the shadows moving like last time? He wished Big Lou was here.

"Should we really be driving farther away from the only exit?" Victor asked.

"If we stop now, then we'll have to walk to Melissandra," Gen said. "We want the van as close as possible if shit gets out of control."

Celina gulped again.

"Is that crazy bitch wearing a corset?" Victor asked. "What psycho wears a corset to a drug meeting?"

"I told you she was different," Blaze said, bringing the van to a stop. He thought about hitting the gas pedal instead of the brake and plowing her over, but there'd be ramifications. She had thugs working for her. He felt them lurking in shadows, so he put the van in park.

"There's 'different' and then there's 'bat-shit-crazy-comic-book-super -villain.' Does she have superpowers? Shoot laser beams out of her eyes or breathe fire or some shit like that?"

"She might be one of us," Genocide said with a tone that implied eve-ryone in the van was a super villain. Blaze shivered from the feeling he got around everyone he had met recently, except that Robert guy. Was that what Gen meant? Did she feel it, too?

The four of them exited the van, Blaze taking the lead with Gen next to him, Victor and Celina staying behind them. Melissandra's eyes widened, and her shimmering red lips spread like spilled blood to display each one of her glistening teeth. Blaze didn't like that, not one bit. And Victor was right, she was wearing a deep red corset over a full body, black latex outfit. Imprac-tical high heels as well. He'd have a difficult time taking her seriously if it weren't for the sense of dread bone-deep within him.

"Oh, you came back, Blaze!" Melissandra said as she stepped for-ward, her hands reaching for him. He wasn't sure if her squirming fingers were priming to embrace or strangle. "You brought your maddening aroma with you. And you brought others who smell just as insanity-inducing. Kill or fuck, kill or fuck, I can't make up my mind. But you…" Melissandra gave a wicked side glance to Gen, and then strode toward her.

Fists clenched, Genocide went rigid, but held her ground. With an eye-fluttering look of ecstasy, Melissandra inhaled deeply. She ran her index finger over her bottom lip and then pointed at Gen. "You, Sister, smell the best. I must confess – you're here sooner than expected. Helluva determination you got. I can see why Mother gifted you."

"Sister?" Victor muttered. "Well, this shit got real interesting."

"Mother didn't gift me anything," Gen replied.

"Wait… You knew you had a sister?" Victor asked. "Where was this information during emotional sharing time in the hotel room?"

"I didn't know. I didn't really know. It's… It's complicated."

"Oh contrary, my canary, it's very simple," Melissandra sang. "You have what I want."

"I don't want it, and I'd gladly give it to you if I could."

"Give what?" Victor asked, tone clipped, her words coming faster. "What are you two talking about? Some family heirloom? Like a tea set? A picture of grandpa? The good silverware?"

"It's not an heirloom, Victor. It's not something I can give. Like I said, it's complicated."

"You sure about that, Sister?" Melissandra asked as she stepped away from the group, back to the center where the lights shone. "I believe if you die, I then get the gift."

Blaze reached behind his back and gripped the handle of the gun, moving closer to Gen. He didn't want to be overly aggressive, but wanted to make sure Melissandra knew he was packing. "I came back to drop off the van and get paid."

"Not so fast, my fuck-toy murder victim," Melissandra purred. "The show is about to begin."

The darkness moved around the shelving units to the left and right of the warehouse. Blaze had known it all along – her thugs were hiding back there. He drew his gun but pointed it at the ground. Didn't want to wave it around like a lunatic, afraid the shadows would be quick to use theirs, but wanted to be ready to put a bullet in Melissandra should the time come.

Celina whimpered. She aligned herself with Victor, and they both shifted closer to Gen and Blaze.

The shadows stopped, but more movement came elsewhere. Behind Melissandra, a door opened and more darkness seeped into the room, dimming the lights.

First came the squeak of rolling wheels. Blaze squinted, trying to discern the figures shaped like men, but they didn't move quite right, bad actors pretending to play a part, pushing two large, wheeled frames into the light.

"Oh, no!" Celina yelped.

"Fuck!" Victor shouted.

Orion and Robert. Stuck on spiderwebs.

Two wooden frames held the webbed Orion and Robert. A wet patch discolored the front of Orion's pants. Snot and tears flowed down his face accompanied by hitched sobbing. His body twitched and shook so much that Blaze thought he might be having a seizure. Robert wasn't shaking, but his wide eyes and pale skin betrayed his fear.

*Wait, how did they get stuck to webbing? How is it strong enough to hold a human being?*

Gen stepped forward. "Let them go, Melissandra. We can work something out."

"Fuck that!" Victor yelled. "Blaze! Shoot the bitch in the head."

Blaze pointed the gun where Victor suggested, but his hands quaked too much for him to aim. "Let them go!"

Melissandra put her hands on her hips, the posture of a scolding authority figure. "Now, now tasty treats, no talking back! I hate that. You're not really going to have me ruin this outfit, are you?"

At first, he thought she meant she was upset about getting blood on her clothes. Nonsensical, but nothing she had said tonight made a lick of sense. Then both sides of her pants ripped. One of the fasteners shot from her corset. The sleeves of her latex top stretched, expanded.

*What the fuck is happening? Is this some kind of trick?*

"No, my fly, I will not let them go. Nor will I let anyone go." Two spindly black legs raised from her right thigh, destroying her pants while two more shredded the left leg. Her coreset pop-pop-popped off as her torso morphed and ballooned. Like her legs, each of her arms split into two thin, black appendages. A spider! She was turning into a spider! Just like the ones in the barrels. However, she still maintained the head, shoulders, and chest of her human self.

On her four hind legs, she scuttled closer to Orion and Robert. Orion grimaced and pulled away from the frame, his chest barreling outward as he tried to free himself from the webbing. Robert remained still, as if all hope was lost.

The two figures who had wheeled in their captives had already mutated into human-sized spiders and scurried from behind the frames. Scraping noises came from both sides of the main aisle – more spiders among the shelves. How many, Blaze couldn't guess.

Small, black chelicerae sprouted from Melissandra's cheeks. She ran her tongue over them, then used the spider legs sprouting from her shoulders to point at Orion and Robert. "These two I'll eat. *You* will be my mate. Or maybe the other way around? All these smells are filling my head with buzzing noises. The girl food, I'll kill and feed to my men. Then I'll—"

A crack of thunder cut her off, and a plume of red goo sprayed from her back.

Blaze looked around the room, then up to where he thought the shot had originated, to the catwalk above.

Calista Lindquist.

The barrel of her smoking gun was almost as long as she was tall, and she had it propped on the banister. With glee in her voice, she waved to everybody below and said, "Hi, kids! Who wants to die next?"

# CHAPTER 41

*March 31st, Los Angeles*

Celina never wanted to go home so badly in her life. The desire to snuggle under her favorite blanket on the couch with a good book felt so strong it made her joints ache. There was comfort in her home. Warmth. Familiarity. And most importantly, safety. Crime lords did not exist in her happy home. No women with guns trying to kill her. No spiders. No people who *turned into* spiders!

The darkness of the warehouse started to close in on her, constricting her peripheral vision. She focused on Melissandra who had transformed into a half-spider monstrosity, the most terrifying thing she had ever seen in her life. Until a bullet tore through her. The way her body jerked, the way the bullet tore pulpy chunks of muscle and bone from Melissandra reminded Celina of what happened to her sister. Caused by the same woman.

Calista Lindquist.

"Hi, kids! Who wants to die next?"

Bitch. That bitch was the reason Celina couldn't go home. The reason why home wasn't safe anymore. No couch, no favorite blanket, no good book because of Calista Lindquist. And the bitch was having fun!

Calista whooped as she fired her weapon two more times, direct hits to Melissandra's chest, geysers of blood erupting from her back. The strange spider creature tripped around in a circle and collapsed to the floor like a hunk of meat in a butcher shop. On her back, her eight spider legs curled inward.

Shrill whistles filled the air mixed with rapid clicking noises. The spiders.

High school biology came rushing back to Celina. She remembered learning that spiders were a noisy bunch, some communicating with sound, tapping the end of their abdomens to produce a faint ticking noise. Some hissed, others make more of a purr. The clicking came from strigulation, the rubbing of their front legs together, similar to crickets. Melissandra's group screeched and clicked for their fallen leader. Then they spread out.

Goosebumps prickled Celina's skin as spiders skittered along the floor and up the shelves, headed for the person who killed their queen. Celina couldn't begin to guess at their number, a dozen? Two dozen?

Their numbers didn't seem to bother Calista. The psychopath held another weapon, an automatic gun spraying bullets. She laughed and shouted obscenities as the human-sized spiders rained down from the catwalk. But not all the spiders charged after Calista.

Celina had thought that witnessing her sister's murder would always be the most intense situation she ever lived through. That experience was reduced to "unpleasant" status as five spiders crawled closer to her and her friends.

Strength had grown within her ever since meeting Victor, uncovering a level of bravery she never knew she possessed, but everything inside her shriveled like a salted slug as these monsters scurried closer. Not even Victor could have prepared her for this moment, and Celina imagined the anguish from being paralyzed and eaten alive.

Blaze stepped up and fired his gun twice. Two bullets pulped the head of the closest spider. The spider behind the one he killed jumped at him. Blaze dove to the side and hit the ground hard. He dodged the attack, but scabbled along the floor as two other spiders converged on him.

Celina screamed. This was too much. She was going to die. Her friends were going to die, starting with Blaze. Until Genocide did something confusing. She took off her jacket and dropped her skirt.

And then turned into a spider.

Just like Melissandra, Genocide's legs split into four spider legs as her arms split into four more. Chelicerae sprouted from her cheeks as her eyes bulged and blackened like marbles. Transformation complete, including a red hourglass on her back, Genocide leaped on top of the spider closest to Blaze and sank her fangs into it. She scuttled off the dying spider as its legs curled under its twitching body, and faced the next spider. They circled each other, front legs raised and jabbing at each other. Along with the rapid gunfire, Celina heard spider's clicking as they rubbed the bristles on their hind legs together, like predators rubbing greedy hands before descending on their victim.

Two more spiders crept closer to Celina.

"I saw something over here!" Victor yelled as she crouched by Genocide's discarded clothes. She fished through the pockets of Genocide's jacket until she found the lighter. "This way!"

Celina moved as one of the spiders jumped at her. It narrowly missed and slammed into the van. She screamed and ran after Victor. *Don't look back. Don't look back.*

Victor sprinted down an aisle between two sets of shelving. She stopped close to the end and picked up something from the floor. Whipping around, she flicked the lighter. "Duck!"

Celina dropped and slid across the concrete floor just as a line of fire whooshed over her head.

Holding a spray can, Victor coated two spiders in flame. Screeching, the creatures retreated up the shelves, leaving a trail of crackling cinders and free flowing red ash behind.

"The shelves are on fire," Celina whispered, stunned that she was still alive.

"They are," Victor said as she helped Celina to her feet. "Hopefully, it spreads fast enough to kill all those fuckers."

Celina followed Victor, the two of them running the length of the wall, colored in unfinished graffiti. Cans of spray paint on the ground told Celina where Victor got the accelerant.

The women continued to sneak along the side wall toward Orion and Robert, and then down an aisle, the floor littered with forgotten tools and a half dozen metal pipes.

"Grab a pipe to use as a weapon," Victor said.

Celina grabbed one that was over four feet long. Thin enough to tightly grasp, and sturdy enough not to bend. She then grabbed another useful tool.

"A hand saw?" Victor asked.

"To cut down Orion and Robert."

"Okay. Follow me."

The women hurried, and stopped at the end of the aisle to assess their situation. Orion and Robert hung only ten feet away, but two spiders were creeping closer to them. Victor rushed out from the shelves, blasting them with her ersatz blow torch. They caught flame and retreated, spreading fire as they ran.

Celina sprinted toward Robert. Judging by how the webbing pulled Robert's pants, shirt, and skin, Celina assumed the entire web was made from the sticky variation of spider silk. Getting Robert and Orion down from the frame took priority over removing the webbing itself, so Celina used the saw to cut away the contact points, starting at Robert's feet.

She cut away small chunks of wood, hoping to keep the webbing from clinging to the blade. After sawing away a few pieces, the webbing started sticking to the blade. She fought the urge to pull at the tacky globs and continued sawing away at the contact points. More web-strands detached from the frame, freeing Robert enough for his foot to touch the base of the platform. Suddenly, his body tensed, and he yelled, "Celina!"

She turned in time to see the spider leap at her. Screaming, she fell backwards and tightened her grip on the pipe, jamming its end into the center of the spider's cephalothorax, piercing the exoskeleton. Blue tinted slime oozed down the pipe and over her hand as the creature shook, legs flailing. Venom dripped from its fangs, splashing the floor next to Celina's head. The tips of its legs scratched and cut Celina's arms as it tried to gain purchase and bring its head closer to her. Reacting out of fear, Celina swung the saw toward the spider's waist, the thinnest part of its body, and started cutting.

Adrenaline fueled her muscles and turned her arm into a piston. Globs of blue, mucus-like blood gushed over her arm and splashed her chest. Mashing her lips to keep it out of her mouth, she cried and whimpered while cutting. More than halfway through, the spider went limp, and its legs curled inward.

Celina released the saw and grabbed the pipe with both hands. Under a sheet of flowing goo, she used all her might to push the thing aside and stood up. Stomping her feet and shaking her hands, she screamed. No words, no vowels, or syllables, just long, lung-clearing shrieks. Blue slime still clung to her hands no matter how hard she waved them or wiped them on her clothes. All she saw was blue blood and spider fangs.

Until Victor's face appeared.

"Celina! It's me! It's Victor! Can you see me? I'm right here. I'm right here."

Yes, Celina finally saw Victor's eyes, her face. Felt Victor's hands on her cheeks. Heard her say, "Breathe. Please, breathe. I know you want to go away, but come back."

"Okay… okay…" Her throat hurt as she spoke, but she nodded to let Victor know she heard her. "Okay. I'm here. I see you."

Eyes shimmering and locked onto Celina's, Victor exhaled a sigh of relief. "Good. You had me worried. You are a total bad ass, by the way. Robert's free and we're working on getting Orion down. Once we do, we're going to jump in the van and get the fuck out of here."

Celina nodded again and looked at Orion. The panic in his face matched the panic flowing through her body and it broke her heart. Gooey webbing still clung to Robert's shirt and pants as he helped Blaze pull Orion from the frame. Relief rushed through her, hot and palpable. No, the heat wasn't from within her – the air around her was warm and getting hotter. The fire!

The shelves on both sides of the warehouse crackled as the fire consumed them. Celina's heart crashed against her ribs as flames jumped from one set of shelves to the neighboring unit. "We have to go."

"Oh, you're not going anywhere, Princess!" came from an aisle between two shelving units not yet ablaze. Calista.

Handgun pointed at Celina, she sauntered out into the open. "I've fucking had it with monsters. I've killed an entire generation's worth of them, and now I have to deal with their kids. I thought I started with you; thought I blew your fucking brains out at that diner."

"That was my sister." The words fell out of Celina's mouth, and she had no idea why.

"Humph. Well, that makes sense. Time for you to join her!"

"No!" Victor yelled as Calista pulled the trigger three times.

Celina brought her fists to her chest and jerked after each round. It took a moment for her to realize she wasn't in pain. She didn't see blood.

Calista had missed!

Blaze reached behind his back and withdrew his gun. Calista threw her gun at him, smacking him in the cheek. His head snapped back, and she closed the distance between them in a blink. She smacked the gun from his hand and delivered a gut punch hard enough to double him over.

Victor's reactionary tackle knocked Calista off her feet, and she grunted as Victor drove her to the ground. With a spin and a twist, they were both on their backs. Victor wrapped one leg across Calista's chest, knee under her left armpit. Her other leg swung over Calista's neck and left shoulder. With a twist, Victor pulled Calista's right arm by the wrist.

"Heh," Calista chuckled. "Nice arm bar."

"I can't believe after our night together you're trying to kill us."

"Oh please. My body is like ninety percent scars, and you didn't have any questions?"

"I did. I was just being respectful."

"Respectful? Ha! I think I had you too distracted to think straight. Anyway, this is going to end poorly for you."

Victor pulled harder. "Not from where I'm looking."

"Two things: first, my shoulder has been dislocated so many times that I doubt my arm is technically attached to my body anymore. Second, even though you were a lot of fun the other night..." Calista rolled toward Victor, pushing her legs out of the way. Wresting her arm away, Calista jumped on top of Victor. One knee on Victor's chest, Calista grabbed the knife from a sheath strapped to her calf and raised it in the air. "... you don't have any moves I haven't seen before."

"No!" Celina yelled as Calista stabbed, aiming for Victor's face.

The knife tip struck the floor hard enough to create a few sparks.

"What the fuck?" Calista screamed as she stabbed three more times, each time hitting the floor. She swung again, but instead of her blade, she led with her fist and connected with Victor's cheek.

"Mother fucker!" Calista yelled as she stood. "I have to be able to kill one of you bastards!" She drew the other sidearm holstered to her thigh and swung around, aiming at Orion.

Robert jumped in front of the young man with his arms extended.

Calista shot three times

Robert gasped and looked down at his unharmed torso.

"What is happening?" she screamed as she pulled the trigger again and again, advancing closer to her target until her gun offered nothing more than impotent clicks. She dropped it and swung at Robert. Hands up, he blocked her, but she continued to attack, her strikes faster and her screams louder. Robert couldn't keep up with her speed. A right jab to his jaw dropped him.

Calista turned to Orion, the fire in her eyes blazing hotter than the inferno consuming the warehouse.

"Leave him alone!" Celina yelled over the sounds of the roaring fire. The high ceiling and open floor encouraged the smoke to rise. The hot air thick, it was harder to breathe and Celina felt certain that two of the exterior walls had caught flame. The catwalk groaned as it shifted.

Calista paused, her torso heaving with every breath, and then grabbed Orion by his shirt.

Celina had never seen a more maniacal look in someone's eyes before.

With her hand around his throat, she squeezed. "Or what? What will you do? I'm going kill him and then figure out a way to kill the rest of you."

Celina searched for a weapon. The pipe she had earlier lay under the spider carcass, but other tools were within reach. She grabbed the closest one.

A hammer.

Raising it over her head, she took a few steps forward.

Calista released Orion and he dropped to the floor. Wide-eyed, trembling fear replaced the look of mania as she took a step backward. A quick shake of her head as if waking from a nightmare, her brows furrowed as she smiled. "Jesus, you looked like your father for a second. No matter. I killed that fucker and I'll kill you—"

Calista's statement ended with a cry of pain as a set of spider fangs sank into her shoulder from behind. The spider pulled Calista to the ground and turned, exposing its back and the red hourglass.

Genocide.

Two sets of shelving gave way and a portion of the catwalk collapsed. A thick cloud of dust engulfed Genocide.

"Genocide!" Celina yelled.

"Get in the van and go!" Genocide yelled back.

Limping and coughing, Celina and her friends clamored into the van. Not even bothering to close the doors, Blaze threw it in reverse and zoomed toward the exit, plowing through the smoke and flame.

Celina watched the inferno through the windshield, wiper blades on and pushing aside debris. Through rolling oranges and yellows, a spider-shaped silhouette kept pace with the van. Genocide? It had to be her!

The wheels hit the parking lot and Blaze brought it to a tire-squealing stop, far enough away from the collapsing building.

A woman sauntered toward them. In human form, naked and carrying her skirt and jacket.

"Genocide?" Celina said, jumping out of the van.

The rest followed Celina's lead.

Addressing Blaze and Victor, Gen stopped and said, "Still want to fuck me?"

Neither of them answered.

"That's what I thought." Genocide said. She stepped into her skirt and started to walk away.

"Where are you going?" Blaze asked.

"Home."

"But—?"

"No, Blaze, we're done here." With that, she put her jacket on and disappeared into the shadows.

"Everyone okay?" Celina asked.

"Nothing a bottle of vodka and a hot bath couldn't fix," Blaze said, hands on his hips while stretching his back. "How about you? Are you okay?"

"I'll have nightmares for the next decade, but... yeah. I'm... I'm okay."

"Good. Very good to hear."

Blaze moved on to Victor, then checked on Orion, and finally Robert, ending with a handshake and a back-clap.

"What a friggin' weirdo," Victor whispered to Celina as they both watched Blaze.

"I still think he's nice," Celina replied.

"He's not. Trust me, he's not. But... are you really, okay?"

The warehouse's roof collapsed, the impact sending a slight tremor up Celina's legs. The flames flared but settled into a steady burn with the occasional crack or pop, inky black smoke cascading upward. Celina had stood in the middle of that and escaped. Just like what had happened to her this past week. She thought escape was impossible as her life burned down around her. Yet, her she stood with others like her. "As much as the idea of someone dying upsets me, I'm relieved that Calista is gone."

"Hey, Victor!" Blaze called out. He stood beside the rental car, admiring it. "Is this one of those limited-edition Mercedes with the different driving modes?"

"It is."

"You rented this to drive across the country?"

"Nothing but the best."

"Do you get the add on insurance rider when you rented it?"

"I did. Why are —?"

Blaze held up the key fob.

Robert patted his pants pockets. "Son of a— He pickpocketed me."

Victor sighed. "Mother fucker."

Blaze unlocked the door, jumped in, and drove away.

# CHAPTER 42

*April 1st, Los Angeles*

The quartet had driven the van back to the hotel last night, everyone silent. They went to bed, agreeing that a good night's sleep was in order. Miraculously, no one had any nightmares, or no one admitted to having any.

In the morning, with the threat of being hunted gone, there was nothing else to do except go back to their lives. After a brief conversation, Celina said she was going back to New York, but was still going to look for the other people on the list. Victor agreed to help Orion buy a car to start his new journey, wherever life would take him.

Victor still didn't know how she felt about Robert. At the warehouse, he had stepped in front of Orion to protect him from Calista, and even though she had unloaded a full clip from her Glock, not a single bullet hit him. No one was that lousy of a shot. Although... Calista had also shot at Celina and missed. Missed again when she tried to stab Victor in the face.

Those thoughts remained in her head as she gave Robert a farewell hug. She felt a bit of a naughty tingle – his muscles were tight under his sport coat, and, damn, did he smell nice. Should they cross paths again, she might have to show him what she had shown Calista. Nah. She loved Celina too much to do that to her. Unless she gave express written consent? Well, judging by how tightly Celina squeezed when it was her turn to hug him, that consent wouldn't be signed anytime soon.

"Come by the gallery any time you find yourself in Philly," he said. "I would love to meet up again for non-life threatening reasons."

Celina blushed and tucked a lock of hair behind her ear. "I will."

Robert leaned to the side and said, "Orion, please continue with your art. You have an amazing talent."

"I will," he replied from the kitchenette. Leaning over the sink, Orion crunched through his third bowl of cereal. Since he hadn't returned the milk to the fridge, Victor assumed he'd consume a fourth in the immediate future.

"Bye," Robert said to Celina.

She watched him leave, then shut the door.

"You dirty little whore," Victor whispered to Celina, causing her cheeks to go fire engine red. "God, I'm going to miss making you blush."

Looking down, Celina chuckled and tucked another lock of hair behind her other ear. "In a weird way, me too."

The smile faded from her face while she continued to look at her feet.

"Don't be a stranger," Victor said.

"I won't. You either! Face-to-face calls at least once a week."

An exuberance glowed within Celina. Victor was going to miss that. "Yes. Absolutely."

Celina pounced with a hug so strong that Victor had a difficult time breathing. It was worth it. "Damn, girl, I'm going to need to see a chiropractor."

After releasing Victor, Celina stepped back and wiped away stray tears. "So... I guess this is it?"

"Guess so," Victor said. She wanted to speak from her heart, but sharing emotions meant exposing herself, which meant a weaker position in negotiations. Emotions equaled a loss in profit. But these weren't negotiations, were they? Celina wasn't a business deal. And having allies was never a bad thing. Right?

As Celina turned to leave, Victor grabbed her arm. "Wait."

Celina faced Victor with a glimmer in her eyes

Victor cleared her throat and said, "I... I didn't get much sleep last night. My body completely shut down, but my mind... my mind is still trying to piece together this puzzle and how I fit into it. There's no mystery as to why Calista was hunting us. Your father, Orion's father, Gen's mother. It's a tiny, tiny leap in logic to assume that one of my birth parents is a monster. I can't stop thinking about that. If I'm the child of a monster, does that make me a monster? I mean, come on, I have a lot of monster traits. I love money. I like sex a lot. More money. Booze good. Money, money, money. I sometimes feel way too good when I make a man cry. Money, sex, money, booze. When I have a rare moment of introspection and look at myself, and see what motivates me, it's worrisome. Then I look at you. Your father was an absolute terror. Yet, you are a *good* human being. Waaaaaaay better than most people on this planet with normal, not monster parents. I don't feel like a monster when you're around. And I want to keep you in my life."

Victor reached into her pocket and pulled out a key ring with four keys on it. She took one off and held it out to Celina. "Make Vegas your new home. Make my apartment your new home."

Celina smiled as tears rolled over her cheeks. The big bright one that went from ear to ear and showed all her teeth. "You're not a monster! I've been having the same thoughts, too, worrying that there's one lurking inside me, somewhere deep, one that will come out if I change my routine. Then I look at you. You have no routine and you're stronger because of that. You use your strength to lift up the people around you, not push them down. You've thrown me into uncomfortable situations, but you've helped me deal with it afterwards. And you may love money more than you should, but you're generous with it."

A tingle raced from behind Victor's nose to her eyes, an unfamiliar sensation, and she didn't like it. "I think I'm about to cry."

"You're allowed to cry."

"No, I'm not."

"Stop being a bastard."

"Suck my dick."

"Not even if it's as gold as Blaze's jacket."

Victor wiped away the few tears that had escaped as the women shared a laugh. She then held the key out again. "So, are you going to take it?"

Celina took a deep, contemplative breath. She addressed the key, "I… I… don't know. I like my job in New York."

Victor shrugged. "Then bring it to Vegas. Call Anson and Branson and let them know you want to open a Roll & Role Café franchise. You have seed money and Bouch & Becker will go in on it with you, fifty-fifty."

Eyes still glistening, Celina looked at Victor. "Are you sure you'd be okay with me taking up your personal space?"

Fighting not to laugh at such a ludicrous statement, Victor said, "My living room is bigger than this entire suite and I have four bedrooms. I use one bedroom as my fuck fort, and another as my home office. Honestly, I've had sex in my home office more than I've used it as an office."

Celina's face soured as if biting a lemon peel. "How many times have you had sex in my room?"

"None! That's what I'm trying to say. The other two rooms are completely empty. I don't even use them for storage because my life is so vacant that I have nothing to put in—Wait. Did you just say, 'My room?'"

Celina giggled as she snatched the key with both hands and bounced up and down on the balls of her feet. "My room!"

"God, you're so fucking weird. But... are you one hundred percent sure? We're talking about disrupting the status quo."

"This past week, all I wanted was to go home and curl up on my couch with my favorite book, drink my favorite tea under my favorite blanket. I can still do that, just in a different home. I'm not disrupting the status quo; I'm altering its parameters."

"So... Ummm...?" Orion said from the kitchenette. "Does that mean I can have the other room?"

"Oh, God no!" Victor said.

Orion hung his head and slouched, and Celina smacked Victor's shoulder. "Don't be mean."

Victor huffed and said, "I didn't mean it like that. I meant I'm way too young to keep an eighteen-year-old boytoy in my apartment. Maybe when I'm old, like thirty."

Celina reacted this time with a punch to her shoulder. "I'm only a year older than you."

"Ow! Settle down, old lady. Don't worry, I'll install handles in the shower for you. Just make sure you don't get granny-smell everywhere."

A second punch. "Ow! God, for a nerdy café owner, you punch hard."

Celina cracked her knuckles and smirked. "Don't forget, I stood toe-to-toe with an assassin."

*Yes, you did.* Victor smiled and gave a playful punch to Celina's shoulder before turning back to Orion. "Look, kid, I didn't mean to be harsh. Sometimes my mouth does its own fucking thing. Just because I'm saying no to you as a roommate doesn't mean I won't help. First, are you absolutely sure you don't want to take off and explore the world?"

"Yeah. I mean, like Celina said, there are others like us. She and I might never have met our birth fathers, but we know something about them. There's a connection. The three of us, heck, the six of us, are all connected. Where else in the world could I find a connection like that? Plus, if we do find others, then we'll explore the world together... as friends?"

Victor sighed. "Yes, kid, we're friends." Her words sparked a massive smile from Orion, one accompanied by droplets of milk rolling off his chin. "Go shower and then I'll rent another car and the three of us will drive back to Vegas. I'll help you find your own place and enroll you in high school so you can get your diploma. You can be Celina's first employee at her café and earn your own way through life, you slacker!"

Orion hugged Victor and then ran to the bathroom.

"Ugh. I just got hugged by boogers, snot, and slobber."

"You do know he's eighteen, right?"

"Doesn't mean he's an adult. Now that he's going to be a part of our lives, we need to be careful."

"From Orion? I think he's the only human being nicer than I am."

"That may be true, but don't forget, once we leave this hotel room, he's using his new identity. That'll bring up hell-questions."

"Hell-questions?"

"Who the hell are Conner and Madison and how the hell do they have the resources to do what they did? Who the hell are they protecting him from? What the hell is living inside his head?"

Celina looked at the closed bathroom door as if watching a movie play out. "He's such a nice kid."

"Hey, I'm not saying he's not, but if we're going to keep contacting people on that list, then we need to prepare for whatever attention we attract. And I mean more than just whoever Conner and Madison are afraid of."

Frowning, Celina whipped around to Victor. "What do you mean? Calista's dead."

"Yes, but I got a pretty good look at Louis. There was a hole clean through him and very little blood, nowhere as much as there should have been. He could've been moved from wherever he was killed, but I'm almost positive he was killed right where he lay. The only thing I can think of that makes those kind of holes? A big ass laser, and I don't remember Calista bringing one of those to the warehouse. Even if she did, Louis looked like he'd been dead for a few days. I'm no dead body expert, but...."

"Calista was in Chicago at the time."

"Exactly."

"You think someone else killed Louis?"

"Also, exactly."

"Should we tell Robert, Blaze, and Genocide?"

"No. I'm having trust issues with all three of them."

Celina rubbed her chin and frowned. "I can understand Robert. As charming as he is, I think he's hiding something. But Blaze is nice."

"He stole my fucking car!"

"Technically, it wasn't your car. Plus, you said you had the insurance rider. And I'm sure he had a good excuse."

Victor rolled her eyes so hard it hurt. "Oh, God, your taste in men is awful."

"Hey! It's not like that. I feel like he's a good person stuck in a bad situation."

"Sure, you do."

"I do. But Genocide? Is it because she's a...?" Celina finished her sentence with a shiver.

"A mutant spider thing? Sort of. When we were in Chicago, in Genocide's neighborhood, how did we find Murphy's body?"

"Do you really think she did that?"

Victor shrugged. "She's a pretty cold individual. Nothing about last night freaked her out. She killed Calista without a second thought and remained perfectly calm while walking out of a burning building. When you

271

and I first met her, we pressed her hard. Maybe she didn't like that we knew so much about her and killing Murphy was a way to scare us off. Double extra bonus 'oh fuck' – the police haven't contacted me. She was easy to identify and trace back to me. I have a hard time believing Gen would have the Chicago police department in her back pocket, so that means she and her minions cleaned up after we ran."

Celina nodded. "Okay. Anything else you want to scare me with?"

Victor sighed. "West Virginia. You said you hallucinated Calista. Was the woman you saw that night the same woman in the warehouse?"

"Yes. I have no idea why I hallucinated her or how." Celina shivered again.

Victor placed a hand on Celina's shoulder. "Don't worry. Together we'll figure all of this out."

Celina nodded. "I agree. We'll be careful about how we move forward. We'll go slow and do as much research as possible."

"I like this plan."

A wry smile twisted across Celina's face as she held up her new key. "But first... I need to plan the decor for my new room. And my half of the apartment."

"Your half? I'm letting you stay in one room. One room."

"Pink. My half of the walls are going to be pink. Accented by unicorns."

"One room, that you're never allowed to leave."

"How do you feel about Care Bears? You like them, right?"

"What the fuck is wrong with you?"

"Obviously, something fundamentally deep and disturbing if I'm your new roommate!"

The women shared another laugh. Celina's eyes lit up and she pulled out her phone. "I have to call Anson and Branson and let them know the good news."

Warmth bloomed behind Victor's chest as Celina skipped to one of the bedrooms to make the call.

Yes, she made the right choice, no doubt. But what about her own future? Could she continue to go through life without knowing who her birth parents were? Could she live knowing that a monster could be lurking inside of her? What about the voice that saved her life from Calista? She hadn't heard from it since then, but that didn't mean it was gone. Whatever she chose to do, she wasn't going to do it alone. For now, that was good enough.

# CHAPTER 43

*April 1st, Los Angeles*

"She's not dead!"

Blaze winced and moved his phone away from his ear. Jerry had yelled so loudly that Chelsea looked up from her meal, across from Blaze in the diner booth. He offered her a comforting smile and gave her a slight wave to let her know everything was fine.

"She is," Blaze said into the phone. "I saw her get shot in the chest three times."

"I don't know, dude. She's an evil bitch and evil bitches don't die."

If Blaze were to close his eyes, he'd be able to see the splashes of blood spraying from Melissandra's back. The way her chest caved from the bullet impacts. The way her head snapped back and how her hair flowed. How her spider body fell. How the legs twitched and stopped, curled inward. Her blood was red, different than the bluish goo from the other spiders. Because she was still partially human, maybe? "Trust me, she's dead. If three bullets to the chest didn't kill her, then the burning building crashing down on her certainly did."

"Yeah, I'm still not buying it. And who's this new crew you're working with?"

Blaze had stretched the truth a bit for information flow purposes, but he hit the important notes: found Big Lou dead, found others who wanted Melissandra dead, met with Melissandra, and someone else who wanted her dead had shot her. "I'm not working with a new crew, and it doesn't matter if you buy it or not. I'm passing along information in case you wanted to come back to town."

"Well, I don't."

"Yeah? Where are you now?"

Silence.

"Okay, Jerry, I hear you loud and clear. Be safe."

"Always. That's why I'm here and not there. You be safe, too, Blaze."

Jerry hung up and Blaze tucked his phone back into his jacket pocket. It still had a faint odor of burning building. No matter. In a few days, all of it would be a distant memory, and he'd be on his next adventure.

Chelsea finished her dinner, and slouched back against the booth seat, her head next to a taped-up hole in the upholstery. "Thanks for dinner again, but I think I should really give you a blow job or something."

"That's not necessary."

Chelsea sat up and leaned her elbows on the table. Eyes wide and with a twitch in her upper lip, she said, "A hand job? Jesus, Blaze, even a kiss with tongue. I need to do something to you. You heard what Marcel said the last time, right?"

Blaze smiled, soft, yet confident. "I did. But there's no need to worry about Marcel."

"No?" Marcel appeared beside the table, his voice so deep it rattled the silverware. "Why do you not need to worry about Marcel?"

Chelsea recoiled, sliding all the way to the wall.

"Because he won't hurt anyone at this table," Blaze answered. Marcel grabbed Blaze by the jacket with both hands and lifted him out of the booth to the surprised gasps of nearby patrons. Noses almost touching, he growled, "Rumor has it Big Lou is dead, and Jerry skipped town. You're pretty fucking confident for a little man who lost his bad-ass friends."

Blaze reached into his pocket. Urged by Chelsea's sobbing from the booth, he held up a key fob and said, "Why would I need their help when I have this?"

Marcel did a double take. Still frowning, he lowered Blaze to the ground and released him. "What's this?"

"This is what I promised to find for you. This is also the fee necessary for you to forget Chelsea and never contact her again. Correct?"

Marcel grunted as he snatched the fob from Blaze. He glared at Chelsea, still withering under his gaze, and nodded for her to join Blaze. Avoiding eye contact with Marcel, she slid from the booth and stood behind Blaze.

She whispered, "I don't know what to do now."

Blaze pulled her around, and slid his arm around her shoulders, guiding her toward the exit. "Yes, you do. We're going to the bus station and I'm buying you a ticket home while I buy myself a ticket out of here."

"Where you going, Blaze?" Marcel asked.

Blaze's first thought was to tell the pimp to fuck off, but why ruin a perfectly good mood?

"Chicago."

# CHAPTER 44

*April 2nd, Chicago*

"…and I killed the bitch."

Genocide finished her story and stretched out in her office chair, feet on her desk. She arrived on the bus this morning and thought about getting some rest. Not happening. She had slept for most of the bus trip and would have been restless had she tried to stay away from the club. A much-needed shower and a solid breakfast, then back to the club. This place was more of a home than her apartment and it felt good to be back.

Lucas stared at her, his mouth gaping. Even Ven looked a bit flummoxed. Lucas spoke first. "So, the two crazy women from the other day weren't so crazy after all?"

Gen smirked. "The jury's still out about their sanity levels, but they were correct about all of it. About them being different, about a killer hunting me."

"The killer you killed," Lucas said.

"I pumped enough venom in her to paralyze a horse."

"Good," Ven said. Swiping away at his phone, he stepped forward. "Well done. Now, back to the problem at hand."

"Come on, man," Lucas said with a flustered tone. "Let the poor woman take a minute off, huh?"

Gen pulled her feet from the desk and leaned closer to look at Ven's phone. "No worries, Lucas. I'm happy to be back."

Ven snarled at his blue haired bandmate. "See? She's happy to be back."

"What did you two find out while I was galivanting across the country?"

"The latro supply dried up almost immediately, so it seems Melissandra was the sole manufacturer."

"Well, that's good news."

"But the rec remains on the streets."

"Well, that's bad news."

"It gets worse." Ven finally got to the picture he was looking for and showed it to Gen. Taken from a darkened street, the image was of two brown spider legs poking out from an alley. "There was supposed to be a raw material delivery for rec the day after you left. Obviously, that didn't happen, but we watched the place. A couple suspicious characters came by, so we followed. While tracking them, I saw a spider, but it scurried into the alley. When I got there, it was gone."

"That's a different shade of brown than one of our kind. So, the idea of another breed of spider moving into our area has moved from speculation to fact?"

"Looks that way," Lucas answered.

"Fuck." Gen messaged her temples.

Lucas grabbed Ven's arm. "I think we hit her with enough for now."

Ven yanked his arm free. "She's the queen of the black widows. She can handle it."

"Yeah, nothing a fifth of top shelf can't solve," Gen said. "Maybe two bottom shelf fifths, depending on what else you got."

"We need a new drummer."

Lucas looked to the heavens and laughed as he shuffled to the door. He opened it and gestured for Ven to walk through. "Okay, that's enough for today. She knows we need a new drummer."

"We need a new drummer, and he should be one of us."

"He?" Lucas asked, the playful tone in his voice indicated that he was about to say something to irk Ven. "Why does it have to be a he? Couldn't the drummer be a she? Or someone who doesn't identify as either?"

A rumble emanated from deep within Ven as he turned and puffed out his chest. His upper lip curled to make room for the protruding spider fangs. "Not what I meant."

Lucas's shit-eating grin remained unchanged.

Gen sighed. "Put those things away, Ven. I know what you meant."

Ven did as ordered and walked through the office door. Before he left, he grunted and said, "The new drummer should be one of us."

Lucas waited a few seconds after Ven left and shook his head. "He is so not progressive. He's so not perceptive either. You look miserable."

Gen offered a smirk and a half-shrug. "Just a long past few days. Kind of weird to think there are monsters other than us spiders out there. Hell, it's kind of weird to think of spiders other than black widows. My brain always knew both were possibilities, but my heart is having a hard time accepting it."

Lucas nodded. "Yeah, I know what you mean. The head knows what the heart ignores."

"I'm writing that line on a cigarette."

"Sounds good. Just let me know if you need to talk, okay?"

"Yep."

After Lucas shut the door, Gen's body went limp, finally giving in to the weight of the world on her shoulders. That weight, the whole world, could be summed up in one word – gift. That was how Melissandra described Gen's burden. A gift. How untrue. A gift was something to be enjoyed, cherished. A gift could be given back if the one receiving it didn't wish to keep it, and Gen would happily give this "gift" away if she could. The fate of the entire species rested upon her, and that was in no way a gift.

Hell, it had only been a couple of years since she learned she wasn't human, that monsters were real, and she was one of them. After her mother had introduced herself, she explained, "There are different clusters of half human, half spiders and you are the queen of the black widows. Only the queen can reproduce, there is only one queen, and the queen only produces daughters."

Gen appreciated the way nature kept things in check to keep the population under control. The males of the species were always made, never born. Drones and warriors, as Gen's mother labeled them. Lucas and Ven were warriors, able to maintain either form instinctively – spider or human – while drones were mindless workers who had trouble staying in one form or the other. Melissandra could convert human men into males of their species, but she was born infertile. Only Gen could reproduce. And she didn't want to.

All she wanted to do was make music and perform. Her heart beat to a drum and her veins strummed inside of her like bass cords. Now she owned a portfolio of businesses and properties worth millions that she had no idea how to manage. She thanked every deity she could think of that her mother had done an amazing job setting up the businesses which practically ran themselves. Gen used her time since inheriting the assets to learn about them, but had zero confidence in herself to make good decisions should a crisis happen. She educated herself with the businesses and ignored what it meant to be the sole perpetuator of an entire breed of creatures she barely knew anything about. Never once in her life had she entertained a flicker of maternal longing, sneering at the entire industry dedicated to the commercialization of motherhood. Now, if she couldn't accept motherhood, then an entire species would die when she died. Knowing other monsters existed, hunters out there wanted to kill her, and another breed of spider lived within her territory all made the pressure suffocatingly worse.

Gen did the only thing she could think to do.

She cried.

# CHAPTER 45

*March 24th, New York*

Robert ran the tip of the glass cutter along the surface of the drinking glass. He wasn't sure if this was going to work, but he had adjusted the thermostat of the hotel suite while he had been gone. It was now sweltering, and he set a glass of ice water on the counter.

Satisfied that the scoring was deep, but not deep enough for his soon to be guest to notice, he put the tool away and rinsed the glass. Careful not to break it, he dried the glass and returned it to the cabinet. Just in time – a pounding came from the door.

Calista Lindquist.

"Jesus, it's hot in here!" she said as she entered. "Tell me it's hot in here and not just me. I'm only forty-seven. Way too young for menopause. "

"Although it's typical for the change of life to happen between the ages of forty-nine and fifty-two, it's not uncommon to occur as early as forty-four. Whether or not that's what you're experiencing, I forgot to adjust the thermostat after checking in, because I was in too much of a hurry to complete your little assignment." Robert concluded by taking large gulps of ice water.

Calista sneered as she moved into the kitchenette and opened the cabinet. She took the first glass available, the one Robert had altered, and filled it halfway with tap water. After a few gulps of her own, she said, "It's a little fucking weird that you know that, but considering who your father is, it's not surprising. Speaking of my little assignment... Did you find out where she'll be tonight?"

"Yes. She's having dinner at a small restaurant called The Signpost, close to the café."

"She told you this?"

"Not in so many words, but the restaurant came up in conversation. Simple human psychology and all that." Robert took another swig of water.

Calista drank as well. "Good enough for me."

"You couldn't find out where she lives?"

She shook her head. "Her mailing address is a P.O. box and wherever she's living isn't under her name."

"You couldn't go to her café and do your own recon?"

Calista drained the glass. "No! Because when I finally see that bitch, I'm gonna fucking kill her. I don't think it'd be good for anyone if I cut her open and threw her guts around a crowded café."

"You had me find out where she was going to eat dinner so you can shoot her in the head. How is that any different than killing her where she works?"

"There's a difference between shooting someone from a neighboring building and tossing their entrails around like Mardi Gras beads!" She tightened her grip on the glass. "It's like you don't even know me!"

*Oh, I know you.* "I really don't see the difference. Both options are loud, messy, and very public. I thought you liked to take care of monsters in the shadows."

"The difference is I won't get caught."

"No? Still seems risky to me. What makes her so special? Why take that risk?" Robert knew the answer, but he also knew the questions would get her to do what he wanted her to do.

"Why is she so special?" Calista's eyes widened as she got louder. "Why is she so special? Because she's the daughter of my first kill! Because she's the daughter of—! Ow! Fucking fuck!"

The glass broke in Calista's hand. A stream of blood flowed from small lacerations. She set the base of the glass on the counter and quickly dug two pieces from her palm. "Fucking cheap ass hotel shit."

Robert handed her a dish towel that she wrapped around her hand. "Or maybe you need to control your temper."

"Fuck my temper and fuck you. It's my temper that has allowed me to be successful all these years."

"Well, you still haven't killed my father yet."

"He's not a monster. Well, he's not my definition of a monster."

Even though Robert had admonished Calista about her anger, a rush of heat burned up his neck and flushed his cheeks. "If you don't believe my father is a monster, then you haven't adequately done your due diligence. He is a monster, and he needs to be removed from this world."

Calista smirked as she sauntered to the door. "Now who has the temper? Don't worry, I'll kill Daddy Dearest for you. But you shouldn't convince me that he's a monster. If he's a monster, then that means you're a monster. If you're a monster, then you know what I'd need to do."

The door latched shut behind her, and Robert picked up the glass. About a half ounce of blood pooled at the bottom. More than enough. The lights suddenly dimmed and the temperature dropped from eighty to sixty. Right on time.

Robert took the glass to the center of the hotel room and placed it on the desk next to his journal and a small pile of crystals he had shaped into jewelry. He flipped the journal open to a blank page and said, "You know you don't need to go through these theatrics on my account."

The lights remained dim as every shadow oozed along the walls, ceiling, and floor to the far corner of the room, forming black veins that pulsed to an unseen, evil heartbeat. A pair of yellow eyes opened from within the darkness followed by a smile of yellow teeth, blocky and broken.

The witch had arrived.

"If I didn't make such a grand entrance, how would you ever know it was me?" She punctuated her statement with a blood curdling cackle.

Robert was in no mood to placate the witch's ego. "I got what you said I would need."

The darkness rippled, a malevolent pool of black ink, as the witch's face emerged, gnarled skin twisting in grotesque ways. Her body remained in the cold darkness, but she reached out with a withered hand, paper-thin skin wrinkled on bone, and touched the blank page of Robert's journal. "Always so serious, just like your father."

"That is the only similarity, I assure you."

The witch whispered in an arcane language, her words scraping across the hotel room walls, as her crooked fingers slid over the journal.

Letters formed on the page one at a time, maroon in color, forming words like wounds as if the paper were sliced open flesh. The witch cackled again. "That is a bold claim. Untrue, but bold."

"Taunt me all you'd like, just come through on your end of our deal."

Finished cutting words into the journal, the witch withdrew her hand. "Yes, yes, the pedestrian request that I kill your father."

Robert looked over what she had written in his journal. A new spell. "This is a protection spell? What exactly will this do?"

The darkness moved across the wall from one corner of the room to the other. Robert hated the showmanship.

"The spell will infuse the hunter's blood with the crystals. The hunter will not be able to deliver a killing blow to whoever wears theses crystals."

"Fair enough. Why haven't you killed the hunter yet? You must have had plenty of opportunity over the years."

"I have my reasons, boy. You're smart, but you think yourself cleverer than you are."

"I'm clever enough to master the spells you've given to me." Robert took one last look at the spell and closed the book. "What makes you so sure that Celina will find her way to me? I just sent the hunter to kill her."

The witch cackled again, and Robert's guts twisted from the sound. "I'm the one who delivered the list of names to the hunter, but I haven't given her all the names. I've hidden many from the list, including Celina's twin sister."

"You're willing to sacrifice one of your grandchildren?"

"It's time for the children of monsters to meet, and some sacrifices need to be made."

"Well, you are a vile witch, after all."

The witch's face jutted from the darkness, stopping inches from Robert's, her cobweb-like hair whipping forward from the momentum. The smell of rotting leaves nauseated him. "Don't push me, boy! You are merely a convenient tool, not a necessity. Lest my oath to kill your father is no longer meaningful to you, then you best watch your tongue."

"My apologies."

The witch's face receded into the darkness like a craggy stone sinking into thick mud. "Apologies mean nothing to me. You have your spell. Be sure to use it."

"Will you be around when the children of monsters meet?"

"There is much to do before I introduce myself to them."

"Where will you be should I need your assistance?"

The darkness freed the witch's face so she could give Robert one last leering smile. "Not that it concerns you, but I'm going to Los Angeles to kill another of my grandchildren."

With that, the darkness disappeared, but her cackle echoed long after she left. Robert waited until the lights returned to normal brightness and the room temperature normalized before he was satisfied that she was actually gone. He reached into his pocket and pulled out a small plastic bag. In his other hand, he had a few strands of the witch's hair, plucked from her when she threatened him. Her hair squirmed like worms, and he dropped the wiggling strands into the bag and sealed it. He had no idea what he'd do with them yet, but when he saw an opportunity, he took it. Surely a spell existed that he could use to gain an upper hand. That was for later, though. Now, he had to go home to Philadelphia and prepare to meet Celina again.

Want to know more about Celina's father?

Want to learn how Calista Lindquist started?

Then check out:

# Hammer and Blood

www.fortresspublishinginc.com

# Viktor Bloodstone

is

Brian Koscienski

Chris Pisano

Jeff Young

www.novelguys.com

www.ingramcontent.com/pod-product-compliance
Lightning Source LLC
Chambersburg PA
CBHW051531260626
47170CB00003B/882